Saga Hillbom

TODAY DAUPHINE TOMORROW NOTHING

ISBN: 978-91-519-0887-8

Copyright © 2019 Saga Hillbom

Cover Design © 2019 Germancreative, Fiverr

Cover image: Shutterstock

First published in June 2019

This is a work of fiction. Some names, characters,
places, events, and incidents are wholly or partly
based on historical facts, while others are entirely a
product of the author's imagination. Real events and
characters may be portrayed in a certain way for the
purpose of the story.

Thank you, Robin, for always giving your honest opinion and providing me with the necessary guidance

"I believe that the histories that will be written about this court after we are gone will be better and more entertaining than any novel, and I am afraid that those who come after us will not be able to believe them and think they are just fairy tales."

Elizabeth Charlotte, *Duchesse d'Orléans*

Table of historical figures frequently mentioned

Including full name, important titles, and relations

Adélaïde

Marie-Adélaïde of Savoy
Princess of Savoy, *Duchesse de Bourgogne*
Later *Dauphine* of France; sometimes known as the *Petite Dauphine*
Married to Louis; daughter of Victor Amadeus II

The King

Louis XIV
King of France and Navarre 1643-1715; sometimes known as the Sun King

Louis

Louis de France
Duc de Bourgogne
Later *Dauphin* of France; sometimes known as the *Petit Dauphin.*
Married to Adélaïde; son of the Grand *Dauphin*; grandson of the King

Madame Maintenon

Françoise d'Aubigné
Marquise de Maintenon
The King's morganatic second wife

Charles
Charles de France
Duc de Berry, heir apparent to the Spanish
throne 1701-1707
Son to the *Grand Dauphin*; grandson to the
King

Philippe
Philippe de France
Duc d'Anjou
Later Philippe V, King of Spain.
Married to Maria Luisa; son of the *Grand
Dauphin*; grandson of the King

Madame
Elizabeth Charlotte (House of Wittelsbach)
Princess Palatine, *Duchesse d'Orléans*
Married to Monsieur

Monsieur
Philippe de France
Duc d'Orléans, previously *Duc d'Anjou*
Married to Madame; brother of the King

Nantes
Louise Françoise de Bourbon
*Mademoiselle de Nantes, Duchesse de
Bourbon, Princesse de Condé.*
Legitimised daughter of the King and
Madame Montespan.

Blois
Françoise Marie de Bourbon
Mademoiselle de Blois, Duchesse de Chartres
Later *Duchesse d'Orléans*
Legitimised daughter of the King and
Madame Montespan

Maria Luisa
Maria Luisa of Savoy
Queen consort of Spain
Married to Phillippe; daughter of Victor
Amadeus

Grand Dauphin
Louis de France
Dauphin
Eldest son to the King and the late Queen

Chartres / Orléans
Philippe
Duc de Chartres, later *Duc d'Orléans*
Married to Blois; son of Monsieur and
Madame: nephew of the King

Maisonblanche
Louise de Bourbon de Maisonblanche
Baronne de La Queue
Illegitimate daughter of the King and a
mistress of little importance

Madame Montespan
Françoise-Athénaïs de Rochechouart
Marquise de Montespan
Favourite mistress of the King and mother
to several of his legitimised children

Vêndome
Louis Joseph de Bourbon
Duc de Vêndome, Marshal of France,
military commander

Noailles
Françoise Charlotte d'Aubigné
Duchesse de Noailles
Niece of Madame Maintenon

Victor Amadeus
Victor Amadeus II (or Vittorio Amedeo
Sebastiano di Savoia)
Duke of Savoy, later King of Sardinia and
Cicely
Father of Adélaïde and Maria Luisa

The Chevalier
Philippe de Lorraine
Chevalier de Lorraine
Monsieur's infamous lover 1658—

Conti
François Louis de Bourbon

Prince de Conti, previously *Comte de La Marche* and *Prince de La Roche-sur-Yon*
Titular King of Poland for a short period of time
Nante's lover and father to at least one of her children.

PROLOGUE

11th February, 1712
Château de Fontainebleau,
Fontainebleau, France

The air in the *Dauphine*'s bedchamber was stagnant with the odour of used bandages and the broth that stood on the nightstand. The curtains had been drawn to prevent the rays of moonlight from spilling through the windows—a vain attempt to create a comforting atmosphere for the King's favourite, who lay slumped in the enormous bed between silk sheets, the rashes making her once so exquisite face a grotesque sight.

Adélaïde craned her neck and beckoned the *femme de chambre* to her side. 'Will you bring me Madame Maintenon? I should like to speak to her before I die.'

The bluntness in her words made the *femme de chambre*—who could hardly be a day older than seventeen—bite her lip, her eyes round as buttons. 'Of course, Madame. Of course.' She picked up her skirts and slipped away, her little steps tapping against the floorboards. The temporary slit in the door as she left the room allowed a patch of blinding light to cut through the heavy shadows in the room, but the door closed within seconds, and Adélaïde was once more enveloped in the musky darkness.

*Four hundred and one, four hundred and two...*Adélaïde counted the seconds that passed before her visitor arrived; each second seemed to last an eternity. The figure that strode towards the bed was not Madame Maintenon; it walked with the stride of youth and was draped in clothes more fashionable than the King's wife would ever choose. As the woman closed the distance between herself and the bed, Adélaïde recognised the thick neck and small, rounded chin that belonged to the *Duchesse de Noailles*, Madame Maintenon's niece. *How odd. I can't remember the last time she paid me a visit.*

'My aunt is taking her bath, Your Royal Highness. She'll be present as soon as she is properly dressed. I thought I might come in her place, just for the time being, unless you mind.'

'No, no...I don't mind, not at all. I'm pleased to have some company. Come, sit.' Adélaïde attempted a faint smile, but her lips merely twisted in a strange grimace.

The *Duchesse de Noailles* lowered herself on the chair that the *femme de chambre*, who had returned together with the *Duchesse*, placed by the bedside. The *Duchesse*'s face was obscure in the flickering light of the candle she was clutching in her hand, her knuckles white, but the creases on her forehead were the unmistakable marks of several days of fretting. Her powdered fontange coiffure lacked any ornament; the only jewellery that she had bothered to adorn herself with was a cross with glistening emeralds resting at the base of her throat, hung on a thin gold chain. In all her simplicity, the young woman was more beautiful than Adélaïde had recalled.

'How are you feeling, Madame?' Noailles inquired. 'Is it...is it safe to be near you?'

'The illness is contagious—the measles, the doctors say. If you wish to leave, you have my permission, though it should comfort me to have you stay.'

'Then I shall stay.'

'I think perhaps I've been sorely mistaken. I thought I would be Queen, I always did, and I was so close, but not anymore.'

'I pray you, don't say such things, Madame! You have many years left! And your husband would only be weakened in his own illness if you were to leave him.'

Adélaïde shook her head, the tears that were trickling down from the corners of her eyes soaking into the pillow as though it was a sponge. 'I don't. I don't think I have many hours.'

Noailles said nothing, for it was obvious to anyone that the *Dauphine* was right in this—but Adélaïde was not searching for sweet-faced lies to reassure her of the opposite.

'Don't tell them I pitied myself, please don't tell them such things. Oh, but I do, I pity myself and I pity Louis. But don't tell them that.' Adélaïde reached out a hand to stroke Noailles's cheek and fumbled in the gloom with the swaying movements of fever until the *Duchesse* caught her hand and cupped it in her own. 'Farewell, beautiful *Duchesse*. Today *Dauphine*, tomorrow nothing. In two days utterly forgotten.'

CHAPTER I

4th November, 1696
Montegris, France

They called him the Sun King, and when Adélaïde beheld the man in front of her, she knew he could not be known by any other name.

Having climbed down from the extravagantly decorated carriage—an intricate construction covered in gold and draped in heavy velvet—she stood erect in the damp November air. The cold bit her cheeks and temples, bringing forth a youthful blush; the breeze tried to ruffle the stiff coiffure. Adélaïde clenched her small hands, which were hidden in the folds of her skirts. The blood pulsating in her ears felt deafening. *If he does not like me, then I shall make him like me. I refuse to be a burden—not to the King of France, nor to the court. I'll make them happy.*

The smile on Louis XIV's fleshy lips grew wider until it reached his eyes. Adélaïde blinked repeatedly as she caught sight of the blackened stubs where his teeth must have been once upon a time, but she did not flinch. Despite the crooked nose and folds of fat underneath his chin—attributes not usually found on a handsome face—the King radiated charm and authority at the same time. A periwig of the same cocoa-brown as the horses drawing the carriages framed his face and formed countless curls on his broad shoulders.

Adélaïde felt the tension drain gradually from her frail body. Her hands unclenched. There truly was something in those dark eyes before her that mimicked the brightness of the sun itself. *And anything he wishes to shine on will live in brightness.*

'Madame, I have been waiting most impatiently to receive you.'

'Sire, it is the greatest day of my life,' the young girl answered and dipped into a deep curtsy as elegantly as she could manage.

The man—three times her size—did not hesitate, but scooped her up immediately, chuckling to himself. 'Come now, Madame, there is no need for such formalities with my dear granddaughter.'

Of course, there was every need, but none of the spectators were as brazen as to remark on this aloud. Their eyes scanned the freshly arrived

Petite Dauphine-to-be with the razor-sharp judgement required in such a situation. Eventually though, the disapproval was exchanged for reluctant acceptance. Her light chestnut hair could easily be styled in the French fashion; her slightly Italian accent could be extinguished by practice; her feeble figure could perhaps be mended if fed properly, until suitable for childbearing.

Indeed, Adélaïde of Savoy's faults were not necessarily permanent, and they were not many, to tell the truth. All this was of little significance though, for the Sun King already appeared enchanted by his grandson's bride, and the King's approval was the only approval that carried any true significance.

'May I present my son, the *Dauphin*, and my grandson, your fiancé, the *Duc de Bourgogne*?' The King glided back a step, giving precedence to another man.

Adélaïde ran her eyes up and down her father-in-law-to-be. The *Dauphin* was dressed in plush, dark velvet, and on his head towered a periwig so voluptuous and powdered that Adélaïde began to fear it might tumble down on her, spoiling her gown with chalk. The *Dauphin* walked slowly, his face jiggling slightly with every step. As he halted to make a shallow bow, his eyes met Adélaïde's. They reminded her of those of a sheep: not at all unkind, but apathetic and rather unintelligent.

3

After the *Dauphin* came his son. Adélaïde filled her lungs with the biting air and raised her chin so that she might observe her match properly. Louis. One Louis out of hundreds at the court of Versailles, no doubt. But this would be *her* Louis, the man—no, the boy—that would transform her into a valuable piece on the French chessboard. *My ticket to everything I could ask for. I hope he is kind.*

'Welcome, Madame,' Louis said. His voice was abnormally high-pitched, only to dive on the second word. However, a careful smile flit across his lips.

Adélaïde curtsied for the third time, and pressed down a doughy lump of disappointment. Perhaps a great prince did not have to be handsome; perhaps he was allowed to have a beak-like nose and a crooked shoulder. The rules on the chessboard were not the same for men as they were for women, and she knew it all too well. Kings and nobles did not depend on dainty beauty the same way their wives did.

The formalities proceeded according to protocol. The train of carriages began their journey to Versailles with a jerk as the horses settled into a trotting pace.

A strange warmth spread throughout Adélaïde's body as she pressed her face against the window, waiting to behold the buildings and gardens she had been told so much of. She slid her hands between her skirts and the ice-cold

4

leather seat, shifting her weight impatiently. The Sun King had been charmed; she had seen it as clearly as she now saw the real sun reflecting in the glass, bathing the floor of the carriage in light. She had been so terribly anxious thinking of the meeting; now that the moment had been mastered, Adélaïde could not understand how she could possibly have failed.

It did not matter much that the King's son appeared similar to a bland turnip, or that his grandson carried himself with an awkward air. What difference did it make, when she would have the greatest palace in Europe to serve as her playground?

Adélaïde practically chirped, beholding the enormous buildings from the carriage window.

The fountains burst with cascades of sparkling drops every second. The grass—worn by the cold but still maintaining some of its summer colour—wound in intricately rounded patterns. The black and golden gates towered, inspiring awe in those who happened to pass by, marking the threshold to that peculiar world they guarded. Adélaïde's neck ached from her attempts to broaden her view through the window. She found herself unable to stop marvelling at the vast differences that separated the buildings before her and those of the Royal Palace of Turin, where she had spent so many years. Though a deep-rooted fondness of that chalk white, comparatively

5

simple place remained, there was no denying that Versailles was the gem of Europe and in lack of proper competition.

The clopping of the horse hooves ceased and the entourage halted with a slight jolt. The footman opened the carriage door with a click, offering his hand to lighten Adélaïde down on the cobblestones.

The courtyard swarmed with curious men and women—all decked to their teeth in silk and taffeta, rouge and precious stones. Their glances seemed to pierce Adélaïde without mercy, as if scanning every centimetre of her figure. Soldiers in decorative uniforms followed the series of carriages now parked within the gates, their horses neighing and flapping their tails. Adélaïde flinched despite the distance between herself and the powerful creatures. There was something about them—perhaps the incomprehensible musculature, perhaps the way their black, spongy nostrils flared—that frightened her.

She proceeded through the fluttering, colourful mass of courtiers, resting the equally colourful bouquets of flowers placed in her hands against her lower arm so that she would not risk dropping a single one. The flowers covered her torso and arms; the clusters of leaves tickled her nose.

Ushers waited stone-faced on each side of the massive, swung-open door. Adélaïde drew a breath, placing one slipper inside the palace, then the other. *Finally.*

Of course, not everything was quite the shimmering dream it appeared to be. The sparkling bubble quickly burst, revealing a far more simplistic—though not unpleasant—life.

Adélaïde of Savoy was enrolled into the Maison Royale de Saint-Cyr to complete her education and prepare her for her new role. This came as no surprise; she had been made aware of it before her arrival in Montegris, but the brief sense of disappointment was undeniable. It would be another year before her marriage, and until that day she would be in the care of the *Maitresse générale des classes*, the woman who was head of the class mistresses.

The school in Saint-Cyr held a fine reputation. It was a rather new institution, founded by the King's wife, Madame Maintenon, who did not possess the title of Queen, for the marriage had never been officially recognised, but that of Marquise de Maintenon.

Adélaïde studied the older woman's face with a warmth sparking in her chest. In Adélaïde's eyes, Madame Maintenon was the essence of both dignity and kindness, ambition and intelligence. Naturally, if she had asked the men and women who frequented the halls of Versailles for their opinion of the Marquise, the condemnations would have rained as thickly as the praise. Some called her greedy, others said clever. Who is to say which declarations were made in envy and which in the pursuit of favour? The only aspects of Madame Maintenon every member of the court found themselves agreeing on was her devotion to God, her passion for education, and the change she had brought about in the King.

Louis XIV's affairs were no secret. At least, they had not been in his youth—now, they simply did not exist. Louise de la Valliére, Madame de Montespan, all those fair-skinned, soft-limbed young mistresses...they were nothing, now that the glamorous moment of adoration had passed. Madame Maintenon, on the other hand, had taken the permanent place in the King's heart, and would not be nudged from her position.

One would not have expected it if one merely casted a glance upon her. With her sixty-one years, the youthfulness the King loved in women was long gone. But the petite chin, strongly marked lips, straight nose, and thick hair, made her a pleasant sight nonetheless, not to mention the strong character that lay underneath the beautiful surface.

Adélaïde quickly came to learn the ways of Saint-Cyr. Upon her arrival, she was immediately clad in the required uniform: a plain dress of brown muslin, accompanied by a white bonnet tied with red ribbons. The ribbons were meant to represent the class to which she belonged: the youngest group at the school. Once she had passed her eleventh birthday, the ribbons would be exchanged for green ones; the older girls were marked with yellow or blue.

Adélaïde had never possessed a great interest in fashion, and so she did not mind the change of clothes terribly. However, the harsh transition from Versailles—those splendid rooms that she had only been allowed a glimpse of—to Saint-Cyr stung like a needle.

CHAPTER II

The girls were hustled out of bed early; Adélaïde pulling the blankets up above her ears in a fruitless attempt to remain in the warm atmosphere of dreams. It was the very first morning since her arrival at the school, and the sharp daylight flooding the dormitory made her eyes feel sore. She could not for her life remember where she was or what on earth she was supposed to do. Then, the scattered puzzle pieces came together and assembled to one picture in her head. *Yes, of course. Classes...the catechise, maybe? Will they be reporting my every move?*

Adélaïde swung her legs over the edge of the mattress and touched the icy floor boards with her toes; the cold progressed through her legs and up her spine like rats' feet. She grimaced.

'The Italian has lost her wits,' one of the younger girls said with a snicker.

Adélaïde brushed it of like dust, but the queasy feeling in her stomach only grew. *The Italian. Surely I am more than just* The Italian?

10

That she, who truly did her best to please those around her—to make them as merry as she wished the whole world to be—and who were to be the *Duchesse de Bourgogne*, should be called something so diminishing felt foreign to her. That there should be any ill will at all seemed unnecessary, and she had always failed to grasp why certain people had it in their nature.

Once the morning prayers had been held in the school chapel, breakfast was served in the refractory. Adélaïde smiled to herself as the steaming hot, thick porridge slid down her throat. This was one simplicity she enjoyed rather than disliked. She scraped the plate fervently, making certain not to miss the last of the melted dollop of butter.

The other girls glanced at her through downcast eyelashes as discreetly they could. Their faces—some bony, some plump; some spattered with blisters and blackheads, some smooth—twitched with wonder every now and then. Before them sat the Princess of Savoy, according to rumours already the King's new pet, eating like a sloppy farmer's daughter. And yet she possessed a strange charm which they could not quite put their finger on.

'Are you going to live in Versailles?' one of them asked. Her dress was tied with red ribbons, and as she spoke a wide gap in her teeth became visible.

'Yes,' Adélaïde said, lifting her eyes from her porridge. 'Are you?'

The other girl shook her head so that strands of hair broke loose from underneath the white cap. 'My brother says my husband and I will live in the country. I think he knows that—he knows many things.'

'The country can be very dull.' Adélaïde frowned, but broke into a smile seconds later. 'You can come live with me instead.'

The two of them exchanged a look of pure joy. *How easily problems can be solved if one only puts one's mind to it. Adults ought to try it sometime.*

'I'm Françes Talleyrand-Périgord.' The gap-toothed girl's arm shot out across the table.

Adélaïde blinked in surprise before shaking her hand. 'Marie-Adélaïde of Savoy.'

The most valuable friendships are often formed by complete coincidence, and this was one such. The classes that followed—catechism, reading and writing, arts, arithmetic—floated by with the ease of a rippling brook. Adélaïde did not feel the weight of them, nor how the repetitive information bounced off her mind, for she had acquired a companion who would laugh at her and with her, who would chime in whenever she made a remark about this or that, who would play hide and seek under squeals and fits of laugher when no one was watching. Françes proved to be

12

quite the playmate even by Adélaïde's standards, and in some ways, she came to fill the role that had previously been occupied by the *Duchesse*-to-be's younger sister, Maria Luisa.

In the evenings, Adélaïde often excused herself from the board games and hushed chatter in order to write letters to her grandmother and mother in Savoy. She had never had a natural talent for chess, and although conversing with Françes made her feel giddy and light-hearted, the pen and quill possessed an irresistible charm.

The landmass that lay between herself and her family no longer made Adélaïde's chest ache—she was too convinced now that France was where she truly belonged—but the love and fondness she felt remained nevertheless. How could one erase such emotions in a matter of weeks? It was simply impossible; not the finest jewels in the world could disturb them.

Adélaïde was surprised when she realised that the letters to her grandmother, Marie Jeanne Baptiste, were far more frequent than those to her mother. It was always her to whom she longed to write and tell about dull lessons at Saint-Cyr as well as all the thrilling gatherings at the palace. She would put the pen to the paper, and the thoughts would pour out in black on white, until it felt as though her head had been sapped of everything she could possibly have to say. Adélaïde suspected—with a sinking feeling in her stomach—that the teachers and mistresses were only too glad of this, for they did not take any great pleasure in listening to her chatter, and would rather let the paper carry that burden.

Françes was eager to listen, of course, but she already knew everything about the school, while she knew nothing of Versailles. Thus, the conversation was doomed to be either a result of complete agreement and thereby dull, or something similar to a monologue from Adélaïde's side. One of the things they did speak of at length, though, was the three Bourbon boys: the King's grandsons.

Naturally, Louis, the *Duc de Bourgogne*, was the eldest of them, and although he was not a particularly interesting child, he was nevertheless the main character in Adélaïde's and Françes's minds simply because of the impending wedding.

After him came the two younger brothers: Philippe, *Duc d'Anjou*, and Charles, *Duc de Berry*. One might have thought they would be of similar personalities, being related so closely by blood, but Philippe and Charles could have originated from two different worlds—the former was grave, an overly pious boy with slight oddities that were somehow both subtle and worryingly intense; the latter was like a firecracker bursting with mischief and lively childishness, and almost eight months Adélaïde's junior.

Regardless of the princes' various charms and flaws, Adélaïde cherished the rare moments in their company that she was granted, because it was with the three of them that she would someday ride high on the wheel of fortune, and it was with these three she might grow old and grey.

CHAPTER III

C an you not act like adults?' Philippe
said, scratching the slight cleft in his
chin. Aging had come prematurely to
the *Duc d'Anjou*; he possessed that strange
nature which turns thirteen summers to
thirty, lips locked in a sombre line.

'You always spoil the fun,' Charles
replied.

Louis, who was sitting on the ledge of
a fountain with the catechise resting in his
lap, lifted his glance. 'I do think we ought to
stay here, until Madame Maintenon is ready
to leave.'

Adélaïde studied the three brothers,
tilting her head. Although she had never
mentioned it to anyone but Frances, she did
not enjoy Philippe's company more than that
of an old rag. Of course, Louis shared the
other boy's interest in the church—but at least
her fiancé rarely hesitated to accompany her
in her and Charles' games, since he knew how

much it would please her. *At least he has other attributes to him than those of a statue.*

The four children had been allowed to accompany the King's morganatic wife on a walk in the gardens as part of their monthly time together, but Madame Maintenon was now caught up in admiring a new kind of lilies, which one of the gardeners was brimming with pride to present. The remaining members of the group, who possessed no interest whatsoever in lilies or any other flower, had thus been left to their own devices, and this presented an excellent opportunity to escape the rules' firm clasp.

'Come, Adélaïde, we'll go. I'm tired of waiting.' Charles pulled at the ruffled lace sleeve of Adélaïde's dress, and she complied.

'Louis?' She flashed him a blinding smile.

Louis slipped the catechise onto the stone brink and heaved himself down, joining the two others while his brother remained stubbornly behind.

'They're just children—' Philippe began, but his words fell flat as he seemed to realise how pointless they were in changing Louis's mind.

Adélaïde followed Charles through the web of gravel paths, holding onto her fiancé's sweaty hand with a tight grip—an intimacy never allowed under more public circumstances—and together they speeded across the lawn, which was usually a forbidden area to step on.

Two elderly ladies had just abandoned their tea and pastries on a decorative table farther down the garden. As the three children caught sight of it—the servants not having had the chance to clear away the remnants of the sweetmeats—they were beyond restraint.

Adélaïde sank her teeth into a soft petit-choux, unintentionally squeezing out the filling so that a dollop of cream and marmalade landed on the grass by her feet. Charles snickered and smeared some cream on her cheek with his forefinger. Adélaïde shot him an irritated look, but smiled after a fraction of a second. *At least he's far better than serious Philippe. What's the use of manners when there's no one watching?*

'Father told me of the treaty they are hoping to negotiate,' Louis said. 'I trust you are pleased, Madame?'

'Of course I am! Why, just to think of all the soldiers who can go home to their wives and children.' A dreamy expression swept over her face.

'Yes—but the marriage, I mean.'

'Oh, that too!' Adélaïde tucked the remnant of the *Petit*-choux in her mouth and sucked her finger tips with a lapping smack like a common wench who had never seen such delicacies before in her life.

Louis ate slowly, fervently trying to think of something to say that might extend the talk of marriage. The girl in front of him was just that—a child—but she would not always be. 'Will you be happy, Madame?'

'Versailles is truly beautiful. And your grandfather treats me kindly, Louis.' A faint giggle escaped her lips. 'I'll be happy as a lark in springtime.'

Louis merely nodded. Was there nothing he could say to plant a seed of romance? Perhaps not; perhaps it was as his father and grandfather had both told him on several occasions—that he had been made for the factual army and the state, not the decant game of court gallantry or the art of irresistible charm.

Charles helped himself to a second pastry, for the young couple appeared to have forgotten his presence. He pulled at Adélaïde's sleeve, his baby pink lips turned down. 'Let's go back to Madame Maintenon and the others. They will be terribly cross.'

Adélaïde nodded, though she knew Charles's concern was hardly related to Madame Maintenon's good graces, and the trio trotted back with grass stains on their shoes.

Upon their return, they found that Madame Maintenon's attention had left the lilies and was instead occupied by two other women, to whom she was chatting idly, well aware that her protégées had not gone too far off.

The women were considerably younger than herself, both dressed in extravagant gowns that were on the verge of garish and hardly to their advantage: white, voluptuous furs draped their shoulders, protecting the glistening silk underneath, while large hats decked with feathers sat in their fontange coiffures and jewellery in shrill colours adorned their wrists and earlobes.

Though they were equal in beauty— with perfectly oval faces, plump lips, blush the colour of cranberries, and hair like high crowns of silk coils—one of the women appeared superior, for she thrust her chin forward and placed herself slightly in front of her companion. *They must be sisters, yes, I think I've seen them before. They're like two beautiful blackbirds against the snow.*

Madame Maintenon gave Adélaïde a sharp look, reminding her of her manners, and Adélaïde sank into a shallow curtsy.

The two ladies mimicked the move, and the foremost of them—who, one might argue, was also the most compelling to behold solely because of her airs—spoke. 'Louise-

Françoise, *Duchesse de Bourbon* and *Princesse de Condé*. Pleased to make your acquaintance, Madame.' She flapped her hand towards her companion. 'My sister, Françoise-Marie, the *Duchesse d'Orléans*. I would have thought you remembered—we were formally introduced at your arrival.' She gave Adélaïde the same glance a huntsman might give a deer while pondering how he might best skin and cook it.

'I recognised your face, Madame, but I'm afraid I was a little absentminded when we first met. I beg your pardon,' Adélaïde replied, embarrassed.

'Well, Madame, don't forget it again.'

Adélaïde bobbed her head, uncertain as to whether she ought to say anything, but the sisters had made their departure before she had the chance.

Charles whispered in Adélaïde's ear. 'Mademoiselles Nantes and Blois. That's what we call them.'

'I'm not sure I like them, at least not the one who spoke to me…Nantes? Is she always like that?' Adélaïde whispered back.

'The King's bastard daughters. Nantes is used to being the brightest one at court. She doesn't like you much, either. And now she's almost twenty-four years old, too.'

Charles's blunt words made Adélaïde gape like a fish, quite literally, but she said nothing of it. *Will they make my life a torment? Are they, no, is* she *so easily offended? And how could I ever compete with someone who carries herself with such authority?*

CHAPTER IV

C hristmas arrived little more than a
month after Adélaïde's arrival in
Montegris. By then, Turin seemed a
far-away place, as if it had only existed in a
dream or in a former life, and she no longer
felt any sincere longing. She always wrote to
tell her mother and grandmother of how
home would never cease to hold a dear place
in her heart, but the truth was that Versailles
held the dearest place there was, and its
people were climbing rapidly in her good
graces. Even her grandfather, Monsieur, had
somehow become an object of deep affection,
despite his occasionally brazen jokes and
tendency to flaunt every scrap of indecency he
could find in his own life or the people around
him.

Adélaïde found herself seated next to
Madame—Monsieur's German princess for a
wife—and was pleased at first, because the
woman was one of the few at court who did

not crinkle their noses at Adélaïde's hearty appetite. On the contrary, Madame set quite the example herself. However, the *Duchesse d'Orléans* soon proved to be a disappointing table companion because of her attitude.

'I was thinking about something just yesterday, Madame,' Adélaïde began. 'Do you think people will remember us? And miss all this?' *I don't see how anyone could escape it.*

'Hmm. I'm not certain they ought to.' Madame tucked another piece of pheasant, dripping with clear grease, in her mouth and chewed with a zealous expression. She turned to Adélaïde once more. 'I believe that the histories that will be written about this court after we are gone will be better and more entertaining than any novel.' Another bite, followed by a short pause. 'Those who come after us won't be able to believe them, and think they are just fairy tales.'

'Surely not, Madame. I'm sure the world won't be so frightfully dull in the future.'

Madame cast a disdainful glance over the room. 'Look at them, child. Look at the decadence. And the King's old drab pretending she's so demure, so sober.'

Adélaïde shifted her weight on the chair and plucked at a raisin in the bread on her plate. They reminded her of little black bugs. 'I wish you wouldn't talk about Madame

Maintenon like that, Madame. She has been most kind to me, and clever, too.'

'Pah! Clever—clever women never draw the winning lot. Although, I suppose she has.' The older woman pressed against the corners of her mouth with the napkin, then proceeded with cleaning the double chin.

'I think I drew the winning lot.' Adélaïde could not help herself, but smiled with something similar to pride. 'Don't you think so, Madame?'

'Perhaps, girl.' Her voice was dry. 'We'll have to wait and see if anything comes of it. My brother the King is fit to reign still— and Christ knows this court is scattered with potential princes.'

'I *will* be Queen, Madame. I promise you that.'

The conversation faded at that; Madame Liselotte returned to gorging on pheasant and Adélaïde returned to watching the potential princes and princesses at the head table. There were the King's illegitimate—though acknowledged— daughters and sons; there were his favourite generals and officers; there were more *marquesses* and *comtes* than she could count on her fingers or remember the names and titles of.

One whom she quickly recognised, though, was the Prince of Conti: a handsome young man with a cloud of finely spun, dark locks hovering down his shoulders, dressed up in ridiculously decorated clothes. If Adélaïde had her information straight, he was the brother-in-law to one of the King's daughters by Louise de la Valliére.

Conti and Nantes were soaked up in each other like two sponges; Blois sulked next to her sister, without doubt wishing she also had an admirer wrapped like a silk thread around her little finger. She might have had, of course—being a Légitimée de France—but she had perhaps been in enough stormy weather to last her a lifetime because of her marriage to Madame's son. Even now, the disdainful glances passed between the two women. *Is there never anything but bitterness in these people?*

Adélaïde pinched her cheeks hard enough to make the blood flow to them and give her what she hoped was a rosy look, and turned instead to Charles on her right. 'Which one is your favourite?'

'Ice cream.' He had streaks of said dessert around his lips.

'I meant the dances.'

'Well—then I don't know. They're all so precise. It's no fun when everything has to be *just so*.'

'I thought you'd dance with me—I know it would be jolly.' Adélaïde could not hide the note of disappointment in her voice.

Charles seemed to struggle for a second, but nodded. 'Only with you, then. As long as you don't step on my toes.'

And dance they did. Despite Charles' blunt steps and Adélaïde's own fluttering ways, the King clapped his hands as the two children tripped about the room between the more gracious men and women, contrary to every rule of etiquette. It was obvious to every pair of eyes at the banquet that they both had paid more attention to games than education in dances and manners—though at least the girl appeared a natural at times.

To her delight, Adélaïde remained at Versailles during the time between the Christmas celebrations and the New Year. The latter was welcomed with a greater spectacle than the former; the occasion was not affected by the same religious spell, and the path was clear for the exchange of lavish gifts.

Once the intoxicating mirth had filled its purpose and the court was beginning to return to its normal state, Madame Maintenon scuffed Adélaïde back to Saint-Cyr like a mother hen with her chicken.

After the overwhelming Christmas and New Year's celebrations, returning to Saint-Cyr felt

like both a punishment and a relief to
Adélaïde.

A constant chill permeated the
buildings, despite the crackling fireplaces and
thick robes. The demoiselles had exchanged
modest gifts, none of which could match the
ruby necklace Adélaïde grazed with her
fingers occasionally—one of the King's
generosities. She discovered a certain
gratitude for the school's strict code of dress,
for she could not have endured the glares
from the other girls had she been obliged to
wear it, nor the bulky weight of the stones
themselves.

When Adélaïde awoke the morning
following her return, the bed in the left corner
of the dormitory was gaping empty. The
covers and sheets had been smoothed so that
it looked as if they had never been used; the
pillow lay in its precise place. There was not
so much as a dark hair against the crisp
whiteness to indicate that there had been a
girl tucked up in it only last night.

Adélaïde presented her concern to one
of the Mistresses once she had taken her
breakfast in the refractory with the other
demoiselles.

'Mademoiselle Talleyrand-Périgord has
been taken to the infirmary—she is not to be
disturbed,' the Mistress said.

Adélaïde stiffened. *The infirmary.* Illnesses had always been one of her great enemies—not because she had often been ill, but because the phenomenon itself frightened her beyond comprehension. The way a human body could simply succumb to a vicious nature, crumple and decay... Even if it truly was God's trials, it seemed unfair.

'I would like to see her,' Adélaïde said.

The Mistress only shook her head. It was not possible, she said; that a future *filles de France* should be allowed in the same room where small pox—for this is what the illness was—ravaged. 'The King would not permit it, I'm afraid. Think of your health, Madame, not to speak of your skin.'

Adélaïde lowered her eyes; tears welled and burned. *Surely, there must be something that can be done...surely the King or Madame Maintenon can send for a credible doctor if only I asked?* She said nothing more to the Mistress though, but turned on her heel, and her steps echoed in the corridor as she scuttled after the other girls. A stubborn tear spilled over the rim of her eye, soaking her lashes. Adélaïde wiped it away swiftly. *Françes will be quite alright, yes, this is all paranoid nonsense.*

Despite the temporary conviction that such was the case, the classes in arithmetic and Latin that followed proved to be near impossible to endure. Even theatre—which always sparkled so brightly compared to the less creative subjects—demanded a focus Adélaïde could not seem to summon. The Mistresses constantly showered her with reprimands that were on the verge of growing grim, but none of them could push away the daunting images that took place in Adélaïde's head: images of pox-ridden faces and hands spattered with vomit.

Eventually, the surging temptation became too prominent to ignore. Once the candles had all been blown out, and the last sliver of sunshine had faded, she slithered out of bed and steered her steps towards the infirmary. The floor sent chills through her feet up her spine; the wood threatened to crack or squeak, revealing the figure who tripped over them. Adélaïde wrapped the blanket—which she had pulled with her from her bed—tighter around her narrow shoulders as she made a shortcut across the courtyard. The infirmary had been placed almost impossibly far from the dormitories, to prevent diseases from spreading. In that moment, Adélaïde cursed the architect, who must have been believed himself to be so terribly thoughtful.

She swung the door to the infirmary open with the utmost care, only making the crack wide enough for her to slip inside. If it had been any wider, it would have given away a shrill creak, just like every other door in the school.

The room bathed in darkness. Adélaïde's eyes had slowly adjusted during the walk, though, and she managed to distinguish the bedposts from what appeared to be a black void.

'Frances? Frances?' she exclaimed—if one can exclaim when whispering. She threaded down the aisle between the otherwise empty beds.

The object of her search was slumped under the fifth cover she reached. The girl's hair lay spread around her head on the pillow like a fan—a fan that appeared to have been dipped in filth and left to dry. A few strands rested on the bumpy cheeks where clusters of small knots had risen. Adélaïde had been bracing herself for this sight during every hour of the day, yet the blot of desperation in her chest expanded a thousand times when she ran her eyes over Frances. *How can such a drastic change occur in little more than twenty-four hours? She wasn't entirely well last night, but still...*

'How are you feeling? It's me, Adélaïde.' She climbed into the bed and shifted her weight until she rested comfortably next to the other girl.

Frances's eyelids fluttered. 'What are you doing here? The nurse—'

'But it's the middle of the night! Can't you tell? I only wanted to talk to you; the nurse mustn't find out.'

Frances drew a shaky breath. 'Do you— Do you think I shall be horribly disfigured? My brother won't be happy, Adélaïde.' She reached up two fingers and brushed them against her pox-smitten skin. 'He won't be able to find me a good husband.'

'Well, I don't care about that, so you can still come live with me at Versailles. And when I'm Queen, no one will be allowed to spend much time on vanity, anyhow.'

Françes did not answer, but rested her head in the curve between Adélaïde's shoulder and throat.

Eventually, the sun bled through the clouds outside the windows, and daybreak arrived. Adélaïde hauled herself down from the bed as quietly as she could, placed an ephemeral kiss on her friend's cheek—near the temple, where the pox had shown the most mercy—and made her way back into the dormitory where the other demoiselles were still asleep. It was pure luck, though, that none of them had woken and discovered not just one, but two empty beds, and reported the oddity to the *Maitresse de classe*.

Adélaïde shuddered to think of the harsh words and perhaps even punishments that would fall upon her if this should happen—and so she did not return to the nursery the following night. Instead, she began placing subtle queries in the occasional conversation with the teachers and mistresses, rotating the object of her questions so that no one would realise just how often she asked about Françes's health.

The replies she received were, at first, not very different from what she had seen with her own two eyes. Towards the end of the week, however, fragments of good news were pouring into the daily routines: a trickle of hope just bright enough to reinforce the conviction that everything would sort itself out nicely. The pus in the rashes was seeping away; Françes's forehead was not as burning hot as it once had been; the nurse had succeeded in feeding her a cup of hot bouillon without having to sweep up the vomit seconds later.

This progress did not last longer than a few days. Adélaïde's eyes were plastered to the plain, sharp-edged coffin that the two men loaded onto their cart before slapping the horses with the reins and removing it from the grounds of Saint-Cyr. The wood was fresh; it still smelled distinctly of sap. In the courtyard stood two members of the staff, giving the departing cart one last glance, their black frocks undeniably suitable for the occasion.

Adélaïde had only ever experienced a cramp in her foot before—but now it was as if her whole chest was contracting painfully, and then there was the constant burning in her nose that warned of oncoming tears. The tears had already come and gone, though, and left was a forlorn dryness. The sentiment might have been bitter, but she was not yet capable of bitterness.

The pox had taken a vicious turn, the nurse told her. It had been God's will that Françes should join him in his kingdom. Adélaïde wondered to herself how God could want such a thing—perhaps he envied the humans for having friends—but she said none of it aloud. Speaking in blasphemy would not bring a dead girl back to life. *Though if it could, I would say anything, no matter how offended God would be.*

Sorrow was a stranger to Adélaïde; a foreign phenomenon surrounded by mist that had now hit her like a galloping horse. Her little sister, Maria Anna, had been lost in infancy, but it was many years since, and Adélaïde only had hazy memory flashes of the tragedy. Now, she could not seem to grasp it—it did not fit into the delicately sculpted picture that was her world. That picture solely contained colour, merriment, frolics, and mutual adoration, not empty beds or cold coffins. She found herself aching for her grandmother once more, to the familiar columns of the Palazzo Madama.

Perhaps I should never have left...perhaps I would have been happier living oblivious to all this, perhaps all the splendour in the world is not worth it. But it must be.

It was this reasoning she clung to like a lost man might cling to a sole lantern in a dark night, and it was this reasoning that eventually brought her back to her regular senses. In parting from her family, she had found a new one waiting for her; despite losing Françes she still had two newly found friends in Charles and Louis, and others were certain to follow.

CHAPTER V

Early in March, the King was struck by one of his impulses; this time, he wished to make one of the regularly occurring masquerade balls a particularly lavish occasion. It would do the court good to be livened up, as the winter was clinging onto France like a stubborn child, he said. The objects of his so-called concern—the courtiers—threw each other long glances and squinted at their allowances, trying to find room in the budget for another elegant costume.

Adélaïde did not squint, nor did she grant her costume a thought. The King had already picked out one of creamy silks and emerald embroideries—but she only felt excitement regarding the mask that came with it. The masquerades were Adélaïde's favourite gatherings; she had only been allowed to attend one of them since Christmas, but there was no doubt of it. What could be more delightful than a room full of grown men and women transformed into little children thinking no one recognised them because of their diamond-studded masks? *When I am Queen, there shall be one every evening, and no one will ever truly grow up. Maybe that's the trick.*

The sun sank, making room for a compact canvas of darkness and a moon as bright as a chip of bone. The light of the chandeliers, however, remained on its post throughout the evening, casting its reflections between the mirrors and precious stones. Adélaïde held her fan in height with her eyes—as always when in the hall of mirrors on an occasion like this—and did her very best to keep track of the real people in the room. Their images in the glass still confused her at times, especially as they seemed to glide across the floor to the opposite side of the room without making a sound.

Even Charles had been allowed to attend. Adélaïde measured him with her eyes and noted that he had grown another two fingers since she last spoke to him two months ago. A crease appeared on her forehead. It was simply not fair that he—who was only ten years old—should be able to look down on her.

'Blois is looking, well, like a cloud of rain,' Charles said, a smile reaching his eyes.

'I wish she'd be merry at least when the King says so.'

'Perhaps someone needs to make her laugh. Or shout.'

'We ought not to be cruel, Charlie.'

The young boy pulled a mischievous grin. 'You don't like her any more than I do—you just won't say it. I stole a box of firecrackers from my grandfather's birthday—'

Adélaïde covered her mouth with one hand. 'Firecrackers! Do you think—'

She interrupted herself as two figures approached: the two figures in the room who inspired the most respect. The King shone like a piece of pure gold; Monsieur carried himself in a more solemn nuance of blue that appeared black from certain angles. Adélaïde couldn't help but to feel sorry for her own grandfather, who took such measures to not outshine his older brother. *It must be terribly dull to be the moon and not the sun.*

'What frolics is it you plan, my doll?' The King asked with a twinkle in his eye.

'Nothing to concern you, Sire.' Adélaïde smiled. 'Are you happy with the ball? I think it's just splendid, I really do.'

'Hm, yes. It's the shadow of what we had going on back in the day—wouldn't you say so?' He turned to Monsieur, arching an eyebrow.

Monsieur nodded. 'I remember one or two…interesting occasions.' His skin resembled aging parchment in the light from the chandeliers. The *Duc d'Orléans'* fifty-eight years were tugging at his heels, although his spirit appeared unmarked by time. 'Brother, when will you let go your firm grasp of the past? Versailles will always be glorious, but your own golden days are long gone.'

'How dare you speak to me thus?'

'You know it as well as I do, Sire. We must look ahead. The absolute monarchy won't last forever—no matter how much I wish it could.'

'Hold your poisonous tongue—don't you know your words are as good as treason?' The King's voice was rising by the second like an imposing thunderstorm. 'You never understood the politics of this nation; that's why I've kept you from them whenever I could.'

Monsieur abruptly turned from the three of them, took a few long, determined steps across the Hall of Mirrors, and halted by the side of a man whom Adélaïde had come to know as the Chevalier de Lorraine. His face was sculpted in refined lines so as to make it not handsome but beautiful, despite being only a few years younger than Monsieur himself. The Chevalier was infamous at court for his evocative nature, devoid of scruples, and for something else, it seemed, though no one had ever told Adélaïde what it was.

Monsieur tapped the Chevalier's shoulder with two fingers. When he turned, the King's brother yanked him closer by the arm. Then, he blatantly kissed him for several seconds.

Adélaïde did not notice her own lips forming a silent '*O*'. It was as if a wind had swept over the room, extinguishing every voice and every breath, until only complete silence remained. The demonstration would have been scandalising enough to have both participants drowned in gossip and disapproval if they had been a married couple. Adélaïde had never seen anything like it and found herself stifling laugher bubbling up in her chest.

The King himself was not amused, not in the least. Neither was he baffled, it seemed, for he simply clenched his jaw and nodded towards the door without so much as a word of reproach. Monsieur pulled the Chevalier with him and made his departure with a smug expression. When the ushers had closed the door, the atmosphere quickly recovered.

The King turned to his grandson and his doll. A mask of cold stone had settled on his face, but it cracked and crumbled as he looked at the two children. In its place was now the old man they both adored: the man who, to their narrow knowledge, was incapable of cruelty. 'Never mind my ill-mannered brother. The Italian Vice is a vicious thing—you must take care not to be infected. Now, let's see if they can bring us some sugared pears, hm?' A sliver of humour appeared in the King's eyes, and he disappeared to personally give the orders about the pears.

Adélaïde met Charles' glance. His face possessed a knowing expression, though Adélaïde could not understand why her little brother-in-law to be was so much better informed as well as being taller. Now that she thought properly about it, she found herself envying the shield of black lashes that rimmed his eyes, too. *Envy is not a becoming emotion...not in anyone, but especially not in a young lady.*

'The Italian Vice—yes...' Charles remarked.

'Won't you tell me all you know?' Adélaïde knew her hope was in vain.

Charles grinned and shook his head so that the periwig's coils bounced. 'It's not for a lady's ears. Let's get to it with the firecrackers instead.'

'I'll tell Louis.'

'Louis is a bore,' Charles muttered. 'He always spoils things.'

'Don't be so unfair—he's your brother. And we won't hurt her, surely? We'll just make her laugh,' Adélaïde said and smiled, her cheeks aching from it.

After a minute or two of Charles' arm-nudging and his fiancée's eager words, Louis at last joined the small group. Some fifteen minutes later, a sparking sound increasing rapidly in volume could be heard from underneath the cushion of Blois's chair. Shortly thereafter, the explosion was heard, and the woman who sat on said cushion plunged forward, tumbling down on the floor with her face shielded by skirt hems and men's stocking-clad calves. The remnants of the chair itself—a blackened, burnt skeleton of furniture—fell on its side, smoking.

A tumult broke out. An older lady and two men scooped Blois up from the floor after a moment of reluctance. Adélaïde felt a sting of regret, then the ripples of laugher shook her. Even Louis curved his lips in a strange way and beamed at her.

The victim of the firecrackers did not laugh, as had been their intention. She merely flushed poppy red, tried to brush away the burnt patch on the back of her dress without success, and excused herself from the gathering.

Nantes slapped her folded fan against her thigh repeatedly. As opposed to her sister, all colour had drained from her cheeks. 'Sire, I believe we ought to catch the culprits of such a cruel joke! *Sire?*' she said, turning to her father.

The King took another bite of the sugared pear he was holding between two fingers and frowned. 'And who would that be, Madame?'

'Is it not obvious, Sire?' Nantes threw a toxic glance towards the three children; Conti, who was fixed by her side, frowned.

Adélaïde wished nothing more dearly than to shrink into invisibility—perhaps she had gone too far for her beloved protector to tolerate. Of course, it would have been one thing if the boys had done it alone, but they were, after all, boys.

'You should be happy, Madame, to have such a refreshing breeze at court. The girl is harmless, and the *Duc*s also. We could use something to liven up this place to what it once was,' the King concluded, and Adélaïde breathed a sigh of relief.

Nantes pressed her exquisitely sculpted lips together. 'Yes, Sire. Then I shall be happy.'

The incident at the masquerade ball came with consequences—not the firecrackers, which went unpunished by the King to the courtier's astonishment, but Monsieur's indiscretion. Adélaïde's curiosity had been sparked, and refused to dampen without having been satisfied first. She had never before considered the possibility of two men; the concept of love itself was difficult enough to grasp. *Does it only exist within the holy bounds of matrimony, or can it only flourish outside it? Am I supposed to love Louis that way already? And are there rules as to whom one might love?* Her father had conduced numerous affairs, but to her knowledge, they had all been with young women of his own choosing.

Adélaïde decided to clear out the questions in her head by making a subtle inquiry to the one person she dared approach with the familiarity that was needed. She carefully lowered herself onto Madame Maintenon's lap, resting her hands between the folds of her own mulberry-coloured gown.

Madame Maintenon's thinly tweezed eyebrows arched slightly in surprise—without doubt, this behaviour did not resemble any she had previously encountered from one of her students. However, she did not resist Adélaïde, but wrapped one arm around the girl's waist to prevent her from accidentally slipping off.

'Please tell me, Madame, how I can best please your husband, the King?' Adélaïde asked, meeting the Marquise's' eyes.

'You please him already—I have rarely seen His Majesty so enchanted.'

'If it is so, then I'm blessed. But you truly must help me, Madame, for I fear my Italian ways don't please the court, do they?'

Madame Maintenon waited several seconds before giving her answer, making Adélaïde's stomach flutter. However, when she spoke, she did it with a voice so calm and soft it might have been soaked in honey. 'The court needs a bit of variation, my dear. If I were you, I wouldn't worry about such harmless things, when the inhabitants of Versailles have grown so stagnant that a breath of Italian air would only do them good.'

'But—' Adélaïde hesitated. She had a sneaking feeling she might be about to bring an unpleasant matter to the surface. 'But the King seemed so aggravated when he spoke to his brother, Monsieur—when Monsieur kissed that man.' A blush rose to her face at the mere mention of something as intimate as a kiss. 'He said to me that the Italian Vice was...that I mustn't be infected.' *Almost as if it was the pox or the measles.*

The older woman shifted the girl's weight on her lap with a delicate movement to avoid growing numb. She then flicked her tongue across her lips, trying to find the right words. 'The Italian Vice does not mean you can't be, well, Italian.'

'What is it then? The King sounded awfully grave.' Adélaïde's eyes widened in pure curiosity.

'It is—it is more commonly known as sodomy. Oh, how I hate to speak to you of such gruesome matters—they aren't suitable for impressionable young ears. And you oughtn't think of any sort of passions—'

Adélaïde felt a thrill rippling through her body. She had heard the word *sodomy* before, though her knowledge of its meaning was limited. The temptation of making further inquiries pulled at her; an invisible force urging her to satisfy every wonder and fill every blank patch in her mind, but she restrained herself.

Madame Maintenon had grown noticeably rigid and although she said nothing of it, Adélaïde was certain it would be for the best to let the subject slide. Perhaps she could observe her grandfather's scandalous habits closer by making herself slight.

'I believe it's time for your bath,' Madame Maintenon said.

'Can I have heated water this time, Madame?'

'Once you're married to the *Duc*, you can have all the warm water you like, though I recommend you not to bathe too often, or to do so in milk. Until then, it will only do you good to live simply.'

Adélaïde returned the Marquess' smile. With every passing day, her eagerness to become a full-fledged *fille de France* grew and grew until it felt as though it filled her completely. *Just to think, that only nine months remain! Oh, but nine months is such an eternity.*

CHAPTER VI

They say that waiting can be the worst part of one's life, but that having something to wait for is worth the suffering; Adélaïde found this to be as true as anything. The nine months did not go by smoothly, in fact, they resembled a track covered in bumps and pits. Of course, the court did not feel the jolting as the roughness passed, but then they had no insight into the Italian princess's mind; they were the audience to a seemingly perfected show.

The balls were held, the hunts organised, and the ceremony maintained. Occasionally, Adélaïde would make an appearance—when she did, she was glowing, for the King held her dearer than ever, and Versailles offered better entertainment than ever.

When she was shuffled back to Saint-Cyr though, the glow faded and was replaced by a pensive shadow. The good-natured girl remained, but the bubbling spirit was sapped away every time. Perhaps it was the gloom of Frances's death that still made the air at the school stagnant, perhaps it was the fact that none of the demoiselles were particularly eager to set up any jolly games. They were no longer curious of her—the Italian guarded no dark secrets yet, they had discovered with dismay—thereby she was merely a target of bitterness. Why would she one day become a *Duchesse*, and eventually a Queen? Why not them? Why did she, a delicate child of eleven with awful table manners, carry favour with the royal family and nobles?

Adélaïde could not offer any satisfactory answer to these questions, although they were never actually voiced. All she reckoned was that once her twelfth birthday arrived, she would not waste so much as a glance on looking back on the cold baths and cold stares.

On the 7th day of December, 1697, the day after her birthday, Adélaïde had been dressed up in her wedding gown and escorted to the chapel: the court's doll in every sense. The chapel practically vibrated from the deep tones rising from the organ's massive pipes. The music soaked the lavish room like a thick syrup, filling Adélaïde's ears and adding to the throbbing of her head. She gasped for air as discreetly as she could, daring to place her hand on the bone-hard bodice in a hopeless attempt to ease her own breathing. The corset was laced tighter than any she had ever worn before. The fabric—lined with busks of whale bone to enforce the straightness of the waist—seemed to squeeze her flesh together as if it wished to extinguish her completely.

When I'm Queen, no one shall wear such torturous garments, Adélaïde vowed in naïve determination. She brushed her fingertips over the clusters of diamonds and rubies, while resuming her stride down the aisle. The precious jewels with which the dress was adorned, and the heavy velvet robe attached to her shoulders, weighed as much as the young bride herself. The sleeves carried flaring layers of lace and gold brocade; her hair hang in thin ringlets down the frail curve of her shoulders.

The courtiers allowed present at the ceremony raised themselves on their toes in order to catch a sufficient glimpse of the opulent riches. Perhaps, they mumbled to one another, perhaps she was the brightest shining bride in Christendom—and yet the dress resembled a costume made ridiculous because of her childish aura. It was beautiful and expensive enough to make every bone in the noble women's bodies ache, but the girl looked like a wide-eyed little deer in it.

Adélaïde halted as she reached the altar. Louis lifted his eyes from the marble floor and studied his bride in something that could only be called awe. A few steps behind him stood the King himself, dressed in crimson red, eyes twinkling with contentment. *At least His Majesty is happy...and when he is, I am. I should be, no, I really am.*

The minutes dragged by; the ritual of matrimony was seen through. Adélaïde's eyes darted across the room. The primary thought passing through her mind was the desire to escape from the shell-like corset that trapped her body. Second came the delirious joy and triumph, fluttering violently in her chest and adding to her already slightly dizzy state. *Duchesse de Bourgogne. A fine title, a worthy title.*

The new *Duchesse* watched her fiancé's— no, her husband's—Adam's apple bob up and down several times. He drew a deep breath, offering her his hand and Adélaïde placed her palm on the back of it. As the organ continued to fill the air with its imposing notes, they threaded carefully through the chapel once more.

The state banquet that followed displayed a dizzying array of dishes lining the starched table cloths: chestnut and truffle soup, pheasant, scallops and oysters, salmon on a marble-like block of salt, hare stew, soufflé, candidate fruit. It appeared there was no end to the Sun King's imagination and appetite, nor to the cooks' capabilities.

The undressing ceremony was unlike anything Adélaïde had experienced before, despite the thousands of times both servants and ladies had helped her with her garments. There was something far graver in the atmosphere, a promise of both greatness and duty.

After the undressing, Adélaïde was led into the bedchamber, where Louis was waiting for her along with the most prominent men and women of France. The courtiers peeked over one another's shoulder, their lips turned upwards, eyes exuding curiosity. Their pasty faces appeared to push forward from every direction, although no one moved more than a centimetre.

The King raised his voice. 'May the *Duc* and *Duchesse* enjoy a happy and fruitful marriage, and may they produce an heir.' The words were a pure formality—there were to be no *producing* this night, or any night the following two or three years. The King had expressed this wish so bluntly, so forcefully, that no one dared take it as anything but a strict order. His doll was to remain a doll, a child. There could be no babies for a few years yet, anyhow.

Adélaïde shifted between the silk sheets; it seemed to her that she was sinking deeper into the thick mattress for every second. It was softer than any she had slept on before. Above her head towered the burgundy canopy embroidered with French lilies in gold thread.

She could feel Louis' eyes returning to her continuously. His breaths were heavy; curls of dark hair plunged down across one brow. *Has he been anticipating this moment, or does he find me repulsive all of a sudden?* It was impossible to tell, for his face was a solid mask of plain concentration.

One by one, the courtiers trailed out the door in forced silence, like a vividly colourful swarm of butterflies. One of the men—Adélaïde believed him to be the *Duc de Maine*—was unfortunate enough to trap the hem of one of the ladies' gowns under his shoe, and a series of tripping and hushed apologies followed. Once every one of them—including the King and the bishops—had made their departure, Monsieur poked his head through the doorpost.

'Nephew?' he hissed with a smirk on his lips. 'Don't compromise your marital rights, though my brother would have it otherwise.' He then withdrew his head, and Adélaïde listened to the clicking of his shoes as he hurried his steps to join the cluster of people farther down the corridor.

Adélaïde heaved herself up against the plush pillows and clasped her hands in her lap. She flashed her new husband as sweet a smile as she could muster despite tumult of feelings poking at her insides.

Louis bit his lip before reaching up to place a kiss on her lips, adhering to Monsieur's bawdy advice, but missed fatally and sank back after brushing his mouth against her chin.

Adélaïde could not prevent herself from giving up a rippling giggle. 'Do you kiss many girls?'

Louis's cheeks and temples took on an angry, pink blush. At the same time, his expression softened. It was difficult to be cross with the girl drowning in pillows next to him. 'No, Madame. I hunt with my grandfather, the King.'

'When I'm older I shall let you kiss me,' Adélaïde promised. It felt like a poignant promise; she knew her marital duties were nothing but duties, but a kiss could be something more genuine.

Louis opened his mouth to answer, but fell silent. Instead, he nodded several times, before flipping the cover off his chest and swinging his feet over the edge of the mattress. 'Good night, Madame. Sleep well.' He strode across the room and disappeared through one of the side doors that was hidden in the tapestry.

'Thank you,' Adélaïde said to the wall and glanced at her nails, resisting the urge to bite them. It was a terrible habit, her grandmother always said.

She pulled her knees up to her chin and tried to identify the feeling in her stomach. *He is not very romantic. He is kind enough, and perhaps he does not mind me, but...*She did not get any further before being interrupted by her own yawn and the shroud of exhaustion lowered itself onto her. Adélaïde stretched out her scrawny legs under the cover and slid down until she was resting comfortably. *It is quite alright. We can always be friends—one can never have too many friends.*

CHAPTER VII

The detailed account of the wedding night—which, one way or the other, reached the King's ears within the span of twelve hours—did not please him. In fact, one seemingly insignificant detail was the cause of an outrage that could compete with those he had sometimes suffered over far more serious matters in his youth.

'Were my instructions too difficult for the boy, perhaps? He was never...never that type, not like you!' Louis XIV snapped his fingers in the air before his brother's face.

The *Duc d'Orléans's* lips curved; his dark eyes twinkled. 'It was nothing. You have become a prude of late, brother. Where is the sovereign with the herds of mistresses?'

'He has found God—not that it concerns you. The *Duchesse de Bourgogne* is as good as my grandchild, and I intend to have her treated as such!' He swung his hand in a wide bow and was millimetres from knocking down the Prussian vase on the mantelpiece, had it not been for the servant who leapt forward with an alarmed expression.

'She *is* my grandchild, and I never objected.'

'That, dear brother, is perhaps part of your perversion.'

A cold wind swept over Monsieur's face, hardening his eyes and giving his skin a white tint. 'Don't link my preferences to my view on marriage. I only wish for you to have another set of heirs to your throne—that's why you scooped the girl up from that Italian rat's nest in the first place, no?'

The King cracked his knuckles. He could not stand this kind of insolence, however true it might have been some time ago.

Only to the servant, who stood stiffly by the fireplace while awaiting orders, did it occur how these two old men resembled the hot-livered boys fighting over silly things that they had been once upon a time. Anyone who had spent more than a week or two in the Palace of Versailles knew their clashes were commonplace; the bickering took place both behind and outside locked doors with the same frequency that the ladies purchased new shoes. However, it seemed they never resulted in anything that could not be solved in a matter of minutes—save the fundamental disagreement concerning Monsieur's love life.

'Hold your tongue in the future and we shall say no more of it,' the King said. 'You know nothing of the female anatomy if you're hoping for children at this time in their marriage.'

'Very well. I'm sure you're experienced enough in the field.' Monsieur's voice was dry as flour.

'I'm the monarch in this room.'

And on that note, the quarrel faded into nothingness. Not a word of it was ever retold to Adélaïde, nor to Louis, which was lucky, for the situation was already delicate. Louis found himself in a pit of despair and frustration, unable to convey his emotions or mould himself into the charming romantic—and his wife wondered why she had not fallen deeply in love, before pushing the thought away and carrying on with her games.

CHAPTER VIII

The first year and six months floated by like syrup: sweet but slowly. And too much of a sweet thing can sometimes begin to numb the tongue, which was what happened to Adélaïde. Every day that offered something particularly lovely— meaning practically *every* day—began to numb her sense of humble appreciation until the loveliness felt like a granted right that could not and should not be questioned by anyone. This childish indulgence might have been an obstacle, had she not been surrounded by people who had been fed the same medicine, the same syrup, for years or even decades.

The only misfortune came when one of her dogs, a dear little thing with pink paws and chestnut fur, took ill with food poisoning and had to be shot with one of Monsieur's pistols to end its suffering. Adélaïde was quite shaken by the incident, but the dog was soon forgotten, as the court moved to Fontainebleau in the late summer months of 1699.

Naturally, Adélaïde had visited the leisure palace before, but on those occasions, the court had not remained for as long as she might have wished. Fontainebleau was, of course, smaller than Versailles, but the curved stone stairs and countless chimneys had their charm, especially when the evening sun's golden rays warmed the buildings.

Adélaïde tripped through the high, rich grass on light feet despite the tightly strapped shoes that made her toes ache horribly. Thousands of dew drops landed on her salmon pink satin skirts; melting glass beads being absorbed by the luxurious fabric. Adélaïde gripped the folds of her dress and hunched it up to reveal stocking-clad ankles—a brazen gesture made innocent by the sheer youth she exuded.

There was a certain softness in the air—a softness which tends to make itself present on the doughy, warm days of August. It defines the long hours spent soaking in sunshine, wading through a lukewarm spring of water, breathing in the heavy scent of ripening fruit. It dulls the sharp reality until it begins to resemble a painting, colours floating into one another and mixing together. It was that softness which surrounded the cluster of courtiers now heading across the green in an unusually unorganized manner. Thin, white sheets had been placed out under the shadow of an oak. Around them were chairs and small tables laden with plates spilling over with delicacies; the servants had had a busy morning preparing the scene. Flaky, golden brown puff pastries filled with rich strawberry cream; colourful sweetmeats coated in powdered sugar; hot chocolate; ripe fresh fruit already polished with silk handkerchiefs; duck liver pâté on bread.

Adélaïde ran her eyes over the countless options, yearning to enjoy as many as she could before being gently slapped on the fingers by Madame Maintenon. *She doesn't know what she's missing.*

'A fine display—and a fine day for an outing, or what say you, my doll?' The King whipped the grass with his mahogany cane, striding forth with the slightest trace of that natural grace that so often leaves as old age approaches.

Adélaïde slowed her pace so that she might walk by his side. 'Yes, Sire, it's most splendid.' Her lips curved into a genuine smile.

'The—' A fit of coughs interrupted the King, riding his chest violently. '—the landscape reminds me of a charming collection of stories I shall have sent to you. *Histoires ou Contes du Temps Passé*. Tales and Stories of the Past.'

'Monsieur Perrault wrote them, didn't he, Sire?' Adélaïde flashed the old man an attentive glance.

The King smiled to reveal the gaping hole where his teeth had been in his youth. 'Indeed he did! Now, you will tell me exactly what you think of them, and we shall see what he has to say for himself when we point out any fault of his, eh?'

A look of playful conspiracy passed between the King and the *Duchesse de Bourgogne*. It did not last long, though. As Nantes walked past, she gave Adélaïde a harsh nudge with her hip, causing her to stumble over her own feet, tripping comically before straightening herself up once more.

'I'm certain *Madame la Duchesse* has more important aspects of her education to tend to, Sire. Extinguishing that Italian accent must surely be a priority compared to reading fairy tales, no?' Nantes arched an innocent eyebrow, smiling sweetly at her father.

The King only grunted incoherently, offering Adélaïde his arm as to make sure she did not trip again. The sweet, almost pleading look drained from Nantes's face; the blush on her cheeks was washed away by invisible rain.

Adélaïde swallowed a thick lump of triumph and equal discomfort. Mayhap she had not been as courteous towards her husband's aunt as she ought to have been, but then it was not her fault that Nantes was illegitimate. It was not her fault that Nantes held a lower rank, and above all, it was not her fault that the woman should be so frightfully unpleasant to speak to.

The lavishly adorned group arrived at the prepared picnic. The King sank down on the lush cushion of the *fauteuil* with a heavy breath and loudly cracking joints.

Maintenon followed her husband's example—though in silence—and the remaining members of the party who possessed significant rank took their rightful places on the *tabourets*. Adélaïde felt a sting of aggravation. *Can't the rules of etiquette take even the shortest break, when the summer is so lovely, and Versailles so far out of sight?*

A pair of porcelain hands—much like those on Adélaïde's new dolls—placed one of the puff pastries, resting upon a linen napkin, in her lap. Adélaïde offered the lady a brief smile in return. She could not recall her name, but what a wonderful person the young woman must be, to notice her yearning glances! Adélaïde sank her teeth into the sweetmeat with a crusty sound.

Maisonblanche let out the faintest sound, like a squeaking rat, but was silenced by a stern glance from the woman next to her. Adélaïde took another bite; the pink cream left a thick trace between her Cupid's bow and nose. It did not occur to her any longer that the King always ought to be the first one to eat.

The tense silence, interrupted by ruffling skirts and flapping fans, was quickly broken as the King himself accepted a plate ladled with food and set to the daunting task of finishing every crumb.

During the course of the picnic, Louis gradually inched closer to his coral-cheeked wife. His clothes felt stuffy in the heat, the periwig made his scalp itch, and the confusing choir of voices crept inside his head and seemed to him like one buzzing mass. He reached out two slender fingers to tap his wife on the shoulder.

Adélaïde turned. 'Yes?'

'I should like to walk with you—if you don't mind, dearest.' The words carried a genuine warmth, but could not escape the stiff tint that defined Louis's voice.

'Sire?' Adélaïde turned her face up to gaze into that of the King. 'Do I have your permission to walk with my husband? We shan't be gone long.'

The old man scoffed. 'Permission granted. And Louis—' His grandson froze in the midst of squatting up to his feet. 'Keep your hands behind your back.' He knew, however, that the subtle warning was quite unnecessary.

Louis pushed the low, wispy branches of the oak aside, allowing Adélaïde to pass swiftly underneath them. She kept her neck erect at all costs, so as to prevent the wax-packed, chalk-powdered coiffure from swaying and causing her to lose her balance with its considerable weight. Louis allowed his eyes to rest on the prominent dimples in her neck for a moment. 'I pray you are well today, Madame.'

'Quite well, thank you. Although I must confess, I've had such horrid pains in my abdomen and back ever since I woke.' Adélaïde's voice gave in to the faintest tremble and she gave her cheeks a quick pinching to bring back the colour.

'We must have the doctors sent for, Madame—to bleed you.' Louis's eyebrows came together in a frown.

Adélaïde wondered if this might be the right time to inform her husband that said brows needed a thorough tairiling, but decided against it. Instead, she shook her head and gripped his hand in her own small, cold one. 'Please don't, Louis. I can't stand it when they do, and it would be such a shame to spoil your grandfather's day.' *And my own day. Bleeding is such an awful process.*

Louis hesitated for a mere second, and nodded. He then yanked Adélaïde's hand away from his own with as much gentleness he was able to summon, and placed it so that her fingertips rested on his arm with the lightness of a butterfly, according to protocol. Thus, the young couple resumed their walk through the cluster of trees. Patches of sunlight glinted through the lacework of leaves above their heads, dancing over the grass. The lively voices from the fluttering, bright courtiers remained constantly in the background: a reminder of how rare solitude was.

'What do you think about them, truly? Nantes, Conti, Blois...' Adélaïde tilted her head to gaze up at Louis.

'They're of my grandfather's blood, hence I respect them.' Louis shrugged as if to express the simplicity of the matter. 'Nantes can be vulgar, I know, but I don't deem it my place to say.'

'I think she wishes to rise above her station, don't you think so, too, Louis? I know I use Italian words sometimes—and I try not to, I really do—but surely my accent isn't *that* obvious?' Adélaïde's eyes darkened and her lips pressed tightly together.

'On the contrary, dearest Madame.' The young *Duc* had run out of words. Though he wished nothing more than to comfort the girl on his arm, to talk at length of how charming she was compared to his numerous aunts—not so much because it was true as because she wished to hear it—it was as if his tongue was suddenly a useless lump of clay. He clenched one hand until the bone shone through the skin. Perhaps God would someday grant him the gift of charisma.

Adélaïde, however, did not pay any attention to Louis's shortness. Instead, she shrugged off the gloom, cocked her head to one side, and offered him a mirthful smile. 'I don't care what they think, though. One day, I'm going to be Queen, and they will be old, sad women with no right to reprimand me!' She grew serious again. 'Oh, but you mustn't tell anyone I said something so spiteful.'

'My lips are sealed,' Louis replied. The two of them had returned to the sheets and chairs. Louis bent down to place a stiff kiss on Adélaïde's cheek, and withdrew with powdered lips.

'Louis! Sit down, child,' the King exclaimed, and his grandson obeyed without further ado. 'Come here and sit on my lap, my doll.' He patted his thigh.

Adélaïde scurried forward, treading carefully though the labyrinth of voluminous skirts, out-stretched legs, and buckled shoes. She then placed herself on the King's lap and reached out for one of the sugar-coated confection on his plate.

On the night following the picnic, the King was in a particularly good mood, and requested a performance. The task, as expected, fell to one of his favourites.

Adélaïde tapped her fingers against the piano keys, without pushing them. A little whirlwind of nervousness stirred in her stomach, for there were more people assembled in the salon to judge her musical skills than there ever had been before, and the King's eyes were as attentive as those of an excited puppy.

Her throat itched. *Strange. Like a thousand ants crawling up and down. Dear God.* Adélaïde swallowed twice in an attempt to reduce the itching, then pressed the keys, letting the first notes of "Canon de Pachelbel" float throughout the room. Once her lips parted to give voice to the lyric she had crafted so carefully though, the words were cracked and practically coughed forth. Her mind darted, fingers slipping on the keys.

The courtiers flashed each other glances; their eyebrows arched. Surely, the *Duchesse's* performance had not been this inept the last time, or the time before that?

Adélaïde's heart leaped in panic, but she forced herself to sing the next sentence, although the melody of the piano began to falter and her voice was now half-choked. Her throat burned and she ceased playing and massaged it with increasing desperation. The room stared as she at last abandoned the song and succumbed to coughing and hissing.

After a few seconds, the King's chair creaked as he began heaving himself up—but two men of lower noble rank scuttled forward before he had gotten on his feet, doubtlessly seeing their chance to win the monarch's favour by assisting his twitching favourite by the piano. The coughs were violent now, riding her aching lungs, ceasing for a second or two only to return when the itching did. With a tongue as dry and thick as plaster, Adélaïde rose from the piano stool and fled from the drawing room without accepting the two men's assistance. As the door slammed behind her—ushers too baffled to react properly—the ripple of murmurs grew stronger, but the sound was shut out.

Adélaïde ran, though the agony made it difficult. She ran until the softness of her bed welcomed her in her bedchamber, and pulled the layers of sheets and embroidered covers above her head so that they created a protective bubble from the rest of the palace. Gasping for air, she finally managed to calm her coughs, remaining quiet through the burning pain. *I've already made an utter fool of myself...what would they say if I began whining too?*

A minute, perhaps two, passed in her warm bubble before the doctors arrived with their concerned frowns, portfolios, and trains of peeking courtiers. As they took turns examining her, asking her questions she could barely answer without her voice cracking, Adélaïde's eyes wandered to one lady in particular.

Nantes stood leaning against the window sill, slouching, secure in the knowledge that no one would pay her any attention, her head tilted to the side. A thick garland of hair, powdered iron grey, fell across one shoulder. Her mouth was locked in an amused smirk, as if it was an effort not to break into laugher.

'It seems to me as though Your Royal Highness has ingested some sort of itching powder—perhaps extracted from rose hips or a stronger herb,' the King's personal physician said.

'I agree, Madame. I fear there is nothing to be done but wait for the effect to subdue,' the second doctor chimed in, scratching his hawkish nose and looking over the thin silver rim of his round glasses. 'Perhaps a glass of warm milk or cream would help soothe the itching.'

Adélaïde sank back into the plush pillows again, not because she was tired, but because she wished to slip away from the court's peering eyes. The cream was ordered, stirred with tea and honey, and the people were chased away from the door to the bedchamber.

Only Nantes lingered. 'Unfortunate, Madame, and on such an occasion! But don't concern your little head over that. I'm certain they have had their entertainment by now.' On that note, she flicked the grey coil over to the other shoulder and made her departure.

The immediate agony ceased in a matter of hours, though a faint tickle remained, as well as a queasiness originating from copious amounts of soothing beverages. One of the doctors went as far as to bleed her, although there were hardly any other signs of disease.

Adélaïde made sure to clasp both rubies and diamonds to her wrists and neck— for once—before making any public appearances the next morning. For the first time, she realised just how much protection they offered: instead of suppressed giggles she was given envious glances; the focus shifted from her humiliation to her riches. *It is petty. Shallow. It works.* Once the danger had blown over, Adélaïde discreetly unclasped the jewels, relieved to escape their weight.

CHAPTER IX

Adélaïde tip-toed through the dark passages with a speed rarely used before in the *Château de Fontainebleau*. The blood rushed in her ears, hear head pounded with fright—yet she was certain there were no footsteps following her. The *femme de chambre* lay sound asleep, no doubt.

Adélaïde halted before the door giving access to Madame Maintenon's private apartments. Her hands trembled the slightest, making it difficult to scratch the lacquered wood with her finger nail. Naturally, there was no reply. An impenetrable lid had been put over the entire palace, it seemed, making it impossible for anything but the night itself to exist. Adélaïde pushed the door open in a swift movement. She tripped across the lush carpet with muffled steps and continued through the set of rooms until she was standing by Madame Maintenon's stout bedpost.

The figure underneath the covers turned softly, erupting into petite snores. Adélaïde did not see the King, and she thanked the skies for this. She did not wish to trouble him with this particular matter—it was too shameful, too monstrous to be uttered in anything more than a whisper.

'Madame?' Adélaïde gave the woman a gentle poke. 'Madame?'

Madame Maintenon awoke only after a series of increasingly desperate pokes and nudges, and as she heaved herself into a sitting position, a drowsy glaze remained over her obsidian eyes. 'What on earth is the matter?'

'I-I am afraid I shan't be Queen after all.'

'You had a nightmare?' Madame Maintenon asked and took the icing cold little hand in her own.

'No, Madame, it wasn't a dream. I think—I think I'm dying.' Adélaïde's voice broke towards the end of the sentence and she swallowed several times before uttering another word. 'I've had pains in my body throughout the day, and all of yesterday, and now there—there is blood, too. And I don't think it has anything to do with the itching throat I had yesterday evening.' She lowered her eyes in shame. 'I've never heard of anything like it, and I swear I've done nothing to make it happen!' *Unless God sees some fault in me I haven't yet discovered myself.*

71

The glaze on Madame Maintenon's eyes slowly lifted; she pulled the silk sheets up to her chest and patted the covers by her feet. Adélaïde obeyed and crawled up on the bed.

'I think I know what has happened to you, little *Duchesse*. And no—' She held up a hand, 'You are not dying, that much I can promise you.'

'Truly?' Adélaïde's eyes grew wide as orbs; the tremble in her voice was exchanged for a glint of hope.

'If I am right, then what you are going through is something that happens to all young women—and you must learn to live with it.'

'I don't understand.'

The night eventually shifted into dawn, and the first rays of crisp morning sunshine bled through the slit in the curtains. Meanwhile, the King's wife filled the *Duchesse de Bourgogne's* head with all the knowledge she had to offer of the female body. Some details remained unspoken— perhaps for the best—but once the corridors of Fontainebleau sparked life and light, the mysteries that had clouded Adélaïde's mind had been replaced by knowledge.

She returned to her own rooms through the passages linking the chambers together, and slipped between the bedsheets so that the *femme de chambre* might find her where she had left her.

The days that followed the unpleasant discovery were nothing short of excruciating. Adélaïde found that the physical discomfort was petty compared to the fact that she had passed the hallmark of becoming a woman—all while she was convinced she was still a little girl, especially in the King's eyes. She thanked heaven that her marriage had not been consummated yet, and would not be for another year and a half, for once that day came, she would be faced with the paradox of living two lives: one in the role of the young woman producing heirs, one in the role of the child who amused and softened the old monarch.

Adélaïde had never realised the struggle that lay ahead until she had the benefit of Madame Maintenon's thorough teaching. *It's so terribly unfair. Why should such a burden be placed on my shoulders, and not on a man's?*

The summer carried on though, as summers tend to do regardless of individual dilemmas. Fontainebleau shimmered in the heat; the peacocks, who had been temporarily imported for the duration of the King's visit, strutted across the greens, and the courtiers strutted alongside them. Under the surface simmered forgotten rumours brought back to life.

The *Prince de Conti*—who had been styled King of Poland but found himself unwelcome and been forced to return to France—had made a brief visit to the court.

Nantes lingered more often than not, finger tips placed on the crook of his elbow, radiant. Adélaïde could not recall her looking so filled with joy even back in the day when Conti's presence at court had been a regularity. *Perhaps the wait and the absence has made the reunion even sweeter.*

Although the courtiers loved to indulge in gossip—even the rare good-natured ones—few dared to speculate openly in this particular affair, for fear of the King's wrath. His daughter may be illegitimate, but she was not to be made a laughing stock. Hence, Adélaïde sought out Charles.

'I bet they're *lovers*,' he said gleefully.

'Well, I am sure no one bets against you.' Adélaïde had learned some time ago to not blush at these remarks of his.

'Want to take a look?'

'Charlie! No—' Adélaïde twisted her hands. 'But I was just thinking about the...the incident. A few weeks ago, if you remember.'

'How your throat was as sore as a skinned cat? It was funny.'

'It was horrible! Anyhow, I think now would be a good time for...revenge, I suppose. And don't tell me it's ghastly, because I already know it, but she started it.' Adélaïde brushed away a strand of hair that had stuck to her cheek and sat down on the silk ottoman.

Charles grinned, placing himself on the other end and drawing up his legs under him. 'I don't think it's ghastly—I'll help you. We'll pull her down from her high horse—just a little bit, I mean.'

A new, soaring enticement fluttered in Adélaïde's stomach. She had never before intended any true harm by the giddy frolics and childish pranks in which she had joined Charles, but this was different. Her cheeks still burned as fiercely as her throat had, when she thought back on the evening in the salon, and she had not yet dared to sit down by a piano again for fear of repeating the failure. *I know they snicker at my etiquette, but I won't have them laugh at my music. Not that.* 'We can always have a look, surely?'

Charles nodded, serious all of a sudden, and slipped off the ottoman. Adélaïde allowed him to pull her to her feet in an unseemly manner and smiled to herself. When one asked assistance from the *Duc de Berry*, one never had to wait long, at least not if the matter concerned anything he saw a glint of entertainment in.

The usher by Nantes's rooms stood erect at his post. 'Forgive me for saying so, Your Royal Highnesses, but the *Duchesse de Bourbon* is not in her chamber at the moment.'

Adélaïde raised herself on her toes so that she would not have to crane her neck to look at him. 'I know. She sent us to fetch a few documents for her.'

Charles twisted the thick gold ring on one of his fingers, which had been a present from his father two months previously, on his thirteenth birthday. 'I'm sure you wouldn't want to refuse us entrance. His majesty would not approve—'

Adélaïde threw him a glance. The petty speech was not necessary, for the man had already swung the door open. Swift as weasels, they proceeded inside, until they were standing in the midst of the superfluous bedroom. Heavy velvets and embroideries clad the walls; every single object had been ingrained with gold; the pleated canopy almost caved in under the weight of the bundles of frays. *It ought to be beautiful.* A strange sadness stung Adélaïde. *It ought to be beautiful, but she's used all the luxury in the wrong way.*

Charles immediately set his sights on the drawer by the middle window. Sheets of paper— plain and scribbled on—and various trinkets were scattered over the floor as he began rummaging through the drawers.

Adélaïde began scooping them up, fervently trying to rearrange the papers. While doing so, she soon stumbled across the object of their little search party: tens, no, hundreds of sheets covered in ink, all carrying a faint scent of rich vanilla, littered with declarations of love, of longing, even of passion, signed with a simple "François".

Adélaïde stared at the letters in her hands with blank eyes. *So this is what love is?* She could not imagine anything else. That woman...that wry, snobbish creature had untangled that great thing which Adélaïde herself was so anxious to find. That woman possessed a blessing that could barely be comprehended, and Adélaïde could not for what her life was worth understand why that blessing had not fallen upon *her* yet.

'Put the rest back and help me carry these.' Her voice trembled slightly.

'Whatever you say.' Charles scrambled together the remaining papers and things from the floor, shuffled them back in the drawer, and took part of the stack in his arms. 'She'll know someone was here when she opens the drawer. Unless she has a head made of pâté.'

'It doesn't matter—she shan't be able to prove anything. Please let us go before she comes back.' Adélaïde's eyes darted to the door.

That evening, as members of the court began to assemble for card games and music, they were met by a scent of vanilla. All across the salon, sheets of paper lay spread on the cushions and tables, even on the glossy floor. Adélaïde made herself as small as possible by the King's side as ladies and gentlemen alike began scooping down to retrieve the fragments of letters, sheer curiosity twinkling in their eyes. Not many seconds passed before the compact silence— previously only interrupted by the ruffling of skirts and the clicking of shoes—was shattered by a hundred hissing whispers. It had been far too long since they last got their hands on something this juicy; a few were as bold as to fold a paper sheet and tuck it in their pocket as a souvenir.

Adélaïde watched as the King lowered himself onto his *fauteuil* with a heavy grunt, and felt as if someone had cut off the blood to her limbs and head. His brows furrowed; the bracket of lines around his mouth hardened. He reached out a hand and slowly picket up a paper from the table next to him.

In the midst of it all stood Nantes: eyes glazed and absent, cheeks flushed crimson, shoulders square and rigid, one of the sheets crumpled in her clenched hand. The otherwise crowded room had created a sort of space around her, an invisible barrier. *She knows. She is going to slap me, right here and now.* Adélaïde swallowed.

But Nantes did not move a finger, she merely remained frozen on the spot like one of the marble busts. Then, she turned on her heel in a swirl of argentella lace and marched out of the salon without so much as a curtsy to the King. A wave of dread swept over the spectators, for this incorrect exit was almost as bad as the letters themselves.

'Clean this rubbish up,' the King ordered through gritted teeth, and the servants with the wine flagons went to work after a moment of hesitation. 'I believe we shall have a pleasant time in the gallery. The view of the gardens is incomparable.'

In the blink of an eye, the courtiers seemed to regain their composure. Nodding and smiling, they allowed the papers to sail to the floor, and trailed after their master to the other room—which was, in truth, quite unsuitable for an *appartement*.

The *Prince de Conti* took a hasty leave, returning to some family estate or other. The scandal, of course, had been nourished and therefore prospered—but after a week or two it had filled its purpose and fell flat. Nantes's little girl, Marie Anne, remained a constant reminder of what had been, but as she was naught but a baby of eleven months she could hardly ever be seen in the halls of the palace.

Adélaïde found herself sitting once more with Charles on the ottoman, this time feasting together on crunchy almond biscotti. 'You don't think I ought to apologise?'

'No! You said it yourself—she started it. And it was fun. Are they really supposed to be this hard?' Charles glared at his half-eaten biscotti.

'I love them, they taste just like the ones my grandmother's cooks made.'

'You're too pretty to apologise, anyways.'

Adélaïde could not help but smile at this. 'Don't be silly.'

Charles scowled. 'Am not! My brother doesn't know how lucky he is.'

'Louis has been so kind to me.' Adélaïde frowned. 'It just...well, for some people it takes a little time to get to know one another.' *At least I hope that's all there's to it.*

Charles leapt forward, smacking his lips roughly against hers, then pulling back with a bewildered expression. 'Bet you he doesn't even dare to do that.'

'Charlie—' Adélaïde felt her cheeks burning but could not decide if it was a feeling of flattery or revulsion. *It's not right, not even the slightest.*

'Oh, don't be such a prude!'

Adélaïde spent a moment wondering whether she ought to scold or laugh, then decided on the latter—it was a far easier thing to do. The incident slipped like water through a strainer.

'Well, I am going to try, at least.' On that note, she raised herself from the ottoman and departed.

Nantes was alone in her rooms, except for three maids and an usher. Dressed in a dark blue *deshabillé* that was draped loosely over the soft contours of her body, she looked strikingly similar to her mother, *Madame de Montespan*, in her golden days.

Nantes was leaning back in a chair whilst the maids attended to her toilette in preparation of the dinner: one was kneeling on the floor and buckling a pair of shoes on her mistress's feet; two others were perfecting every coil in the coiffure.

Adélaïde halted by the threshold. Although it was not a rare thing that ladies of rank should receive visitors during their toilette, she felt like an intruder. 'Your Grace.'

Nantes did not bother to raise her glance from her freshly manicured nails, but nodded faintly.

Adélaïde forced her legs to take a few steps forward. 'I—I'm frightfully sorry for—well...'

'What exactly, Your Royal Highness?' Nantes savoured every syllable.

Adélaïde felt the good will slip away bit by bit. *Perhaps it was a mistake to come. Perhaps Charles possesses more common sense than I give him credit for.* 'It was unfortunate that your private endeavours should be so widely known.'

This time, Nantes stood up, brushing her maids away with a flick of her hand. Slowly, torturously slowly, she strode towards Adélaïde, sweeping the silky *deshabillé* closer to her skin.

'You,' she began, 'you are like one of the pugs.'

Adélaïde stared at her.

'See, you sit by their feet and let them pet you, looking so terribly endearing, and then—' Nantes lips curved in a joyless smile.

81

'—then you bite. And the wound becomes infected.'

'Pugs cannot be blamed for their biting if they're kicked, Madame.'

Nantes tilted her head back, laughing. 'Witty, are you now? Little baby slut.'

Adélaïde drew a breath. That word was what the ladies of the court whispered about their husbands' favourite mistresses; a dreaded insult uttered only behind spread fans. And here it was, like a slap in her face. She could not in her wildest imagination think of a suitable answer. 'You—you'll never be Queen, Madame. The King loves *me*.' She sputtered through a haze of tears.

An ebony hairbrush came flying through the air and Adélaïde took a swift step to the right. Then, she retreated to her own chambers, where Charles was finishing up the crumbs of the almond biscotti.

Those were the last words—save curt, necessary formalities and greetings—exchanged between Adélaïde and Nantes for months. Despite the harsh exchange, it was as if a weight had been lifted from Adélaïde's chest; she no longer suffered any guilt for exposing the letters, for they were once more evenly matched in the game of hurt and hurting. As the late summer shifted into autumn and eventually winter, she found herself preoccupied with another matter: that of her marital duties.

CHAPTER X

Adélaïde drew short, sharp breaths. *This is when it truly begins.* She pressed the sheet—which suddenly felt almost sheer—to her breast, waiting. Oddly enough, she recalled the same feeling from when she had stepped down from her carriage in Montegris, little more than three years earlier, greeting the King. That moment had been a similar trial, for it had been equally fateful, equally demanding of perfect execution. Then, the goal had been to win the King's immediate favour so that her new life might be a pleasant one. Now, it was to truly settle into the role of being a wife and beget children of her own. It seemed to her the first task had been a thousand times easier to accomplish.

Adélaïde allowed herself to sneak a glance at Louis, who was smoothing the folds in his chemise, feet dangling over the edge of the massive bed. *He will always be sweet. Always love me.* The thought proved a greater comfort than she could have suspected—it was true. There was something else, though, something far more pressing. *What if I'm barren? No.*

'You look pale—I hope you're not ill?' Louis swung his legs up on the mattress, lying on his side so that he might look at his wife.

'No, not that I know of.' Adélaïde forced a smile. 'Remember...remember on our wedding night, when I said I would let you kiss me when we were older?'

'Yes.' His face wore its usual, stiff mask, but his eyes shone warmly. His hair was almost as dark as it had been on that night, still framing his temples in the same way. Seventeen now, he had not yet grown handsome, and would probably never do so—but Adélaïde did not mind in the least.

'Well, you may.' She smiled without having to force it this time. Her grandmother's advice returned to her: *You don't need romance to do your duty, you only need the right attitude and the grace of God.*

Louis returned the smile, slowly, and shifted closer. After a moment of fumbling, he found her lips in the dark room; a series of shallow kisses followed. Adélaïde took as deep breaths as she could manage. Then, she lay limp as a dead herring, waiting again. When Louis had finished, he slumped back on his side of the bed with a relieved smile—Adélaïde

85

suspected he had been under pressure to preform—and clutching one of her hands, he drifted into sleep.

Adélaïde lay wide awake, surveying the embroideries on the canopy. She could not for her life imagine how men—and some women, too, it was rumoured—could find any pleasure in what she had just endured. *Perhaps it would be different if the circumstances were more...more spontaneous. But tasks rarely are spontaneous, I suppose.*

The gold thread in the fabric above their heads glistered like silver in the pale moonlight slithering through the slit in the curtains. A bird chirped outside the window. Adélaïde ran her hand over the bare skin on her stomach underneath the chemise. *How long will it take?* She removed her hand and rolled over to her side, so that her body fitted closely next to Louis's. Though she remained awake throughout the better part of the night, Adélaïde was eventually reconciled to the situation, convinced that she might well have made a worse match. The *Duc de Bourgogne* would not hurt her, and though the act was not the most pleasant thing she had experienced, it was based on a mutual understanding.

Louis's weekly visits to Adélaïde's bedchamber continued without disruption throughout the months that followed. Each time, his eyes shone with an unusual mirth; his movements and his speech grew more relaxed and knowing. In the daylight, however, he quickly settled back into the role of the frustratingly awkward husband.

The King sometimes gritted his teeth when the subject of heirs arose. 'There is no rush, my doll. Don't listen to them—' He gestured towards the courtiers. '—you're still a child yourself.'

'I'm not so certain they agree, Sire.'

'Fools, the lot of them. Come here and read me a passage or two.'

To distract herself, Adélaïde ordered for a set of canvases, paintbrushes, and paint to be sent to her room. There, she set out on a mission to master the art of painting—which proved to be a far more difficult than she had anticipated. The colours did not blend properly; the nuances appeared too similar to one another; the inspiration was meagre. Adélaïde soon realised that however much she adored ingenious artwork, theatre, and music, she could never aspire to create any of it herself, except for a few pieces of lyrics every now and then. It was one thing to behold and relish; it was another to craft it.

Nevertheless, she persisted with the canvases in her chambers, practicing, the paint spattering her hands and causing several maids and ladies to exclaim in horror over her carelessness.

CHAPTER XI

Adélaïde did not know the hands that had ground the paint now so awkwardly daubed across her canvas.

Those hands were sprinkled with countless freckles and carried blisters from the monotonous work. A young girl—hardly older than the *Duchesse* herself—surveyed them as she stood packaging the paint by the counter in her father's shop. Colette did not fancy the brown spots, nor did anyone she knew. She wished she could wash them away as if they were stains of the paint, or perhaps cover them with white lead like the fashionable women did. Perhaps the same remedy could be used for her bright ginger hair.

The bell above the door tinkled and a customer in sombre attire entered. The woman was draped in amber-coloured taffeta, but the fabric showed signs of a decade's diligent use. A broad nose dominated her face; deeply carved lines surrounded her eyes.

Colette pulled her eyes away from her skin and acknowledged the woman with a small nod. 'Can I help you with anything, Madame?' she asked.

'I would like to place an order.' The woman approached the counter in a wobbling walk that brought a goose into Colette's thoughts.

'Father?' Colette called. 'Father, there is a customer to see you.' Slightly louder this time, her voice cracking a little.

An older man of short but sturdy statue, with greasy streaks of silver hair framing a rather noble-looking face emerged from the back room leading to the inventory. His statuesque expression immediately twitched into that of a welcoming and proud craftsman. 'Yes, Madame, let us see what we can do for you.' He then extracted an arc of paper, a pencil, and a splotched quill container from underneath the counter.

The woman began listing her order while Monsieur Auclaire scribbled down her every word on the paper. 'Carry on with the packaging,' he mumbled to his daughter.

Colette was just about to reach for the paint once more when she felt the bitter taste of metal on her tongue. *Not now. Dear God, not now.* Seconds later, she gasped for air as that feeling grabbed her: the feeling of almost— *almost*—slipping on ice or missing a stairstep. She cleared her throat carefully. 'I'm just going upstairs for a moment, Father.'

'You're staying where you are—the work is not finished yet.' Monsieur Auclaire's nose crinkled slightly, as it always did when he was on the verge of harshness. Then he smiled at the woman and continued taking her order.

'It won't be long. Please...' Colette did not have a chance to finish her plea before her vision blackened and the convulsions began to ride her limbs mercilessly.

When the light returned, she found herself on the creaking floorboards of the back room. As she pulled herself to her feet, she had to press a hand to her scalp to dull the burning pain. It was not a result of the seizure, she knew from experience, but from her father's jerking at her hair in order to remove his distasteful daughter from the customer's view.

Colette drew a breath in sheer relief, for there was no pool of vomit or urine on the floor. Such things occurred less often for every year that passed—but the seizures themselves had not ceased yet. *Mayhap if I pray harder, they will. They have to...*

'When is this going to end? When will you learn to control your wicked nature?' Monsieur Auclaire spit out the words, flicking his tongue over the bright pink lips. 'You scare away the customers, girl!'

'I can't control it—I've said it dozens of times! And I tried to excuse myself, but you insisted—' The resounding slap cut Colette off mid-sentence and flung her head to the left, leaving a prominent mark as the blood rushed to her cheek. She inhaled shakily and allowed thin garlands of hair to fall over her face, hiding the tears reflexively welling up in her eyes.

'Luckily for you, the Madame didn't withdraw her order before making her departure.'

Colette nodded.

Monsieur Auclaire continued; it was as if someone had extinguished the anger in his voice by drowning it in ice water. 'Go upstairs and help your mother fold the linens.' He ran a hand through his hair and Colette half expected it to emerge covered in oily patches. Her father then returned to the part of the house serving as boutique.

Colette scrambled up the staircase, running one hand over the lacquered rail. The numbness in her cheek was drifting away, only to be replaced by intense needles of pain. *I have to try harder. I have to find a way to manage those strange seizures—there must be a way.*

'Colette?' Madame Auclaire beckoned from the bedroom she shared with her husband. Colette hesitated before obediently entering and halting in front of her mother, who was sitting at the narrow table by the window, her hands occupied with slicing letters open with a silver knife. The knife was one of the household's most valued possessions; Madame Auclaire had prided herself on it for as long as Colette could remember, especially before Monsieur Auclaire's trade had begun paying off and they lived in the more rural parts of the city.

Madame Auclaire tucked a strand of strawberry blond hair behind her ear and put the knife down carefully on the table. She had been much renowned for that beautiful hair in her youth—this was one of the stories she most enjoyed sharing with her children—although it had had a stronger tint of red in those days. 'You're awfully flustered, dear. Come, sit, and help me with the correspondence. Your father is a busy man. Come.' She gestured for Colette to take a seat on the other, equally uncomfortable chair.

'Yes, I know. And my brother? Can't Bastien be of some assistance?'

'He is busy also. Men are busy. Now, won't you be so good as to help me answer a few of these letters? These are from clients—and these are private matters.' She pointed at two piles that could not be discerned from one another.

Colette nodded, defeated, and reached for one of the letters. Only then did Madame Auclaire seem to notice the harsh, pink mark on her daughter's cheek, for she bit hard in her lower lip and placed a gentle hand over the mark, the wistful gesture conveying regret. However, she said nothing, for she was not at all surprised and had learned early in her marriage that there was no use in even commenting on her husband's behaviour.

*Tell me you'll make him stop. Tell me that it will go away. Just tell me something...*Colette swallowed her disappointment as the older woman remained stubbornly silent and removed her hand to proceed with her task of writing replies. She cursed herself for being so foolish as to think that her mother might have exchanged the submissive kindness for something more useful, then cursed herself once more for thinking badly of a woman who lived under constant threat of being treated poorly if she dared to utter a word that did not please her husband.

In truth, the only member of the Auclaire family who had never experienced this dread was Bastien, the oldest son and the apple of his father's eye. Perhaps he had achieved this status solely through his sex, or perhaps it was because he had been the only surviving baby out of three from an earlier marriage—the other two dead from tuberculosis. Whatever the reason, Monsieur Auclaire obviously prided himself on Bastien and was taking every measure to sculpt the ambitious young man into the ideal heir to the family business.

Though Colette might have despised anyone else who held that position out of years' worth of bitter jealousy, she tolerated Bastien, because she had long since discovered that it was impossible to hold any grudge against the one person who would—on rare occasions—act as her defender when their father crossed the line. She knew, however, that it was not because he loved her dearly but because he possessed the same, deeply lodged desire to maintain morals and decency as she did, and because he was accustomed to speaking his mind.

Bastien was engaged to the daughter of a cloth merchant though, a dark-haired girl with a tendency to sneeze every other minute, and it was only a matter of time before he would shift his priorities to setting up his own household and building his own family. *And then Mama and I will be left alone. God only knows how we'll manage. Dear God, do have mercy.*

A curt knock on the doorpost attracted Colette's attention. The handsome figure of her brother appeared as though summoned by her thoughts of him. Bastien cleared his throat and slid a hand through his neatly combed, red hair, then spoke with a voice like cool, rippling water. 'Father sends his apologies. You mustn't upset the customers, 'Ette, but he was perhaps a little harsh in reminding you.' His eyes wandered to Madame Auclaire for a second or two and softened; he then turned on his heel and was gone.

Colette did not doubt the apology was entirely Bastien's doing, or perhaps even something he had made up; hence the consolation was as good as non-existent. Her mother, however, swallowed it without question, and a careful smile spread on her lips.

The day proceeded in relative idleness. Colette and Madame Auclaire finished their task of writing letters and moved on to mending and washing clothes that had been ripped or stained as a result of walking along the muddy streets, then hung the garments to dry in the February sun. The woman who functioned both as kitchen maid and house maid was given her instructions for the evening meal, and the four family members gathered around the dinner table in their usual manner: silence.

If a randomly chosen man or woman from the streets outside had been asked what they saw through the window, they would most likely have answered that the group was nothing out of the ordinary, and they would have been right.

However, Colette was convinced that if she could only escape them, her life would improve immensely. She kept her eyes on the soggy stew on her plate, moving the spoon in absent-minded circles against the porcelain, while wishing herself far away for the hundredth time. *Someday I shall leave, and find happiness...find justice and freedom and all those lovely things...*Although she knew deep down that this was naught but an illusion fit for a fairy tale, it was a hope necessary to keep herself from drowning in a sea of despair.

CHAPTER XII

Colette suppressed the apprehension that bubbled up inside her when her mother announced that they were going to the market.

Madame Auclaire stuck her arm through the basket handle, then straightened the white cap on her head. Her tongue flicked across her lips in concentration as she arranged every strand of hair in perfect symbiosis, placing them carefully behind her ears, and surveyed her reflection in the spotty mirror once more.

'Mama—'

'I am on my way, Colette, if you would only calm your horses!' Madame Auclaire finally decided that she was satisfied and followed her daughter out into the bustling street.

A shining black carriage with gold carvings passed by, and an older gentleman peeked out behind the half-drawn curtains.

Colette followed his eyes and felt a sting of offense as she saw the blunt grimace on the man's face. It was obvious he did not find the view very agreeable, though the *Rue Bertin Poirée* was far from the worst sight that could have met him. The houses were tidy—indeed, they did not contain more than one or two families each—and the street did not stink notably compared to other parts of the city, nor were the walls of the buildings littered with beggars. *There really is nothing to grimace at. He ought to smile.*

Colette shot the old man a glare, although she was not certain if he caught it. She could feel something of her mother inside her at that moment: a plain refusal to consider herself anything less than fortunate, a refusal to realise the faults in her own living conditions.

Madame Auclaire seemed unaware of any of these reflections. She hooked Colette on her other arm while carrying the basket and drifted towards *Les Halles*.

The market was as busy as always. Booths and tables crowded the square; hardly a cobble stone could be discerned between the sweeping skirts and frocks, the livestock and merchandise. Voices flooded the area as salesmen and merchants informed the Parisians of how exquisite *their* goods were, how reasonable *their* prices were, or how many eggs *their* hens could give.

Colette did not quite know where to look. It was an unsafe place to be if, well, if something should go wrong. *There's so many people that can see me.*

'Let's see now...' Her mother unfolded a crumpled list of groceries. 'We may as well begin with the fish.'

'Yes.'

Arms still linked, the woman and the girl pushed their way through the wall of warm bodies until they reached the line of fishermen, who busied themselves with gutting their trouts and herrings. The fishes lay skilfully slashed open, their flesh gleaming white or pink in the sunlight, eyes like glass and mouths gaping. The stench surrounding them was almost too strong to endure.

While her mother dug out a few francs from her skirt pocket, Colette scanned the marketplace for an old acquaintance: Gêróme Cochet. *He ought to be huddled up here somewhere.* Gêróme was a young man— though he looked a decade older than his years—with prominent cheekbones, bony arms, and a clucking laugh. Colette had never seen him take one step without Tod, the wolfhound who looked like a dirty rag rather than an animal, but then she had never seen him walk much at all. He often sat slumped against the house walls, inspecting his dirty nails, waiting in vain for some higher force to pluck him from his misery. *Yes, there he is.*

Colette threw a glance over her shoulder to make sure that her mother was occupied in small talk with the fishermen, perhaps even beaming in their flattery, before trailing off to the man and the dog.

Gêróme offered her a weak smile as she approached; despite the squalor and the poor diet, his teeth were straight and impeccably white as if he had devoted every waking minute to caring for them. It was an odd detail in his appearance, a small miracle, even. Colette caught herself thinking—not for the first time—that he might have been handsome in another life.

'How are you holding up?' she asked.

Gêróme buried his hands in Tod's tangled, silver grey fur, and tried to sit up straighter. 'It works.'

He always says that. It works. Colette extracted a piece of bread from her skirt pocket and handed it to the young man. 'No work?'

Gêróme took the bread, staring at it as if he had forgotten the question. Then he placed it on the ground beside him without eating so much as a crumb. 'No, no work, Mademoiselle. My leg won't cooperate, I'm afraid. *Ca craint.*'

'Your leg?'

'See for yourself, Mademoiselle. It was only a little cut a few days ago, by Christ.' Gêróme let out a sigh, closing his eyes. Tod swept with his tail and tramped on the spot, then laid down and rested his head on mud-caked paws.

Colette bent down to look properly at Gêróme's leg, which was bared up to the knee, and had to swallow several times to refrain from running back to Madame Auclaire, or simply turning and vomiting on the ground. The limb was one big, blackened lump with patches discolouring in red and purple. The flesh was swollen, the skin gleaming like tar. Colette had seen it before, on her brother's finger to mention one occasion out of many. *Blood poisoning.*

'You...' Her voice trembled. 'You can't save that, Gêróme. You should have kept the cut clean—or so I have heard.'

'Can't save it?' Perplexity gleamed in his eyes.

'It's as good as dead. It has to go, or it might spread until *you* have to go.'

Gêróme shook his head so that the blond hair whipped his cheekbones. 'It will be fine, Mademoiselle. I couldn't find a handy man to do it, anyhow.'

Colette's lips parted, but Madame Auclaire grabbed her arm before she had a chance to reply, nudging her away towards the bakers. Her face was pale as a sheet. 'Do not speak to them. They're not the same as we are, Colette. Poor beggars—'

'They're people, Mama.'

'Do you want to live in the slums? No? Then don't associate with it.' Madame Auclaire's voice was high-pitched like a mouse's squeal and she pressed a hand against her bodice as if gasping for air before collecting herself.

Colette clenched her teeth but said nothing. *Maybe they'll have taken him away the next time. Maybe to some far-off mass grave.* She shuddered.

Mother and daughter returned to *Rue Bertin Poirée*, the basket brimming with groceries and lips tightly pressed together in two unyielding lines.

Three days later, when they once more strolled arm in arm to *Les Halles*, Gêróme was nowhere to be found. Tod was wagging his tail slowly, his big, wet nose searching along the house walls for something eatable. Colette considered throwing him one of the freshly purchased lamb chops from the basket, but decided against it, knowing that her mother's loose tongue might well result in a pert slap from her father once he found out.

These things happen. However deep that knowledge was carved in her, she could not seem to shake the feeling that there must be more to life than scraping your pockets for coins and feasting on crumbs, before growing black and blue and leaving behind you a poor dog who had no pockets to scrape for coins in. *There simply must be*...But there was not, not for the Parisian masses. It left her twisting and turning in her sheets during the evenings; it projected nightmares during the night, nightmares of succumbing to the looming threat of poverty.

CHAPTER XIII

Colette's lungs were burning and her throat felt like dry, cracking parchment. Strands of hair grazed her face and made it impossible to see clearly ahead.

This was worse than it had been for years. *He never saw before. It was only one container.* She relived the moment once more while pushing her way through a narrow alley: slipping the paint down her apron pocket, feeling the cold spread throughout her body as she met her father's piercing eyes, turning on her heel...The stash of sketches that she kept hidden under her mattress needed colour to come alive; the blue paint had been used to the last drop and she had been desperate enough to steal another container from the inventory.

Monsieur Auclaire did not tolerate thievery—especially not in his own children. His daughter had long since concluded that this was rooted in three fundamental things: he was a man of conventional principle, he was unwilling to see so much as an *écu* go to waste, and finally he believed that painting was a futile pastime. Of course, he worshiped the artworks themselves, but artistry was for the truly gifted and for those with obscene riches—not for the likes of himself who needed every waking minute to earn enough money. He sold the paint at an expensive price, as anyone in that trade would, but the produce he needed to make it was almost as expensive.

Colette continued through the alley, emerged into the light on the other side, and ducked around the corner of a red brick house. *La Seine's* stench gave her a wave of nausea, as always, but there was no room for such pettiness. Monsieur Auclaire's hovering footsteps were closer now than they had been mere seconds ago. His clunking shoes beat against the street like an expression for all the vile threats she knew he would have shouted after her, had the street not been crowded with people.

The surroundings confused Colette, because although she was accustomed to finding her way in the heart of Paris, she could not remember seeing these houses before if her life depended on it—which it did not quite, but close enough. In a frenzy, she continued along the bank of the river, before ducking in between the buildings once more. Two women with baskets hooked on their arms pulled their skirts close so that the hems would not be stepped on, glaring at her as she dashed past them.

Before she knew it, Colette was standing in front of her own home once more. *I must have been running in a circle.* Monsieur Auclaire's footsteps had faded away and could no longer be heard. Colette took deep breaths, trying to slow down her heartbeat, which felt like a pounding hammer against her ribs. Then she threw a glance behind her, before opening the door to the shop and carefully making her way through the house and out on the backyard. In the very same moment as she stepped out on the sun-steeped stone, the fear grabbed her again.

'—that wretched girl!' Her father's voice was like cool, black marble. Floor boards creaked; Bastien's voice answered something in an appeasing tone, but Colette could not distinguish the words. She darted across the yard, instinctively climbed inside the delivery wagon, and pulled the covering down to shield herself from the eye of the beholder.

Cowering, trying to make herself as small as possible by pure willpower, Colette waited—and waited. Shoes stomped in the yard and in the shop, but after a few minutes they died away and left her in silence so intense that it quaked. The wagon was not the most comfortable of hiding places, but the enclosed space gave a sense of security, and Colette rested her cheek against the stubby wood. She had no intention of crossing the path of her father's wrath—or any aspect of the world outside the rough covering—until enough time had passed to make the consequences milder.

A sudden jolt pulled Colette back into consciousness. The wagon was moving rhythmically, horse hooves beating against the cobble stones, wheels creaking. A shiver ran down Colette's spine as she realised the situation's graveness. She dared not move or even shift her weight for fear of being discovered. Her father was undoubtedly driving the vehicle, his legs spread and his hands clutching the reins. *If he knew I was here, not to mention that I've accompanied him on one of his delivery errands...*Colette suffocated the vivid image in her head before it had the chance to grow truly terrifying.

The sharp paint fumes stung in her nose. Her eyes slowly adjusted to the dark, but the sight that met her was only what she had known was there: containers of paint packaged in creamy paper and tied with ribbons, stacked on top of each other.

Colette listened closely to the sounds of the street. The hectic chatter and neighs of horses slowly thinned out until only the breeze and the creaking sound of the wagon's wheels remained. Paris seemed to have faded in the distance; even the air that floated in from a slit in the covering was crisper and cleaner than that of the city centre.

The minutes dragged by in a daze. Colette remained as still as a sculpture, her limbs aching because of their crammed position and with a tickle in her feet where the blood flow had been cut off. Eventually though, the wagon's pace slowed before stopping completely.

Words were exchanged outside, though the voices were muffled by the covering. Then Colette felt the wagon sway as her father jumped down from his seat. She crawled forward between the neatly wrapped packages until she was able to peek out at the front of the wagon. The scene that played out before her eyes was in no way unusual to the courtiers, but nevertheless it nearly took Colette's breath away, for in her eyes it was the most bizarre thing.

Her father, Monsieur Auclaire, stood with his feet planted widely apart, hands clasped behind his back, speaking in a formal tone to two other figures. Said figures were clad in expensive fabrics—Colette did not know enough of such clothing to recognise the names or qualities of the material—and voluptuous periwigs warmed their scalps. Yet it was not these strange men who attracted Colette's wholehearted amazement; it was the background to their conversation. Solid, ineffably polished stone interrupted by large, sashed windows, and behind the glass panes a room heavily adorned with gold and vivid colours. *It can't be...but what else would it be, then? Like a fantasy world...*

Naturally, Colette had heard brief descriptions of her father's deliveries to the Château de Versailles, but they had always been distant fairy tales. She had always allowed them to remain just that, because how was it possible for such a place to exist when half of Paris was a puddle of poverty and filth? How could such a beautiful thing stand so close to all the undeniable ugliness?

A knot of disgust dimmed the euphoric thrill. Colette did not know which emotion to heed, so she withdrew her head from the slit in the covering and shuffled backwards again. Three pairs of footsteps grew distant; there was the thumping sound of a door closing. They had proceeded inside—perhaps so that Monsieur Auclaire might receive his payment. Colette's heart leaped. Before stopping to think properly, she had slid out from her hiding place, flung herself down onto the ground, gathered her skirts above her ankles, and sprinted across the courtyard.

Along the towering wall, past the windows, making a sharp turn through a narrow gateway—and she reached the back of the building. Colette pressed against the cold stone, as if to make herself invisible, and took deep breaths. Once her lungs had caught up, she allowed herself to lift her gaze.

The endless gardens stretched out before Colette's eyes: rich greens twirled and flourished, intertwined with bright gravel paths and fountains cascading sun-chinked water. Along the gravel paths strolled sets of exquisitely clad figures, the ladies' fingertips placed decorously on their walking partners' arm. Colette caught herself frowning at the ridiculous sight, for it was as though they were porcelain figures ready to break unless handled with the utmost delicacy.

Colette chewed her lower lip, barely noticing the metallic flavour on her tongue as a drop of blood emerged. She smoothened her skirts and patted her hair, which had been tousled by the short sprint. *Perhaps I could pass as...well, as some sort of servant. Surely, those high and mighty creatures must be too self-absorbed to pay any attention to someone like me. But I ought to go back. I have to. He will leave without me unless I get back in the carriage right now.* A breath caught in her throat. That was it. Monsieur Auclaire would be long gone within half an hour, and because he had every reason to believe his eldest daughter was still cowering somewhere in Paris, he would not pay any thought to her absence in the wagon. In that very moment, a vertiginous thought—no, a plan—began taking shape in Colette's mind. *They will think I have run off, after the beating. They would be right. But they would never dare come looking here. And why not? Why not stay?*

Colette did not reflect upon the matter any further, for fear of being discovered before Monsieur Auclaire's departing still loomed over her shoulder. She inhaled for several seconds and strode down the stairs to the gardens below, her hand practically caressing the smooth rail. She wiped the dust that had assembled on her palm on her skirt, before proceeding forward past a pair of nobles. The gentleman flashed her a faint glance—his eyes momentarily covered shifting in a hungry expression—but neither of them said a word. Colette felt a thrill of relief, although she had never really expected to be spoken to.

The mild April warmth rested against the nape of her neck; the wind played with a few loose hairs. Colette summoned all her effort to absorb the loveliness that had hit her in the face so suddenly—but was interrupted.

A large entourage approached the gravel path on which she was standing. In the very front walked an old but nonetheless glamorous man of broad build and commanding presence. He occasionally supported himself on a shining walking stick of dark wood, but carried himself upright. Behind him came two women—perhaps in their late twenties—frenetically fanning their pale faces. After them followed three men; lastly came four servants and a cluster of guards in decorative uniforms.

Every one of these figures could easily have attracted attention, at least the nobles, but Colette's eyes gravitated towards the young girl on the old man's arm. Locks of brown hair framed her childlike face and piled up on her head in an intricate coiffure, which Colette believed was called a fontange. Her skin was pale; her face reminded Colette of a marble statue crafted by one of the amateurs, for the artist had not quite managed to chisel the beauty of a Greek goddess, only close enough. The girl kicked the gravel coquettishly as she walked, stirring up tiny whirls of dust around the mauve-coloured slippers.

Colette tore her glance from the girl and glued it to the ground as the entourage passed. She did not know a great deal about the hierarchy of Versailles, but the man who strode at the front without question held a position on the top of the pyramid, and it only seemed appropriate that a supposed servant girl should lower her eyes at almost anyone.

Once they had passed, Colette remained as if nailed to the spot.

CHAPTER XIV

After regaining her wits, Colette sneaked inside one of the buildings and walked rapidly until she reached what she assumed was part of the servants' quarters. The clatter of brass pots and spoons echoed through the corridor; the walls were lined with identical doors. *It's like one, massive machine being run by hundreds, or maybe thousands of people. Like clockwork.*

Footsteps clicked against the marble floor and Colette's glance darted around in search of a temporary hideaway. For lack of a better alternative, she tried the handle on one of the identical doors, it opened, and Colette dived inside without another thought. The space she emerged into was dark as charcoal—not a single candle lit up the walls—but she knew from the distinctive odour that it must be some sort of linen closet. As she stretched out her arms to try and judge the size of the room, her hands collided with shelves lined with folded cloth, which confirmed her suspicions.

How can any household need so many sheets and napkins? There must be hundreds...and this is only one room of many. Of course, it's probably not one household but several...

The light flashed in Colette's face as the door to the linen closet swung open. A pair of pale, almost transparent, eyes peered inside—belonging to a young woman with a rat-like face, dressed in plain white and red cotton robes. Her tongue flicked across her lips as if preparing to say something.

Colette's heart raced as she pushed past the maid servant—for that was what the woman must be, considering her modest clothing and mere presence in itself—and steered her steps down the corridor with one goal only: to escape from this tangled mess before anyone else even laid eyes upon her. She did not get very far, though; surprisingly strong fingers held her back by her sleeve.

'You'll tell me what on earth you were doing in there, Mademoiselle, and I might not call the guards on you. And I don't just mean in the closet.'

Colette turned, suddenly nauseated. 'I—'

'Well?' The young woman stuck her hands to her hips, thrusting her chin forward.

'I'm looking for employment, Madame. I'm a hard worker, truly.'

'It's Mademoiselle—Mademoiselle Barnette. Employment? There's not much of it in a linen closet, I can assure you.' Her voice was tinged with amusement, though a commanding tone still lay underneath.

Colette wrapped her arms around her chest. *There is no turning back now, no more half-witted lies.* 'Don't you need more servants? A palace as grand as this could hardly have too many of them.' It was shot in the dark.

'Well, Versailles does not run itself; we do. You really are in luck then,' Mademoiselle Barnette gave up a sound somewhere between a scoff and a laugh, 'because the girl who used to sleep in our chamber, Therese, she left to get married to some dusty farmer. The Superintendent is worried we won't get all the marble hearths cleaned in time every morning.'

'I—'

Mademoiselle Barnette interrupted her with another shower of chatter. 'Can you imagine that? I mean, we are not exactly the lazy lot, and still...'

'Then...you might take me to her? The Superintendent?' Hope sparked in Colette: a tickling hope of new beginnings, fired by these extraordinarily lucky circumstances. *I shan't ever go back—not to the Rue Bertin Poirée, not to the damned shop, not to the market place...I won't give them anything to complain about.*

The spark grew to a flame as the maid nodded reluctantly. Colette trailed eagerly behind her and together they made their way through what appeared to be a labyrinth of corridors and staircases, before arriving by a grand wooden door.

'This is the ground floor of the South Wing,' Mademoiselle Barnette explained. 'The Superintendent of the Queen's household lives in the rooms behind that door—though, since the Queen is no longer among the living, she's responsible for other parts of the staff these days. There, on your right, lives Monsieur and Madame *du Maine.*'

Colette did her best to memorise everything she was told. She was then instructed to wait outside the door while the maid entered to have a word with the Superintendent.

'You'll be filling Therese's place for the time being—but you better not make any mistakes, or you'll be out on your ears. And don't expect any high wages or comfort, because you're awfully lucky she accepted you without any references. We really must be in desperate need of a work force,' Mademoiselle Barnette said upon returning.

Colette's heart hammered in her chest. *Can such a thing be? To work here, in a place like this? God is peculiar, no, God is good.*

Mademoiselle Barnette continued: 'I shall show you our bedchamber now. Come.'

It was a small room—perhaps nine square meters, made to appear even smaller by the crowding furniture—in the attic of the South Wing. In the unlikely event that one was promoted to *femme de chambre*—a chamber maid—Mademoiselle Barnette informed Colette, one would lodge closer to one's mistress or master.

Two beds, draped with worn, sage-green fabric spattered with tiny blossoms, had been practically built into the walls of the room like alcoves. Between them stood a fireplace in black marble, which was covered in a thin layer of dust and ash, contrary to those that were seen and used by the courtiers themselves. In the centre of the room stood a table and two chairs crammed together.

Colette strode forth a few steps and sank down on one of the beds, spreading her hands on the coarse cover. This was nothing like the splendour she had witnessed during her brief moments in Versailles's *real* apartments, but it still held a slightly higher standard than what she was accustomed to in Paris. Of course, there was the ever-present smell of too many people living in the same space, but at least the stench of the Seine was not trickling through a cracked window, at least the sharp paint fumes were not sticking in her nose and lungs.

'Marie and Josephine ought to come any minute now, since the lot of them will have gone to bed. You can call them by their first names if you like—we don't waste as much time on formalities when we work. I'm Jeanne—forget Mademoiselle Barnette.'

'I thought formalities were everything here.'

'To those who matter, of course, and if you're speaking to anyone superior or inferior. But we are all maids of one sort or another, so why bother, when it only steals away time that could be used for minding our business?'

'I suppose so.' Colette leaned back and fell down flat on the bed with a *thump*. 'And you don't tire?'

Jeanne's eyebrows came together in a wrinkle and seemed glued to her forehead. Her otherwise so bland, forgettable appearance changed in a fraction of a second because of this very wrinkle; it somehow expressed every bit of her personality that Colette had seen so far. 'Well, Marie and I are tired. Not Josephine. She's always so *content*, so *perfect*. I oughtn't to be here in the first place, nor my sister, considering—'

A scrape on the door post, then two more girls pushed through the crack in the door, the last one closing it behind her. The two were as different as a dog and a cat: one short, with pale grey eyes and hair the same shade as Jeanne's, the other awkwardly tall and lean, obsidian hair slicked to her scalp beneath the white cap and a swarthy complexion. They both stopped in their tracks at the sight of the new, younger girl on the bed.

Colette fumbled until she was on her feet again and managed a painfully unpolished curtsy.

'Girls, this is Colette Auclaire. She shall be filling Therese's place, as long as she can keep up the work. She'll sleep with you, Josephine.'

'Pleased to meet you,' Josephine—the tall, dark one—mumbled.

'Why, that's all very sudden. We usually hear word before a new maid is hired.' Marie frowned in symbiosis with her sister.

Might they be twins? I could hardly tell them apart even without that strange expression. Colette spent the following quarter of an hour engaging in small talk, or rather answering fervent questions, with the Barnette sisters, while Josephine sat on one of the chairs making tiny stitches in her needle work under massive concentration. An elaborate set of lavender was slowly taking shape under her slender fingers; the shades of green and purple shone in the warm light from the candle on the table.

There, in the dusk, Colette parried dozens of inquiries, some plain curious, some suspicious. The answers she gave were more often than not cut short by the next question, and therefore she did not offer any superfluous information about herself in spite of them.

'And you father? What does he think about your new position?' Marie said and removed the cap from her hair, braiding her thin mane.

'He's very pleased, I think. It was his idea, of course, otherwise I would not be here in the first place.'

'I see. Well, they won't be receiving any extra money back at home, unless you want to go dressed in rags and live without any leisure whatsoever. The pay isn't exactly what one might desire.' Jeanne followed Marie's example, and soon they had crept down in the other bed in their chemises and with one pigtail each flung over a shoulder. 'You forgot to bring any luggage.'

'I...'

'You'll have to tell us more tomorrow. Now, we really should get some sleep.'

A few minutes later, the twins were breathing heavily, and Colette turned in her bed. Josephine remained by the candlelight with her needle work, but looked up as she noticed Colette's wondering glance. 'I wait a little while to sleep.' Her voice was as timid as that of a mouse. 'I snore frightfully—best to wait.'

Colette never managed to forget the view that met her the next morning as she helped removing the shutters from the Hall of Mirrors. The sun had only just broken through the clouds, painting the sky with strokes of warm yellow and coral pink, illuminating the contours of the gardens below. Patches of sunlight danced on the marble floor, which was waiting to be swept clean of every dust particle. Colette could have sworn she heard the rippling *rat-a-tat* of the fountains outside—at least she could see them clearly where they stood, dominating the peacefulness of the early morning hours.

However, the fascination soon faded away, replaced by weariness, as Colette found herself kneeling on the floor along with seven other house maids, scrubbing the stone with flannel dipped in a lather of hot water and soap.

By the time they had finished the task, her knees and feet were both numb, her fingers—although hardened by the years of grinding paint—sore and wrinkled like raisins from the water.

As though they were one body, the maids proceeded to wipe clean the remaining surfaces and polishing the mirrors, until Colette was silently cursing the very idea of spot-free glass. When she took a few steps back to inspect the result of their work, the cursing escalated in her head. *There is no real bloody difference—it was just as clean when we arrived as it is now.* But it had to be done nonetheless, naturally, and once she gazed out the window to absorb the rising sun one last time, it was worth it.

Three hours later, little past eight o clock, the fire places rinsed and lit anew, Colette finally sank her teeth in the bitter rye bread, which was covered in a layer of duck fat, before washing it down with the lukewarm mead. *Oh my...*The drink was stronger than she had expected.

The oblong servants' table was littered with more of the same breakfast, and the table was lined with men and women of all sorts. Colette was beginning to memorise the vast number of positions one might have in this giant household: house maid, chamber maid, laundry maid, valet, scullery maid, kitchen maid, assistant cook, cook, footman, hall boy, lady's maid, gardener, wet nurse, butler...The list seemed to continue in eternity. Some of them she had not seen yet; some worked in a completely different part of the palace and would probably never cross her path. Far from everyone belonged to the royal family or the palace itself; a lot of people were employed by *marquises* and *comtes*, or even nobles without titles.

The same applied to the courtiers, or as she had begun referring to them as, *the upper shift*. Colette's thoughts often strayed back to that moment in the garden, when she had been staring right at what she had later understood had been the King and his entourage. *It feels almost surreal now...*

'Jeanne?'

The young woman next to Colette turned with crumbs tumbling from her lips. 'What?'

'There was a young girl trailing by His Majesty's side yesterday. Do you know who that might have been?'

'Oh yes!' Jeanne brushed away the crumbs and smirked. 'That's the *Petite Dauphine*, his favourite. Marie-Adélaïde of Savoy, *Duchesse de Bourgogne*, if that means anything to you.'

'I heard about her, I think, a few years ago. I heard she is very pretty.'

'You'd know that best yourself, I suppose. I never saw her upfront.'

Blood rushed to Colette's face. 'Yes—yes, she is.'

'I wouldn't pay them much attention if I were you. We are only here to make their surroundings nice enough. Beyond that, they're untouchable. In fact—no, never mind.'

Colette let the subject slide, with the notion that she would find out the grounds of the Barnette sisters' bitterness concerning their position soon enough, as they hardly ever seemed to shut their mouths.

With each passing day, each week, Colette felt herself becoming one with the rooms in the central building. Her duties, though extensive, did not stretch to the wings, where the members of the court who had little but not enough royal blood running in their veins had their apartments. The mornings were bliss, as were the evenings, but during the bustling day time she often felt the familiar anxiety creeping up. *What if I have a seizure, and they report me? What if they throw me out?* There were plenty of flashing lights in the mirrors, plenty of sudden noises that might trigger one of the nasty attacks. But there was nothing to be done about it.

Jeanne's words at the breakfast table proved truer than Colette could have anticipated: *the upper shift* was untouchable. The invisible wall between servants and their masters was far more prominent here at Versailles than the wall between the estates had been in Paris. There, it had been considered ill-behaved to speak to anyone below oneself; here, to speak to a superior without first being spoken to was a punishable offense.

Yet despite this, Colette began to observe them whenever she could, fascinated by the world she discovered while dusting a Sèvres vase and listening to a conversation through a nearby door.

The King's personal bothers and affairs were, of course, publicly known. His gout, his bad teeth, his bickering with his ministers, the whispers that lingered after far-gone escapades of his youth.

Then, there was his daughter by *Madame de Montespan*, the *Duchesse de Bourbon*, whose own daughter was rumoured to have been conceived by the King of Poland.

There were quite literally bared teeth between the King's sister in law, Madame, and the King's youngest daughter, the *Duchesse de Chartres*. Colette learned from the more experienced maids that the dispute was rooted in a marriage hated by some and desired by others. Furthermore, there were the tensions between the military men, and a series of assumed amorous connections. A few of the servants went as far as to whisper about Monsieur's indulgence in what was known as the Italian Vice.

In this golden web, Colette quickly forgot her own worries—both the seizures and her family at home—and was irrevocably caught up.

CHAPTER XV

The apartments of the *Duchesse de Bourgogne*—the rooms that had originally been meant for the Queen of France—stood empty. Not a single maid was brushing the dust off the mantelpiece; not one usher was waiting by the doors, for they had all been dismissed for the moment, as the *Duchesse's* possessions would soon be prepared to be moved to Fontainebleau for the summer.

Colette walked slowly through the Grand Cabinet of the Queen and into the Queen's bedchamber, her feet sinking into the lush carpet which muffled her steps. She brushed her fingertips over the fragile china vase that stood on one of the cabinets, enjoying not only the glossy surface but the very thrill of doing something strictly forbidden. Did the *Duchesse* ever stop to do those things—to touch and admire the ornaments in her chambers? No, Colette could not imagine it. After all, they were neither forbidden nor fascinating if they belonged to you and would do so for the remainder of your lifetime.

The *Duchesse* had been entertaining herself by other means, though. By the window facing the gardens stood an easel, and upon the easel a canvas splattered with bright paint. A palette with dollops of blues and greens had been placed on the windowsill, and paintbrushes lay scattered nearby. Colette cringed as she realised the spots they would leave on the white, lacquered wood. She moved closer to the easel, her eyes wandering across the unfinished painting. The motif was that of a lake surrounded by clusters of trees against a plain, powder-blue sky. It was—to tell the truth—not a skilfully executed piece, no, the sharp lines indicated the eager brush strokes of an amateur; the pigments had not been blended properly to obtain the right nuance. The image lacked depth—a depth difficult to describe, and absent in the lake on the canvas.

Colette twitched with the temptation to correct the faults of the painting. *A few dashes of white here, a stroke of shadow there—it could be done easily.* She threw a glance towards the open door, but not a soul could be spotted. Then, she filled her lungs with air until her chest began to hurt, exhaled slowly, and gripped one of the paintbrushes from the windowsill. There was something indescribably satisfying about watching the painting gradually shift until the lake, the trees, and the sky seemed to come alive, yet there was the looming guilt of altering another person's work. *It's for the best. She will scarcely notice the difference, caught up in pleasantries…*

'Pardon me? What are you doing?'

Colette swung around so that a tiny drop of paint splashed onto the carpet. Her heart made a loop to the base of her throat as she stared into the powdered face of the *Duchesse de Bourgogne.* Her curious eyes surveyed Colette; her hands were still clutching the fabric of her scarlet red gown to avoid tripping over the hem. Judging by her expression, she might as well have walked in to see a pet monkey playing the harp.

'I—' Colette pressed out. 'I must have gotten lost, Your Royal Highness. Please do forgive me.'

'Is that my painting?' The *Duchesse* advanced a few steps into the room.

Colette swallowed one, two, three times, before she was able to reply. 'Don't send me home, Madame.' The words came as a mere whisper. *Please, please…*

The other girl did not answer, but her eyes widened farther, and a quaint smile spread on her lips—full lips the same colour as her gown, Colette noted absentmindedly. 'It was not so very good before, was it? But now—now it's different. Better. Won't you show me what you did?'

'Madame?'

'Oh, do! I need something pretty to show The King.'

Now it was Colette's turn to put on the face of complete confusion. She must have misunderstood somehow—but what was there to misunderstand? Though she wished nothing more sorely than to scramble back to the servants' quarters and hide her flushing face, she could hardly disobey the request. Her eyes darted across the room and found a velvet-padded stool, which she hastily pulled forward to the easel.

The *Duchesse* sat down on the stool without further ado, straightening her back, eyes fixed on the canvas. 'You may begin.'

'See—see this?' Colette dipped the paintbrush in the white paint once more and added a few stokes to the painting. 'The sun ought to be coming from up here, so...so naturally the waves would gleam—here.' The ludicrous situation drove her to the verge of smiling, because despite the initial terror, the King's favourite courtier did not bite. As the

131

minutes flew by, the tension seeped away from Colette's chest and was replaced by ease.

'It's so pretty! Thank you—you don't know what it's like to have them watch your every move. People can be awfully cruel sometimes.'

'No, Madame, I don't know what it's like.'

'And of course, they want sons.' She swallowed. A wet blanket had been pulled over the lively *Duchesse*. 'And I have not given them so much as a daughter. And—'

'Stop it!' Colette did not take the time to realise what she had said before flinging the paintbrush to the carpet and bursting into full outrage. 'Can't you see the splendour you spend your days in? Open your eyes! If babies and art are your greatest concerns, then I suggest you take those sparkling slippers on a trip through the streets of Paris and discover for yourself what reality looks like!' Her breaths quickened; her intestines felt like one cramping knot. *There is no returning now. Dismissal? The Bastille?* Colette had no clue what the punishment might be for extreme insolence.

'I—' The *Duchesse* began. A glaze of tears covered her eyes, and Colette suspected they were an indoctrinated response to yelling. 'I am sure it cannot be *that* bad. The King...he tells me the people of Paris rejoice in these times...' A plump drop trailed down her cheek, leaving a wet trail in the powder.

'They starve, Madame. They pay their taxes so that Versailles can import new flowers and oaks from Germany, but they live in filth. At least—at least I've seen those who do.' Colette clenched her fists. Now, when she had already allowed it to escape, the anger was rapidly sapped from her body and replaced by a desire to wipe the pearl-shaped tear from the other girl's jaw. She had never realised such a great deal of a person's beauty could consist solely of their joy. With eyes gone red at the lids, and with quivering lower lip, the *Duchesse* suddenly appeared stripped of all finery.

In that very moment, she had the familiar, metallic taste on her tongue. *Dear God. Dear God, not now, not now...*

Adélaïde watched in horror as the maid servant collapsed on the floor in a mess of sprawling limbs and jolting head. Her eyes dried in a matter of seconds; she shot up from the stool and took two stumbling steps back. The servant's eyes rolled back so that they shone milk white. Within seconds, though, the convulsions ceased and the girl lay motionless.

Adélaïde had never witnessed anything like this, but she had heard stories about those inhabited by wicked spirits, those cursed by Satan. *Could it be true? Surely not.* Although she would rather be whipped than to admit it to the King or Madame Maintenon, Adélaïde harboured the slightest doubt concerning Satan, and even God. She simply could not see the point of dedicating one's every thought to invisible powers, when one could laugh and dance instead.

Squatting down to her knees, Adélaïde crept closer to the limp body again. The girl's chest was heaving up and down rhythmically; she appeared to be sleeping soundly. Her copper-red hair was slicked against her scalp by the roots from the sweat that had broken out on her temples and forehead.

'*Svegilati! Svegilati!* Wake up!' Adélaïde repeated the Italian word—it was the only word she could summon. But the servant did not wake up at her command. Adélaïde folded her legs underneath herself and plucked at the fuzzy threads in the carpet, waiting. *Should I fetch someone? Should I return to the salon?* To her own bafflement, the only answer she found was a resounding *no*. There was something pinning her down, something keeping her from letting the servant out of her sight for so much as two seconds.

A few minutes dragged by before Adélaïde was rewarded for her waiting.

The servant's eyelids fluttered before the confusion cleared off her face and she raised herself on her elbows. Her eyes widened as they wandered over the room and landed on Adélaïde's face; her skin grew paler so that the freckles appeared in strong contrast. 'You cannot tell anyone what happened,' she hissed.

Adélaïde shook her head, the fright still pressing urgently against her ribs.

'I—' The servant scrambled to her feet and started for the door.

Adélaïde regained her normal breathing. 'Wait!' She picked up her skirts and lunged towards the other girl. 'I...I'm sorry.'

'It's me who ought to apologise, Your Royal Highness.'

'Well—thank you, then. For the painting.'

The servant nodded after a moment of hesitation, before escaping from the apartment. Adélaïde remained standing on the spot for what must have been minutes, though it felt like an eternity, in the attempt to absorb both the blunt outburst and the convulsions. But however deep she dug, she could not muster any one word that summed up her emotions; they swam inside her like scattered puzzle pieces that refused to fit together.

To take my sparkling slippers on a trip through the streets of Paris...only imagine! And why would I? Surely, the conditions aren't so horrid as she would have me believe. And if they are... Adélaïde suffocated the thought, shoving it to a place in her mind where she knew she would not find it by mistake. She had enough worries already—worries that were *not* silly, regardless of what some freckled maid thought.

Returning to the *appartement* in the Salon of Mercury, Adélaïde also returned to a sense of security. The warm atmosphere, stinking of fifty individual perfumes, enveloped her; the glow of the candles in the chandeliers embraced her. The King was sitting on his *fauteuil*, surrounded by men with strong opinions and luxurious silk stockings: the *Duc de Vendôme*, the Comte de Tessé, and a man whom Adélaïde could not quite place, but who might be of the house of Rochefoucauld. The King turned as she entered the room, patting his thigh.

Adélaïde complied and sat down on his lap. She could sense the glances of exasperation that passed between the circle of men, but brushed them off.

'—and I hear he has not many months to live,' said Vendôme, twining a coil of his periwig around one bony finger.

'It is no great wonder! The inbred bastard has never been fit to rule a country,' Tessé chimed in.

The King flashed them a stern glance while taking Adélaïde's hand in his own. 'Mind your foul tongue—need I remind you my granddaughter is present?'

Oddly enough, the courtiers did not adhere to his scolding, but proceeded to pour out their dislike for Carlos of Spain. They spread their legs on the padded *tabourets*; those who stood clasped their hands behind their backs and raised their chins. It was not so much poise as it was habitual scorn for the Spanish ruler.

'*Con comme ses pieds!*' The declaration was followed by a ripple of chuckles.

'And you wish Phillipe to take his place on the throne once he has passed, Sire?' Adélaïde asked out of mere courtesy. She could not imagine being less interested in the Spanish succession at this moment; her thoughts remained in her own chambers and with the freckled servant girl.

'Precisely, my doll. Your brother-in-law is quite well suited for the position, wouldn't you say?'

Adélaïde crinkled her nose. 'At least he can have his own, dull court.' She then smiled sweetly to soften her harsh words.

'Hm! Perhaps you are right. But we must have him married—we certainly cannot have him...misbehaving himself.'

Rochefoucauld cleared his throat and arched a plucked eyebrow. 'Might I ask whom you had in mind, Sire?'

The King's eyes gleamed. He turned to Adélaïde as well as to Rochefoucauld. 'You may indeed. There have been negotiations concerning your younger sister, my doll. Maria Luisa of Savoy.'

This grabbed Adélaïde's full attention, forcing her to let go of her straying thoughts. *Maria Luisa, three years younger than me, to be chained to a depressed, cold husband who jumps into bed like a maniac with every girl he can lay hands on? Sent off to faraway Spain...Spain, which can't possibly be as charming as France...*She could only remember Maria Luisa as a girl of seven playing in the gardens in Turin with golden locks bouncing on her shoulders. 'But Sire— surely there must be someone better suited?' she asked anxiously.

The King frowned. 'I had expected it would please you to be closer to your own sister by marriage.'

'Everything you do pleases me, Sire—' Adélaïde widened her eyes, gazing purposefully into the old man's face. '—but I would be wretched if you chose a girl too inexperienced for the position.'

'His Majesty is capable of making decisions, Madame,' Vendôme broke in with a slippery voice, cocking his head.

'You seem to be placing words in the girl's mouth. Is it not natural that she should care for her sister?'

Vendôme closed his mouth like a blubbering fish.

Hope sprung in Adélaïde's heart that she might be able to convince the King to choose another bride for his second grandson, but the time was not right, not with a small audience soaking up every word. 'Do I have your permission to retire, Sire?'

The King grunted, gave her a quick peck on her hand, and Adélaïde got on her feet. She did not bother to pay the three men any goodnights or salutes, but walked with rapid steps back to her own rooms.

CHAPTER XVI

The following morning, Adélaïde caught a glimpse of red hair and slim, freckled hands polishing the mantelpiece in one of her rooms. Two older, pale women in similar dresses were dusting of the furniture. She leaned against the door post in absolute silence—painfully aware that she ought to be in the gardens with Madame Maintenon, taking her daily dose of fresh air—and traced the curve of the servant's neck with her eyes. The girl appeared both old and frightfully young at the same time, for she hunched her back as if afraid, but walked with energetic steps at the same time.

Adélaïde shifted her weight—a fatal mistake, because the threshold had not been oiled properly, and gave forth a loud squeak as if she had stepped on a rat.

The servant's head spun around, and her eyes widened as she caught sight of Adélaïde.

One of the other women raised her glance and dropped down in a plain but habitual curtsy, her eyes glued to the floor once more.

Adélaïde flashed them both a smile, though she could not for her life identify what lay behind it, before turning on her heel and speeding towards the gardens with lips still curved and the hem of her gown hauled up above her ankles. Once the blazing sun struck her face, she smoothened the folds in the satin and tried to take those petite, silly steps that created the illusion of gliding forth.

Madame Maintenon waited propped on a chair by a white table with chiselled flowers, laden with a generous array of biscuits and two tea cups. She was draped in her usual sombre black; Adélaïde marvelled as to how she could endure the heat in such a costume. Madame Maintenon pressed her lips to a thin line as Adélaïde approached, but the reprimanding mask soon faded, revealing a hint of a smile.

'Pardon me, Madame—my mind was elsewhere. I'm afraid I forgot the time,' Adélaïde said, seating herself on the other chair on the opposite side of the table. She then plucked two biscuits covered in pasty, green icing and placed them on the napkin by her cup.

'Don't—' Madame Maintenon broke off as it was already too late. Instead, she removed her gloves and gestured for one of the servants to pour them each a cup of chamomile tea. 'How are you today, my dear? Anything pleasant you would like to share with me?'

'I am not sure it is a very pleasant thing, Madame, but I rejoiced to see the King on the road to success last night.'

'I presume you mean his plans for the Spanish throne.' Madame Maintenon bit into one of the glossy biscuits, crumbs raining down on the napkin without so much as a single one landing on her black clothing.

'I—' Adélaïde hesitated. 'I don't like it. Why is it that we can't leave Spain to the Spanish and England to the English, and put our minds together to make *France* as splendid as she can be?' She elaborated on the question to herself: *Because what is there, if not Versailles?*

'Because, my dear, the King has ambitions—as any man, or woman, ought to have. And I'm afraid all our hearts desire different things, though only some of them can be pursued. Only those of the truly privileged.'

'It seems to me, Madame,' Adélaïde said, growing increasingly melancholy, 'that not even they—we—can pursue them. I can't

142

talk to the people I wish; Monsieur can't love whom he loves; Louis can't execute the political reforms he spends his days thinking about. Not even—'

Madame Maintenon smiled that certain placating smile that so often comes to elders when speaking to the young about troubles they know they cannot do anything about. 'Whom is it you cannot talk to?'

Adélaïde did not get the chance to formulate a smooth enough answer, because in that moment, the King approached them with his impressive entourage swarming like flies behind him, and requested that his wife and granddaughter-in-law join him on his walk in the gardens. Naturally, there was no such thing as declining.

Adélaïde took her place by the King's side, however, her mind was elsewhere, and she knew it would be until she managed to resolve the emotional tangle she was caught in.

CHAPTER XVII

A hand with nails bitten down to the skin latched onto Colette's arm as she was climbing the Ambassador's Staircase after one of her daily chores. She froze in her step, but the grip was not a harsh one. The *Duchesse* gave a half-smile, loosening her fingers. A fragrance of ripe strawberries surrounded her; stains of red sullied her cheek and the corners of her mouth.

'Is anything the matter, Your Royal Highness?' Colette pressed forward.

'Well—only I wish you would tell me what happened when...' She wiped the stains away with her sleeve. 'It frightened me.' She lowered her eyes.

'I can't, Madame. I don't know myself...I wish I did, but I don't.'

'Did it hurt? *Does* it hurt?'

Colette swallowed. *This conversation isn't supposed to take place.* 'No. Everything

144

just...disappears. The worst part is the seconds before—when I know I'm losing control.' The last words were little more than a whisper.

The *Duchesse* nodded. 'And what you said was true? About Paris?'

'Yes, Madame. It is not Versailles—you know that much, of course—and the people there are not the likes of you.'

'Surely that does not make them unhappy?' Her eyes were wide; Colette noticed for the first time their almost black colour and the short eyelashes that had been painted to appear more prominent.

'Would you be happy, Madame, if you had to work from sunrise to dawn to feed seven children?' Colette caught the harsh tone in her own voice. 'I beg your pardon.'

'Won't you tell me your name?'

'Colette Auclaire, Madame.'

The *Duchesse* smiled, revealing bright teeth. 'Then you can call me Adélaïde, for I don't believe friends need titles. We are friends, no?'

Colette stared at Adélaïde, as the other girl now so unceremoniously had become. *Friends?* The thought was absurd. 'Yes, *Ma*—Adélaïde. I don't mind having a friend.'

'*Eccellente*!' Adélaïde clapped her hands. 'Put that thing down.' She pointed to the bucket Colette was carrying, and once

145

Colette had complied with the instruction, Adélaïde pulled her into a clapping game that had been popular amongst children for decades. It seemed the nursery rhymes were not so different in Paris and the Royal Palace of Turin. *Clap, clap, clap*...Colette's lips curved, looking at her own, well-kept nails. Despite all the inequity in the world, this was one tiny aspect in which she was luckier than the *Duchesse*.

'I do like your freckles. I've never seen anything like them—of course, the women here are all coated in powder, so one never really knows.'

'I wish I had a bit of that powder.'

'Nonsense! It would be too dull.'

The clapping game had ended after being repeated numerous times. Colette squatted down and retrieved the bucket, clutching it in her hand. 'I have work to do now.'

Adélaïde cleared her throat. 'Yes, well, you must come and visit me when you have the time. There are strawberries, if you want, or cake—'

'Thank you.' *When I have the time? Do those moments exist*?

The two girls parted ways on the staircase, and one proceeded up with a clattering bucket, while the other descended with the long train of her skirt sweeping the marble behind her.

These brief encounters occurred a few more times over the course of the following month, but ceased after an unusually firm scolding from Madame Maintenon.

'You simply cannot run about befriending *servants*! I know you're not daft, my dear, so don't pretend you don't know it as well as I do. They're *maids*.'

'Madame, I thought you encouraged friends. And I'm not daft—I know what they are, what she is, but everyone else is always the same. The same snobbish, scheming...' To her own surprise, tears were burning behind her eyes and stinging her nose.

'Adélaïde!'

Adélaïde froze. It was not often, if ever, that the older woman used her Christian name. 'My apologies, Madame.' *I really am sorry—but it doesn't mean I'm wrong.*

Pushing, pushing...she was floating in delirium. The next moment, a pair of hands was holding something twisted, something unrecognisable before her: a lump of flesh covered in dark spots and with too many limbs sprawling in every direction. The creature could hardly be called a baby.

Then her grandmother was by her bedside, shaking her head. 'That won't do, my dear. That won't do.' The old lady kept shaking her head, double chin jiggling, with a sorry smile on her withered lips.

The misshaped child was wrapped in linen, tight, tight, until the limbs ceased their flailing. Adélaïde saw the marble faces lined up at her feet: the King, Louis, Monsieur, *even* Madame *Maintenon stared at her with eyes so cold that they might have turned boiling water into ice.*

Adélaïde snapped awake with a high-pitched squeak, desperately trying to adapt her eyes to the dark room to scan every corner and make certain that there was no truth in what she had just seen. Louis was sleeping in his own chambers tonight; she longed for his heavy breaths, if only to confirm that everything was in its order. There were no marble faces or icing cold eyes. They would not throw her out head first for giving birth to that...thing.

Adélaïde slid her hands under her chemise and slowly caressed the area around her navel—soft, a bit swollen from last night's banquet, but certainly not the stomach of a pregnant woman. That in itself brought on a wave of relief, but a different kind, a relief interrupted by guilt. *Oh well...there's no rush. His Majesty said so himself.*

The sheets lay crumpled by the bedpost, kicked off during the quaky, warm night, the curtains hung heavy and dominant by the windows. Not so much as the clicking sound of dog's claws or the buzzing sound of servants could be discerned.

Adélaïde climbed out of the bed and sighed with pleasure as her feet touched the cold floor. She dressed herself soundlessly in the *deshabillé* flung over one of the chairs— one of her favourites, with the colour of apricots and subtle rims of silver brocade at the hem and sleeves—and tip-toed barefoot through the passage to the Peach Salon and from there to the Hall of Mirrors.

Versailles appeared to have been purged of inhabitants—it was a rare sight, and one that Adélaïde found particularly enchanting. However much she loved seeing the courtiers strut and play and laugh in the golden haven that would someday belong to her, they also snickered and smelled and made sour faces. Without them, the rooms seemed to be resting in complete serenity.

Adélaïde halted as she entered the Hall of Mirrors, struck by absurdity, seeing the lonesome figure that disrupted said serenity: a young girl with her hands pressed flat against one of the windows, standing still as a statue. Her gaze was pinned to something on the horizon, absent. Despite the considerable distance between them—the length of the room, to be precise—Adélaïde knew by the sight of the red hair glinting under the white maid's cap who it was she had encountered.

The girl did not seem to take any notice of the *Duchesse* as she tripped closer on light feet. Not until they were standing with only a meter of floor between them did the maid escape her trance-like condition.

'Your Royal Highness—'

'It's alright. Do you fancy the night?' Adélaïde tucked a strand of hair behind her ear.

'I'd rather call it the morning, Madame.'

'And I rather you didn't call me Madame, if you don't mind. Don't you remember we are supposed to be friends?' Adélaïde felt a rush of excitement at this returning opportunity to lay off every trace of formality; she almost could not believe her own, strange-natured luck. *Madame Maintenon may scold as much as she likes.*

Three months had come and gone since they last spoke, and yet she could sense the same fluttering in her stomach.

Colette drew little circles on the glass pane with a finger, a tinge of a smile playing on her lips, the first rays of sunlight illuminating her face. 'I often watch the gardens from here, early on, before the others come to clean.' She turned from the window to meet Adélaïde's glance. 'Why on earth are you up?'

Because I dreamed of the most grotesque failure that could fall upon me. Change the subject. 'It's beautiful. I think one must just...suck out all the beauty from life that one can find—like when you're eating crab, or lobster—or otherwise all the nasty things might get the better of you. Don't you think so?'

Colette opened her mouth slightly, but she remained silent for a little while before replying. 'Well, I've never had crayfish, nor lobster, but that sounds like a nice thought. I'm not sure I agree, though.'

'No?'

'Everyone loves beauty, I think, but surely there is more to care for. Progress, justice...those grand things. Reality.'

Adélaïde could only nod and marvel. 'Did your mother tell you that? Or your father, perhaps?'

Colette shook her head, slowly. 'My father only cares for his trade, every *écu* he can scrape together. My mother only cares about her façade.'

'Oh,' Adélaïde began. 'My father only cares for Savoy—though I don't blame him, of course. But the King...the King cares for *me*, so I suppose it doesn't matter much what my father does.'

The red-headed girl's smile faded, leaving a tight-lipped expression. Adélaïde bit her tongue. Perhaps it had not been so very wise to flaunt her own privileges, her own luck, but she needed to hear the words spoken out loud if only to chase away the nightmarish pictures that still swam in her head.

The harsh rattling of buckets caught both girls' attention, as numerous house maids dressed in similar garments and with sleep-glazed eyes entered the room carrying their cleaning tools. They all stopped in their tracks, seeing the two figures by the window, before putting the buckets down and dropping into automatic curtsies.

Adélaïde looked at them in confusion. *What are they doing up at such an early hour? Don't they have breakfast, at least, before tending to their work?*

'Should I go...?'

'Unless you want to help us sweep the floor,' Colette said, before covering her mouth with her hand, a frightened gleam in her eyes. 'I'm sorry.'

Adélaïde grimaced. 'I'm afraid I don't know how one does that.'

The maids exchanged glances, faces stiff and eyebrows arched. Adélaïde tugged at her *deshabillé*, suddenly feeling out of place in her own home, her own rooms, under the eye of the servants. This was their hour, their domain. She—a greater lady than they had ever so much as *touched*—had somehow been reduced to an object of awkwardness and inconvenience. Pulling the apricot silk tighter, she turned on her heel and began tracing her own steps back to the Peach salon and then her bedchamber, only exhaling the breath she had been holding once she had closed the door after her with a subtle *click*.

'I told you that you shouldn't pay them too much attention. What did she want with you, anyhow?' Marie said, the familiar frown settling in on her forehead.

'Nothing to bother you with.' Colette crawled into bed, the mattress squeaking without mercy, and folded the covers by her feet. The sweat was trickling down her back and under her arms. Because there were no windows to let the sun in, the air was stagnant, and it seemed that every last drop of September heat had been absorbed in the palace walls. With three other girls in the room and no proper ventilation, Colette was grateful there was any air to breathe in the first place.

153

Josephine tore her eyes from the needle work in her lap, the dark shields of lashes concealing the expression in them. 'Was she terribly cross?'

'I don't see why! If everything was as it ought to be, Marie and I would even be allowed there day-time, don't you think?' Jeanne turned to her sister, who nodded eagerly.

'Well, she wasn't cross in the least, and that's that. And I wish you'd just tell what it is that's so special about the two of you—your father, is it?'

Marie bit her lip, a barely noticeable smile on her face; Jeanne heaved herself to a sitting position on their bed and crossed her legs underneath her. The sisters exuded beaming pride—made obvious by the way their eyes shone and the straightness of their backs—and they savoured every second of knowing but not telling and of the knowledge itself.

'Do you know who the *Duc de Harcourt* is?'

Colette nodded after a moment of hesitation. 'I've seen him once or twice, I think—that old man who always sniffs his handkerchief?'

'They never speak of it at court, naturally, but he slipped up a little back in '79. Made one of the wet nurses with child.'

154

'She—the wet nurse—died in child fever, at least so we were told, but Madame Colbert was so kind as to raise us and make sure they kept us on in the household once we were old enough to carry a bucket.'

Madame *Colbert...ah, yes, the assistant cook. I think she gave me a caramelized apple some time ago.* The Barnette sisters' confession began to sink in, and Colette could do little but chew on her lower lip until a drop of blood erupted and languished away on her tongue as she stared at the young women on the opposite bed. *They do have that same button nose as the Duc.*

'You oughtn't to say anything of it—it's not proper,' Josephine whispered from her chair, as if afraid to repeat what had been said, should the walls have ears. 'We all have our place, and I truly think you should consider yourself fortunate.' Her face was as calm and smooth as ever; the obsidian eyes reflecting the candle light like massive, black pearls.

Marie crossed her arms over her chest, pushing up her ample breasts like a dove ruffling its feathers. 'Well, you see, I don't agree at all. Sure, we all have a place to fill, but my place is not here in this...this crammed cave for a bedroom!'

Josephine withdrew from the conversation at that note, exchanging the needle work for polishing her nails with a tiny rasp.

'I think—' Colette drew a deep breath, trying to muster enough courage to take up the peculiar subject. '—I think the places we are given should not be dependent on birth or rank, but by merit and good intention.' Once the words had been spoken, she pulled her knees up to her chin in an attempt to make herself as small as possible. *Father would have beaten me if I had said anything of the like at home. It's too daring.*

Jeanne's frown deepened until one could have hid an *écu* between the wrinkles. '*Mon dieu!* You sound like quite the maniac.' The sisters rolled over, and without another word, they appeared to have fallen asleep, although Colette doubted it was anything more than a way to get rid of her. She clutched her knees; it felt as if a swarm of butterflies were fluttering violently inside her chest, about to break her ribs from the inside in their desire to escape their cage.

CHAPTER XVIII

In the beginning of November that year, 1700, the news of Carlos II's death reached the inhabitants of Versailles. The Spanish King had been little less than thirty-nine years of age—though this early passing was no wonder, considering his many deficiencies—and Adélaïde could not help but pity him.

The sinister aura that surrounded the deceased laid the foundation of whispered rumours and frightened glances around court; these were hardly dampened when the physician performing the autopsy made a peculiar statement: *His body did not contain a single drop of blood; his heart was the size of a peppercorn; his lungs corroded; his intestines rotten and gangrenous; he had a single testicle, black as coal, and his head was full of water.* Whether any of this was true or not, it sent cold shivers down Adélaïde's spine and out every fingertip. The description sounded as though it belonged to a creature of Hell rather than a man appointed by God—but she doubted any religious principle could be applied to this situation.

Because Carlos II had not left any children to succeed him as ruler, his passing gave rise to the question of who would become the next King of Spain. Although Archduke Charles—second son of the Holy Roman Emperor—had previously been suggested as heir, the dead king's will had been changed, and now named Philippe *Duc d'Anjou* as his successor.

The Sun King, Louis XIV, was quite naturally overjoyed, and the high-ranking men in his presence shared this attitude. Vêndome, Tésse—they all straightened their backs, implying dignity and quiet triumph, while shooting each other gleeful glances. Precautions and second thoughts rained from every direction, but there was no satisfaction in declining the offer that had been just out of reach for so many years, and so they were all silenced.

On November 15th, the King officially accepted the Spanish throne on behalf of his second grandson, who had no objections. Adélaïde marvelled at her brother-in-law, now Phillipe V of Spain, her eyes wide in disbelief, lips slightly parted. *King? Dull Phillipe? And he only seventeen!* However much she reprimanded herself, the envy boiled hot in her chest, burning, and she had to remind herself constantly not to say anything inconsiderate to his pasty face.

Had Philippe refused, the claim would have passed down to his younger brother though, and this insight helped Adélaïde endure the thorns of jealousy. If Charles had been swept from her side...she would rather lose a thousand Philippes. Besides, the *Duc de Berry* had never been cut out for politics or the administration of a nation, and he knew it as well as everyone else did.

'I pity him, I do,' Charles said, rolling three dice on the card table. 'I could never go to gloomy Spain. Heir Presumptive, though— that's not such a bothersome thing to be.'

Adélaïde smiled, watching him inspect the cards in his hand, which were spread as a perfect fan. 'I'm glad. You shall have to marry, you know, regardless of those things. Is there anyone you fancy?'

'I fancy you.'

'*Sciocchezza.* Don't say those things.' *And for God's sake don't let anyone hear you say it.*

'Well, if I'm not allowed to fancy you, then I don't fancy anyone.' Charles slapped his cards on the table and folded his arms across his chest, ignoring the game. 'Though I suppose—' A cheeky smile crossed his face. '—I suppose anyone would fill the purpose as long as she's not a nun or a warty witch.'

'I'll speak to His majesty, see what he can make of it. There's plenty of girls in Christendom, Charlie, and I bet they're delightful.'

'Maybe.' He pushed his chair from the table with a screech against the lacquered floor and sauntered over to the billiard table, where his oldest brother was poking randomly at the balls. The two boys were soon engaged in a game; Adélaïde remained in her chair, still brushing off Charles' sneaky approach. *We'll find him a nice princess for a bride— then he'll return to his full senses. I never did encourage it...*

Tension stirred in Europe, holding the countries in a firm clasp, tickling their rulers' ambitions and pointless old grudges. England was not willing to enter a war concerning the Spanish succession, it seemed, but the Holy Roman Empire and the Dutch Republic remained in opposition of the newly declared, French choice of regent.

Charles of Austria was put forth as the man who ought to have inherited the Spanish throne in Philippe's place—indeed, it was not long before the fifteen-year-old second son of the Holy Roman Emperor proclaimed himself

King of Spain. The clash was inevitable; not even the scullery maids were ignorant of this fact, and Adélaïde understood from listening to the King talking with his ministers and diplomates that war lurked around the corner.

No bride was found for Charles, or, to be fair, there were a hundred brides to pick and choose from, but none seemed to suit the King or his youngest grandson. Many of the eligible girls were simply too young; the daughters of Blois and Nantes might have been a fit match, but they were only seven and five years of age. There was no rush, though, not apart from Adélaïde's own concerns. Charles would have many years ahead of him, begetting sons and extending his influence, once time had matured his spirit.

Another marriage treaty was beginning to take form, though: that between Philippe and Adélaïde's twelve-year-old sister, Maria Luisa. Jaw clenched, fingers cramping as they gripped the pen, Adélaïde sat down by her desk to address a letter, because if the King would not adhere to her pleas of finding another princess for the wedding, Maria Luisa might.

I only pray you to consider the match with the utmost care, for, in honesty, my brother-in-law is no pleasant man. I wish for your happiness, dearest sister, and I cannot help but think you would find it sooner with another husband. Your delightful spirit ought to be set to work elsewhere, and not be wasted in a conflict that can only see bloodshed at its end. Be as kind as to have a word with Father, and write as soon as you find the time, she wrote.

Adélaïde folded the paper, dabbed it with a few drops of lavender water, and pressed her seal in the dollop of hot, crimson-red wax. *That ought to do it.*

The reply that arrived by a messenger shortly thereafter was far from satisfactory though, and Adélaïde sought out Louis with a foreign feeling of hopelessness.

'She appreciates my concern, she says, but if Philippe asks, my father is not likely to decline the offer. And she doesn't believe she'll be unhappy either, because it all sounds *exciting*.' Adélaïde patted her horse's muscular, warm neck as they rode a few meters behind the King along with the rest of the hunting entourage. Rain was pouring down as if someone had emptied a giant bucket in the skies, soaking their clothes until the fabric lay glued to their skin and no one could suppress their shivers. The biting November air had crept under Adélaïde's cloak and was now making its way up her spine.

'I do hate to see you in such distress, Madame. Dearest.' Louis pushed his hat farther down and the little pool of water that had gathered on top of it dripped down on his shoulder.

'As long as you are on my side I shan't be too distressed. Are you?' Adélaïde flashed him a smile, teeth chattering, already knowing what the answer would be.

'Always.' Louis hesitated. 'Surely you know I...' He fumbled with the reins, holding his horse to keep it from galloping off. '...I...I love you frightfully much.' Once the words had been uttered, his face stiffened again and he returned his eyes to the road ahead.

'I know that—thank you. I love you too.' *But there's a difference between loving and being in love.* Adélaïde leaned over as far as she could without slipping of the saddle, and placed a kiss on her husband's stubby cheek, overwhelmed by a rare pittance for her spouse.

'Come up here and ride next to me! You too, Louis,' shouted the King from his silver-grey stallion and gesticulated with his hand. In spite of the weather, the Sun King shone, bright in spirit after the successful hunt. He had taken down several quick-footed deer with his own musket, and had spent the journey back to the palace chuckling to himself. When the young *Duc* and *Duchesse*

163

sided with him, the King said: 'A fine day, eh, my doll?'

'The finest, Sire,' Adélaïde replied while wiping away the powder that had gone liquid in the rain and had smeared down on her throat and jaw.

'Your Majesty—Grandfather—I would like to discuss with you the possibility of delegating some governmental power to the provinces...' Louis was in his rightful element.

Adélaïde zoned out from the conversation; although she was far from indifferent to politics, this was hardly the time nor place to discuss it. *A cup of hot chocolate, a dry chemise, a fire in the stove...*Painfully slowly, the distance between themselves and Versailles decreased minute by minute, until, at last, the hunt had officially come to an end.

Adélaïde squeezed the King's liver-spotted, wrinkly hand and promised to make herself presentable in time for dinner, before scurrying up to her chambers.

CHAPTER XIX

Colette had barely finished scattering the lavender on the surface of the warm, rich milk in the bathtub when the door flung open, revealing a *Duchesse* leaving a trail of drips as she walked. Colette straightened her apron and cleared her throat. 'One of the chambermaids has taken ill—'

'Oh, well...do I have to bathe? I feel quite wet enough already.' Adélaïde removed her cloak and hat, letting them drop to the floor in a pile.

'Madame Maintenon wants you to take care of your skin, and besides, it's warm.'

'Then I don't mind in the least.' She lifted her arms slightly, like a bird preparing to fly, and waited behind a screen while two other chambermaids stripped her of the heavy skirts and began unlacing the corset. Finally, she emerged from the screen wrapped in a thin bathing sheet and with the fontange coiffure brushed out completely.

Colette stared at the loose curls that fell over the *Duchesse's* shoulders—it was the first time she had seen her in such a natural state. *She looks almost like a commoner.*

The two chambermaids that had undressed Adélaïde were dismissed, with the instructions to return within the hour to dry and dress their mistress, and to bring the hair stylist and lady's maid with them. Colette fetched the soaps and scrubbing brushes from one of the cabinets, and set to work once the other girl had lowered herself into the bath tub with a satisfied sigh. The thick goat milk—at least Colette thought that was what it was, but it might as well have been from a donkey—made the sheet bellow and float to the surface; the lavender filled the room with a strong fragrance. *I wonder how many Parisian families that milk could have fed.*

'How was the hunt, Madame?'

'You don't have to call me that. It was perfectly awful, thank you.'

Colette's lips curved in a smirk. 'I can't see why His Majesty would want to drag you all out in that weather.'

'He likes shooting his deer and his pheasants.' Adélaïde crinkled her nose. 'And we can't deny him our company—I wouldn't want to.'

'I'm glad he'll never request *my* company.'

'Oh, no, you mustn't say such things. He can be terribly kind, too, you know.'

'Everyone can be kind when they want to.' Colette selected one of the softer brushes and began scrubbing Adélaïde's arm, then proceeded up to her shoulder and collar bone. The skin was as smooth as cream, except for the line of tiny, symmetrical birthmarks that trailed along the upper arm, and she could not help but to run her fingers across them for an extra second or two.

'That tickles!'

'Pardon me.' Blood rushed to Colette's face.

Adélaïde only shook her head, smiling, and sent a splash of milk flying in her maid's direction so that the floor became spattered with white. 'There!' she laughed.

Colette opened and closet her mouth several times, searching for words, but all she could manage in response was an equally rowdy splash, and before she knew it, the bathroom was in a disarray.

However, nothing could have prepared her for being pulled close, almost tipping over the edge and into the tub; nothing could have prepared her for the cold, plump lips that pressed against her own. It lasted only a heartbeat or less, followed by silence that was too heavy, too long. She did not stop to gather her stirring thoughts, but leaned in on her own initiative this time. The kiss, which lasted longer this time, was eventually interrupted by Adélaïde's rippling giggle.

What's so funny? Me? Colette leaned back on her heels and pushed herself up from her squatting position. 'I—I'm sure you can manage washing yourself.'

'Please do stay.' Adélaïde's voice still bore a trace of laugher.

'I can't—' Colette gathered her skirts, tripping backwards over the slippery, milk-spattered floor, and made her way out through one of the side doors. As she scurried down the corridor, her face felt as if someone had set fire to it; she clenched her apron with both hands. *You're insane. Insane. As if the seizures weren't enough—now you'll only have one more thing to fret over, one more thing they might throw you out for! Stupid cow.* And yet she could not entirely disregard the downright pleasant flashbacks that kept coming back to her: creamy skin, lavender fragrance, gleaming eyes, cold lips...*Go away.*

Later that evening, after the banquet had been seen through and the guests had all fluttered off to their—or someone else's—chambers for the night, Louis entered Adélaïde's bedchamber after scratching at her door with his fingernail. The candles shone through his chemise, thin as crepe paper, illuminating the

168

contours of his torso and arms. Louis draped himself in a frock of green and silver brocade while waiting for his wife to go through her toilette. A *femme de chambre* massaged her skin with a mixture of olive oil and lemon juice until she seemed to shine.

'You may go now,' Adélaïde said to the maid—and older woman, perhaps in her mid-forties, with a broad jaw and stubby neck—and rose from her chair.

'Have you recovered from the rain?' Louis asked, leaning against the bedpost.

'Absolutely.' She offered him a subtle smile. 'There is something I would ask of you, though.'

'Anything.'

'One of the house maids, a Mademoiselle Auclaire. I would like to have her made one of my chamber maids permanently, if that is alright. You know the managing of the households better than I do, Louis.'

Louis hesitated; he knew even less of this matter of organisation than Adélaïde did, but did not dare to say so. 'I'll have a word with...someone. You'll have your maid, I promise you that, dearest.'

It won't hurt anyone—it's not such a horrid thing to have a new friend, or a bit of fun.

'Will you come to bed? I thought we might...try again. The court is beginning to grow impatient.' Louis stared at his hands, looking almost apologetic. 'It *has* been a year.'

'Of course, I...' Adélaïde swallowed, then climbed into bed and sunk down in the plush pillows. She felt very much like the little girl she had been on her wedding night, too small for the great bed, but back then this particular pressure had been as good as non-existent.

The rehearsed performance took its turn, and Adélaïde tried to concentrate on the scattered kisses Louis placed on her cheeks and mouth, for they held something vaguely similar to warmth in them. *The court is beginning to grow impatient...it's true.* The nasty feeling of chasing time crept onto her; her fifteenth birthday was days away, and yet it was as if her youth was galloping off without giving anything in return. *Soon I shall be an old, childless woman of twenty-five...*Adélaïde beat the thought away furiously. It was not true in the least, she knew, only the paranoia and melancholia that sometimes visited late at night but would be gone once the morning sun cracked through the curtains.

'Sleep well,' she told Louis.

'You too. You too.'

'Why is *she* made a *femme de chambre*? She's only been here for a few months—you haven't promoted me since I was a wee girl!' Marie exclaimed, aiming her pleading glare at the Superintendent. It was no use, though, and Colette could only watch as she was given one of the few things she did not desire, and which everyone else in the lowest ranks seemed to yearn for.

House maid to chamber maid...of course, it was no great advancement, but it meant being trusted in the innermost bed quarters; it meant being spared some of the cold during the winter; above all, it meant a slightly higher wage. Those few extra francs were a pleasant thought, but Colette knew she would have to spend them on new garments if she was to be appropriately dressed for the position. It would have been something entirely different to become a *lady's* maid, but one did not simply rise that far above one's station, regardless of lascivious bathroom kisses.

'The *Duchesse de Bourgogne's* household, is it?'

'Yes.' Colette gathered up her few belongings, preparing the short move to one of the rooms closer to the Queen's apartments.

'I didn't think she bothered to meddle in any of those things. None of them do, as far as I know.'

'Perhaps you don't know everything, Jeanne.'

Jeanne threw up her hands as if to fend off a physical attack. 'I was only speculating, nothing more. Surely it isn't a crime to wonder?'

Colette answered by clutching her things to her chest and pushing past her bleach-eyed former roommate, following one of the other chamber maids to her new lodgings. *Can't they all just mind their own business? I've got enough to worry about without their sneaky inquiries.*

Adélaïde clasped her hands, smiling broadly so that her teeth—that were unusually well-preserved compared to most of the courtiers—showed like lines of sugar cubes. 'Now we can be closer,' she explained.

'I'm not sure being closer is such a splendid idea.' Colette's chest twisted at the harshness in her own voice; she wanted nothing less than to be cruel.

'Oh—' The *Duchesse's* smile melted away. 'Don't you like me at all? I know I'm silly sometimes, but not everything has to be so terribly dire, and...'

'It's not that.' She swallowed, hard. 'Actually, it's the contrary, don't you see? I think I would come to like you far too much. And that's not an option, is it?'

'Do you think it's wrong?'

I wouldn't know, but it doesn't matter what I think, because as good as everyone you ever saw would do their utmost to gossip and shatter and prosecute. 'It's different for you—you've got a *King* treating you like a...like a little porcelain doll! You're not at risk of losing anything, not really.'

Adélaïde's eyes hardened, adding an odd attribute to her soft face. 'I have a reputation.'

'But you'll still be *Dauphine* soon, and after that Queen, even with a shred in that reputation, won't you?'

'Well, it's too late now. I can't exactly tell them to reposition you again, it would look suspicious.' She spread her hands and sank down on the edge of the bed, shoulders slumped. 'I never meant to trouble you.'

'I know that.' Colette carefully lowered herself next to Adélaïde. The thick cover—sparking with colour and glittering with golden thread—felt strange under her hands: something forbidden suddenly available to her touch. *The mattress must be three times as thick as mine.*

173

'I have to go now.' Adélaïde rose again, breaking the spell. The forbidden was beyond reach once more. 'I'm sure you have work to do, not that I don't enjoy conversing with you, but you shouldn't fall behind with your...chores.'

Colette nodded and made her departure. As she closed the door behind her, the illusion that she had been stuck in like a cocoon had been cracked open, torn to pieces, but no butterfly had emerged. Only now, when she had uttered the words aloud, did she fully realise what a ridiculous impossibility she had been playing with. Two parties of the same sex were absurd enough. Two parties from different estates, from the highest top and the lowly middle of society, was as good as a joke.

CHAPTER XX

'ifteen years old! Can you believe it, darling?' chirped a shrill voice at Adélaïde's ear, belonging to some ingratiating lady or other. Adélaïde did not bother to turn and answer, but stared at the gleaming plate in front of her. Under normal circumstances, the desire to please would have been far too strong to ignore, but today it was as if that desire had been sucked out of her along with the excitement over her birthday.

The deep-sea oysters, the Beef Madrilène, the cherry meringue galette, were exquisitely cooked as always—better, even, considering the occasion—but they might as well have been plaster. *You're not at risk of losing anything, not really...*That was what she had said. Adélaïde chased the thought away for the tenth time that evening and shifted her attention to the large snowflakes drifting down against the jet-black sky outside the windows. Some stuck to the glass panes, where they melted within seconds; others landed on the ground, where a thick, cotton-white coat was building up. W*e could go sleighing tomorrow, if it stays during the night.*

'I *will* not speak to that woman!'

Adélaïde turned to see Madame—crumbs flying in every direction as she spoke—and her son, the *Duc de Chartres*, locked in a deadly glare. Madame*'s* exclamation could refer to a number of women, but this time it appeared she was once more targeting Blois. Her voice was thundering now, and the colour of Chartres' face was similar to that of the purple grapes on the table. Blois herself looked like a marble bust: cold and unyielding.

'There will come a time, Madame, when you shall have to accept what is—for everyone's good.'

'The dowry was not worth it,' his mother persisted.

'It came in handy,' Chartres hissed, perhaps becoming aware of the looks they were attracting from the other guests. 'Now, let's enjoy the dinner and speak further another time.' The protruding vein on his throat pulsated as he turned to his plate.

Madame pressed her lips tightly together; the King pressed his lips tighter, sitting by the head of the table, holding a half-eaten hard-boiled egg between two fingers.

Adélaïde inched closer to him, making an effort to look as sweet-faced as he liked her to be. 'Sire? I pray you aren't upset.'

The old man—now with sixty-five years on his back—shook his head, then ate the last bit of the egg before answering. 'You are the one who ought to be upset, my doll. After all it's your birthday party, is it not? That impertinent sister-in-law of mine, she has never taken the time to appreciate all the benefits of that marriage.' He plucked another egg from one of the silver dishes. 'Over eighty thousand *louis d'or*! Not worth it...pah!'

'The party is delightful.' Adélaïde forced a smile. 'You're always good to me, Sire.'

'That's the right spirit.' The King patted her cheek, his dark eyes glittering in the light from the chandelier.

The candles slowly burnt down, and when the party moved to the Salon of Diana for entertainment and gambling, only burnt stumps remained, dripping wax on the floor below. The court was merry, save the bickering trio of Madame, Chartres, and Blois, but not even Charles's coaxing charades or Louis's toasting could bring forth any genuine joy in Adélaïde. *Over eighty thousand* louis d'or*, and God knows how much spent on this* *evening. What would Colette say about that kind of money? Something awfully judgemental, no doubt about it.*

Once the guests began to realise—much slower than one might have wished—that the object of the celebrations was only half-conscious of their flattery and their efforts, they turned to gossiping about more interesting matters instead. Was there any truth in the rumours of an incestuous relationship between Chartres and his adored daughter? Was that a new type of gown? Who would receive the greatest command over the troops, should a war break out over the Spanish throne?

Adélaïde rubbed her temples, her head aching from the champagne, the sugar, and the never-ending chit-chat. She excused herself through a series of awkward mumblings, the men and women on either side of her raising their eyes to behold this odd spectacle that the King was somehow allowing, and retreated to her bedchamber. As she picked up the engraved hand mirror to survey herself though, it revealed an intricately folded piece of paper. A thrill went through her spine; her fingers worked quickly to unfold the note and read its contents. The words were few and scribbled with an uncertain hand, as though the author had very limited experience in writing, but they were enough.

Adélaïde walked slowly despite the excitement that was rushing within her, admiring her surroundings, for the moon-lit gardens were to bright and too dark at the same time to be overlooked. She swept her glance over the blanket of snow crystals reflecting the cold light of the moon, which looked like a chip of bone against a black painting, following the sharp contours of the shadows that the hedges and bushes cast on the ground. The landscape she had watched with longing from the bustling inside of the palace had become real and crisp, the air hurting her lungs in the most refreshing way possible. Her shoes sank deep in the white powder; she gathered her skirts in a knot in her hand to keep the hem from getting soaked.

The fountain that the note had spoken of—Adélaïde knew it instantly, since the cherubs were easy to recognise even in the dark—stood as stout as always, but she saw no figure by it. Adélaïde's heart leaped. *What if it's just some cruel prank? What if I made some error while reading the note?* Her curiosity urged her to continue though, and as she rounded the fountain, a scrawny silhouette became visible.

'I wondered if you got my message. I'm freezing—'

'I only saw it once I came back to my chamber.'

'Oh.'

'You look like one of the statues come alive.' Adélaïde hesitated, painfully aware of how ridiculous her words sounded when spoken aloud. 'Like...like some winter nymph.'

Colette laughed; it was a light and melodious laugh that Adélaïde realised she had never heard before. 'Don't be silly, you're just flattering me. But I have been thinking, and...well, I just don't think opportunities should be allowed to slip by. I've never wanted to kiss anyone before, you know, and I don't know if that kind of person is going to come along very often.'

Adélaïde could almost feel her face flush pink as a piglet, and prayed the moon did not show it too clearly. 'I've been kissed plenty of times. But never like that.'

Step by step, they had both advanced, until Adélaïde was close enough to count the freckles that were sprinkled across the other girl's cheeks and nose. The kiss that followed was more collected than the one they had shared in the bathroom; it brought some warmth in the freezing weather. Adélaïde backed up, sitting down on the edge of the fountain, gasping as she felt the coldness of the stone through her layers of clothes. She reached up to caress the pale skin on Colette's arms as they melted together again, before pulling back to get a proper look at her. Colette's lips were the same colour as withering lavender, and although she was smiling, shivers were giving her goose bumps.

'You ought to go inside, get some warm blankets and a cup of hot chocolate,' Adélaïde said.

'If I go inside, they'll notice I've been out, and I cannot imagine they'd reward that with hot chocolate.'

'I won't have you freeze to death.'

'Would you let me stay in your chamber for a little while? Until I've returned to my natural colouring and can go down?'

Adélaïde bit her lip. *She's terrible at coming up with excuses. But that's alright.* 'I would. I shall tell them I wish to be alone for a moment—they can't deny me that, not on my birthday.'

'That sounds...splendid.' Colette braided her fingers with Adélaïde's in a way that reminded Adélaïde of Françes—only this time, there was a far greater underlying promise that came with it. *I shan't feel lonely again, I refuse to. Not even when Charles is away, or when I can't speak freely.* The aspiration was a pleasant one, and Adélaïde

181

vowed to herself that she would do everything in her might to keep the freckled chambermaid with her as closely as would be possible under the court's hawk eye, that she would grasp this strange chance to explore another mindset than she was accustomed to.

The spring that followed was, without conceit, the most emotionally rewarding months Colette had known for many years. True, she had already watched the seldom seen merriment that somehow flourished at the court just as the flowers and greenery flourished in the gardens in springtime once before, but this was different, for now she was suddenly a part of it. She had moved from being the envious onlooker, marvelling at both the luxuries and the intimate intrigues, to being an active participant of all this— although only one person other than herself knew about it.

Colette did not hesitate to admit to herself that there came numerous benefits with being the lover of the *Petite Dauphine*: Adélaïde regularly bestowed upon her small but precious gifts and confectioneries from the royal table. She even took the risk of bringing Colette to the menagerie, a favourite place of hers, which the King had renovated back in 1698 and granted her free access to. The menagerie was wondrous. Striped horses, exotic birds with strange-looking beaks and feathers in popping colours, giant creatures called elephants—these were the sights that met Colette and immediately nailed her to the spot where she was standing, stunned. *If there are such beings as these, then there must be a land somewhere far off where they are the common species. And if there is such a land, then the world must be too large to grasp.* The thought both thrilled and frightened her.

Despite the material perks of the affair, Colette knew that what truly mattered was the unmistakable warmth that sneaked upon her every time she laid eyes upon her *Duchesse*. Every time she stole a kiss, or was granted one without asking, it made all other gifts seem insignificant to her happiness.

It was a tricky business though, even trickier than she had expected. Only now did she realise just how suffocating the courtiers were; they would always gather around Adélaïde like a swarm of buzzing insects, always unwilling to leave, whether it was due to protocol or their own desire to be near the King's pet. Hence, the two girls found it easiest to meet during the night, either in Adélaïde's chamber or in one of the passages close to the Hall of Mirrors. The path one had to take to get from Colette's room to the oblong hall was shorter than it had been when she was a housemaid, since her current room lay in the main building and not in the South Wing, but it made little difference since the risk of being discovered had always existed.

Colette's true concerns were of a different nature though. The relationship in itself was against God's will, and this tortured her more than she could find words for. How could she, who was already stained with wicked seizures, be granted mercy if she allowed herself to partake in yet another sin? *But I can't help it. I don't want to help it.*

During one of those nights—this time sitting cross-legged on Adélaïde's bed, bathed in soft candlelight—she decided to bring up the delicate subject.

'Did I tell you I received a letter today? From my Lady Mother,' Adélaïde said. She twisted a coil of hair around a finger.

'You told me just now.'

'Anyhow, she has come down with a healthy baby boy—finally. So you see I have a little brother now, whom they shall baptise Victor Amadeus, naturally.'

Colette tilted her head. 'Are you happy about it?'

'Of course! Father needs a second heir, I suppose.'

'You don't look thrilled—your eyes are all gloomy. I know you want a child of your own.'

'I know I sound frightfully mean-spirited, but my father has already had six children, though not all of them by my Lady Mother—' She blushed at this, lowering her eyes for a second. '—and I can't see why God should not grant me at least one. To grant the court some satisfaction.'

Colette leaned back until her head hit the pillows and drew a deep sigh. *They are somehow softer each time I rest on them...how is that possible?* 'Well, we can never know God's ways, can we? Some things we only have ourselves to blame for.'

'What do you mean? I never did anything to anger Him—never hurt anyone!' Adélaïde exclaimed as loudly as one can exclaim when whispering.

'You don't believe this angers Him? Have you not thought of it?'

Adélaïde bounced down on her elbows next to Colette, frowning, her chemise bulging like a cloud around her body. 'If God is not pleased by love, then what is the point?'

'You—you shouldn't say that! It's blasphemous, it's...' Colette struggled to find the right words and clenched her jaw. *Blaspheme is the last thing we need, the last drop. How come you can't see that?* 'Perhaps it would be for the best if we spoke about something else.'

Adélaïde giggled. 'You could read me some of *A Midsummer Night's Dream*—I told you about the man who wrote it, didn't I? William Shakespeare. You have to practice your reading sooner or later, surely.'

Colette sat up again and reached for the book at the end of the bed, then flicked the pages to where they had left off a few days ago. 'I know a bank where the wild thyme blows, where oxslips and the nodding violet grows. Quite over-canopied with luscious woodbine...' she read.

They did not get through more than a few paragraphs before Colette's eyelids felt heavy as lead, threatening to fall down any minute. But to fall asleep in the *Duchesse de Bourgogne's* private chambers was unthinkable; to be found having dozed off together on the bed as the servants and ladies of the court came for the dressing at daybreak would be catastrophic.

Colette covered her mouth with her hand and yawned twice, her muscles longing for rest. 'I have to go now, Adélaïde.'

'Won't you stay just a little longer?' The *Duchesse's* eyes had the familiar sleepy glaze, but she rarely admitted wanting to retire from these precious occasions.

'You know I can't.' Colette lowered herself carefully so that she might enclose the distance between them, and pressed her lips against Adélaïde's cheek once, then her mouth twice. She then swept her frock—which had been waiting on the floor—tight around her shoulders and slipped out through one of the passages that she knew so well by now. As she closed the door, she could feel a pair of almond-shaped eyes watching her from the grand bed.

CHAPTER XXI

Adélaïde pinned Colette against the rugged oak trunk and laughed as their teeth clattered against each other in a misdirected kiss. She dug her fingers in the other girl's hair, pulling out the pins that kept it in place under the ruffled cap and dropped them in the grass below. 'Won't the Superintendent report your absence from your duties?'

'Everything is perfectly clean. What does it matter if I'm in my room with a piece of needlework or—' Colette paused to engage in another urgent kiss. '—here with you?'

'It makes all the difference to me.' Adélaïde had to push down the laugher that threatened to bubble up as Colette placed a finger to her lips and hushed; everything seemed comical, somehow, in the most liberating way, as if all the dilemmas in the world had been turned into jokes and all the suffering had been turned into amusement.

It's too good to last, surely. But maybe it can...

Adélaïde abandoned every rational thought as they sank down on the lawn, which had been cut and trimmed earlier that day and gave off a strong odour that was unique to spring. The surrounding trees shielded them from unwelcome eyes, stretching their branches like bony fingers and creating a lace pattern of leaves over their heads. Although far from rampant or overgrown, the cluster of trees was as natural as they came at Versailles, and the distant splashes from the *Grand Canale* only added to the illusion of wildlife.

'All that tumbling about might give you grass stains on that exquisite gown, Your Royal Highness.'

Adélaïde snapped out of the delirious fondling, the blood rushing in her ears and her heart beating almost violently against her ribcage, and stared at Blois's feet, for she did not dare raise her eyes. The other woman's shoes were the tiniest, most pointy creations Adélaïde had seen; toes squeezed together under a ridiculous assemblage of lace and straps.

'—It would be such a shame to spoil it,' Blois continued, her voice dripping with glee. In that moment, any potential onlooker would have been struck by the astonishing similarity

189

between her and her older sister, Nantes, though the *Duchesse de Chartres* was usually the more tolerable of the two.

Adélaïde's lips parted but not a sound came over them. *It is all over, oh why, why...*

Colette though, who had scrambled to her feet and begun to rearrange her hair under the cap with flick fingers and the look of a hunted deer on her face, spoke. '*Madame la Duchesse*, I hope we can forget this...awkward coincidence.'

Blois's eyes grew round; the lowly maid had not even bothered to curtsy. Perhaps she had lost her rightful place along with her chastity. 'You cannot speak to me thus.'

'Pardon me.' Colette glued her eyes to the ground, the alarmed expression replaced by one of pure humiliation.

Adélaïde wished she could soothe her, but the situation called for absolute flattery and obedience, at least if the scandal was to be prevented from leaking out and colouring the court with indecency. 'That string of pearls—the large, salmon pink ones—you can have it if you wish,' Adélaïde said, referring to one of Charles's elaborate gifts, which she had seen not only Blois but a number of women practically drool over.

'I thought a bribe ought to be suggested in a subtler manner.'

'Don't you want it?' *Of course she does. Thank you, Charlie.*

The *Duchesse de Chartres* fell silent, then offered a brief nod before turning on her heel in those instruments of torture disguised as shoes. Just as she was about to slip through the wall of branches though, she flashed a glance across her shoulder and said, 'That's alright for now, then. But even pearls can lose their shine eventually.' Then she was gone, as smoothly as she had appeared.

Colette's eyes burned on Adélaïde. 'How easy for you, to whisk away every problem with a string of pearls.'

'Don't be upset, 'Ette, I didn't want her to spread rumours.' Adélaïde reached for the other girl's hand, but it was pulled away before she had a chance to stroke the freckled skin.

'I know *why* you did it.'

'I don't understand you—one minute you adore the riches like any person would, and the next you are unhappy because of them.' Adélaïde frowned, not in anger, but in genuine confusion.

'At least I can see the absurdity in it all.'

'But there's no such thing, 'Ette! They're lovely, and why should we not have them? Besides, the pearls were a gift from my brother in law, the *Duc de Berry*. I don't think he'll even notice they're gone.'

Colette folded her arms tightly across her chest. 'Is he still terribly fond of you?'

'Are you still jealous of nothing?'

'Are you still married? That's not what I would call nothing.'

'That's not fair.' Adélaïde swallowed. 'It was never my choice—and you knew it the first time you saw me. You must know there's nothing I can do about it!' *Would I if I could?*

Colette nodded after a moment of hesitation, defeated, and thus it appeared the turbulence had blown over.

Blois kept her promise, at least for the time being, and Adélaïde soon forgot the imposing threat of her secret being exposed, as she dared to feel certain of her bribes' efficiency, and it seemed even more distant as the King brought a clique of courtiers with him to the *Château de Marly* when summer approached. Naturally, the *Château* provided its own household, and only those servants who stood closest to their masters and mistresses in rank—lady's maids, wet nurses, hairdressers and the like—were brought from Versailles. This group did not include any chambermaids, and so Adélaïde was smacked in the face with both excruciating longing and a certain relief. *There won't be any dangerous temptations for a few weeks now, perhaps even months. And they do say the wait just makes it sweeter.*

The beige, square building appeared compressed and rustic compared to Versailles—although this was balanced out by decorative red marble and gold—and the twelve pavilions housing the potential guests were small enough to resemble cottages in Adélaïde's eyes. They ensured a rare privacy, an opportunity to flee from the usual protocol, which the King appreciated as much as anyone. When Adélaïde pointed out to him that he himself often reinforced said protocol during the rest of the year, she simply received the answer that 'even the Sun needs some shade'.

CHAPTER XXII

The sun was beating down on the animals and courtiers alike as they rode across the grounds of Marly, the air vibrating with the stench of the hunt and the June heat.

Monsieur smacked the reins against his horse's cocoa-brown withers, which was glistening with sweat. 'My son is no concern of yours.'

His older brother shot him a glare before returning his eyes to the winding path they were following between the bulky tree trunks and exuberant leaf crowns. The King's cloth of gold frock reflected the sun in a way that was most certainly intended, so that anyone who laid eyes upon their monarch would be automatically blinded. Now, he grumbled: 'You forget, brother, that he's my son-in-law as well—my dear daughter's comfort and reputation is as much at stake as your own wealth.'

'Your daughter! She was the one who pushed for the marriage, Sire. She ought to be content.'

'Does Madame have such great influence over you that you have forgotten the dowry?' the King said, a shadow of a smile crossing his face. He knew Monsieur's sore spots better than anyone, and the very mention of his wife was one of them.

'Madame has nothing to do with my views, Sire.' Monsieur's face was beaded with shiny droplets. 'But the fact remains that your daughter was quite lucky to climb above her station of illegitimacy.'

'Lucky to marry a scoundrel who gambles every *écu* and spends more time at the filthy bordellos of Paris than at Versailles?'

'Philippe has done his duty—Mademoiselle Blois has been blessed with children enough to carry on the line.'

'And without doubt he has done the same service to a number of lowly born women, spreading his seed like a dandelion in the wind!' The King's voice rose to a roar; the men behind them froze in their saddles and exchanged nervous looks both with one another and with the horses, who seemed to sense their masters' unease.

The *Duc d'Orléans* only smirked though, a youthful expression in strange contrast to his silver eyebrows and the deep creases at the corners of his eyes. 'Sire, I sometimes wish you would remember your own days of philandering, for it was not in another lifetime that you kept Montespan and Vallière, and who knows how many others in your bed.'

The King gritted his teeth. 'You mistake your position gravely, if you think you have the authority to speak to your king in such manners.'

'Have you so soon forgotten the misery of your first wife, Marie-Thérèse, as you flaunted your mistresses?'

'You will silence your tongue if you know your own good!'

Monsieur shifted his weight in his saddle and gave his horse another smack with the reins so that the mare surged forward, ahead of the Sun King himself. The gesture could not have been clearer; the men behind them murmured once more, but the King allowed it to pass. There was a limit to the struggle he was willing to put into leashing his younger brother, and as the years had advanced, that limit had grown higher. His blood was boiling, but they had both been instructed by their doctors and physicians to put as little strain on their senses as possible. If only the world—the world and their strength—had been the same as it had been thirty, forty years ago! Without doubt, the quarrel could have been settled or at least stemmed by a good set of fencing.

However, this was no longer an option, and during the banquet that night, Adélaïde could almost touch the trembling tension between her grandfather and her dear King. The previous argument, which one of the men in charge for the hunting luncheon later retold to her, sparked and flamed up again—and this time it was only silenced when a servant awkwardly informed the King that the entire court was listening to the sound of their disagreement through the thin walls to the adjoining salons.

'Poor little sister,' Nantes snickered at Blois while flapping her fan. 'As if your dowry was not big enough—pah! I should have thought that would have made you a content wife.'

'I am *content*, Madame,' Blois said.

'But your husband is not, not as far as I've heard, at least. And it has little to do with the money—'

Adélaïde pressed her palms against her ears as another round of toxic comments were fired; she had long since stopped keeping count of all the times she had listened to the two sisters' jealousy and resentment to one another being played out. *Is it really that difficult to get along, to be kind?* She did not give so much as a thought to her own strives with both Nantes and Blois, choosing blissful denial rather than ransacking herself.

What had appeared to be naught but a temporary storm of disagreements abruptly changed into a pit of darkness. The *Duc d'Orléans's* health had been deteriorating, true, but when the bleeding of the brain came, the court snapped silent in shock. Monsieur lay limp in his bed at Saint-Cloud, where he had retreated from Marly; physicians leaned over his body and peered through their silver-rimmed spectacles. The man's heart had not yet ceased to beat—for more than twelve hours he had lain unconscious but nonetheless alive—and this was the state the King found his brother in when he arrived at dusk.

Adélaïde felt the tears burn in her own eyes, but they had already begun to roll from the King's and Madame's. *Is everything forgiven now? Everything forgotten?* It appeared so, for they were both flat on their knees by the deathbed of the brother and husband they had spent so many years belittling and bullying.

Adélaïde dropped down next to the King and eyed him carefully, then rested a hand on his arm. 'Sire, I pray you, don't cry. It pains me to see you like this.'

'My dear,' he said, squeezing her hand until she had to swallow to refrain from gasping with pain. 'I cannot believe I shall never speak to my brother again.'

'He loved you—still loves you—very much, Sire.'

'He did not always show it.'

And you showed your love even less. Adélaïde's voice quivered as she spoke again, desperately searching for the right words to avoid offense and lies at the same time. 'You ought to get something to eat.' It was true; neither of them had had a proper meal since the small entourage of carriages embarked to Saint-Cloud earlier that day, and the King had been unable to stomach anything they had offered him on the journey, which was odd considering his usual appetite.

'Always taking care of me...' Louis XIV shook his head, his back hunched over the bedside. 'You go, my doll, for I shan't be with you until my brother has drawn his...his final breath.'

Adélaïde obeyed reluctantly and retired to the chambers that had been hastily prepared for her in the Orléans residence. Once her maids had left her, she pulled back the curtains from the windows again so that the sun might wake her early the following morning, and so it did, giving her the opportunity to visit her grandfather one last time without curious eyes watching.

Both the King and Madame had eventually been persuaded to leave the *Duc d'Orléans's* room, and Adélaïde dismissed the attendants the minute she entered.

'Monsieur?' She tapped his chest with a finger one, two, three times. 'Monsieur, can you hear me?'

The *Duc* remained perfectly still and Adélaïde's hope sank like a rock. *Of course he can't say anything, of course he won't open his eyes, you silly—*

'Are you...happy?' His voice was thick and strained, as if speaking required a greater effort than anything imaginable. The left side of his face hardly moved as he spoke; lameness possessed it.

'At court? It's a marvellous place, Grandfather, though I'm afraid I sometimes forget it.'

'...seen it in the 1660s. The fêtes. The Chevalier...'

Adélaïde stiffened at the mention of Monsieur's infamous favourite—his lover—the devilish Chevalier, whom she had spotted by his side so often. She knew, though, that their companionship had been a thousand times more fierce and intense back in their youth. Adélaïde had been told the stories in the shape of whispers more times than she could count, and they had never failed to fill her with a tickling sense of scandal.

She plucked at the cover on the bed, unable to look at Monsieur's closed eyes. 'I should have told you some time ago, I suppose, but I never have. I *hope* you don't mind. You see, I don't think His Majesty is right to treat you poorly because of all that. I don't think any of it is right...And I have the same secret.' Adélaïde held her breath without realising it, her stomach twisting and turning as she waited for some form of response.

Monsieur appeared to have returned to his state of unconsciousness though, and not a single word came over his swollen lips.

Adélaïde arose from the floor and brushed the non-existent dust from her gown, before sneaking back to her own chambers. *I won't ever have the courage to do that again—I couldn't even do it properly with only a half-dead man listening. Coward.* She clutched the damask of her gown as she walked, her knuckles whitening, fighting to suppress the shame that came flooding from every direction.

At noon that same day, the *Duc d'Orléans's* faint heartbeat finally faded completely, marking the beginning of the ceremonial mourning period, which would stretch its long shadow over an entire year. The courtiers draped themselves in dense black, as were the rooms they inhabited, while the King himself enjoyed the privilege of a violet mourning shroud.

During the funeral service at Saint-Denice, Adélaïde leaned over to whisper in the *Grand Dauphin's* ear, overcome by an urge to share her thoughts. 'I think my greatest loss is the bond to my mother, now that I reflect over it. And the court will be a dire state for so long.'

'The Moon to the Sun King has sunk beyond the horizon, Madame. The night shall be far darker without moonlight—but you must do your best to navigate nonetheless,' her father-in-law said.

Adélaïde rewarded him with a half-smile. His wisdom surprised her; the *Grand Dauphin* was not known for being insightful, nor exceptionally comforting.

'Thank you.'

A tragedy rarely comes alone, and a few months later, Europe watched yet another disgraced monarch succumb to death; this time, it was the exiled King James of England, who had slowly withered way from life as well as from the power he had once held. Louis XIV recognised James's son, James Francis Edward, as England's rightful king, as did Spain and the Papal States. The boy was three years younger than Adélaïde: a beautiful child with plump lips and headstrong ambitions. It appeared to Adélaïde as if every youngster in Europe except herself was suddenly being granted kingdoms and courts of their own, although this was far from true. *He's not really King until the British parliament has acknowledged it, and they won't do that*, she reminded herself.

What truly grabbed her attention during the autumn of 1701, however, was the second proxy ceremony between Philippe and Maria Luisa, which took place at Versailles in the middle of September. Seeing her little sister's face for the first time in almost five years soared her to the skies with joy, but her heart sank again as she watched Philippe drool over the girl as if she had been a decadent dish at his grandfather's table. His immediate obsession with his bride was taken for devotion by some, but Adélaïde failed to see anything but a man who was so consumed by both piety and suppressed sexual desire that whoever became his spouse would be doomed to live with a highly unbalanced person for the rest of her life.

The marriage proceeded nonetheless, as was unavoidable, and Maria Luisa set off to the city of Barcelona with a courageous smile on her soft lips, leaving Adélaïde whispering a prayer between gritted teeth.

The year that followed Monsieur's death was a crossing of gloom and joy. The year of mourning was no easy thing to see through, not least because of the pressure to mourn when one would rather cast off the black velvet. Her grandfather's passing had left Adélaïde close to tears for weeks, snivelling over the connection to her lady mother that had so suddenly been broken off, contemplating how she might have committed the same folly as the rest of the royal family and not appreciated the *Duc d'Orléans* enough. But a *year*? It was too much, regardless of how pensive she tried to act.

The court's joy derived from many things—the usual things—but Adélaïde's own joy depended greatly on her little sister's success as the Queen of Spain. Although she was quick to jealousy regarding young monarchs and their kingdoms, seeing as she herself had not yet come to rule one, Adélaïde loved and pitied her sister far too much to feel anything of the sort. Maria Luisa wrote frequently about how she enjoyed acting as regent in the country while Philippe was away touring their Italian provinces, and according to the ambassadors' reports, Spain appeared to have found a true ruler in this girl who was not yet fourteen. Adélaïde fished for details of the marriage itself, but received none. If her brother-in-law was as perverted and dull as she suspected, his wife refused to admit it, undoubtedly for fear that the letter might fall in the wrong hands.

Despite these ailments, Adélaïde smiled more often than she had even when she was a little girl, although now her smiles came from completely different pleasures. The greatest of them, she had concluded, was to watch the sun turn Colette's hair into the most fiercely red colour, like a candle shining through red paper, while they lingered around Adélaïde's private chamber during lazy July afternoons. With the servants and the courtiers all dismissed, they had one or two such interludes every week. Adélaïde discovered that the greatest beauty lies in the simplest things as long as it is the *right* simplicity. If someone had asked her to elaborate, she doubted she could have given any answer, but she knew she had found that peculiar puzzle piece she had been searching for ever since her engagement to Louis: love.

Colette would often pick up the paintbrush by the window—the brushes and the other painting supplies were more hers than Adélaïde's at this point—and let it dance over the canvas with the confidence of someone who has found their true purpose, a confidence that Adélaïde rarely saw in her at other times.

The landscapes that flourished under her fingers were often more compelling than those that they had been made to resemble. Colette was disappointed, because she sought realism, while Adélaïde was delighted, because she sought perfection. In the end they would wind up on the ottoman instead, having put their differences concerning the artwork aside, to engage in activities that required less brain activity.

Then, of course, their time together would have passed once more and their duties called—whether it was a tea party or the sweeping of the bedroom floors. As long as Blois received her regular, opulent bribe, everything ran as smoothly as one dared hope, and the bribes in themselves were never really a concern since the jewellery and the exotic gifts still arrived in a steady stream from both Charles, the King, and every corner of the court.

CHAPTER XXIII

Towards the end of August, 1702, Adélaïde's heart leaped as she realised she had not had her monthly bleeding. When one of the maids had to run for a porcelain basin so that she might vomit twice in three days, every trace of doubt vanished. Adélaïde had acquired greater knowledge of the symptoms of child-bearing than she could have wished for, through ladies with kind intentions as well as through her mother's anxious letters; even one or two gentlemen, feeling terribly confident in their authority as men, had told her indelicately what she had to expect once she conceived. There was no question of if, but of when, because implying that the direct succession line of France might be broken was too treacherous a thing to voice.

And I have! I did it! Now, every obstacle has been taken care of. The rush of maternal feelings she had been expecting shone with its absence though; the joy was merely based on triumph and relief from being one significant step closer to fulfilling her duty. Perhaps this was because she was still caught up in her own childhood.

'Are you certain?' Louis whispered after she had spilled the fortunate news to him and him alone.

Adélaïde nodded, her lips curving in a broad smile as she watched her husband's dark eyes sparkle. Louis seemed at a loss for words, pulling her indecently close in lack of any sufficient ones. Adélaïde smelled the fabric of his frock, her nose against his shoulder, and was grateful that they were alone for once, because she did not wish to declare her condition to the entire court. They dissected her private life enough already; they would have the gossip they lived and breathed once she began letting out her gowns and wearing maternity corsets. She made up her mind there and then that the only people she would tell, save her husband, was Madame Maintenon and Charles—and Colette. Colette would have to be told.

Adélaïde waited by one of the sculptures in the Hall of Mirrors that same night, shadows and trickles of moonlight animating her bare arms with harsh lines and bright patches. When the scrawny girl approached with tapping steps and hair gleaming red, Adélaïde leapt forward, taking her by the arms.

Colette flinched before recognising her face, whacked out of balance. 'You frightened me! Careful!'

'Oh, forgive me—you won't believe it!'

'What?'

Adélaïde's laugh echoed against the exquisitely painted ceiling; she then remembered the intended secrecy of the meeting and lowered her voice to an eager whisper. 'I think I am with child at last.'

'Truly?' Colette frowned, her brows coming together like one dark line.

'Almost certainly. You're happy, no?'

'The *Duc* must be overjoyed.'

'He was—' Adélaïde took a step back, examining the plaster-pale face before her, her own excitement dampened. 'But you're not?'

'Of course I am.' Colette nodded repeatedly. 'I just...I just wasn't aware he was still bedding you.'

'I don't feel for him what I feel for you, but don't you see, it is not my decision to make—there has to be children.'

'I know that!' Colette folded her arms, clutching herself as she spoke. 'And if you've finally succeeded, then I shall be as happy as anyone, but I hate being reminded of that. It might be stupid, or selfish, but...' Her voice died out; her lips remained parted, highlighted by the moonlight like two shreds of white against her shadowed face.

'It's not my fault I have the position I have, 'Ette. I wasn't the one who negotiated the marriage.'

'Would you refrain from it—if you could travel back in time and decide for yourself—and everything that has come with it?'

Adélaïde hesitated. Versailles and the world within the palace walls had gradually grown in her affection, and the answer to Colette's question made Adélaïde realise this more than anything else could have. *Not in a million years, not if it meant losing Versailles...losing everything. Not even for you.* The thought was as though someone had thrust an iron-studded boot in her stomach, but the pain did not cease. Adélaïde stood rigid, lips sealed, unable to express neither her love nor the harsh truth.

Colette hesitated for a second, then wrapped her arms around Adélaïde in a strange embrace. *She knows, she must know.*

The two girls remained thus for several minutes, swaying back and forth as one being, their reflection cast in the mirrors lining the walls, each contemplating the nature of their relationship, both unable to untangle the knot that it was.

The pregnancy proceeded in its due course without showing any odd or ominous signs. Throughout September and October, Adélaïde discovered all the gory details of child bearing which she had been told of, in addition to an array of other symptoms and emotions. However much she searched for that reputed maternal instinct though, she found nothing. *Of course I shall love it—I shall love it dearly, once it arrives. But a mother? Strange.*

Louis, having been admitted to the High Council that same year, ten years younger than his father had been when he had achieved the same political milestone, spent even more time than before discussing foreign as well as internal affairs with his grandfather. Their opinions still differed greatly, yet the King seemed to enjoy their conversations, perhaps because the *Petit Dauphin's* interest in such matters was one of the many redeeming qualities his son the *Grand Dauphin* did not possess.

Adélaïde went as far as to voice her own views, which were similar to those of her husband, though she coated them in enough sugar to make the King overlook the fact that a girl of seventeen probably knew less than his trusted advisers. Louis argued for a less absolute monarchy and more power to the colonies; Adélaïde took on the role of transforming these ideas into something the King could listen to without erupting in a fit of rage. A few years ago, she would not have been so supportive, but bit by bit she had absorbed the stories that Colette told her of the third estate. As long as she could be Queen over a Versailles lacking nothing in the way of glory, she would gladly be a champion of the people of France, allowing them their share of the pie—that the pie was not infinite and that the people's gain would be her own loss did not occur to Adélaïde.

Charles, however, could not be bothered to participate in the debates. His spirit was still that of the ten-year-old Adélaïde had befriended when she first arrived in 1696, only more experienced in every imaginable frivolity, and he would rather place hairpins in the ministers' chairs and watch them exclaim with pain as they lowered their ample bodies onto them. Adélaïde could not help herself; she provided him with the pins, giggling behind her fan, once more pulled back into the childhood that was her natural state. *It's a good thing I have someone to keep me young, to help me keep us all young. Age is such a frightful thing, not solely to the body but to the heart.*

On the other hand, Charles's light-hearted mischief easily swayed towards pure impropriety and even nastiness that could make Adélaïde take a step back. This mostly happened when he had had too much to drink, surrounded by too much merry company, when every boundary seemed to break. One such evening, towards the end of October, built up to consequences Adélaïde could not have imagined in her wildest nightmares.

CHAPTER XXIV

Charles leaned back, shifting his weight so that the chair wiggled back and forth. The deep red, almost black, wine in his crystal glass splashed against the edge, threatening to stain his starched, white culottes beyond rescue.

'Careful with that!' Adélaïde laughed. She popped another ripe strawberry in her mouth, savouring the sweet flavour. The wine had gone to her head, too, and she felt as if looking through a dimmed glass; the contours and sounds in her surroundings were fuzzy and the colours too strong.

'Whoops!' Charles tittered as he deliberately emptied his glass on the floor, before bursting into a fit of laugher and taking Adélaïde with him. Some poor servant hurried forward to scrub the liquor off the floorboards before it made a permanent mark, but neither of them paid any attention to the man, or to the other courtiers. *They're too busy enjoying themselves to care. For once.*

'No bride in sight yet, Charlie?'

'Don't call me that—'

'You could use some nice girl by your side, and I could use another friend.' She reached for yet another strawberry.

'Oh, won't you stop nagging, when you know I'd marry...marry *you* if it wasn't for *perfectly proper* Louis.' He flashed her one of those piercing looks—as if he could peel off her layers of skirts just by using his eyes.

'Charlie, stop it!' Adélaïde chimed out with a bubbling laugher, unable to summon any graveness.

Charles held up a finger, signalling for the servant holding the wine carafe to refill both their glasses, then leaned in to whisper in her ear, his downy chin tickling her cheek. 'Why don't you ever let me...let me in on things anymore, huh? Not even telling me who...who your lover is?'

'No one!' She slapped his arm lightly.

'You've been walking around with that...that stupid grin on your face for months, years even. Isn't the baby...only told me 'bout that a few weeks ago.'

Adélaïde managed to gather her scattered thoughts through the fuzzy lens, realising the threatening tinge her friend's voice suddenly bore. 'I don't need any man other than my husband to keep me content, Charlie.' *There—the model wife has spoken. And it's no lie: I don't need another man.*

She glanced over to see Louis sitting by one of the gambling tables, engaging in one of his few bad habits, fingers flicking between cards and little towers of silver coins, his clothes as neatly buttoned as always. His grandfather stood behind his chair, one wrinkly hand resting on Louis's square shoulder, and the two men were conversing with ease over some political matter— Adélaïde could not distinguish the words, but she could guess well enough. *At least he's the father of the child, and that's what truly matters.* Her heart ached, a rush of guilt sprung upon her. *What he doesn't know won't hurt him—or any of them.*

'I think you do...you just don't know it yet,' Charles said, his chapped lips brushing against her neck.

Adélaïde swallowed the lump in her throat and rose from her chair, tripping across the room on unsteady legs like a new-born foal and sought refuge in a group of rosy-cheeked ladies. *If only we could be eleven again.*

The evening progressed in the usual manner. The dark hung like heavy velvet outside the windows; the guests eventually grew numb to the pleasure of each other's company and the delicacies on silver platters; the mass of people dwindled from the room like sand from an hourglass. Adélaïde followed their example, retiring to her bedchamber with certain relief.

The wine had lost its immediate effect and left her with a throbbing head. Louis was already sound asleep in his own room—as to not wake her when going hunting at dawn—and Colette was not on duty at this hour.

She crept into bed after undressing, staring blankly at the pages of a frivolous novel, unable to focus on its contents, having abandoned the cup of hot chocolate that one of the maids had brought up from the kitchen. The scent itself made her stomach turn.

Click. One of the side doors swung open with a subtle sound. A figure stumbled in, periwig missing, his dark hair in a disarray, the cravat untied and hanging loosely around his neck. 'We meet...again,' Charles said, fumbling with the words. His breath reeked of a liquor unknown to Adélaïde; he must have continued drinking for quite some time since she last saw him.

'Charles?' She lifted her head from the pillow with a grimace.

'Have you missed me?'

'I'm not in the mood for games—I'm exhausted. *Stanco.*'

'Give me...give me a kiss.' He took three determined steps forward, then climbed into the bed with a steel-eyed expression.

Adélaïde closed the book with a thump and pulled the sheets closer around her body. Tiny shivers of alarm were starting to run down her spine. 'Go to bed, your own bed, please Charles.

'Don't you see? Don't you see you're meant to be *mine*?'

Adélaïde stiffened, frozen, her arms glued to her sides as Charles began placing hungry kisses on her neck and mouth, gripping with both hands at her chemise. Her throat felt like one doughy knot that made speaking impossible, screaming unthinkable. *He needs to shave. And chew some mint leaves...what* is *that on his breath?*

The seconds ticked by, and the knot in her throat grew as her chemise was yanked up, until she felt as if something was suffocating her. Then, in a flash of clarity, Adélaïde wrapped her fingers around his wrist against her bare hip and twisted it with all the force she could summon. Charles shrieked in pain as she held it bent in an unnatural angle, her nails digging into his flesh until they drew blood—only then did she release her grip and untangle herself from the sheets, tumbling down on the floor.

'Little...bitch,' Charles growled and clutched his lower arm to his chest in an attempt to relieve the pain. 'Since when did you...become such a prude? Friends 'aving a good time—'

'Friends?' Adélaïde's voice cracked. She backed to the opposite corner of the bed chamber. 'I thought so, too.'

Charles crawled out of bed, still clutching his wrist, and shot across the room so that his face was only a hand's width away from hers. 'You used to be fun.' Spit landed on her nose as he spoke.

'Is this your idea of fun?'

'I—' He did not get any farther before she had turned around and was scuttling towards the door. Adélaïde felt the shove in her back before she had taken more than a few steps; a whimper escaped her as she was flung against the sharp edge of a drawer with greater force than she could have imagined a drunkard would be able to muster. A numb pain spread through her abdomen as she collided with the furniture and crumbled to the floor. Before she had the chance to draw a proper breath, he had thrust a gold-studded shoe in her stomach and kicked, until Adélaïde felt more like a soggy rag than a human being. *Don't let him see you cry—don't give him that. Don't—*After taking a few long breaths, she raised her eyes.

Charles took a few steps back and stood by the side door he had entered through, his face covered in harsh shadows, but despite the dim lighting in the room, Adélaïde had no trouble distinguishing how his glance darted back and forth from her to the door, or how he chewed his lip before fleeing through the passage. The very moment the door closed behind him, Adélaïde let the tears stream down her cheeks in warm trickles—not so much over the intense, cramping pain in her stomach, but over something she could not quite distinguish. *It didn't happen. It didn't. Why would it?* She rested her cheek against the plush carpet, giving up the thought of getting herself back in bed and tidied up, for it all seemed utterly meaningless.

The sight that met Colette and her two fellow chambermaids, Louisa and Celestine, as they entered the Queen's bedchamber to draw the curtains from the windows to let in the morning light engraved in Colette's mind and never left her completely even years after the incident. A crimson red sea had been released onto the beautifully crafted carpet on the floor, soaked up in the fabric and the wood underneath. The source of the crimson lay limp as a sack of flour in the midst of it, clad in a torn chemise.

What appeared to be a slaughter at first glance, though, turned out to be both that and something entirely different—whether it was for the better of for the worse, Colette was unable to judge.

A small choir of fussing voices broke out between Louisa and Celestine as all three own them dropped to their knees next to their unconscious mistress. *Please, dear Lord*...Colette tangled herself in a hundred silent prayers, hushing at the two other women to lower their voices.

'Go to the Superintendent, Louisa. Have her call on the doctor, or Madame Maintenon—anyone. Understand?'

Louisa nodded, wide-eyed, picked up her skirts and sped out of the room. Colette remained on her knees, which were growing numb, stroked Adélaïde's hair out of her face, grateful that Celestine was too overcome with shock to remark on the absurdity of a commoner touching the bare skin of a member or the royal family.

Everything was tidied up and properly arranged once the doctor and the ladies of rank—Madame Maintenon, the Superintendent, and Maisonblanche, who had come along uninvited out of sheer curiosity—arrived. The carpet was rolled up and carried off by two servants; the *Duchesse de Bourgogne* was lifted into her bed, where

Colette and Louisa assisted with exchanging her chemise for a clean one, and the doctor set to work under dire silence.

'I am afraid the child is lost, Your Grace,' he said, washing the blood off his hands in a basin of water.

'And her Royal Highness?' Madame Maintenon looked almost as pale as the object of her concern.

'Her Royal Highness has lost a great deal of blood, Madame, but it's possible this has served to balance the fluids within her, should the miscarriage have been brought on by an evil humour.'

'Monsieur, I am not interested in the *Duchesse's* fluids—I want to know if you can save her.'

'Naturally, Madame, but I shall need a midwife to assist me.'

Madame Maintenon shot a look over her shoulder and Celestine took the hint, making her departure to send for said midwife.

'This certainly is a most unusual situation, and not one fit for your eyes.' Madame Maintenon drew a deep sigh, her breath quivering slightly. 'You—' She nodded at Louisa. '—you wait here with the midwife once she arrives. Your friend can continue her work.'

Colette opened her mouth to protest, then remembered the circumstances. It was a miracle that anyone of such high rank, except Adélaïde herself, should speak directly to her or the other maids. *Please let me stay, please let me wash her properly. She looks so awfully small.* Colette forced down the internal screams that were bouncing and raging within her and stepped out through the Grand Cabinet to the antechamber, but did not take up her chores. Instead, she rounded a corner to keep herself out of sight from the ushers, and stayed there, pressed against the wall, rigid as a stick. To keep herself from scratching the tapestry in distress, Colette began counting in her head; she had just reached little over two thousand when Louisa and a midwife with a creased face hurried past.

The midwife was carrying her instruments—and in Louisa's arms rested a bundle of white cloth, its contents beginning to bleed through. Colette's stomach twisted as she stared at the bundle. *Is that the baby? What would it look like?* She peeked around the corner, only to discover the ushers on their posts as always. *They would never let me in—it's pointless.* With a cold pit in her chest, Colette retreated to her own chamber to wash the blood off her hands before returning to her duties like Madame Maintenon had instructed.

Versailles must continue in the ever-present rhythm that was the core of all their lives; the grandeur must be upheld; no one must know about the unfortunate situation of the *Duchesse de Bourgogne*. And indeed, no one did know. Colette had expected the servants to be abuzz with gossip over the latest tragedy: that of the King's darling and the little heir that might have been—but it appeared Madame Maintenon had taken measures to ensure the story did not reach too many ears. It was for the best, of course, because the anti-*Bourgogne* faction might well have used it for their own benefit, claiming that the loss of the child had been brought forth with vicious intent. No, the *Duchesse de Bourgogne* had come down with a nasty flu and had been prescribed bedrest for a few weeks at the very least.

Because of this, finding out how Adélaïde was recovering was next to impossible. Colette poked in and dissected every whisper and every detail that might indicate the most basic things about the *Duchesse's* health—but it was fool's errand. Few knew, and those who did know would hardly share their knowledge with a curious chambermaid.

CHAPTER XXV

Adélaïde spent a week in grave physical discomfort, then another two in mental agony. Once the bleeding had slowed until it was no worse than her monthly course, and the bruises on her abdomen had begun to fade, the shock clung to her, and after the shock came the disappointment with its tearing claws. *Was it my fault? Maybe. No. I can conceive again...the doctors said so. But he really did it, he—*

She wanted everyone to know, to realise, but she could tell no one. As she lay in her bed with the curtains drawn, contemplating, the past and the future seemed cluttered together. Paradoxes pulled her in different directions until she finally gave up on trying to figure out what it was she wanted the most. *It doesn't really matter, does it? I must try and smile, yes, and dress up nicely. The King will be happy when I do. And I must pray for another child.*

225

The loss of the baby had, up until now, seemed like an insignificant detail, for the scene that had resulted in it had been what truly hurt. The more she thought about it though, the more she realised the enormity of her loss: not only her dignity and one of her dearest friends, but the little heir that had raised her even higher on her pedestal. Regardless of whether she had felt any strong maternal attachment to the child, it had already taken too long to conceive in the first place, if one were to adhere the unwritten rules of a political marriage.

*As soon as Louis is allowed into my chamber, they will all be pushing the matter again...*Adélaïde turned on her side and curled up so that her knees pressed against her chest. They were knobby for the first time in her life; she had barely had the appetite for more than a few savoiardi—oblong, Italian biscuits—every day, and Madame Maintenon had expressed her concern several times while paying a quick visit. The small bulge on Adélaïde's stomach had long since sunken into nothingness like a punctured souffle, and now she could graze her finger over her ribs and count the first three. *None of my dresses will fit properly—I'll look terribly queer for a while.*

Once the proper amount of time had passed since the incident, the physicians declared that the *Petite Dauphine* was officially recovered from her so-called flu, and that she might therefor receive visitors other than Madame Maintenon, including those of the opposite sex. Because Colette, Louis, and Madame Maintenon had been the only members of the court to know about the pregnancy—except for *him*—and only the doctors and presumably a couple of chamber maids had found out, there was no need for elaborate explanations. Those who knew thought she had slipped and hit herself on the drawer, and this was the story she stuck to for the time being.

Adélaïde wondered in silence if she would have the courage to tell even Colette the full sequence of events. They had not spoken to one another since a few days before that night. Although there had been no disagreement between them, Adélaïde had promptly asked for locks to be put on the side doors as a way of soothing her own paranoia, hence there was no possibility of meeting, and she secretly relished not speaking to anyone but Madame Maintenon for as long as she could get away with it. She knew she would have to face them all eventually—her lover, the King, the courtiers—but it would have to wait just a little longer.

Louis came sooner than Adélaïde would have wished. Late one night, he entered awkwardly through the main entrance, not being able to access the room through the usual passage, and lowered himself next to his wife. He asked no questions regarding the locks or her pale expression. The room was too dark, anyhow, for him to notice.

Despite his crooked shoulder and beak-like nose, there was still something in Louis's face that reminded Adélaïde of his younger, more handsome brother; perhaps it was the abyssal darkness in his eyes; perhaps it was the contour of his jaw. Regardless of which, it made her flinch at his touch as he brushed his fingers over her arm and prepared to perform his duty—anxious to get another child in her belly, no doubt, after the *unfortunate incident*.

Adélaïde felt the bile rising in her throat and pressed one hand against her mouth, the other gripping the sheets in alarm. *Don't be him. Don't touch me.*

Her husband frowned, withdrawing as though he had been burned, then propped himself on one elbow so that he might look at her properly. 'Is something the matter, dearest?'

Adélaïde shook her head, slowly removing her hand from her mouth, tears stinging her eyes. 'Nothing. Only, I'm afraid I'm not quite recovered, *capito*? There are still some complications

'Oh…pardon me, then. The physicians told me everything was in its order—but I wouldn't know enough of women's ailments.' Louis blushed, and in a heartbeat, Adélaïde saw the young boy he had been on their ceremonial wedding night, when Monsieur had spurred him to give her a peck on the cheek in defiance of the King's orders. He was still that boy, she realised, and he was still as different from Charles as he had been five years ago. *Charles*…The mere name sent a wave of disgust throbbing through her body.

'Just give it some time, will you?' Adélaïde cupped his large, warm hand in her own. 'We will have an heir, I promise.'

'It's—' Louis struggled in search for words. 'It's not that which concerns me, dearest Madame, but that you should be so downcast. You used to thrive, to…to grant everything a smile. But I haven't seen you smile for too long.'

'I'm all out of smiles presently, but don't fret, they will be back.'

'We must have a ball, then, a masquerade. You would like that?'

'I would like nothing better.' Adélaïde's lips curved, much to her own surprise, and she rested her cheek against the warmth of her husband's chest. *If I must appear in public, if I must lay eyes on his face, then it might as well be behind a mask,*

229

and with a piece of gallant music to help me keep my spirits.

It was impossible to sleep that night, just as it had been every night the previous couple of weeks; every time her eyelids fluttered close, Adélaïde was jolted awake by the slightest noise. *Was that the door opening? No. Was that it?* Even with Louis's erratic snores constantly present, she felt as if the whole scene might repeat itself right there and then—but this time, she would not escape alive.

Sleep-deprived and half-hearted, with dark shadows under her eyes and a dress that hung from her shoulders like a sack, Adélaïde entered the ballroom on her husband's arm a few days later. Though she had been sullen on the way there, a spark lit up her face as the bright colours flashed before her. Elaborate costumes and masks adorned with feathers poking in every direction; an underlying ripple of cheerful voices that flooded through the room. *It's almost as delightful as it used to be...all these grown men and women playing hide and seek behind their masks. I suppose I'm one of them now.*

'Look at that, the colour back on your cheeks! We are delighted to see you up on your feet again, dearest,' the King exclaimed, pausing the dance, causing the entire room to freeze still, awaiting his signal to continue.

Adélaïde did not have the heart to tell him that the blush had been applied in bold strokes by one of her maids, and was anything but natural. 'I could not bear to be absent from such a glorious gathering, Sire. You really have outdone yourself.'

'Anything to bring out that smile of yours, my doll. Now, Louis—' The King turned to his oldest grandson, who had been waiting his turn in humble silence. 'There are a few issues I would like to discuss with you later.'

'Yes, Sire.'

'Good. Continue, if you please!'

The room was once more set in motion, the participants of the dance moving in intricate patterns around one another. Neither Madame nor Madame Maintenon were among them; they were both comfortably seated on *tabourets*, as far from each other as was physically possible.

And yes, there *he* was. Surrounded by a small hoard of girls in glossy gowns and intricate jewellery, both fake gems and real, competing for his good graces.

Louis was caught up in a strangely fervent conversation with the King, doubtlessly concerning some political matter, and Adélaïde took a deep breath before gliding over to the *Duc de Berry*. She would

231

have to seek out the confrontation sooner or later—if she did not seek it out, it would come for her instead—and she knew she might as well get over with it.

Charles's mouth twitched as he laid eyes on Adélaïde. She noticed every detail painfully clearly, from how he brushed something off his emerald-studded coat, to how his expression shifted again and again before settling on the same smile he had worn every other time they had encountered one another.

'You really *are* a prude—I never thought that before, you know,' he said and winked.

'I'm not a prude.'

'Well, let us hope for better success next time. Now, won't you shake off the gloom and have a dance with me?'

That was the final drop that made Adélaïde's goblet of tolerance spill over, the final grain of sand that made the scale to shift from hurt to pure anger. She did not even bother to cast a cautious glance over her shoulder, but took a step forward so that their noses were a mere centimetre apart. Charles did not reek of liquor, as he had done *that night*, but his hot breath still made her eager to vomit on his silk stockings. 'You don't dance with me. You don't smile at me, or flirt with me. If you do—' She licked her lips, mustering all the courage she could find. 'I'll tell His Majesty what you did.'

'Even if you did, they would all know it was *your* misstep. You who wanted it, too. And you know the situation is hardly unique.' Charles was still smiling.

Adélaïde felt her chest cramp as she realised the brutal truth in his words. There was no use in telling him—in telling anyone—that she had had nothing to do with it, for she was a woman, a member of the so-called weaker sex, and she could never win this fight if she fought it openly where everyone could see it. Louis would believe her, perhaps; the King would, if she was in luck. But what good did that do when hundreds or even thousands of people would whisper behind their fans that she was nothing but a whore who had spoiled herself for her husband and did not deserve to be Queen?

'I cannot dance with whomever, Monsieur *le Duc*, for I have promised my husband my company this evening.' *Another lie.*

'So formal, Madame? Maybe next time, then.'

'I should be delighted.'

Charles dropped the subject at that note and returned his attention to the ladies that were flocked around him like so many fluttering butterflies around a flower. *Why can't they see it? Why could I not see it? The ugliness, the arrogance...I'll bring him down—one day, when he least expects it.*

CHAPTER XXVI

Charles hissed in Blois's ear, repeating the question. The King's daughter giggled, infatuated because of the wine and the company of her nephew, and took another sip from the glass that she so often clutched in one hand. Then, the gory details began pouring out; she laid at Charles's feet the story of how she had discovered her father's dainty favourite with one of the maids in the gardens that sun-soaked afternoon two years ago. Blois had not received the regular trinkets and purses of silver—besides, she was in no state to refuse her nephew the information he so charmingly fished for.

Moments later, Colette was dismissed out of hand with no further explanation than that she had not conducted herself with the dignity that being a member of the household required. She dared not press the Superintendent for information, but such a hasty decision could only have been made on the command of someone with unquestionable authority, someone who need only lift a finger to make the court dance after their every whim.

That woman—Blois, as Adélaïde had called her—she knew, of course, but Colette could not for her life understand why the consequences should hit at this hour.

Dumbfounded and clutching the few belongings she had acquired during her time at Versailles, she watched the golden doors slam shut before her face with a solid *bam*. Her lips trembled, desperately pressed together to prevent screams and protests of the most pathetic sort to escape. Not until a droplet of blood trickled down her wrist did she notice how hard she had been digging her nails into the palm of one hand.

Colette swept her eyes over the buildings and fountains bathed in a cold light that gave them a bluish hue. Goosebumps erupted on her bare arms. *What now? Adélaïde needs me, she needs me after everything that has happened, I can't...I can't leave. It's ridiculous.* She considered pounding her fist on one of the countless windows, but lowered her hand at the last second, knowing deep down that nothing good could come of it. She had never before been taken by surprise when faced by misfortune or pure malice—these things had been a natural part of her life since infancy—but it stung nonetheless, it stung worse than any beating or crushed expectation could have.

Carriages stood neatly lined up outside the gates, available for hire, and Colette steered her steps toward them without another thought.

Colette asked the coachman to let her off at the outskirts of the city, knowing her pay would have to suffice for lodging and food as well. *I might as well walk the last bit—it can't be terribly far to the Seine.* However, the distance turned out to be of little importance, since her uncomfortable shoes and empty stomach made the walk a painful endeavour regardless. The streets surrounding the river, the heart of the city, would provide a large selection of rooms though, and perhaps a large selection of employment. These pragmatic thoughts were the only thoughts she could allow herself to think; she grasped after them as if they were Ariadne's red thread and her own dishevelled mind was the infamous labyrinth.

The longing, the fear, the itching feeling of failure, that would have to wait until she had roof over her head and a plate of soup or a piece of bread in her hand. After having been as much a prisoner of the intoxicating world of Versailles as the courtiers themselves for years, Colette felt a thick lump forming in her throat as she passed the squalor in the poorer neighbourhoods. The streets carried a stench: an unmistakable stench caused by faeces and rotten waste. Despite the grey skies and biting November wind that pulled mercilessly at Colette's hair, she laid eyes on several people slumped against the houses, dressed in tattered clothes. Many of the women were young mothers, it seemed, for they clutched linen-wrapped babies to their bosom and stared blankly ahead. The children did not scream or whimper—they lay peculiarly still in the cold.

So this is what France still is? Not the fêtes and banquets, but this...I had almost forgotten.

Colette thanked Jesus Christ when she finally escaped the slums and reached a better part of the city, where a majority of the inhabitants were merchants and craftsmen: those balancing between the working class and the bourgeoisie, those who were not rich but earned enough to pay for a decent apartment and warm meals every day of the year. It was in these quarters that she felt at ease, for it was here she had spent her childhood. Could she return? Opposite powers tore at her; one voice kept repeating that blood must be thicker than water, thicker than anything in this world, and thus they would welcome her with open arms; the other whispered of the unspeakable things her father might do the instant he caught sight of her. The second voice spoke with logic and reason, she knew, while the first possessed naught but wishful illusions. *They must think I had a fit of insanity and ran away—and so I did—to some sinful life. They would not believe me if I told them where I've been, what I've seen. No. One night at a time...*

The night had lowered its black veil over Paris by the time Colette escaped the streets in favour of a tavern that was cheap enough and had room for another guest. Stepping over the threshold was like entering another world, from the crispness under the twinkling dashes of light in the sky to a boisterous bubble of warm light and alien odours. Five chairs were placed in a half circle around the hearth, where logs crackled and spewed sparks, and on the chairs sat five alarmingly similar men with their legs spread wide, hands resting on their full bellies. Perhaps it was only Colette's impression of them that made them float into one picture, but it appeared to her that they all belonged to the same breed of drunkards: ruddy faces, stubby build, greying beards smeared with grease from the meal they had feasted on earlier that evening, and the same ringing laugh. The fire animated their faces with gold and deep shadows. In the tavern they appeared as friendly as dogs whipping their tails, but if she had encountered one of them outside in the dark, Colette would have taken flight.

She leaned her elbows on the counter and waited for the servant girl—a tawny child of perhaps fourteen, who tripped around between the tables balancing a tray of empty glasses, trying to avoid the sticky hands that somehow kept latching onto her —to approach her.

'I would like a room, please, Mademoiselle. And dinner, if you are still serving at this hour.'

The girl looked at Colette through a shield of pale lashes, her brows knitted, without offering a reply. Then, a plump woman with raven-black hair twisted in a knot and wearing an apron that might have been white once upon a time but was now spattered with every kind of stain, emerged from the room behind the counter while wiping her hands on her skirt. Colette concluded that the woman, whose skin was creased by the corners of her eyes and mouth, must be the girl's mother.

'What's this?'

Colette repeated her request.

'An' you're all by yourself? I'll 'ave you know this isn't a house of misconduct.'

'I never thought it was.' Colette felt the blood rushing to her face. 'I only want lodgings for the night, Madame, if you would be so kind. There's nothing indecent about that, surely?'

The woman tucked a strand of hair behind her ear with a calloused hand, frowning in the same way her daughter had. 'If you can pay me honest an' good money, we've got a room with a single bed. I'll have some stew heated up for you.'

'Thank you, Madame.' Colette dug deep in her pockets and extracted a handful of clinking coins, which her hostess quickly tipped into her own palm, counting the sum with darting eyes. She returned a few of the coins, slid the rest in her apron pocket, and nodded before disappearing back into what Colette presumed was the kitchen.

How much did she take? She stared at the remnants of her last wage with a horror she had rarely felt before. *One coach ride, one night in a room, and one dinner—and that's half of it gone.*

What was done was done though, and fifteen minutes later she was seated at a rickety table in a dusty corner of the room, eagerly gobbling up the pork stew in front of her. To call it pork stew in the first place was not quite fair, since she found three pieces of meat in the entire bowl—the rest consisted of broth, gelatine, and turnips. It seemed to swell in her mouth, a tasteless mush, but at least the hunger pangs were ceasing.

The room was the size of one of the linen closets at Versailles, smaller, even, and covered in a thin layer of dust that tickled Colette's nose and itched in her eyes. The bed, which was attached to one of the walls, looked about as fragile as if it had been made of eggshells; she had not yet dared to put it to the test by resting her weight on the mattress. It proved to be strong enough, despite the creaking of the springs, and Colette pulled the blanket up to her chin after licking the last of the stew from the spoon.

Now, the emotions came welling up. *What on earth have I gotten myself into? If I had only stayed true to God's will...If I had only guarded the little virtue I had from being corrupted by lust and tempted by all the finery. Then I would still be sleeping in my chamber. I would still be a part of that world.* These desperate, wishful thoughts did little to help, however, and Colette knew it with the same certainty she knew her own name. The rational side of her once more battled with the spiritual and the self-loathing, resulting in an awful lot of bitter tears.

CHAPTER XXVII

Colette awoke the next morning with stiff joints that made unpleasant noises when she cracked them. She crawled out of the squeaking bed and gasped with pain, having slept with her shoulder twisted in an odd angle throughout the night, too exhausted to notice.

After dressing herself and tying the crinkled shawl tightly around her shoulders, she descended into the common area of the tavern on a quest for some sort of morning meal.

'We only 'ave bread and ale, Mademoiselle. I am afrai' the milk and cheese are all out—we don't make a lot of it this time of year.' The dark-haired hostess leaned on the counter, her head tilted, examining her guest with knitted brows.

'That will be alright, Madame,' Colette said.

'You only paid for a room.'

'Yes—yes, I know.' She swallowed her disappointment. 'I shall be collecting my things in just a moment.'

'Very well, Mademoiselle.'

Colette did as she had promised, and was out on the street again little more than fifteen minutes later. The serving girl had slipped her a loaf of bread—though the crust was dry and sullied with mould—and she chewed her way through it as she walked. Being too caught up in her own mind, Colette barely noticed getting closer and closer to the *Rue Bertin Poirée* until she practically stumbled across the house she had once called home. Silhouettes were moving behind the sheer curtains; muffled voices could be heard from the window. Colette's stomach cramped in alarm as she flung herself behind a corner so that she might watch from a safe distance just as the door opened and a familiar figure emerged.

Monsieur Auclaire's hair was tinted with white, no longer steel grey as it had been the last time his daughter saw him, and the brackets of grim lines around his mouth were set deeper. The glint in his eyes as he looked at the paint boxes stacked up and prepared for delivery was the very same though; it was as though he was surveying his children, struggling to conceal his pride. Of course, if the packages had indeed been his children, he would never have allowed them to suspect any such pride.

Colette's breath caught in her throat as an old woman exited the house and stopped a few steps behind Monsieur Auclaire, waiting patiently for a scrap of his attention. Her mother appeared to have aged fifteen years during the two, almost three, that had passed—not aged well like a fine wine or a cheese might, but as a rapidly withering flower. Her hair was as always neatly tucked under a white cap, but looked thin and brittle. Her once so noble face was overlaid by wrinkles, and she walked with a slightly hunched back and shuffling steps.

Is it my going that has made her so weary? Or is it him? Her glance slid back to her father, who now turned his head to listen to the flood of words that spewed from the woman behind him, his thin lips curved in a smile that did not come close to reaching his eyes.

'So, you see, dearest, I thought I would make something of that cabbage Madame Feuilly offered to give us—perhaps a soup, or a pie. And then your brother wrote to say he might pay us a visit the next time he finds himself in the city—oh, but you mustn't go out without a thicker coat!' Madame Auclaire clasped her hands and stuck her head inside again, then withdrew with a hefty woollen coat hanging over her arms.

'I'm perfectly well, thank you. Put that thing back.'

'It is frightfully cold outside, dearest.'

'Yes. How fortunate, then, that I'm only going down the street.'

Madame Auclaire remained silent but nodded after a second or two, taking the garment with her inside once more, and did not reappear, as if to avoid being dismissed further.

Colette watched the exchange between her parents, feeling sick to her stomach, heart hammering in her chest. What had once been the most natural and unquestioned pattern in her life had—since spending such a long time in another world—changed into a queerly gut-wrenching sight. What appeared insignificant was in fact only the tiniest fragment of a greater picture. *Such civility, compared to what he showed me, such calm. But no affection, not even kindness...how does she bear it, dragging them both through the years? Like a broken clockwork that still ticks somehow. And Bastien is married by now, surely...then there's no one there to make father think twice before raising his hand.*

As she pressed herself against the chalked house wall, strands of hair falling down and blurring her vision, Colette knew there was no going back, not now. Seeing her mother slowly crumble to pieces, watching her father's bony hands knowing what they were capable of...she would rather spend the winter in the gutters. An impulsive thought, it was true, and perhaps one she would come to regret, but it was there nonetheless and could not be disobeyed.

Her shoes clapped against the cobble stones as she retreated through the alley she had come; the layer of ice, thin as crêpe paper, had her slipping several times, but she never tumbled down head first.

However, her flight was cut short as she collided with a man's trunk-like chest, which was clad in a musky overcoat. The man lost his footing, only just managed to prevent falling by gripping a protruding windowsill, and his eyes flicked around in search for the cause of this inconvenience.

Colette's face burned, and she reached out in an impulsive attempt to smooth the crumpled overcoat, her fingers grazing over a small bulge. Spurred by the threat of not having a warm meal or a dry bed that evening, she slipped her fingers inside the pocket, closed them around an icy metal object—perhaps a watch—and pulled back before the man had fully returned to his senses.

'Pardon me, Monsieur! I pray you are not injured?'

'No, no...but you ought to watch your step, Mademoiselle—if not for your own safety, then for that of others,' the man grumbled with a voice that seemed to come from the deepest pit of his massive chest. His hay-coloured moustache fluttered slightly with the rhythm of his panting breaths, and Colette could only observe its movements, clutching the metal object that now lay in her own pocket as hard as she could, pleading to God not for forgiveness but for his help in her crime. *What on earth is the matter with you?*

'Off you go, then.' Then man did not waste another glance on the wench that had interrupted his errand, and continued down the alley with determined steps.

Colette allowed the breath she had been holding to escape in a cascade of white smoke that quickly faded. After rounding two more corners—making certain that her victim had not changed his direction and was in fact following her—she stopped to fish up the object and have a proper look at it. There, cupped in her palms, indeed lay a watch, a far finer example than she had dared to hope. What appeared to be solid silver reflected the crisp sunlight, forcing Colette to squint at her prize; the thick chain lay in ringlets around the watch itself.

How much is it worth? What would I get if I offered it to one of the merchants at

Les Halles? No doubt it would pay for modest lodging and necessary commodities for a few days at the very least, for this was not a regular trinket but a precious possession, this much she had learned about the value of different jewellery and the like from her time at Versailles. The shame that now enveloped her could not change that fact, and Colette resolutely fended it off. *God forgives, yes, and some need more than others. There is no wrong in taking from those who have more than enough already...I know that, if anything.*

That night, Colette sought shelter in a more comfortable tavern than the one she had spent the previous night in, although the price was not much higher, since she had picked the best bargain with greater care and more time on her hands. The coins that she had obtained by selling the stolen watch gleamed in the candle light where they lay on the table in her room, serving as a not so benevolent reminder of the moral battle that was raging in her head. It was wrong to steal, she had been indoctrinated since she was a wee girl—but it could be right under certain circumstances, whispered a voice within.

What would Adélaïde say? No, she would have nothing to say, because she would never have to do anything of that sort. The young *Duchesse* felt as distant now as the moon, and in possession of the same ethereal beauty, for Colette had already begun to build the idealistic imagery of her in her mind. Only a short period of time had passed since she last saw the other girl, yet everything that had connected them felt like a pretence, a dream; Adélaïde had transformed into a hazy figure surrounded by a golden shimmer. Whenever Colette tried to break through that shimmer and think of the figure as an ordinary girl, someone with whom she shared countless very real memories, she merely ended up laughing at herself. How could those memories be anything but an absurd dream? How was it possible to rise so drastically in good graces only to be plunged to the bottom of the heap in a matter of days?

And Colette soon sank deeper yet— not, perhaps, in poverty but in her own morale. The pocket watch was followed by a collection of various trinkets; they ranged from chains and engraved pedants to broken mirrors and used napkins—which were, of course, of no value whatsoever.

Once she had cobbled together enough money from her conquests, Colette changed her room at the tavern for a rented attic room. The landlord asked no questions, though his eyes bore all the doubts in the world, for with every paid rent followed a petty bribe to butter his ego and maintain his silent collaboration. *He knows perfectly well what I am: unmarried, unprovided for, yet paying my way little by little. There can be no mistake there.*

Spending her days literally working her fingers to the bone in a factory did not present the most appealing prospect once she had become accustomed to the relatively light work of picking pockets; Colette hesitated to admit it even to herself, but comfort had taken the upper hand of her conscience the very minute she had faced the streets of Paris. However much she regretted it, Versailles had guided her into corruption as easily as a dog guided by a piece of ham, and it seemed to her that she had already given up enough.

Employment in one of the wealthier bourgeoisie or even aristocratic households was impossible also, for they would hardly take on a girl looking as tattered as she did at this point, and even if they did, Colette felt certain she would not be able to hide her seizures in such a crammed space. She had managed them at Versailles solely because there had been *too many* people, too much going on to pay any attention to someone like her.

As such it was that Colette passed the winter of 1702: wrapped in a blanket like a cocoon, curled up on her bed, resting her chin on her knees, sketching on a sheet of paper covered in smudged charcoal sketches and doodles, which she had acquired in the shop across the street. The room was penetrated by cold from every direction, a cold that pressed through the walls and enveloped her like a heavy mist. The room had no fireplace, hence Colette often moved from the bed to sit on the floor where she would press her palms against the wood to sense the warmth from the apartment beneath.

She knew only a little of the neighbours who lived underneath her. The father of the family—a comically short man with sprouting eyebrows and a melodious voice that rose through the cracks in the floorboards—earned his living as a secretary to some gentleman. His wife, with whom he frequently gibbered, could often be spotted chasing after one of her youngest, her braided hair whipping her back as she scurried about.

Then there were the four children. Colette grew to loathe the creatures more for every minute that passed, for their high-pitched squeals and screams continued throughout better part of the night, and their angelic halos of golden locks did little to dampen her aggravation. Fortunately, she did not have to encounter them very often, as she kept to herself in the attic room.

During the days, she would loiter around the squares and market places, hands buried in her pockets, searching the crowds for easy pickings: those who looked wealthy enough to survive a petty theft without noticing any real difference in their lives, yet ordinary enough to move without any guards or servants trailing behind. The busiest places were the most convenient, quite naturally, because it was easier than one might have expected to push through the wall of overcoats and skirts while slipping a hand inside one or two pockets, escaping on the other side without being caught red-handed. They hardly ever seemed to notice—just like at Versailles, there were too many people for them to react every time someone stroked past them, especially if this someone happened to be a slim girl so pale as to almost appear transparent, with eyes demurely lowered and steps lighter than the snow that fell over the city in the first few weeks of the new year.

By the time she had harvested enough for one day, Colette would shift her attention to the street artists that lined the squares even in this season. They were poor, most of them, but had saved up enough to buy the tools they required to perform their craft. With ink-splotched fingers and expressionless faces, they sketched and painted images as captivating as the finest artwork in the country—only theirs lacked gold leaf imprints.

Others were of higher birth, of course, but they were of a different, more respected sort and tended to have their own studios, and Colette could only catch glimpses through the windows of their rich colours and thick brushes.

She often caught herself wondering whether she would have any success in the field, should she embark on a career as a street artist, but dismissed the thought. *I could never be skilled enough—I would only waste the little money I have on supplies, only to end up earning no profit and stand there like the fool I am.* Therefore, she restricted herself to purchasing three sheets of paper every week and, when there was need, a pencil and some ink, using it sparingly during the evenings that dragged by. Though she missed sinking a brush into creamy azure paint, the practice sufficed to keep both her spirits and her sanity reasonably high.

The motifs changed slowly over the course of months, but one theme kept returning: that of the court. Colette drew their faces, their gowns, their apartments, all through a new perspective. At times, she would picture them side by side with the sights from the slums she had passed through that November day; at times, she would mix the two worlds into absurdity.

The sketched faces that began to form a pile on the floor were never Adélaïde's; at least Colette did not intend them to be. She refrained from approaching it, for while she gladly thought back on Versailles itself—questioning and comparing—the most compelling object of her heart was better left alone, for everyone's good. *And my ink would run out too quickly...her hair is too dark to fill in.*

CHAPTER XXVIII

Adélaïde watched the light from the chandeliers dance in Charles's eyes like fireflies against the night sky. Her grip around the golden fork tightened as she slowly chewed the salmon, then stabbed into another piece. The *Duc de Berry's* glance darted from his father, with whom he was conversing most unwillingly, and locked eyes with her. Adélaïde gazed back briefly before remembering the vow that she had made herself in silence that night at the masquerade a few months ago. She would wait, wait until all she felt for this man, this boy, was cold contempt, because boiling hot revenge never worked quite as well. The thought scared her; she had always been frightened by the mere idea of hate; it did not come naturally to her to be full of vengeance—yet this was different. *If he has transformed me into a vicious being, then it's only another thing that I blame him for. The world can be a kind*

256

*place—it must be—but some people are
obstacles to that world...*

'You look rather sickly, Madame,'
Nantes said, sitting on her right side, with
glee badly disguised in a shroud of concern.

'I am fully recovered from the fever—I
have been for some time now. And how is
your daughter faring?'

'She longs for her father.'

Adélaïde chewed on her lower lip,
recalling the affair with Conti, for a short time
King of Poland, who now resided at a *château*
in the outskirts of Paris, which he had bought
in 1699. The scandal had died out long ago by
court standards, and to Adélaïde's knowledge
the couple had not seen much of one another
since that emotional summer when their
letters had been spread across Fontainebleau.
When she thought back on it, Adélaïde found
no emotions of her own; the spite she felt
towards the King's daughter was still there,
but it was as though all the anger she was
capable of simply had to be directed
elsewhere for the time being. Nantes had been
blissfully passive during the past year.

'I'm sorry to hear that, Madame. But
surely, *Mademoiselle de Clermont* is dearly
loved by her...father, your husband.'

'Of course. Dearly loved.' Nantes
plucked at the napkin in her lap. 'They can be

frightfully irrational, children, I mean. You shall see once you have one of your own. *If.*'

Be nice. You don't need another family member on your vendetta—please.

'Yes. But I think I have seen enough irrationality in adults to know what it is, Madame,' Adélaïde said with a smile as stiff as that of the cherub centrepieces on the table.

'Ah...who is it now that has hurt your tender little heart?' Nantes cocked her head to the side.

In the blink of an eye, Adélaïde had flapped her hand, knocking over a glass of *pinot noir*, and the deep cherry-red spread over the impeccably white satin of Nantes's gown, leaving a mark that would hardly fade even with the help of every laundress in the country.

'How clumsy I am, Madame! You must forgive me, you simply must!'

Nantes's lips parted, but she remained silent, stunned. The King gave her a stern look, his bushy eyebrows arched, until she nodded. 'I know it was not your intention, Madame. May I be excused, Sire?'

'I would like you present later this evening. You may go.'

'Yes, Sire.'

Adélaïde watched Nantes make her hasty departure, and cursed her own sensitivity, painfully aware that it would only

258

complicate her ambitions to tear open old wounds that had just begun to heal.

Adélaïde's thoughts trailed back to the day she had called the Superintendent to her chambers to inquire where that chambermaid of hers had gone, the one with the red hair and the freckles. *Dismissed on the grounds of misconduct and indecency not fitting for a girl in her position, or any good Christian. Her services no longer required. Not a matter to concern Your Royal Highness with.* That was what she had been told; no more, no less. The abyss that suddenly gaped beneath Adélaïde's feet was dark as coal, drawing her closer without mercy. Only weeks before, she had been standing on the top of a mountain, enthralled by the beauty of the view, unaware of the four losses that were to follow: that of her child, her dearest friend, her lover, and her naïveté. She still could not decide whether the third or the fourth of these was the worst, for without Colette there was a massive piece missing from her life, but without her naïveté she did not recognise herself.

Adélaïde had quietly fended off the sobs that threatened to shake her body any minute as she marched directly to Blois, throwing the question at her feet without further ado. She had not even received the answer she had hoped for—that Blois simply wanted Colette gone, having tired of their games—but stood dumbfounded as the older woman confessed that she had been a mere accomplice in the dismissal, Adélaïde dedicated a bitterly thankful though to her brother-in-law for not making the scandal publicly known at court, at least, not even sparking a rumour, but acting with a discretion he rarely used.

Now, as January was coming to an end, the abyss had only grown wider and darker, yet it would not suck her down; she gripped at streaks of light, trying to grasp after something to keep her from sinking. The prospect of revenge truly was the greatest motivator—as she had so often heard it said—but there were cheerful moments, too. When Louis, or Madame Maintenon, returned a smile or stroked her cheek, clinging to the light became easier. Whenever the King patted his thigh to have her sit in his lap as if she were still eleven years old, it became easier to pretend that nothing was amiss. They all reminded her that there were as much kindness in the world as before, if she could only learn to see and cherish it again.

Adélaïde assumed that Colette must have returned to her family in Paris when given her notice, and if this was the case, she would be properly looked after. Colette had never told her much about her father or mother, only random slips of the tongue revealing the family business that earned their bread. Of course, their home could be nothing like Versailles, but Adélaïde doubted their living conditions came close to the squalor Colette had told her was reality in some parts of the city. *She'll be fine, yes, she must be. I only wish I could kiss her goodbye. Would that have been too much to ask?*

Madame Maintenon's voice tore Adélaïde from her reflections. 'Are you listening, dear? I asked about your sister.'

'Pardon, Madame. She's doing marvellously—haven't you heard?'

'It must be quite the strain on her spirit, England and Austria still having the insolence to question Philippe's right to the throne.'

'I think she's tougher than she looks, Madame. But I do wish she could have spent a few years at Saint-Cyr, completing her education, just like I did. Every young girl should.' Adélaïde flashed Madame Maintenon a genuine smile, grateful that she might focus her mind on sweet memories rather than the dire present.

Madame Maintenon was scraping the leftovers of at least seven dishes to the sides of her plate with delicate movements; she had sampled each of them before discarding them as too rich or too tasteless. 'It brings me such joy to hear you say it, dear, it really does.

Saint-Cyr, ah, I remember how you used to run about with that friend of yours—what was her name?'

Adélaïde frowned, searching the back of her mind for the answer. 'Frances, I think. Yes, Frances.'

'Poor thing! And you were heartbroken, such a solemn child, so unlike yourself.'

'But I patched it together, Madame!'

'You most certainly did, and you will again. You can't fool me, dear, but whatever it is that weighs your soul will soon be lifted by the grace of our Lord.'

'I know it,' Adélaïde said and smiled. *But not by the grace of our Lord—by the grace of myself, if anything, though there would be no use in telling you so.*

Madame Maintenon carried on with the poorly treated delicacies on her plate, picking up light conversation with her stepson, the *Grand Dauphin*, about the necessity of finding the right perfume to spray on your leather gloves.

Adélaïde sat through the rest of the dinner with a slightly merrier perspective; the King's wife had succeeded, perhaps without intending it, in strengthening the hope she had already begun to nurture.

Louis came to her room later that evening, and though it still made her twitch,

Adélaïde summoned all her effort to endure her marital duties, not because it was expected of her, but because she knew success in one field would give her enough prestige to succeed in other matters. She then slept soundly through the night without being taunted by so much as a single nightmare. She knew they would return—if not the next night, then the night after that—but those peaceful hours of nothingness were a victory in itself.

Colette picked up her bruised self from the bumpy floor in the attic room and inspected the red marks on her arms; they would shift into purple and mustard-yellow during the day. She remembered nothing of the seizure, as usual, but she could imagine the violence with which limbs must have jolted and collided with the furniture or the floor boards. Her neighbours—the couple with the angel-haired, wailing children—had begun to throw strange glances at her when they passed in the staircase. *I need some herbs, mayhap mugwort, or some charm...And for that I need money.*

With this motivation, Colette twisted her hair into a knot and pulled on a brown beret, before abandoning the spotted hand mirror on her bed and embarking on her daily rounds of the city. The wind hit her in the face the moment she closed the creaking door to

263

the house; her toes were immediately clammy from the slush that penetrated the soles of her shoes. By now she had acquired a form of invisibility as her long hair was tucked underneath the hat and her figure draped in a sack-like cloak that made her look like a young boy. Although the transformation had been unintentional at first, Colette had quickly learned to appreciate the shield against unwanted glances and touches that these clothes provided.

Following the well-known path to Notre Dame, she went unnoticed by the passers-by as any urchin would, placing her steps with calculated care to avoid the worst puddles of dirty snow and rainwater. The cathedral towered majestically, making her feel infinitely small, yet safe, with its white stone and Gothic spires. The gargoyles glared down at her from the building, guarding their domain, leading one's thoughts to mythical creatures rather than God.

Colette knew better than to enter the cathedral. She had had the nasty experience of being shooed out only a few days ago—her shoes dragged in too much filth, they said— but remained a few meters away from the gates, arching her neck to fit as much as possible in her view. Then, she lowered her eyes again and clasped her hands in the folds of her cloak, whispering a prayer for forgiveness and for mercy, two things she knew she would need if she was to survive the following hours of sin. *Perhaps He can't hear me, or perhaps He doesn't want to, but it never hurt to ask. Dear God...*

A quarter of an hour passed before Colette raised her eyes and bade farewell to Notre Dame. She would return soon, without doubt, but already missed this temple of piety more ardently than she could grasp. Now that she had been forced to stoop low in terms of morale, her trust in the spiritual had only soared higher in an attempt to compensate and redeem herself.

After having spent the rest of the morning lurking in the long shades cast by the ships docked along the river bank, waiting for a few drunken sailors to strut ashore—as they were easy victims for her lithe fingers in their intoxication—Colette enjoyed a light meal sitting on the steps of the customs house. It tasted better than one might have expected pickled trout and dry bread would taste, for she had paid for it herself. Of course, the money she paid with came from sold stolen goods, but it was certainly an improvement compared to most of the food she consumed.

Little did she know at the time that her current career was about to come to an end, nor that the beginning of the end would come that same afternoon.

CHAPTER XXIX

The house was two stories high, though it appeared larger because of the pointy roof. The walls were of dark brown bricks; like so many other houses, the rows were uneven and the mortar cracked. The chimney stuck up like a small tower but no smoke came puffing out. Despite the rather poor impression the house made, it was situated on the *Rue Saint Antoine,* one of the wealthier streets, and Colette suspected its inhabitants must have enough money to live in comfort but not enough common sense to take care of their property.

Colette peered through the spotty glass panes, trying to comprehend the complete chaos inside the house. Furniture cluttered the living area—cabinets with peculiar patterns carved on the doors, chairs piled with books and stacks of paper looking as if they might topple under the weight any minute, carpets rolled up and leaning against the walls—so that she could hardly see the floor. Dim light from the numerous candles fastened to the walls mixed with the cool daylight, bathing the room in an unusual brightness. And everywhere, everywhere lay discarded paintings: canvases and sheets of paper with nothing but a few strokes of colour, abandoned on the floor and on the desk, surrounded by paintbrushes stiffened with dry paint instead of having been washed and groomed. Colette felt a whirlwind of dismay in her stomach as she beheld such carelessness for one's tools. *They would be far better off in my hands...some people don't know their luck.*

She tore her eyes from the window and took a few steps forward, passing a door of chestnut, where the owner of the house had nailed a thin brass sign that read *Étienne Lemaigre.* Colette was just about to round the corner of the house and carry on with what she referred to in her mind as work, when another window caught her attention. This window, unlike the others, was swung wide open and the curtains fluttered back and forth in the breeze. On the windowsill stood an array of tins and boxes of paint along with glasses of dirty water and brushes. Less than a meter into the room sat a man—perhaps approaching his fortieth year—with thinning blond hair and an equally thin, tweezed moustache hunched over what appeared to be the outline of a face. His hands were smudged with coal and his concave cheeks carried similar marks. The portrait was naught but the skeleton of the finished product, but there was no doubt that this man knew his business alright.

The temptation had grown too strong to stem; the treasures were sitting at the windowsill as if asking to be taken care of, like a juicy bone held in front of a starving dog.

A memory flashed before Colette's eyes: that day when she had been running from the wrath of her father after stealing a small package of paint from the factory, paint that should have been delivered to some wealthy statesman's wife to give her something to busy herself with, and ended up hidden in the delivery wagon. That time, she had been clumsy and terribly inexperienced— this time, things were different, but the consequences would be far graver than an enraged Monsieur Auclaire, should she be caught in the act. Slowly, slowly...then *quickly,* her fingers closed around one of the little boxes on the windowsill and she withdrew her arm as far as she could before a hand latched onto her wrist and held it in a steady grip. Panic rose in Colette's throat, the same panic she had felt that time all those years ago—as if the air she breathed was full of knots and clogged on its way to her lungs.

'What's this, boy?' The man's grip tightened until Colette could feel the blood supply being cut off and her wrist took on a bluish tint.

'Monsieur—'

'Don't think I haven't seen a common thief before.'

'No, Monsieur. But I was not trying to—'

The man's eyes gleamed dangerously, warning her not to speak another word. Colette could not help but note their vivid, olive-green colour.

'Monsieur, may I suggest you add some more shade under the lady's cheekbones, to give more depth?' She bit her tongue after uttering these bold words, reminding herself that the situation could hardly get any worse.

Monsieur Lemaigre—Colette assumed this must be his name considering the sign on the door—did not move so much as a finger. '*What*, boy?'

'Well—' Colette drew a sharp breath as the man's nails penetrated her skin, then did her best to deepen her voice, and found it was surprisingly easy. '—I think you could add a bit of shade there, and perhaps make her eyes look a little larger, softer. Perhaps use burgundy as a base for the lips. That is, if you're working on commission by the lady herself. If you are, a white lie to make her prettier wouldn't come amiss. Monsieur, you're hurting my arm.'

'Now you're giving me business advice as well as painting advice? Not that it concerns you, but I happen to work for my own pleasure and not on commission—at least not this one.'

Let go of me, please, let go of me. 'Then I suppose it does not matter whether she's pretty or not, Monsieur.'

'You suppose right.' Monsieur Lemaigre slowly loosened his grip and then let go entirely, probably not to ease her pain but so that he might continue with his drawing. 'You know an awful lot about these things for a thief of the street, or perhaps you just think you know.' His right hand moved with swift strokes without so much as a glance on the sketch, and Colette felt a pang of triumph as he—in spite of his words—heeded her advice. She remained standing there by the window, still locked in the painter's claws, although now it was by enthrallment rather than violence.

Once her feet were numb and the sketch as good as finished, Colette realised the folly in staying any longer. The very second she took a step back from the window though,

Monsieur Lemaigre's voice cut through the air like a razor.

'Where do you think you're going?'

'Don't report me to the police, Monsieur. I don't think you can, anyhow, seeing as I never took any of your possessions.'

'You have an odd interest in my craft, boy. Why is that?'

'My...my father manufactured paint...I grew up with it.'

'And now your father is dead, the business is nothing but unpaid debts and a non-existent clientele, and you have retorted to stealing to earn your living.'

Colette opened her mouth to object, then swallowed her words and nodded instead. *Let him think that's the situation if it simplifies things. What does it matter? He's not entirely wrong.* She took another step, and this time she chose not to hear the man calling after her as she dashed through the puddles towards the safety of her attic room, coming dreadfully close to being trampled to death by a horse-drawn carriage.

There was something about the painter that drew Colette back to the window—which was still cracked open—only a few days after the encounter. She did not attempt to snatch anything from the windowsill, nor from the

272

room within, having learned her lesson, but merely peered at the faces that littered the floor: portraits of young and old, men and women, heart-achingly beautiful and gut-wrenchingly ugly. Some were incomplete, others appeared to have been crafted through countless hours of meticulous labour. Colette was perplexed as to how she could have missed them the first time she had been there. *And how can anyone live here, walk here, in this mess?*

It became a habit to visit the house on *Rue Saint Antoine* in the early afternoon every day; sometimes she simply passed, sometimes she lingered for almost a quarter of an hour to study the portraits from afar. Monsieur Lemaigre often paced back and forth in the room by the window or sat in one of the armchairs scratching his scalp through the feathery layer of hair, but Colette made it a priority not to be seen or heard, to avoid another confrontation with the scrawny man. Despite her efforts, though, it appeared Monsieur Lemaigre knew exactly who his secret visitor was, for on the last day of February, the door was open as well as the window when Colette arrived. She was struck by the inconvenience of this; the rain was pattering down on the cobble stones outside and the rain gusted inside with the wind onto the doormat, which was now soaked through, resembling a wet rag that could have been used to swab the floor.

There was no doubt: Monsieur Lemaigre knew, and this was an invitation—a strange invitation, true, but Colette could think of no other explanation as to why anyone would leave their door open under such ghastly conditions. Hence, she stepped inside, avoiding the drenched doormat, and closed the door behind her with a satisfying *click*. A musty whirlwind of scents enveloped her, forcing her to inhale slowly or else be smothered in it: the scent of aging leather, chamomile, and damp logs, dominated by sharp paint fumes. It was as if she had been sucked into a bubble entirely different from the harsh reality outside, and by entering this bubble she had entered the arcane mind of a rather surly craftsman, where she was both an intruder and an observer.

'I see the urchin has peeked his nose inside the cave at last.' The voice came from the end of the narrow hallway.

Colette raised her eyes from her muddy shoes and met the olive-green pair that seemed to pierce hers despite the distance. 'The door was open, Monsieur. I hope I'm not disturbing you.'

'On the contrary.'

Colette tramped on the spot in an attempt to get the blood flowing in her legs and warm herself up before the cold did any permanent damage. *Perhaps he'll let me sit by the fire for a moment...he must have a fire somewhere here, unless he is some kind of supernatural creature.*

'Are you looking for employment?' Monsieur Lemaigre continued with his head tilted so that he might gaze down upon her. 'Don't bother to answer—of course you are, a child in your shoes. How old are you?'

'Eighteen a week ago, Monsieur,' Colette replied after counting on her fingers for a second.

'Hm. You look younger, a little...squeamish, feminine. Of course, it doesn't matter much as long as you can perform the chores that I give you.'

'What chores would that be?'

'Running errands, delivering paintings and writing down commissions, anything that needs to be done that I'm too busy to do. I could use some assistance, and to be frank, I don't think you are in a position to negotiate the wage of your dreams.' Monsieur Lemaigre pronounced these words without contempt or glee, simply as a matter-of-fact, and Colette knew he was right. An honest living, surrounded by artwork, paid little but probably more than the girls in the factories and the laundries earned. *I thought I was putting comfort first by doing what I do, yet*

I've had no comfort. What is there to lose compared to the knowledge I might gain?

'I can perform them perfectly well, Monsieur. Maybe...maybe I could help you with the paintings, too? I'll show you, or I can learn whatever you need me to learn.'

'Don't get ahead of yourself.'

'No.'

'You won't lodge here, at least not to begin with, but you may eat with the kitchen maid—she's the cook, too—if you please. And you will keep those paws to yourself—if I catch you so much as touching my possessions one more time you'll end up in prison, understood? I hope you know the Bastille is no comfortable place, especially not for a skinny little thing like you.'

Colette merely nodded, struck by the unspeakable agony that would await her in almost any prison: places of filth and disease, gambling and prostitution, brutes and murderers, common people up to their ears in debt. Prison was an ugly place, ugly enough to make one long for the gallows. At least that was the rumour that had circulated around Paris—not only Paris, but the rest of Europe, perhaps the rest of the world—since the beginning of time. Whether it was true or not could only be learned by joining the unfortunate lot of prisoners and perish with them, which, naturally, was a path most people tended to frown upon.

'I won't lay a finger on them, I swear, though I do hope you'll let me watch at times. And yes, I should like eating with the kitchen maid very much.'

Thus, they entered a form of partnership, or to be fair, their own miniature hierarchy wherein Monsieur Lemaigre acted the unyielding master and Colette the humble apprentice. Neither of them said the word aloud, but it was a mutual understanding that apprentice was her title, not servant or messenger boy. Though she did execute the tedious duties the painter laid on her shoulders—the chores he had listed that afternoon in the hallway—being in his presence constantly gave her the opportunity to observe, learn, and even sneak in a piece of advice in one of their tart conversations. Monsieur Lemaigre never once acknowledged her comments as being of any help; yet he heeded them more often than not, his lips curving at the result. Indeed, the few times Colette saw him with a semblance of a smile on his fleshy lips were when eying his own work, a habit that might have made him too self-indulgent for anyone to endure, had it not been for the fact that said work could reel in an admiring smile from *anyone* who laid eyes on it. Furthermore, he never so much as once voiced his satisfaction or expected Colette to butter his ego, although she did this sometimes without realising it.

Monsieur Lemaigre continued to live under the presumption that the youth he had taken in from the streets was an orphaned boy and not a former *femme de chambre* who had abandoned her home willingly. He never bothered to look closer at his employee, or notice the slight oddity in the forced deepness of her voice, perhaps because he preferred assuming the truth that suited him best—and Colette refrained from contradicting him, for this truth was the most convenient version for her as well. Though the disguise was sometimes difficult to uphold, it was worth it a hundred times over.

She rarely saw the painter's clients in person since a majority of the commissions were simply slid under the front door in neatly sealed envelopes; Monsieur Lemaigre would visit their houses to make his sketches while they sat for him, then return to the *Rue Saint Antoine* to polish them up and set to work with colours. Only then did Colette see their faces bloom out on the canvas like a butterfly spreading its wings. The women were of particular interest; master and apprentice would both spend considerable time praising their features while speculating both in silence and with one another about the client's life or personality.

Colette quickly discovered that Monsieur Lemaigre was not one of those men who spent every night in a new girl's bed and then blamed the girl for her lack of prudence, or took a stroll down *La Seine* in the dusk to prey on women of the street. He was not married either, nor did he appear to have any sisters or daughters—the only relative she could find any trace of in his house was an older brother who lived in Cannes—yet he possessed a fascination for the female sex.

'Clever creatures, and far more rational than most men,' he once grunted.

'I agree,' Colette responded, secretly relishing this sentiment, wondering if Monsieur Lemaigre would have taken her on if he had known her true identity.

'Methinks they are best admired from afar though, like birds. Too much stir and racket can make birds a flighty, nervous lot.'

Colette frowned. 'Surely we must all live, and that ought to stir us up if anything, don't you think?'

'You would rather have that kind of life than one in harmony?' Monsieur Lemaigre stood up and cracked his finger joints, then brushed off the fragments of dust that had gathered on his waistcoat during the painting session.

Colette was gently rubbing the brushes in a basin of hot water, having made the task a part of her daily chores out of pure concern for the man's tools. 'I think it's too late for me, Monsieur.'

'Ah, yes, the adventurous urchin. You know, there are times when I think you must be hoarding some rich past—but the world is full of children like you.'

'Yes, Monsieur, I suppose it is.' Colette had to bite her tongue as to not say anything she might regret. *If I told him about what I've been through, if I told anyone, they'd say I'm a lunatic, or that it was all fever hallucinations.* 'May I go to the kitchen?'

'Fifteen minutes or so. I have an errand for you to run.'

She placed the last paintbrush in the empty cup that had become the official container, wiped her wet hands on her sack-like overcoat, which she refused to remove under any circumstances, and headed down the corridor to the kitchen.

The cook—who served as kitchen maid as well—was not to be found in her rightful territory. Indeed, Colette wondered about her whereabouts more often than not, for it seemed that the woman with the spotless apron and rust-coloured dress spent the majority of her working hours someplace else. When Colette asked Monsieur Lemaigre, he simply replied that 'Madame Sylvester is free to come and go as she pleases, as long as dinner is steaming hot on the table every day when the clock strikes eight. She does her bit in this house—where's the use in me keeping track of her every step?' The few times Madame Sylvester had encountered her master's new apprentice though, she had left a lasting impression with her swaggering walk, enormous hips, and sagging cheeks where the blood vessels had burst underneath the pale skin so that it looked as if she had been playing with Monsieur Lemaigre's purple paint.

Colette drew a sigh of relief upon finding the kitchen abandoned. She even dared to twirl around the room a few times to fully enjoy the freedom of not being observed by either the painter or his equally sharp-tongued cook. In truth neither of them was vicious people, but together they created such a dense atmosphere in the house that Colette felt as though she was tripping over glass and trying to avoid getting cut.

A set of white porcelain tins decorated with blue dots supposed to resemble cornflowers stood lined up beneath the cupboards. Colette lifted the lid of each one of them looking for something edible. Crackers as dry and white as paper, various grains, dried apricots and prunes, honey, coffee beans...Every tin contained the kind of food Colette had only been able to dream of a few weeks ago when she was living on the paltry coinage she could get for her nicked jewellery. The wage she now earned was smaller, true, but her quality of life had improved a notch.

They're never empty, never touched. Does he eat at all? Or is Madame Sylvester constantly refilling the pantry when no one's watching? Dear God, forgive me my greed. She plunged her hand into the porcelain tins, scooping up their contents until her palms were spilling over, then dropped down on the rickety chair by the table that stood in the middle of the room. At first, she nibbled on the rye bread and chestnuts; then she turned the nibbling into hungry devouring and the food was gone before she thought to have some cheese with her bread or fetch a cup of ale to wash it all down.

Colette glanced at the beaten brass watch on the wall. A quarter past two in the afternoon—Monsieur Lemaigre would be expecting her to return to her duties any minute now. The chair scraped the floor with a high-pitched noise as Colette pushed it back and stood up to clean up the mess she had made on the counter, putting the right lid back on the right tin so as to avoid Madame Sylvester's venomous scolding.

The errand that Monsieur Lemaigre had spoken of proved to be one of greater interest than usual.

'Take this letter to the address I have written on the envelope. There. Now, you take this to a man called Hyacinthe Rigaud—a great man of great talents.'

'Rigaud? I think I have heard that name before.'

'It wouldn't surprise me if you have, despite your origins. He's done commissions for the royal family as well as an array of nobles and merchants. He is an acquaintance of mine, if you must know. We worked on a few pieces together in our youth, and I happened to stumble across him at the *Académie* a few years ago.'

'The *Académie*, Monsieur?' Colette cringed at the childish sound of her own questions, but she dared not take anything that concerned her employer for granted.

'You talk too much, boy. *L'Académie Royale*. Now go, before I have to deliver the letter myself.'

Colette nodded, pulled her beret further down over her ears, tucked the envelope in the pocket of her overcoat, and headed out through the front door. She had been sent as a delivery boy many times before, but never to someone as prominent as the man she was now about to pay a visit.

*Perhaps he has put his paintbrush to the ceilings in Versailles, too; he has contributed to several of the portraits that hang under the chandeliers in the marble halls...*These thoughts quickly escalated to vivid images of the world she had spent so long trying to forget, but she stifled them and remembered that even though Monsieur Rigaud had connection with the court, she was a messenger and nothing more. In the best of scenarios, he would exchange a few words with her concerning the letter or the wellbeing of her master, pop a coin in her palm for her efforts, and dash off to whatever he was occupied with at the moment.

As it turned out, she was not entirely correct in this presumption. Upon entering the foyer of Monsieur Rigaud's grand apartment later that day and being led by a man servant to the salon, Colette found that even the greatest masters can sometimes take interest in the humblest beings who scramble at their feet.

The renowned painter was a man of calm, confident airs and his smile was slightly wry, insinuating that he knew everything about everyone. His complexion was dark, his hair like black wool, his chin clean-shaven and split in a prominent cleft. As he spoke, Colette felt like she was sinking through the floor under the weight of pure awe. This man, whom she was now standing before with a letter crumpled in her pocket, had achieved the highest success one could hope for in the world of art—his skills could not be questioned.

'You bring word from Monsieur Lemaigre?' Rigaud asked.

Colette fumbled to extract the letter and placed it in his hands. 'Yes, Monsieur. He sent me to give you this.'

'Good. Ah, an invitation to dine.' Rigaud skimmed through the note. 'I'll have my servant bring you a cup of ale and something to eat. You look rather scrawny— forgive me for saying it. Monsieur Lemaigre rarely takes on students.'

'Thank you, Monsieur—for the refreshments, I mean. I wouldn't be so bold as to call myself his student, perhaps something similar.'

Rigaud nodded thoughtfully. 'And do you have any interest in art?'

'Oh, yes, naturally. Only a fool does not.'

'Hmm. I suppose so. And why did he take you on?'

'I'm not certain, Monsieur.'

'He has an eye for promising talents— is that what you are? No, in fact, don't answer that. But if you do happen to craft something of your own making someday, I wouldn't mind looking at it. Ask Monsieur Lemaigre—he knows where my studio is.' On that note, Rigaud turned on his heel and marked the end of their meeting, strolling off with his hands clasped behind his back.

Colette stood wide-eyed in the salon, waiting for the servant to bring her the refreshments, processing what she had just experienced. *I talked to one of the great artists. And he was almost polite, almost chatty. And he wouldn't mind taking a look at my own work if I ever come up with something promising. How strange fortune is.*

CHAPTER XXX

Adélaïde did not confront Blois until April arrived. By that time, she had mustered enough courage and sophistication to talk of the things that had occurred between herself and Charles, and Blois's role in the aftermath, without feeling as though she might break into incoherent rambling, or worse, weeping.

The King's daughter had retreated to the Palais-Royal in Paris—a grand building lined with sand-coloured pillars—where she would often go to escape court life; though it was anything but plain, it was somewhat quieter, allowing her to withdraw from her husband's infamous debauchery at Versailles. Adélaïde had concluded over the years that Blois was one of those people who enjoyed the whisper of a scandal, as did everyone around her, but would rather drown herself than play a part in one. Her husband, the new *Duc d'Orléans*, had hardly improved his way of living since that fateful summer of 1702, when his father and uncle had quarrelled so violently over his behaviour. However much Adélaïde blamed Blois for giving Charles the information he needed to shatter the little happiness she had left, she pitied her for having persisted in marrying Phillipe d'Orléans.

The small entourage that arrived at the Palace-Royal on a crisp spring day consisted of the *Duchesse de Bourgogne*, her husband, Maisonblanche, and a randomly selected set of *comtes* and *marquis*. It would have appeared odd to pay the palace a visit by herself, and so Adélaïde had hurriedly scraped together a party of companions who would doubtlessly be delighted at the prospect of spending a few days in the lavish lodgings of the Orléans family. The eleven visitors crammed together in three carriages—although eight additional vessels were provided for their luggage alone—desperately trying not to step on the hem of each other's dresses or get any sharp objects stuck in the men's white stockings. Thus, they rolled through the streets of Paris, past the *Jardin des Tuileries* where the trees were just about to burst into bloom, the entourage being the object of numerous curious glances despite having the curtains drawn in all three carriages.

The welcome they received and the banquet that followed the same night were perfectly marvellous, but did not give Adélaïde any genuine pleasure. It was all the same routine, the same experience she had already had a thousand times, and moreover it was utterly unnecessary to her cause. The dining only prolonged the mandatory courtesies that had to be exchanged between the hostess and the guests before she would be given the opportunity to play her cards and ensnare Blois in her own little court of justice. *Justice, not revenge. That's what this is.*

With this mantra ringing in her head, Adélaïde bided her time until the *Duchesse d'Orléans* made her departure from the salon to retire for the night and followed her through the corridor, grabbing her by the elbow.

'What did you do?'

'I don't know what you're insinuating, Madame. Be as kind as to let go of me.' Blois shook her arm but it was fruitless.

'You told someone, you must have. I'm not trying to be ill-mannered, truly, but you must have. You were the only one who knew— were my gifts not enough?' *Calm, calm...*

'I—' Blois lowered her eyes and a trace of guilt crossed her face for a second before her mouth hardened again. '—I may have spoken out of turn but I don't carry the blame in this whole affair. That blame is yours, Madame.'

'I assume you understand there will be no further exchanges between the two of us—they would never believe you if you told them, now that she's...now that she's gone. You have nothing to use against me.'

'For now.'

'Never again. *Capito?*'

'People slip up, Your Royal Highness, even those who carry themselves with such innocent graces.'

'Tell me you regret your actions,' Adélaïde pleaded, desperate to give her forgiveness both for Blois's sake and for her own inner peace.

Blois tilted her head to the side. 'I shall tell you something better, if you will only let go of my arm. *Thank you.*' She rubbed her elbow, though Adélaïde's grip had in no way been harsh. 'There are people, apothecaries and the like, who can help cure you of that...Italian vice. Other things too, any potion you desire.'

'Is it...is it witchcraft?' A gust of fear swept over Adélaïde.

'Do you believe in witchcraft? Don't be absurd.'

'Science, then?'

'I suppose so, but what does it matter as long as it serves its purpose—whatever that purpose may be.'

'Why are you telling me this?'

'It seems only fair that you should know. It's commonplace to take help from those people, at least in the right circles. Consider it an apology if you wish.'

Every potion I could desire. I don't need to be cured though, I need something quite different. 'You shall have to tell me more about where I can find this person,' she whispered, compelled to lower her voice as she was suddenly painfully aware that the walls had ears; the risk of being overheard was even greater here than at Versailles. A couple of the other ladies still lingered in the salon, stubbornly sipping at their drinks like cats trying to lick the last drops of milk from their bowls; a few of the male guests were playing billiard in another room; then there were the servants.

Blois cast a glance over her shoulder, a glossy coil of hair bouncing against her collar bone—and then she spilled all the knowledge she possessed on the subject. Adélaïde listened attentively and absorbed every hushed word, all while beginning to form a sketchy plan in her mind. *Everything will be well again. It's solely a matter of time. To think I wanted naught but a confession of regret, a confirmation, and now she gives me this!*

Adélaïde dared not make use of the information that same night, nor any of the following three nights they spent at Palais-Royal, although it would have been convenient considering the location. Instead, she spent the hours pondering and contemplating whether it was such a splendid idea after all, and whether she could bring herself to execute the plan that was still only a whisper in the back of her mind; meanwhile, she engaged in the leisure and the ceremonial pastimes that were simply everyday life. She attended mass, praying absentmindedly and watching Louis light up with devotion as the priest read from the scripture, she strolled in the gardens with two or three ladies trailing behind her and chattering continuously.

Above all, she relished being free from worry of being asked to dance with *him*—not so much as catch sight of his blunt glances or dashing smile. Unfortunately, they could hardly extend their visit to infinity, and once the King wrote to notify her that he was *sorely missing the pleasure of my dearest girl's company*, the carriages returned to Versailles like a train of lapdogs called on by their master. The return was like a needle puncturing her bubble of temporary serenity, a wet blanket cast over the joy that usually overcame her when she beheld the grandeur of which she would one day be mistress.

CHAPTER XXXI

The ebony-coloured satin grazed Adélaïde's cheek as she turned up the hood to shield her face from the moonlight, hiding her features in dense shadow. The hooded cloak was new, fresh from the tailor's hands, and fell in perfectly executed lines around her modest gown. It served its purpose better than any other garment she could have thought of; in combination with the flat, silent shoes, she moved as discreetly as a moth through the passages and corridors.

After descending the stairs to the ground floor of the palace, Adélaïde threw one last haughty glance over her shoulder, then slipped out through one of the back entrances that the guards had left unattended, favouring a blunder of sleep. She scurried across the courtyard on her toes to ensure her steps were light enough not to attract any attention— although this precaution was perhaps silly, she refused to take any greater risk than the one she was already taking by leaving Versailles in the dark of night without an excuse. There was no excuse, of course, that would suffice if they caught her, other than blaming sleepwalking and hoping for the best.

Thank God. Everything good so far. Adélaïde climbed into the waiting carriage and sank down on the velvet cushions with a rush of relief that she had seldom felt before in all her life. The coach man had received his instructions; she had paid him a visit earlier that day to place a purse heavy with coins in his palm and whisper a few carefully chosen words in his ear. She was once more baffled by the things money could buy, and more grateful than ever for her generous allowance from the King, though it weighed her heart with shame even so. *I would never hurt him, never hurt anyone, if it wasn't for what he did...he has the blame in this. It has to be done. How else can I ever rejoice? How else can the court be filled with light and laugher, when there's a snake in the grass?* These were the things she repeated to herself to stem the inner conflict that had been evoked in her mind between the sweet-natured desire to do good and the icy hate she still felt. She knew, though, beyond all doubt, that once the carriage began its journey towards Paris, there would be no turning back.

They travelled in utter silence, save the sound of the horses' hooves against the road, the night enveloping them like a veil. Adélaïde almost wished she had brought a maid servant as company, if only to exchange a few words to break the tension, but there had been none whom she could trust as well as she had trusted Colette. They were not unkind, nor too timid, but it was best not to share her intentions with more people than was absolutely necessary—meaning no one. The coach man knew nothing of the purpose of this trip; he had been paid and that was all there was to it.

Adélaïde sat on the edge of the seat and peered out from behind the curtains as the carriage rolled into the city. She had been there a few times before, but never had she been given the freedom to see the common quarters, and certainly not at this hour. The alleys cut through the mass of tightly set houses like thin, black ropes; the walls loomed over the streets as if they were too tall and badly constructed to stand up straight. Between the balconies dangled crumpled laundry that fluttered back and forth in the breeze.

The carriage halted by the bank of the Seine—Adélaïde knew little of Paris's geography, but she could tell this much—and the hooded *Duchesse* emerged. The stench that welcomed her was different than the stench at Versailles, which came from filthy periwigs and the lack of a proper sewage system amongst other things. This was worse; this was the reeking odour of faeces and waste emptied on the streets, rotten fish from the river, perhaps even rotten bodies of beggars decaying behind some tavern or other. Adélaïde crinkled her nose in the way that made the courtiers' hearts soften. 'Wait here— I shall be back before you know it, perhaps in an hour or an hour and half—just stay inside the carriage. Who knows what might roam these streets,' she told the coach man before leaving him where he stood and embarking down the nearest alley. Blois had been so kind as to give thorough directions to the apothecary, so she ought to have no trouble finding his lair, if only she could remember the instructions she had been given.

Thin streams of golden light from one of the windows made it easier to see where she put her feet down, avoiding the filthiest patches and puddles. *Who lives there?* Adélaïde arched her neck to try and glimpse through the window, which was on the second floor, and realised that she had reached her destination. She lifted the fist-shaped piece of iron on the door and smacked it against the wood one, two, three times. *Please open, oh, please don't let all this be in vain…*

Just as her every ounce of hope had begun to peter out, a series of locks rattled from the other side of the door, and it opened with a squeal that made Adélaïde fear the neighbours might wake up. The figure behind the door was the complete opposite of what Adélaïde had pictured when she first gained knowledge of the so-called apothecary: the person who gazed at her under the light of the dripping candle stick was not an old man with a liver-spotted face and a cryptic expression, but a woman whose skin was free of wrinkles and whose lips curved in a calm smile. Hair the colour of copper was swept underneath a nightcap rimmed with lace, though the clarity in her face implied she had been awake for some time, her droopy eyes wide open.

'Pardon me, Madame, I must have knocked on the wrong door. I hope I didn't disturb you—' Adélaïde began, convinced that she must indeed have made a mistake.

'Are you one of them? You need...special assistance?' The woman's voice was as melodious as a harp; it did not even quiver as the hot wax from the candle dripped down on her hand and left a red mark on her skin.

'Yes, yes, I suppose I do.'

'Then you're welcome to come in. Don't worry your pretty head about me,

Madame, I'm used to nightly visitors of your kind.'

'My kind?'

'I think you know, Madame. All very secretive, very fancy—though I must say you're younger than most. Now, don't stand there on the threshold!'

Adélaïde obeyed the apothecary without further questioning and stepped into what she had pictured in her head as a gloomy cellar stacked with potions and tinctures but turned out to be something quite different, just like her hostess.

The room was spotless; not a single stain could be seen on the simple furniture or the pale lavender tapestries. Everything— from the cabinet and the chairs to the vases with white daisies—gave the impression of purity itself, like one might expect a little girl's dollhouse to look. *Why would someone with such lovely taste and enough money to afford it chose to live in a location like this? It's like one of those stones that are rough and dirty on the outside, but when you crack it open, the inside is the finest crystal.*

The woman closed the door behind Adélaïde and followed her guest inside. 'What is it you need, dear? A love potion, perhaps? Or something to ease your monthly pains?'

'I...' Adélaïde fumbled with the words, suddenly finding them too difficult to pronounce, her intentions too shameful to admit. 'You see, Madame, there is someone who has wounded me deeply.'

'Ah.' The woman lowered herself on one of the chairs and clasped her hands in her lap, her eyes intense on Adélaïde's. 'You want to get rid of someone, no? I get that request more often than I would like, but I rarely refuse. It's not my concern what measures people like you take in your games of...what is it? Power? Money?'

Adélaïde flushed red and took to biting her nails. *I would never do it for power...people like me. Am I like that now?* She forced herself to leave her nails alone and meet the apothecary's piercing eyes. 'I have enough of those things, Madame. But if you have something, anything, that might help my situation, I'll pay whatever price you deem fit.'

'I know you will.' The woman turned around and opened one of the cabinets, where she proceeded to scan through the shelves of glass containers until she found what she had been searching for: a tiny tube wrapped in strings of leather, about the size of an almond biscotti, plugged with a piece of cork. 'Pour half of this—it's enough, trust me—in a cup of wine or something similar. The dose will be small enough to go unnoticed, provided, of course, that it's stirred with liquor or food. It will be a few hours before the symptoms become clear, a little longer before death sets in.'

Adélaïde stretched out her hand and received the tube in her palm with a thrill of excitement dampened with guilt. The container was light as a feather; it seemed almost too incredible to be true that such small amounts of poison could end a life, yet she dared not express her doubt to the apothecary.

'Now, to the matter of my price. Those earrings you wear—' The woman lifted a finger and pointed at the glistening emeralds and pearls that dangled from Adélaïde's earlobes with the same calm smile as when she had opened the door. '—they would suffice for this time.'

Adélaïde reached up to touch the precious stones, wondering why she had even bothered to put them on. 'I shall pay you in *louis d'or*, Madame, for I would not like to leave anything that might reveal the fact that I paid you a visit. How much is it you want?'

'How much are the earrings worth?'

'I don't know—I didn't purchase them myself. Take this.' Adélaïde extracted a purse from one of the deep pockets in her cloak and handed it to the apothecary. It contained more than the sum she had spoken—it contained more than one could be expected to pay for almost any tincture in the world—but she was anxious to close the deal so that she might return to the carriage. Without another word, she turned on her heel and escaped out into the night's chilly embrace, speeding her steps until she reached the familiar silhouette of the carriage.

As soon as she had slammed the door shut and sank down on the plush seat, the coach man gave the horses a smack with the reins and the carriage jolted forward. Her head was one bird's nest—both in regards to thoughts and coiffure—presenting a rather dishevelled *Duchesse*, though her appearance was the least of Adélaïde's concerns at that moment. She allowed her head to fall against the window, pressing her cheek against the cold glass, eyes glued to the knobbly trees with clusters of buds that flashed by. Their branches seemed to reach for her, gripping in vain, threatening to make her pay for the sin she was in the process of committing as well as for the list of ungodly deeds already written on her sleeve.

*If Colette was here...if Colette was here, everything would be alright, because nothing else would truly matter. She would kiss me here, and here...*Adélaïde bit her tongue trying to stem the tears that blurred her vision as she remembered the only sin she could never regret.

CHAPTER XXXII

A fortnight after the grim errand, Adélaïde mustered enough self-control to begin making what appeared to be friendly advances toward Charles, and it proved easier than she had dared to hope to lull him into a false sense of security. A few days passed; then she took the leap and discreetly gave him an invitation to her private chambers—of course, the meeting would have to take place in complete secrecy.

Charles made himself comfortable on Adélaïde's bed, rumpling the covers and leaning back on his hands, though he gave no further indication of any indecent intentions. 'Have you come to your senses, then? Finally.'

'I admit I've acted rather...immaturely, Charlie.' The nickname was like sharp glass on Adélaïde's tongue.

'But now you realise your blame.'

'Naturally.' She fired him a sweet smile; his eyes softened just as they used to before *that night.*

'You're too pleasing to the eye to be cross with for long. Marzipan?'

'I would never refuse such an offer!' Adélaïde exclaimed with a cheerfulness so false that anyone with more intuition than Charles would have distinguished it—but he would always hear what he wanted to hear, and she knew that perfectly well. She sank down on the edge of the bed, where her guest was already opening a small package wrapped in silk ribbons, revealing pieces of pink marzipan exquisitely shaped like roses. Adélaïde reached for one of them, chewing the sugary paste in silence, frantically trying to remember what she was supposed to say, ignoring the queasy feeling in her stomach. *It will be worth it, a hundred times worth it. One last night of flattery—then nothing.*

'How fares my brother?'

'Louis?'

Charles frowned at the mention of her husband. 'No, Philippe. I should hope his health is what it ought to be, at least until he's got a babe on his wife. I'm still the heir presumptive, remember? And *Spain* is not where I'd like to spend the rest of my life.'

'From what I hear he's as fit as a fiddle. But my sister is young—it will be some time yet before she has children of her own, methinks.'

'Well. Don't you have anything to drink?'

'I ordered some dessert wine to be brought up. Wait there a minute.' Adélaïde stood up and slowly approached the table where the bottle sat next to two crystal glasses that reflected the warm candlelight in intricate patterns. *You're clearing the path to your own end, don't you see? No, of course you don't.* The liquor glugged as she filled the glasses. Charles had taken to inspecting a loose thread in the cuff of his shirt while he waited, giving Adélaïde the opportunity to retrieve the miniature tube from one of the pockets hidden in the smooth folds of her *deshabillé*, remove the plug, and shake out about half of the contents into one of the glasses. The white powder dissolved in the wine within seconds, leaving no trace on the surface. The sweet liquor appeared so harmless, yet a single mouthful of it would equal certain death for a grown man—at least this was what Adélaïde had understood from the apothecary, and from the discreet research she had done on various toxic substances since then. The powder was, she had come to realise, arsenic: a poison commonly used by kings and criminals alike, famous for its efficiency and accessibility.

Now, the powder would help her take a man's life, all in one sip of the wine.

Adélaïde returned the tube to her pocket, threw a glance over her shoulder to make sure Charles was still not looking, and realised how dangerous it could be to turn her attention away from the glasses. *The right one was meant for him...I think. Yes, that must be it.* 'Here, take this,' she said and offered Charles the right glass, praying intensely that she had not confused it with her own. *That would be awfully unfortunate.* 'If I'm not mistaken, it comes from the vineyards in Tuscany.'

'You should have a servant to pour it for us. Where are they, anyhow?'

'I—I dismissed them for now. I thought we might be alone tonight.' Her voice trembled slightly, for she knew that if this failed, she would be locked in an impossible situation, where the only way out would be to either let him have what he wanted from her, or cause a scene and put herself at risk of his temper. And this time she *had* invited him to her bedchamber; there was nothing she could say that might serve as a plausible defence, not in the eyes of the court. Unless, that was, Charles drank—and he did.

The wine disappeared from the glass as Charles gulped it down, seemingly without a second thought, following it up with two more marzipan roses and a satisfied grunt. Adélaïde watched with her breath tangled and stuck in her throat, eyes wide, not having taken as much as a sip of her own glass. *A few hours until the symptoms appear...if I can only keep his attention averted, if I can only keep him from doing anything stupid for a few hours...*Adélaïde put the wine glass down on the table again, unable to bring herself to taste the sweet liquor for fear that she might vomit if she ingested anything more. Thus, the waiting began.

Four hours later—according to one of the clocks set in an intricate gold construction— Charles was growing more impatient by every minute that passed, so impatient that Adélaïde suspected he would either burst into thin air or recreate the events that had led to this very moment in the first place, unless she gave him keep him at bay and calm the dangerous gleam in his eyes. Only then did she think back on her actions, scanning every move she had made, and froze as she realised her fatal blunder. *Right glass, left glass...no...I can't have...*It was, however, the only explanation. Charles had never received the glass she intended, but the one that contained only dessert wine; the glass with the poisoned contents stood on the desk, still untouched. If Adélaïde had not been unable to drink, doubtlessly she would have been lying in spasms on the floor, emptying her bowels, plagued by fever and excruciating headaches.

The realisation sent chills down her spine, but she forced herself to think rationally about the situation. Before she had the chance to offer Charles her own glass—his glass—there was a familiar scraping on the door: Louis.

'You have to go, Charlie, *now*. It delights me that we're on pleasant terms again but you mustn't get the wrong impression,' Adélaïde hissed under her breath.

'Is it your husband? At this hour?'

'He does that sometimes—when he's feeling lonely.'

'Can there be any faulted impression? I think not.'

'We're friends. Like before. Don't you think it's for the best, so that we might return to the way things used to be?'

'Then you should never have invited me to your chambers in this way.'

'Perhaps not—now *please* go!'

To Adélaïde's surprise and relief, the *Duc de Berry* obeyed, slipping out through a side door with a sour look on his face. Although there had been no doubt about his desires, he was not intoxicated enough to risk being found in her bed by his older brother.

308

Adélaïde had never seen Louis enraged, nor even heard him raise his voice during their five years of marriage, but she had heard rumours that he had been a hot-headed child before his tutor tamed him and religion made him more than agreeable. Simply because he had never—and would never, she was sure of it—direct any anger towards *her*, did not mean Charles held the same privilege.

Adélaïde lunged forward, knocking the poisoned wine over on purpose, just as the door clicked open and Louis entered. The contents of the glass made a nasty stain on the carpet, but it was worth it a thousand times over if she could only eliminate the chances of her husband drinking from it by some wicked twist of fate.

'Are you alright, dear? Were you speaking to someone?' Louis made a rather unattractive sight in his nightgown, the candles highlighting his beak-like nose, but Adélaïde could not have cared less in that moment.

'Everything is just as it ought to be, no worries. I was just...talking to myself—I couldn't sleep.'

'Me neither.' Louis stared at his hands. 'May I sleep here, then? I thought maybe if we tried together it would be easier.'

Adélaïde felt her lips twitch in a smile despite the chaos in her head. 'Of course. Come.'

Louis drifted into said sleep shortly thereafter, while Adélaïde remained awake throughout the latter part of the night as well, when the veil of darkness outside began to shift into pale purple and pink as the break of dawn crept closer. The humiliation was the strongest of all the emotions she felt; the fact that she had taken the blame for another person's abominable actions in vain, with the only result being her own trampled confidence. The snare which she had sought to loosen was now tighter than ever; Charles was convinced that she had come to terms with her so-called folly and that their relationship was now every bit as friendly as it had been once upon a time. If she was lucky he would not cross the line again; if she was unlucky there would come a day when he spun out of control. Regardless of which, Adélaïde had sentenced herself to a future built upon an illusion of comradery, a pretence she had to carry on with until she either learned to forgive and focus her thoughts elsewhere, or until she had used the rest of the arsenic.

The tube rested in the pocket of her *deshabillé* with enough white powder in it for a second deadly dose. *We'll have to wait and see about that...I can't repeat this evening, I simply can't. If another opportunity presents itself, then maybe.*

CHAPTER XXXIII

'Word is your father had decided to turn on France by joining the Grand Alliance,' the King said. There lay no trace of accusation in his tone, yet Adélaïde felt her cheeks burn.

'Yes, Sire, so I have heard. I cannot answer for his foolish actions.'

'Neither must you speak against your father,' Madame Maintenon reminded her. 'You're in a delicate position, my dear, but always remember that you are no less a princess of Savoy than you are a daughter of France.'

'A daughter of France she is nonetheless, Madame.' The King frowned at his wife before turning back to Adélaïde. 'I have no doubt your loyalty lies with your King and with your country, my doll. This old man has enough worries already, no?'

'Naturally, Sire. You receive an awful lot of letters.' Adélaïde was sitting on the King's lap, opening his post with the letter knife at his request, oblivious to this familiarity which no other member of the court could dare to even dream of. Madame Maintenon sat in the armchair closest to them; a few of the most distinguished ladies and gentlemen were scattered around the Salon of Diana. Their glassy eyes observed from afar as they entertained themselves with card games and gossip, constantly alert lest their king should happen to mention anything of interest. The air was—as always—thick with the smell of sweat and concealed filth mixed with bizarre amounts of lavender perfume.

'Well! That's because I have an awful lot of business to keep in check.'

'I'm sure it must tire you, Sire.'

The King smiled, exposing his blackened stumps. 'Sometimes, my doll, sometimes. But I believe we have all become children these past few years, haven't we? You still make me giddy.'

'It should pain me if I didn't. You must let me know, Sire, if I ever bore you or—or if my lack of merriment displeases you.'

'Aren't you merry, my dear?' Madame Maintenon demanded. 'I can't think of anything that might trouble you, though your

313

father has been unwise in the very sense of the word.'

Adélaïde forced a smile. 'Don't waste your concerns on me, Madame. *Veramente.* I'm afraid I've got a headache, if you'll excuse me?'

Once she had escaped the company of the others, Adélaïde tiptoed straight to the King's private apartments, and was allowed inside without a glance from the ushers. The entire palace knew by now that the *Petite Dauphine* went where she wished to go; the guards had long since ceased to cross her for fear of the Sun King's wrath.

Adélaïde steered her steps towards her goal as soon as the heavy doors closed behind her: the marquetry desk in which she knew the King stored both intimate letters and political correspondence of the greatest significance. Pulling out the drawers one by one, she worked quickly, flicking through the stacks of paper in search of any document that might be of use to her father. Despite the enduring love and affection she felt towards certain members of her new family, despite Versailles being the centrepiece of her life, despite her dream of reigning over her own sublime France—the loyalty to her parents and siblings was too deeply rooted in her to ignore. *I oughtn't meddle—and yet I must. And poor Mother...she must know I'm still her loving daughter, that I still care for my origins.*

Victor Amadeus, her father, remained a nearly godlike figure in Adélaïde's imagination. He had been too preoccupied with his numerous mistresses and the Nine Years War—a conflict in which Savoy had fought with the Grand Alliance against France—to be an active part of her childhood, hence her knowledge of him was simply built upon the glorifying tales she had been fed since she was born. When he visited the nursery or spent time in his children's presence during a ceremony, Adélaïde had seen what she wanted to see: a grand man with a façade of titles and clothes in red velvet and gold, his mind on administrative matters rather than the little girls competing for his affections, his face as still as if he was an effigy on his own tomb. Having seen him for the last time when she was only ten years of age, just before travelling to Versailles, Adélaïde had never encountered her father with a more mature perspective; therefore she had never reflected that there might be another, flawed side of the Duke of Savoy.

Once the military documents were in her hand, slightly crumpled, Adélaïde took a blank sheet from the stack of paper lying on the corner of the desk and picked up one of the intricately decorated pencils. She proceeded to take notes of the pieces of information that felt the most important—everything from numbers and equipment to the names of key commanders and strategies—until the blank sheet was cluttered with ink and she knew her time was running out. She then carefully put the documents back in the right drawers, organised the contents of each drawer as neatly as they had been when she opened them, and returned the pencil to its marble holder.

The secretive exchange of information between Victor Amadeus and his daughter continued throughout the autumn; it proved an immense benefit to the Duke, and a chance for the *Duchesse* to form the bond with her family that she had lacked in her early years. Adélaïde still wrote frequently to her mother and grandmother of private matters, but the connection to her father was something new: a treasure previously unknown and a little odd. They barely spoke of anything other than what her father wished for her to find out, but merely seeing his handwriting was enough to make Adélaïde's spirits soar with satisfaction over being able to please a person who had previously been unattainable. The things she let her pencil tell were mostly details though, for there was a limit to how far she was willing to go. Perhaps she had already crossed the fine line of treason in her eagerness, but she soon realised that the most important pieces of information were best left untouched; besides, she rarely stumbled across them at all.

During those months of espionage, Adélaïde crafted a new motto for herself: *Never do one part more harm than what is necessary to bring another joy*. This mantra was constantly present in her thoughts—until her father's letters dwindled to a trickle, then ceased all together. *I am no longer useful to him; he won't bother any longer. But it was lovely while it lasted.*

However, less than a week passed before she was compelled to share a radically different piece of news with not only Victor Amadeus but also with a list of relatives who had been yearning to hear exactly what she now wrote to tell them: a child of the houses of Bourbon and Savoy would be born in the summer the following year, provided that everything went smoothly.

Adélaïde cupped her hand in the air where the bump on her belly would soon begin to form. How strange it would be to have another life in there, stretching her skin...somehow, it felt as if she was cheating the shapeless, bloody baby that had once occupied that same space within her before it had been so cruelly removed. But the physicians had confirmed it: her bleedings had ceased, and the nausea came in waves in the mornings, spoiling decadent breakfasts. Adélaïde recalled one particularly awkward moment, seated next to Louis at breakfast, her mouth filled with puff-pastry, when suddenly the sickness had overwhelmed her and sent her scuttling from the table with no regard to etiquette. Madame Maintenon had visited her later that day, practically vomiting reprimands, though Adélaïde swore she saw a tint of joy behind the scolding façade. The King's wife knew better than anyone the toll the miscarriage had taken on Adélaïde, as well as the fragility of her role at court. A *Duchesse*, a *Petite Dauphine*, was a grand thing, but grand things could be replaced unless they filled their purpose—not that anyone could suspect the King of scheming to replace his doll, but there were always other forces operating, and one could never be certain enough.

I ought to feel victorious, cheerful, all those sweet things—why don't I? Adélaïde knew the answer deep down, of course: she was petrified. The last time she had found herself in this condition, the consequences had nearly driven her into an early grave, both mind and body, and although the pregnancy itself had not been the cause of this, the association was inevitable. Hence, she spiralled deeper into the gruesome abyss of self-pity and bitterness without quite realising it herself.

'We must name him Louis, dear,' her husband said; an unnecessary statement. 'He will be the *Duc de Bretagne*, I believe.'

The line of the French throne was a chain of one Louis following another; to name their first child any different would go against every tradition, unless it was a girl, which no one dared suggest out loud. The child would be Louis Something, the number depending on whether death to his father or grandfather before he was crowned. Adélaïde would whisper the words; they were like honey on her tongue and music in her ears. *First Queen, then Queen Mother...how absolutely delightful. God is kind again.* This thought was the sole ray of light that crossed her mind when she thought of the pregnancy, but it was enough to keep her spirits afloat.

CHAPTER XXXIV

Winter shifted to spring; the buds on the trees broke into full bloom and the air changed from freezing to crisp, to pleasantly warm. The things that occupied Adélaïde's mind did not change greatly, but somehow they felt more distant than before. The War of the Spanish Succession still raged but no one had expected or dared hope for anything else, so this was hardly the source of any great unhappiness. Charles still acted like a cat preying on a particularly juicy mouse, waiting for the hour to come when the mouse would give in and grant him her full confidence—but there was something about Adélaïde's pregnancy that made him less saucy. Adélaïde guessed that it had less to do with genuine concern—as always—than the fact that she was no longer as attractive in his eyes as she had been before nature took charge of her appearance as well as her feelings; her wider hips and oilier skin in addition to the unpredictably shifting emotions were not the most appealing aspects of her person. *Another woman's curse is my bliss, because I would gladly turn into a goblin if it scared him off.*

During the final days of June, 1703, the pregnancy had advanced far enough to force Adélaïde into the preparatory confinement of her private chambers, hidden from public life and tucked down safely in bed. The curtains were constantly drawn so as to create a womb-like environment to enhance the baby's well-being and calm the mother's nerves. This gloom in combination with not being allowed any visitors except the midwives and maids, only nudged Adélaïde to the brink of insanity though, making her desperate for sparkling fêtes and hunting trips in the fresh air. Hunting had, of course, been ruled out since several months back, since riding was considered dangerous for a woman in her delicate condition.

Delicate was, perhaps, not the right word—the only honest descriptions that came to Adélaïde's mind were *gigantic* and *immobile*. It was a while since she had been able to spot her own toes when looking down, her belly resembling a pumped balloon constantly growing another centimetre larger, her skin pitted with marks from the rapid stretching. Although she did not mind the changes in her looks terribly, others seemed to.

'Thank the Lord you are not as stick-like as when you first arrived, Your Royal Highness—things would be far worse then. You have a rather short stature, though...' the women who attended her in the confinement sometimes said. Adélaïde knew they were right but it was a poor consolation once waking became difficult because of the aching in her back.

On the 25th of July, the time was ripe. Adélaïde drew a sharp breath as a wave of dull cramps went through her back and lower abdomen. With it came an intense pressure, as if someone was forging her pelvis apart, stretching her out from the inside. The pain subsided quickly, but returned just as she had allowed herself to relax again. Despite the indescribable distress of being confined to her bedchamber day and night, Adélaïde found some mercy in the fact that she was shut away from public sight, for she could feel her face twist in a grotesque grimace with each wave of ache, which were growing more intense every time. This mercy, however, was a brief one.

The obstetrician—a chubby man in an emerald green waistcoat, whose face was alarmingly similar to that of a pug—clapped his hands together and grinned. 'Ah! It appears to me that Your Royal Highness has experienced the first contractions—that is, the first sign of the birth. Allow me, Madame.' He strutted across the room and opened the main door himself, since the ushers were not welcome in the intimate setting. 'The *Duchesse de Bourgogne* is about to give birth! I shall need another doctor with me.'

The announcement was, of course, not actually meant for said doctor, but for the courtiers. The obstetrician already had two midwives and several maids by his side; the most urgent addition to the group was the spectators. The entire court was vibrant with anticipation and had been thus ever since Adélaïde had gone into confinement and the upcoming birth became the most popular topic of conversation at Versailles. There was the majority, who prayed for a healthy baby boy to secure the line of succession; then there was the minority, who hoped for a stillborn child or a girl, which might elevate their personal prospects of gaining some power. The first outcome would strengthen the King's direct legacy and those who circled around it while the second would plant a seed of hope in the hearts of every other candidate to the throne. Adélaïde swallowed hard as she pictured the monarch's legitimate children by Madame Montespan plotting to put forth their own heirs in the case of her failure.

A hundred people or more poured into the room like a swarm of flies, buzzing loudly and stepping on each other's expensive shoes, eager to find themselves a good spot where they could watch the spectacle that was about to begin. The choir of voices and clopping heels extended to the Grand Cabinet and the antechamber, where the unlucky bunch that had been too slow to obtain front row seats had gathered. Indeed, several of them were already sitting down, contrary to etiquette. *It's like a place of public amusement where all the unwritten rules have been broken and no one seems to mind anymore.* Both the King and Louis had made their way through the crowd to her bedside at that point, but although both their faces were twisted in concern, they made no attempt at interfering with the midwives' work or even touching her. Adélaïde considered asking the King whether he might clear the room of people, but at that moment another fit of pains interrupted her thoughts and made it impossible to focus on anything else.

There was, of course, good reason for the hustle surrounding the birth: not only was it a crucial event, but there had to be plenty of witnesses present so as to ensure that the child was not substituted for another. If the women belonging to the royal family were allowed privacy at times like this, there was always the risk of a daughter being discretely swapped for a son, or a severely disfigured baby exchanged for a healthy one.

The salacious rumours of the late Queen's black child still circulated although decades had passed since the King's first wife, Marie-Thérèse, gave birth to what was said to be the result of an adulterous affair with an African dwarf. The rumours had been stemmed though, thanks to the numerous witnesses who could testify to its absurdity.

Time appeared non-existent; as the labour progressed, Adélaïde found herself pulled into what felt like another dimension. When she thought it must have been dragging on for hours, it was mere minutes—then it lapsed and seconds felt like an eternity. One moment she was fully aware of the clammy tears that trickled down her ruddy cheeks from the effort, then she fluttered into unconsciousness before returning to reality when another pang of burning pain hit, though the pain was different from the one she had felt before beginning to push. Strangled screams of a kind she had never heard before filled the room and it took several minutes before Adélaïde's throat began to throb and she recognised them as her own. Then—when the stifling hot room was beginning to slowly smother her and fire reigned in her head and back as well as in her lower regions—it was all over.

The figurative sheath of tension in the room broke the second the baby slid out into the hands of the midwife and its sex became visible. A few moments passed as Adélaïde struggled to push herself up against the cushions, unable to distinguish what was said around her. Her hands fluttered as she tried to brush away the strands of hair that had stuck to her damp forehead. Then, before she could think so much as a clear thought, the midwife had wiped the baby clean, wrapped it in linen and placed it, warm and wriggling, in Adélaïde's shaky arms.

The baby—its head still splotched with blood and fluids despite the midwife's effort—wailed against her chest, exposing its tiny, red tongue. Adélaïde gazed at the foreign creature, overwhelmed both by its passionate screams and its fragility. Large, almond-shaped eyes the colour of cocoa beans, not unlike Louis's, looked back at her from the wrinkled face through a shield of short, dark lashes; the head appeared abnormally large in comparison to the stick-like arms that spread and stretched for something she could not see; the top of his scalp was covered in the thinnest layer of dark hair.

'A son, Your Royal Highness. My humble congratulations on your successful delivery.' The obstetrician's voice seemed to come from afar as if there was an invisible wall between herself and the rest of the room.

Adélaïde was incapable of tearing her eyes from the child. *A son...my son...how I have been waiting for you. And here you are—looking as though you might break any second. So pure, so new, so lacking of everything foul in this world.* She trailed a finger down the baby's button nose, touching the velvety skin on his face for the first time. The wailing subsided into a quiet snivelling, then silence reigned, interrupted by the occasional gurgling sound. In that moment, everything became crystal clear. There could be no more bitterness, no more hurting, no more scheming, not if she wanted to be an affectionate mother to her son. The very idea of the ugly games she had been sucked into filled Adélaïde with distaste; the world she wished for this baby to grow up in had no room for such things, for it was already brimming with kindness and merriment. *Just like it was when I was younger myself. I must go back, back, back. Cleanse all the dirt from the wound. The things that have caused me pain—the people—will still be there, but that doesn't mean I have to go on like this. I can move on, for his sake.*

Baby Louis's mere existence served as enough proof that clean slates still existed. As he curled his purple fingers, which were the size of those on the hands of the dolls Adélaïde had once played with, anyone who laid eyes on him would have sensed the refreshment a new life brings.

The Sun King's face truly shone like the sun at that moment—but Adélaïde knew the most relieved and joyful person in the room save herself was the *Duc de Bourgogne*, who gaped like a fish and could not take his eyes from the baby.

The courtiers stood on their toes, squeezing against each other in their eagerness to behold the future heir to the French throne, this healthy boy that was the answer to some prayers and the end to others. The ladies flapped their fans with an impressive velocity, sending gusts of stagnant air back and forth, while the men tried to wipe the gleaming droplets of sweat that crowned their temples as discretely as possible. Some of them practically shone with triumph while a few of their opponents gritted their teeth over the *Petite Dauphine's* success in her task, stung by the bitterness one could expect to feel when being shoved a step further away from the throne, despite never being particularly close in the first place.

Adélaïde could not have cared less about them, though, for she was spell-bound by the *Fils de France* whose eyes now seemed even larger and darker than before, gazing at her as though he knew the answers to her every question. Thus, they remained, mother and child, studying one another until the wet-nurse arrived and broke the spell by taking him away to the nursery.

Being a mother was not as dreadfully draining as Adélaïde had feared it might be—at least not for a woman of her status. The wet-nurse fed the child and dried his tears; the other nurses cleaned him; the governess and the tutors would provide him with the finest education possible in the years to come. Adélaïde enjoyed the parts of parenthood that were not so much about responsibility as they were about adoring the child; she visited the nursery as often as life at court allowed, enveloping little Louis in her arms and rocking him back and forth, swaying her hips. Each time she saw him it was as if a swarm of butterflies came to life in her chest, beating their wings against her ribcage, urging her to tell anyone who would listen how her son, her miracle, was not only the future King of France but the most beautiful child born within the walls of Versailles.

Perhaps Adélaïde was simply overcome by pride, but no one dared argue that it was not true.

Louis was as awkward with his heir as with his wife, but equally loving. His prime moments were when he could watch the two of them from afar and congratulate himself on having obtained the happy little family which was so rare amongst the aristocracy, convinced that his piety towards the church had led Jesus to grant him this treasure. Once Adélaïde had put little Louis back in his extravagant crib—which was draped in cascades of lace and decked with golden cherubs—the *Duc de Bourgogne* trotted after his young wife to the next social obligation, and thus they spent their days.

Just as she had hoped, Adélaïde felt the bitterness and pain seep away from her day by day, until she finally found herself standing by the *Gran Canal* in the gardens with the arsenic tube clutched in one hand. *It has to go. I can let it go. I must.* Slowly, slowly, she opened her hand to survey the lethal poison one last time, struggling with the knowledge that if she allowed it to sink to the bottom of the canal, it could never be recovered. Neither could she repeat the trip to the apothecary unless she was willing to take that massive risk again.

His life is not mine to take...only God can be the judge of that. I vowed I would put my mind to other things, and I have. This is the final trial. And in that moment, Adélaïde turned her palm down with a flick of the wrist, sending the tube tumbling down into the dirty water where it landed with a *plop*. The splash seemed annoyingly insignificant in comparison to the dramatic exit Adélaïde had expected the arsenic to make from her life—into a certain someone's mouth—but it went well with the serenity that flooded her senses as soon as it was gone. It had never been for Charles's sake, never, but for her own peace of mind, her own freedom. If the world had been fairer, if it had not been dictated by the whims and pleasures of men, things might have been different; justice might have been done. Adélaïde had given up on justice for the moment though, for she knew this was not a battle she could fight on her own without tearing herself to shreds in the process, and so she had settled on relishing the things she did have, while nurturing a spark of hope deep inside that there would—in some distant future—come a day when the world was transformed.

CHAPTER XXXV

The Christmas of 1703 was not a jolly one in the house on the *Rue Saint Antoine*. Monsieur Lemaigre had taken to his bed on the fourth day before Christmas Eve, and did not rise until two weeks had passed—and when he did, it was as if a higher force had transformed the man Colette knew and had grown fond of into a brittle creature with little to offer the world. His hair, which had already been thin as a new-born duckling's feathers, had faded both in colour and density, and was now naught but a few white strands slicked over his scalp. His appetite, which Colette had thought strangely small before, was now as good as non-existent, extending only to two or three biscuits with his tea every afternoon and steaming hot broth in the evenings.

The cook, Madame Sylvester, did not appear concerned in the least; she merely shrugged her shoulders, scoffed, and reminded Colette that the less Lemaigre ate, the more there was for the two of them to share without anyone blaming them for eating him out of the house. Besides, Madame Sylvester said, the less strength he had in his limbs, the less strict he would be with their duties and chores.

Although this might have been true in some aspects, Colette soon discovered that Lemaigre's mysterious illness meant that she had to assist him more and more, until she herself was executing a majority of the commissions her master received, before he put his signature to the artwork with a shaky hand.

During the year that had passed since that she first peered through the stained glass windows and tried to steal his supplies, Colette had gone from acting as a simple errand boy to handling not only his customers but his work and his finances as well. By adapting her own style slightly, imitating Lemaigre's brushstrokes, they kept the small clientele in ignorance of the unspoken arrangement.

'Just until I am well again. You'll thank me then, that I let you have the experience,' Lemaigre often mumbled after Colette had finished a portrait, though it was obvious it was meant for her to hear. There was never so much as a trace of gratitude in his voice, but she did not need it in order to maintain the quality of her work, nor was she so naive as to believe he would suddenly have changed into a kind man. The pride she took in those last polishing touches to the paintings were enough to keep her spirits high; although she scolded herself for thinking such a thing, she hoped in earnest that Lemaigre would remain ill for some time.

His loss is my gain, though he does not fully know it. And that's for the best. He wouldn't like knowing it.

The only outsider who had any inclination about what was happing within the walls of Monsieur Lemaigre's brick house was Rigaud, who knew his old friend's work well enough to spot the slight differences between a genuine painting and the substitutes Colette made for him. Rigaud said nothing of it though, he merely frowned at her, as he often did, and told her that Lemaigre was as always welcome to dine with him once his health had improved.

Despite being occupied with the commissions and the deliveries for the better part of the day, Colette often found a moment to sneak over to Rigaud's studio to watch his apprentices stare themselves blind at their master's instructions before attempting to copy him. To tell the truth, it was quite entertaining to watch them all fail in one way or another—but this she never voiced aloud.

'You've become quite the regular, no?' remarked one of the young men one late afternoon. His cat-like, grey eyes were unyielding, demanding to know what on earth the filthy boy in the beret thought he was doing in such an exclusive place. His chin was freshly shaved judging by the tiny, red marks, and he wore a vivid orange waistcoat neatly buttoned all the way up to the billowing cravat: he represented the very image of the young bourgeoisie will all the prospects in the world.

Colette secretly detested him, just as she detested the three or four other boys who studied the arts under Rigaud's guidance. *They think I know nothing, because I'm not like them. Because I don't strut around in fancy waistcoats. If they knew I was a woman they would laugh not only behind my back but in my face, too.*

'Monsieur Rigaud doesn't mind me watching. Forgive me, Monsieur, but you're not exactly regular yourself. See here?' She pointed at a sharp line the apprentice had just drawn. 'You should practice more with that kind of pen, otherwise it looks too...too edgy.'

'You forget yourself.'

'Perhaps.'

This was the pattern almost every conversation in the studio followed, but Colette persisted in going, if only to catch a fragment of Rigaud's attention or beam in rare pride on the occasions when he nodded in approval of some painting of hers she had brought to show him. The magic nod was very rare, and thus all the sweeter when bestowed.

It was by a stroke of fortune's hand that Colette caught a glimpse of the Bourgogne seal pressed in shiny red wax on one of the letters lying on a table in the studio, one boiling hot day in August the following year. She recognised it by sight, having watched the *Duchesse* of that territory seal her correspondence with it more times than she could count on her fingers. The seal on this particular letter had not yet been broken, and Colette did not dare to open it despite the curiosity that tickled her.

'I see you have found my latest order, Auclaire.'

Colette spun around and found herself looking at Rigaud's calm, swarthy face. His mouth was, as always, curved in a small, knowing smile; the cleft in his chin appeared more prominent than ever because of the angle of the light that trickled through the shutters.

'Yes, Monsieur. I didn't touch it, I swear.'

'Of course not. Do you know what it is?'

'A...a commission from Versailles? From the *Duc de Bourgogne*, or perhaps the *Duchesse*?'

'Very clever—I wouldn't have thought someone like, well, someone like you would know it, though perhaps I underestimate people's common knowledge. I suppose you are aware already that I painted His Majesty Louis XIV, as well as other members of the royal family, a few years ago?'

'Yes, Monsieur, I know it well. I think everyone does. It must be an honour in lack of comparison,' Colette replied, consciously buttering his ego, although she knew he was a man who only displayed an accurate measure of pride and rarely bragged where bragging was not due.

'I shall travel to Versailles at noon two days from now. I shall take a couple of my students with me—have them learn something from the experience.'

A spark of hope ignited in Colette. *Can such a thing be? Is there a chance?* 'Your students, Monsieur?'

'Yes?' Rigaud looked down on her, the flesh on his throat and jaw melting together like that of a turtle as he bowed his head.

'Perhaps...perhaps you need someone else, too. Someone who can assist your students and yourself, carry your supplies, maybe learn something valuable.'

'Ah! You wish to come? You think the guards would allow you to enter in those rags? I mean no offense, Auclaire, I never have, but the thought is absurd. Surely you must see that.'

Use any measure necessary. Just make him agree, whatever it takes. 'I know it would delight my master, Monsieur Lemaigre, greatly. He's gravely ill, as you know, and lately he has said several times that he wishes he could live through me. If you take me with you, Monsieur, I'll have a grand adventure to retell to him that might brighten up his dire hours.'

Rigaud folded his arms across his chest and appeared to consider the suggestion in a new light. Then, he slowly nodded, and Colette's heart leapt. 'For the sake of my friend, then. But if you persist in wearing *that*—whether it be because you have no money to afford a new coat or because you have figuratively grown stuck in it—then you will wash your hands and face at the very least. Understood?'

Hence the agreement had been made; she had her ticket, bought by something as simple as a white lie. Colette hesitated a

338

moment to congratulate herself, hardly daring to believe it could be true, before scrambling out on the street with her lips parted in a broad grin. *Maybe I won't get to see her, maybe she doesn't wish to see me. But I'll be there...I'll be back, back to see all those things I thought I would never lay eyes on again.* The entrancement was as strong as ever, regardless of all the times she had forced herself to supress it, regardless of how many times she had denied her fondness of the palace. The spell had not yet been broken, only tattered and bruised, and it held Colette in shackles as golden as the embroideries on the canopy of the *Duchesse de Bourgogne's* bed.

CHAPTER XXXVI

I t felt as if the blood froze in Adélaïde's veins the moment the renowned portrayer entered the room along with three young men—boys, almost, and without doubt his apprentices or assistants. The first two were rather similar in appearance: high foreheads, prominent jaws, beaming eyes taking in all the splendour around them, both dressed in colourful waistcoats and crease-free culottes—trying to imitate the aristocracy, no doubt.

The third one, however, made an astonishing contrast, for not only was his attire dirty and cheap, but Adélaïde strongly suspected he was not even a boy in the first place. The assistant's movements were similar to the other two, but there was something unnatural in the act that anyone who bothered to look closer might have noticed. Of course, very few people *did* bother to look closer at such a poor sight.

She can't fool me. But what on earth would have landed her here again, what on earth would have put her in such an odd position? It cannot be. I must be imagining again—it cannot be.

The heavy sprinkle of freckles on Colette's face and hands had faded since they last saw one another—probably bleached under the sun and the turning of the years. Her hair was as prominently red as ever, though tucked under a brown beret and mostly hidden; the slim fingers were entwined behind her back. Unlike her companions, she appeared less dazzled by her surroundings, and more as if she were in the midst of recalling a series of memories, her glance lost in the distance.

Adélaïde leaped sideways behind one of the pillars so that its long shadow shielded her from the visitors' sight. Pressing her palms and forehead against the cool stone, she felt her heart hammer in her chest and heard the blood pulsate in her ears. *Does she blame me? Will she recognise me? Do I want her to recognise me?* The four pairs of clicking footsteps had died out before she dared move from her safe spot behind the pillar and proceed towards Madame Maintenon's lodgings, but Adélaïde hurried her own steps for fear they might return and thereby make a formal introduction necessary. Bows and meaningless flattery from Rigaud and his little entourage was the last thing she desired at this moment. *Thank God I brought no attendants with me. I suppose there's some mercy to be had in that.*

'You ought to pay a visit to your husband, my dear. I'm sure he is terribly bored, standing for hours on end for that painter,' Madame Maintenon told her once they had consumed two cups of sweetened chamomile tea each.

'Louis does not care for the exciting things in life, Madame. I assure you he enjoys the tranquillity.'

'Nonetheless, it would be the act of a loving wife to offer him some company.' Madame Maintenon reached out and touched the tip of Adélaïde's nose, smiling. 'We cannot always do the things that please us the most, dear.'

'I know it, Madame. And I...I shall go, I promise. Just one more cup, please? The porcelain is darling.'

The visit lasted for another fifteen minutes before Adélaïde knew she had stretched it as far as she could without giving the strange impression of not wanting to see her husband. This was not the case—although Louis's company could be dull at times, it was never a plague she consciously avoided—but she would rather give that impression than tell the truth: that the thought of facing a certain painter's assistant made her break into cold sweat and her stomach cramp. The feeling itself brought on a guilt, for she knew she should feel the opposite, that she should be delighted, not nervous.

Nevertheless, she was required to go and thus she went with a small party of ladies at her heels, each one dressed in simple, bright colours just as they knew their mistress preferred them.

Louis stood like a statue in his finest armour, a blue sash hung over one shoulder, the periwig cascading down his back like a brown cloud. One hand pointed in the distance—perhaps Rigaud would paint some scene of the war in the background—while the other rested lightly on the golden hilt of his sword, his body and head slightly turned to the side so as to conceal the crooked shoulder and put his face at its best angle. Although Rigaud was famous for how closely his portraits resembled their subjects, the finished result would probably show a somewhat glamorized version of the *Petit Dauphin*. Anything less would displease the King, who wished nothing more than to have his line of descendants appear as glorious as himself and his ancestors.

When the ushers announced Adélaïde's arrival, Louis's face shone up with the same glow his armour emitted. He lowered the pointing hand and walked towards her, metal clattering, making Rigaud sigh in exasperation.

'I have come to see how you fare,' Adélaïde said, discarding titles despite their large company.

'I lack nothing, dear Madame— Monsieur Rigaud is making progress, I believe. I...I'm glad you have come. Perhaps you would like some sweetmeats?' A coral blush rose on his cheeks.

'Please.' Adélaïde nodded to one of the servants, who brought a tray of candied apples and walnuts within a few minutes. Louis gave the painter and his assistants orders to take a break, and even went as far as to offer to share the contents of the tray with them. A couple of the ladies in Adélaïde's entourage tittered behind their fans at this informality, but Adélaïde was glad to have the rest of the room occupied with their light meal, so that she might steal a look at Colette. The other girl's eyes locked with her own, and in that moment, it was as clear as the morning sky in summer that it would be impossible to pretend as though they were strangers.

*Does she hate me? It doesn't look like it but...*The crunchy sugar-coating on the candied apple melted slowly on her tongue, sweeter than anything she had tasted for a very long time. If it would not make her look piggish, she would gladly have gobbled down the entire tray, although of course this was unthinkable in the presence of Rigaud and the other apprentices, not to speak of the *Duc* and *Duchesse* with their train of attendants.

Colette lowered her eyes once Adélaïde's gaze began burning too intensely. Regardless of whether the other girl held her responsible for anything, the shock must be complete, and things might have changed. Adélaïde was a mother now; she finally had the son she had been yearning to show to the world, and perhaps being a mother had transformed her into a devout wife as well. Perhaps there was no room for a freckled-skinned teenage sweetheart in the *Petite Dauphine's* polished life.

I should have given it more thought before manoeuvring my way in here. I should have thought about these things before, I should have realised it wouldn't be that easy.

Rigaud clapped his hands together. 'With your gracious permission, Your Royal Highnesses, I would like to proceed with the portrait. Auclaire—'

Colette's head snapped up at her master's call.

'—fetch the burgundy.'

'Yes, Monsieur.'

The session continued in silence; Rigaud worked with a frown deep enough to hide an *écu*, and the courtiers thought it best not to disturb him.

Colette tried to keep her attention solely on her master's needs and not stray to the wife of their client, knowing well enough that if their eyes met again, it meant risking that the men and women present would notice the odd connection, a risk she did not dare take. In the corner of her eye though, she could see how Adélaïde shifted her weight on the chair as if she was sitting on rose thorns that made every position uncomfortable.

Five, ten, fifteen minutes passed before Adélaïde rose to her feet and flashed Louis a quick smile. 'I shall go to my chambers and change before dinner. I shall see you there.'

'Yes—yes, of course. I hope you were not...were not bored, dearest Madame,' Louis said without moving his head, standing stiffly just as he had been asked to do, not daring to interrupt the painter a second time.

'Don't worry about me. I'll see you in a little while.' On that note, she turned around and made her departure, the train of her skirts swishing behind her as she walked.

It was not until late in the evening the following day that Colette found the opportunity she had been waiting for, or, rather, the opportunity found her. As she was walking from the *Pavillion d'Orléans* and had begun to climb the Staircase of the Princes—returning from a quite redundant errand Rigaud had asked her to run for him, perhaps with the sole ambition to have a few moments of solitude—an alabaster-white hand latched out and pulled her into a niche behind the banister. The next thing she knew, Colette was staring at the *Duchesse de Bourgogne's* face, which was still that of a young girl despite her twenty years.

'We're going to Saint-Cloud for a few days,' Adélaïde said, breathing heavily as if she had been running to deliver the news. 'I had to speak to you first, before it's too late.'

'I thought perhaps you never wanted to speak to me. I thought perhaps you blamed me.'

'I could never! It was silly of me, trying to pretend you weren't there. I just, well, I was so nervous, I couldn't speak.'

'I've missed those hands,' Colette replied in a low, soft voice, pressing Adélaïde's cool hands to her chest. *And that face, and everything else.*

'Then you are all right? I thought—you look—'

347

'I know, I know. Truth to be told, there's little money to spare after the expenses of supplies and material, and maintenance of the house, and Madame Sylvester's wages…'

Adélaïde giggled. 'I don't know what you're talking about, not in the very least. You must tell me everything, from the beginning.'

'We don't have much time. But if you must know, I live with an old painter—I think he might be dying—and I help him with all sorts of work, mostly portraits. He's an old friend of Monsieur Rigaud; that's why I'm here.'

'And your family? And the…the seizures?'

Colette lowered her eyes. 'They're not important, not anymore. It would take too long to explain everything that has happened these past few years. The seizures, well, I don't think there has been one for months now—I'm praying I might have seen the last of them.'

'How splendid! Maybe they do fade with age. Anyhow, I wish I could show you Louis. The baby, I mean.'

'God granted you your wish at last.' Colette forced herself to smile. 'Is he much like his father?'

Adélaïde did not answer; instead, she leaned in and pressed her plump lips on Colette's chapped ones and closed her eyes, making the kiss last several seconds before pulling back again. It was the first moment of true intimacy Colette had experienced in two years and she clung to the sensation like a love-starved child, overwhelmed by just how much she had been missing. *It doesn't matter if the baby reminds her of its father, or if she has grown closer to her husband, or if the time has changed anything. She's still kissing me...me!*

In that moment, clicking footsteps approached, and a hint of fear flashed in Adélaïde's dark eyes. 'I must go now—you, too. But next time...if there is a next time, then we shall reunite properly, and spend the night, like we used to.' Her cheeks flushed red. 'Promise?'

'Promise,' Colette whispered without hesitation. *Rigaud will be preoccupied for months, considering all the commissions that are bound to pour in now that everyone knows he still has the favour of the royal family. When can the next time be?*

Adélaïde smiled one last time, then turned on her heel and slipped out from the niche, out on the Staircase of the Princes, proceeding down the marble steps as if nothing had happened, her head snapping left and right, reassuring herself that there had been no eye-witnesses to their brief meeting.

Colette returned to Paris with the rest of the small entourage, only to find Monsieur Lemaigre was neither improving nor any worse than he had been when she left him in the hands of Madame Sylvester. He did not come out of his bedchamber to greet her, but she persisted in knocking on his door and entering.

'How was Versailles? A place of dreams, was it? I've never been myself.' Lemaigre was slumped against a pile of pillows in his bed, his hands clasped loosely in his lap, eyebrows arched.

Colette marvelled in silence at his eloquence for almost a minute before replying. 'It was...yes, a place of dreams, one might say. But ruled by etiquette, so rigidly ruled. It always is.'

'Always?'

'I'm just assuming, Monsieur. Will you dine with us tonight?'

'Do I ever dine with my cook and my helper?'

'You never eat properly at all, Monsieur.'

'I suppose not.'

Colette closed the door swiftly behind her and left the thin-haired man to stare at the cracked, pale tapestry. *Were it not for the housing, or the food, or the painting...were it not for those things, I should never say another word to him.* This was not entirely true though, and Colette knew it deep down. There was a thoroughly ingrained sense of duty hat kept her from abandoning Lemaigre completely; she felt as though God Himself was looming over her shoulder, holding a list of all her sins, only waiting to see whether she would commit another one or act the good Christian, caring for the wretched old man. This time, she refused to fail Him; this time, she would obtain some little redemption by doing what was admirable.

CHAPTER XXXVII

Little Louis, the *Duc de Bretagne*, had only just begun to sit up with the support of the nurse's hand on his back, six months having passed since his birth, when the seizures began as well. Adélaïde watched, helpless, as the same symptoms Colette had shown became apparent in her child. The convulsions only came a few times every month though, and the fits were often light enough to pass in less than a minute—still, they left his face purple and his forehead slick with cold sweat, before the nurses managed to return him to a normal state.

Each time the baby regained his rosy cheeks and clucking laugher, Adélaïde exhaled in relief and felt certain that this time was the last time—yet it never was. The physicians declared that convulsions were fairly common in infants and small children and would perhaps cease with the passing of the years. However, they could do little more than pray, and encouraged the royal family to do the same. Adélaïde fretted continuously: what if the seizures lasted into adulthood before ceasing, as they had done with Colette? What if they never ended, or what if the only thing ended was the child's life?

No one can take him from me—it's not possible. Other children die...but he's our heir and God knows that. He shan't take him. I must simply keep my spirits merry.

Despite their concerns, it was easy to think of things other than the baby's health, for messengers carrying news of the war arrived every week, offering the King information regarding his army's numerous setbacks and defeats—these messages came more often than those of victory.

At times, the news of loss made Adélaïde wonder how the throne of Spain could be worth so many years of struggle, with so many lives spilled on the dusty battlefields. The throne of France, perhaps, but surely not every country could be worth dying for. That the soldiers who fought only did so on their greedy kings' command did not occur to her. The fact that she—who stood to gain a great deal by France's military victory whether she had asked for it or not—was part of the elite that the common people as well as the soldiers blamed for their misery, was a foreign thought to her.

According to the reports, there had been twenty-seven thousand casualties from the French and Bavarian armies alone during the Battle of Blenheim: a number almost too large to comprehend. *At Versailles there are five, often ten thousand, including servants and courtiers alike. Twenty-seven...so many children left fatherless.* It felt as if someone had emptied a bucket of icy water over Adélaïde's head, the cold trickling down her spine and giving her shivers.

The Battle of Blenheim, which had been lost in August that same year, was still practically unmentionable at court though; the mere name would cause women and men alike to frown and press their lips into thin lines. The Duke of Marlborough, who had been one of the leading forces of the Grand Alliance, was equal only to Satan himself in the eyes of some of the French commanders, and Vêndome was regarded both with sympathy and contempt for his failures. By the end of 1704—about the same time that Louis's seizures started—the Grand Alliance had captured the towns of Trier, Landau, and Trabach, and rumour was that during the upcoming campaign season of 1705, they would advance into the heart of France itself.

Savoy was still part of the alliance; Prince Eugene, Adélaïde's father's cousin, pushed his forces forward with assiduity, and many spoke of him as the equal of the Duke of Marlborough. Adélaïde remembered his oblong face vaguely, but could not recall how many years it was since she saw him, nor if they had ever exchanged so much as a word. Every time a messenger arrived though, she was painfully reminded of the paradoxical situation she was locked in: championing France's success because France was where she belonged and where she would one day sit on a throne, while praying that her father would be victorious because the grains of fundamental loyalty remained. The period of espionage was over long since, yet she felt the same contradictions pulling her in different directions, like a helpless spectator of a tennis game who cannot decide who she ought to cheer for.

Adélaïde stared at the limb little body, dumbfounded. His eyes were wide open, like the unseeing glass eyes of a doll; his skin had been drained of all colour as if someone had washed the doll too roughly so that the paint had come off. Yesterday he had been smiling, laughing and clucking even, but now his plump lips were as still as his eyes.

She reached out a single finger, quivering, and brushed her fingertip against her son's chubby arm, which was not yet cold. She could not bring herself to cry, nor scream, for the spell was as complete as when he had been born, and there was not room for anything but astonishment.

'What did you—what did you to do him? What happened? Everything was alright, I know it was, I was here only yesterday. What did you do to him?' she demanded.

The wet nurse slowly lowered the hand she had been covering her mouth with but kept her eyes glued to the floor, obviously unwilling to meet the *Duchesse's* intense gaze. 'Nothing, Madame, nothing that could have harmed him. You know of his seizures, the convulsions...There was no remedy this time. It's not uncommon for young children to...to...'

'But he's *mine*. He's my miracle, my heir. It's different—it must be. What about the physicians?'

'With all due respect, Madame, God does not discriminate between the children of royals and the children of beggars.' The wet nurse chewed on her lip with a nervous fervour.

Louis had been watching the exchange in silence, his fists clenched by his sides, his face the colour of cherries as he fought some inner battle to curb the grief that threatened to boil over into violence. He had not suffered from the tendency to burst into fits of rage since he was a little boy; more than ten years had passed since he last raised his voice. Now, however, he struggled to control the river of sorrow that seemed to drown him, and the easiest way to do so was to turn that sorrow into anger. The wet nurse was an easy target, for she was standing closer than the other nurses, and the physicians had left the room to confer with the King.

'This cannot go unpunished. You should have saved him, you should have done something! Out! Go, before I have the guards put you in *La Bastille*—that is where murderesses belong. Out!' His voice broke towards the end of the outburst, threatening to give way to tears.

The wet nurse dipped into a hasty curtsy and fled the nursery like a deer suddenly attacked by a lion it thought was harmless.

Adélaïde gripped her husband's arms in a firm embrace, firmer than she had ever touched him, in an attempt to calm them both. *Breathe. Please just breathe. You can do this.* 'We mustn't lay the blame where it does not belong, Louis.'

He met her eyes and she had to bite her tongue not to remark on how similar they were to those of baby Louis.

'I'm sorry...I'm sorry. I—'

'I'll give you another one, I promise you that. Look, look how perfect he is. That's how our other babies will be, too.' Adélaïde listened to her own words of reason with a queer feeling. They did not belong in her mouth, not at this time, perhaps not ever. She felt her knees folding beneath her; Louis staggered as he tried to hold her upright.

Two nurses and three maids dashed forward, gasping in unison, their hands fidgeting awkwardly to keep their skirts from being trampled on, their faces flushed with panic. According to etiquette, they were not allowed to touch either the *Duchesse* or the *Duc de Bourgogne* without special permission, hence they halted a few meters away, awaiting further instruction.

I will die here, I know I will. I will die right here, right now, for if God could take my child, then there is no reason why he shouldn't take me as well, plunge me into that dark abyss of purgatory. Our other babies...what other babies? Why would they be allowed to live if he wasn't?

The minutes that followed were one swirl of confusion and desperation as servants and courtiers alike whispered loudly between one another; they eventually brought Adélaïde to her own bed, but she could hear them blaming, mourning, gossiping, a few even celebrating, through the thin walls of her chambers. Two women had to half-drag her there while she walked with little paddling steps, like a calf on slippery ice. She wanted to demand their absolute silence but choked on her own words. Some said it was the nurses, others pointed to God—but the whispers that stung the most were those blaming herself.

Of course, no one dared utter a word against Louis, because he was a man, and thus he could not possibly be to blame for any mishap. Adélaïde, however, was a different matter. A woman who had spent so much time with her first-born child should surely have noticed any signs of illness. A woman like her—so pure, so sweet—must surely be hiding a wicked nature behind that lovely façade. Perhaps she had even finished the poor life herself when no one was watching.

The absurdity of these accusations did not seem to occur to anyone, although they only came from a few venomous mouths and were hardly absorbed by the great masses.

As she walked the halls, Nantes thrust her bosom forth and raised her chin another centimetre to emphasise her own grandeur, her painted lips curving in a smug smile.

CHAPTER XXXVIII

You see, Madame, before little Louis was born I thought I would never truly feel like a mother. I know I say I'm no longer young—and I suppose it's true—but sometimes I have the illusion that I'm still the child I was when I married. But then...then when I saw him, I couldn't help myself, and I loved him more than I've loved anything before.'

'I know it, dearest.' Madame Maintenon cupped her warm, dry hands around Adélaïde's.

'Of course I love you, Madame, and His Majesty, most ardently. But little Louis was different, and I was so *proud*. You know I had been anxious I had no son. And regardless of what I had thought it would be like to be a mother it no longer mattered, because all that mattered was that he was mine.'

Madame Maintenon said nothing; words were too flat to deliver the message she wished to give. Therefore, she simply continued stroking the younger woman's cold hands, listening patiently to the brittle voice that came in waves and sometimes faded to a whisper.

'Is the King very angry, Madame? I feared he might be,' Adélaïde said.

'The King could not be more sympathetic, my dear. But it is his wish that you...that you recover from your mourning as quickly as possible. He longs to hear you sing for him again. You know how dull the court was a few years ago when you were absent after your, well, your fever.'

'You and I both know my fever was nothing of the sort. Oh, how I wish there was a remedy for the gloom after the loss of a child! How much easier everything would be. But you must tell my dear King that I shall be with him whenever he commands it.'

'He knows it already. Sometimes...sometimes I fear my husband expects too much from this world and the people in it. Of course, God has given him divine right, but God spares no one from His trials.'

'Don't you think God can be cruel, Madame?' Adélaïde asked, looking at the other woman timidly through her lashes as if to protect herself from the reaction that might come once she had uttered such a blasphemous thing.

Madame Maintenon took a deep breath though, still idle as a sheep. 'God does only what is righteous and what is meant to be. Remember that.'

'I don't see how this could be part of any plan of His.'

'You don't have to *see*—you only have to accept that it is so. Now, call on your hairdresser and we shall make what we can of that bird's nest, hm? It would do the King and your husband good to see you fresh as a daisy at dinner.' She gave Adélaïde a peck on either cheek before rising from the bedside and leaving her to the business of making herself presentable.

The hairdresser arrived half an hour later with the usual array of pins and loose curls, combs and pretty gems to fasten in the fontange coiffure. His manicured fingers danced over Adélaïde's scalp before the mirror, disentangling the mess of hair lock by lock, then combed rosewater through it until it fell like a veil of brown silk from her scalp. She watched her own reflection as the hairdresser piled up the loose curls in ringlets and entwined them with fake hair to add volume, then applied a series of powders and wax-like fat to keep everything in place for several days. The finishing touch were the decorations: jewels, pearls, feathers.

After the hairdresser had packed his things up and made his departure, three servants assisted Adélaïde with applying some powder and blush to her face and finally lace her corset before she stepped into one of her new gowns, which was made of dark damask embroidered with silver thread.

Once the servants had also left her, she spent a good while running her hands over the fabric and following the glittering thread's intricate patterns with her fingertip. *How pretty—like spider web, but glossier. Useless. I wonder what they would say if I appeared uncombed, undressed, in public. At least that would send their tongues chattering about other things than when I'm going to grant them a replacement, a new son.*

Seeing Louis at the table was a poor comfort, for he was as pale as the tablecloth and looked even stiffer than usual in his waistcoat and cravat.

'Are you well?' Adélaïde asked.

'As well as one could hope to be, dearest Madame.'

'Do you fancy my gown? It's new.'

'It is very...very black, dearest. You look very solemn.'

'I hope I do.'

'Of course, yes. Have you tried the salmon quiche?'

'I will, if you would like me to.'

They proceeded with the dinner without another word. The silence was not unkind, but preferable to the exchange of empty pleasantries. *The child brought us together—built a bond that made us more like husband and wife than second cousins. Like it was always supposed to be. And now that bond is broken.* Adélaïde chewed the same bite of quiche for a good while before she noticed how it had turned into a soggy batter in her mouth and forced it down her throat.

The King's appetite, however, was as hearty as always. Crumbs had gotten caught in the billowing folds of his silk cravat and half-eaten boiled quail eggs lay scattered on his plate in the traces of other delicacies. His eyes—alert and clear despite his age—darted to his doll, who was seated on his right side as the First Lady of the court, since his wife was still not his official Queen.

Adélaïde offered him a pale smile. 'Is the food to your satisfaction, Sire? I heard you had the eggs specially send for from a farm outside Marseilles.'

'Ah, indeed I did. Marvellous, truly, you must try one.' The King lifted a finger to call on one of the waiters, who hurried forth to serve her an egg, which was still in its spotty shell so as to be aesthetically pleasing. 'Now, my doll, I know it pains you to talk of it, but you must hear what I have to say about the deceased *Duc de Bretagne*.'

'I'm listening, Sire.' Adélaïde braced herself while studying the turquoise inside of the eggshell after having peeled it off.

'Mourning has its place—a part of a civilized life. But we shall not have the court dire, no, we must aspire to maintain our spirits just as we maintain this display of...of divinity. What would the people think, if Versailles did not sparkle, if the symbol of France appeared lacking in grandeur?'

'Of course. Forgive me, my dear King, if I'm not quite myself. I know you would like me merry once more.'

'I would.'

'But do the people see? Do they truly care? I should think they have tragedies of their own to occupy their thoughts.'

'My girl, the people look to their masters. Their lives are petty in the great scheme, methinks they know it well enough to look to us for guidance. You're young still, and of the weaker sex, but you'll see with time that there is nothing so important as a strong monarch to govern a strong nation. How do you like your egg?'

'It's a peculiar blue colour, Sire, though beautiful.' Adélaïde swallowed her opinions on what the King had just said and began searching for a lighter topic. 'Do you know what would lift my spirits, Sire? If that painter—Rigaud—could be brought back, to paint me. I like my portraits.'

'What you wish you shall have, my doll. If only I could serve you him on a silver platter, ha! It won't be necessary though—he'll come without protest, so don't you fret.'

For the first time since before the mourning period had begun, Adélaïde felt genuine joy pump through her veins. Not only joy, but a rush of excitement and anticipation, like a thousand feathers tickling at once, promising to leave her unsatisfied until she was allowed to meet with the portrayer; or, rather, the portrayer's red-headed assistant. *I shouldn't be thinking about those things at this hour; I should be mourning properly. But oh, if I could only have a second of that embrace to fill me with the life that seemed to have seeped out of me.*

CHAPTER XXXIX

Just as the King had predicted, Rigaud arrived at court at once, the very same day they had sent for him. Colette accompanied him this time as well, her hair pulled up under the same beret and her narrow shoulders hidden by the same filthy overcoat. If she had been by herself, the guards would never have granted her permission again, but there was no refusing someone who came as a package deal with the great Hyacinthe Rigaud.

Adélaïde dressed with a completely different sentiment now than she had before the dinner, and the maids' hands were barely enough to hold all the precious accessories she put on only to remove after throwing a glance in the mirror. The black colours had to stay, of course, but there was a new spark to her appearance, which showed through the natural blush on her cheeks and the swiftness in her steps. Moreover, the gown and the jewels she chose to wear on this occasion would soon be immortalised through the portrait, and were therefore of greater importance than almost any of her other clothes, only preceded by the gowns worn on the most grand ceremonies.

Life would be simpler without all things called style and fashion, it really would. I wish they didn't exist. But they do, and I have to choose carefully. A cross in gold on a chain around her neck to symbolize the Good Christian; pearls and rubies strung around her wrists to symbolize the wealth of the royal family; the mourning train to symbolize her loss; finally, a white rose in her hands to symbolize the purity of youth. Everything was quite in order.

Rigaud worked professionally as always, quickly arranging her sitting on an ottoman with her gaze fixed on something far away, her hands clasping the rose demurely just as one would expect of a young lady. He would add the lavish background later in his studio since not even Versailles could provide them with the dreamlike landscape he sought to capture Adélaïde's so-called free spirit. She, however, could not have cared less about the portrait she had commissioned, nor the background that would go with it, because she only had eyes for the portrayer's assistant.

The other apprentices had been brought, too, watching their master from a respectful distance, all of them the picture of sophisticated young artists. Their clothes were fine enough to hint of their bourgeoisie backgrounds, although they looked a bit too simplistic in Adélaïde's eyes.

'Raise your chin a tad, please, Your Royal Highness. We must have you looking proud.'

Adélaïde nodded and obeyed, and straightened her back as well. Despite the tightly laced corset, she had managed to slump slightly in the chair, which was of course unthinkable on any occasion except for when she was alone in her private chambers.

Colette's face was as expressionless as solemn Greek bust, but she had taken a seat at the front row of the little assembly of young men who were watching their master's every move and working on their own versions in sketchbooks so that they would not risk missing this opportunity to practice with such an exclusive model. Someone who did not know her might have taken this mask of indifference for a genuine reflection of her sentiments, but Adélaïde saw how her otherwise steady fingers trembled as she handed Rigaud a new stick of charcoal, how her glance never once left Adélaïde's bare neck and wrists, as if something possessed

369

her. *She can't hide it from me. If only they knew! What would they say, those boys with their shiny boots and dull faces?*

One, two, three hours passed; Adélaïde's back grew sore and her limbs stiff from trying to remain in the exact same position as though she had frozen to ice. A process that was dreary under normal circumstances now felt like torture, for not only was it completely contrary to her nature to sit in silence for such a considerable amount of time, but there was the itching longing to speak to Colette without being observed. Just as Adélaïde had begun to fantasize about standing up and shooing away both Rigaud and his apprentices without a word though, the painter spoke in his slow, smooth voice.

'That will be all for now, Your Royal Highness. I shall need another moment with you—perhaps tomorrow, if it pleases you—to complete the colouring of your gown and hair.'

'Then I'll come here in the afternoon tomorrow. You may go, thank you.'

Rigaud nodded and began collecting the supplies he had used, scooped down in a low bow, and backed out of the room as was the custom. The apprentices followed him like a tail, all having taken after his example and bowed. The canvas was then carried off by two servants, and Adélaïde was left with only the ushers and another servant for company.

That night, Adélaïde feigned a headache to Louis, ensuring that he would not attempt to visit her. Once the dark had settled outside, she wrapped herself in the same cloak she had taken when going to the apothecary in Paris two years previously, and moved quietly through the passages until she reached the gardens. She had not been able to pass any note to Colette this time, but it seemed to her that waiting at their fountain would be her best chance.

The grass was wet from a light rain; the hem of her skirts and the cloak as well as her shoes were soon soaked as she strode across the lawns, enjoying not having to keep to the gravel paths since there was no one there to reprimand her. The ripple of the water in the numerous fountains filled the night as it was the only sound save for a hooting owl. The fountain—the very same she had visited that first time when the ground had been covered in a thick coat of cotton-white snow and the cold had been giving her goose bumps—appeared as though it had been waiting for her.

Maybe the sculptures know. Maybe they have seen us meet. It's fortunate, then, that they have no tongues.

371

Colette stayed crouched behind the fountain until she was certain that the approaching footsteps belonged to the right person and not to some drunken *Comte* or *Duc* who had ventured out on a midnight stroll. Once she spotted the black slippers with the silver ruffles tripping towards her, she slowly rose and smoothened her crumpled clothes in a futile attempt to make herself presentable—an impossible task even if she had not been in contrast to the fanciful *Petite Dauphine*. The time of being neatly dressed was in the past, not only because of the expense of a new set of clothes but because she had gone too long in her overcoat and beret to feel comfortable without them.

'I hoped you would come. I wasn't sure, but I hoped you would, I thought you might.'

Adélaïde pulled down the hood that shielded her face and smiled, revealing sugar-cube teeth and plump lips. 'Of course I did, I would be a fool not to give it a try. I've missed you, I've missed you more than you can imagine. Are you well? I've missed you.' She leaped forward and swept Colette into a clinging embrace smelling of newly washed fabric and the lingering trace of vanilla perfume.

'I'm not ill, at least,' Colette mumbled against her shoulder, coming to her senses and wrapping her arms around the other girl. 'And you? I've thought about you a little too much, I think—it's not good for me.'

'I suppose you know about...well, about what happened. The reason for my mourning clothes.'

'There have been rumours in Paris but I didn't know if they were trustworthy. Some say they heard the bells toll, but I must have missed it. And I...I prayed that God would have mercy on you and only put you through the trials He knew you could face.'

Adélaïde slowly pulled away from the embrace and carefully freed a lock of Colette's hair from the beret, then removed the headpiece completely so that the rest of her ragged mane came tumbling down over her shoulders. 'God has not been very merciful, but never mind that now. You must tell me, why have you still not cropped your hair? If you are so stubborn to pass for a boy it must be terribly inconvenient to keep it like a girl's.'

Colette shrugged. 'It reminds me of what used to be. It doesn't please you?'

'*Ridicolo!* You always please me and you know it well already.'

The kiss was fervent, sending warm thrills through Colette's body, granting the same long-awaited satisfaction one might feel when drinking a cup of soothing, mulled wine after staying outside in the cold for too long. *As if every trouble and every grief was brushed away in a heartbeat. Perhaps she feels it too—I hope she does.* It was followed by another one and yet another one after that, until Colette was forced to pull away to fill her lungs with air.

Adélaïde smiled again, her eyes twinkling with childish excitement. 'I told Louis I was unwell, so there should be no danger in spending the night in my room, as long as we are quiet and discreet.'

'Like always, then?

'Like always.'

Hence, Colette found herself once more in the apartments of the *Duchesse de Bourgogne* with indecent intentions, and all rational thought was discarded as soon as she set foot in the bedchamber. *I'm sinning again, but it doesn't matter. I'm risking everything, though I have little, but that's alright. As long as I get to fall deeply and devastatingly into this abyss of temptation, everything is alright. Dear God, forgive me.*

She dropped her overcoat and beret on the polished floor, then kicked off her shoes and crawled up on the massive bed in nothing but a cotton shirt, which had been white once upon a time, and a pair of beige trousers.

Colette was infinitely grateful that Adélaïde had already changed to a chemise—with ruffled lace at the sleeves and neckline—under the black cloak, so that there was no need for dismantling a complicated gown or unlacing a corset. Two candles had been lit, one on each side of the bed; their warm glow shone through the thin chemise and animated every contour as if the *Duchesse* was a golden statue.

A strange, half-choked sound escaped Adélaïde's lips: a series of sobs too quiet to wake anyone up but too loud to ignore. Her eyes, dazed with euphoria a few moments ago, were now spilling over with hot tears and the whites had turned pink.

Colette pushed herself into a sitting position, overcome by helplessness. *Now what?* 'Why—whatever is the matter with you?'

'Forgive me.' Adélaïde chirped after air between choked sobs. 'I just wish it could always be like this. Just the two of us, without all the people swarming like flies, without limp little babies...'

'I wish it too, but if there is anything I have learned from these past few years, it's that things are never as one wishes they were, and that it's not for us mere mortals to decide.'

'You didn't see his face, 'Ette. He looked just like a porcelain doll with those large glass eyes. And even when the Lord takes him I can't have you, not properly.'

Colette tugged at her lip, grappling with the words. *How can I make her understand how fortunate she is without sounding like a cold-hearted monster? How can I make her see that her shoulders are not the only ones carrying sorrow in this crumbling country?* She remained silent.

'And then there's His Majesty. Oh, I do want to please him, I truly do, but sometimes I think—' Adélaïde continued but never got the chance to finish her little speech.

'The rest of us he taxes, you know. It cannot be so awfully difficult if your greatest concern is pleasing an old man who already adores you above anything at this...this debauchery court of his.'

'Why do you make it sound as if I were the villain?'

'Because you just sit there, pitying yourself, when you possess all the riches anyone could dream of!'

'My child is *dead*, 'Ette.' The tears continued to stream down Adélaïde's cheeks.

'And I've lived in absolute squalor for years because of the things we did together, because you couldn't just pretend I was made of air, like the other maids. If you had, nothing would have happened and no one would have found out—and I my life wouldn't have been shattered.' Colette put a hand over her mouth to stop herself from blurting out another hurtful word, but the damage had already been done.

'That's not fair,' Adélaïde whispered. 'That's not fair and you know it.'

'Well, few things are fair, it seems.'

Silence settled over the room like a solid lid creating an atmosphere of unspoken emotions; Colette clenched the corner of the pillow in her hand until her fingers ached, trying to make sense of what she really thought and what on earth she was supposed to do now, because she could not bear the thought of spending the rest of the night in a bed where she was not welcome.

Adélaïde must have had similar thoughts, because the next time she spoke, her voice steeped in sadness, she said: 'You ought to go now, 'Ette. The sun will rise soon.'

The sun won't show itself for several hours—but of course you're right. Colette said nothing but merely slid down from the bed and clad herself in a haste, her shirt and trousers rumpled after lying in a pile on the floor. After having taken a quiet farewell of the glowing room and the small figure on the bed, she closed one of the side doors behind her and began the risky trip to Rigaud's study.

The logical solution would, naturally, have been to return to the rooms occupied by the other apprentices, but logic had long since fled her mind. The door to the studio was, to her astonishment, unlocked, and so she opened the door as far as was possible without making any creaking noises and entered sideways through the narrow slit.

The great canvas dominated the room, from which a half-finished face stared into the void: a face Colette knew better than any face, a face she would have relished looking at any other day. Now though, it felt as if her stomach was boiling as she beheld the apple cheeks and the intricate coiffure. Even the white rose—so pure, so impeccable—made her want to rip it from the painting and scatter its leaves like confetti on the floor.

Colette dashed to the other end of the studio, where the tools lay neatly on a table. Paintbrushes, charcoal, paint...Tossing her hair from her face, she gripped one of the small knives meant for sharpening pencils and stalked back to the painting. As she slashed the canvas, the edges of the cuts bulged like torn skin surrounding a wound; she continued to stab and tear with the knife until the portrait was nothing but shreds.

Only then did Colette stop to breathe; her hand fell limp to her side and the knife fell to the floor with a clatter that sent shivers up her spine, for it would be enough to wake anyone sleeping nearby. She backed out of the room, beholding the destruction she had caused with mixed satisfaction and horror, her arms aching almost as much as her heart. Still, the pain was overridden by defiance. She turned on her heel and scurried back the same way she had come. It took her a good while to locate the shared bedchamber she was supposed to sleep in, not to mention the difficulties of treading carefully between the snoring young men to the empty bed, but once she sank down on the mattress the dread left her bones.

*They have no proof as to who did it. They can't accuse anyone, not properly. Not unless she tells them—and she never would. Never. And I was lucky...so incredibly lucky...*The insight dawned upon her as she pulled the sheets over her exhausted body. This would be the last time she would risk walking alone through Versailles at night; she had already escaped unharmed and undiscovered countless times, but one fine day her fortune would turn. *The next time they offer to bring me I must resist the temptation. This can't keep happening. It's not worth it.*

These were not merely the thoughts of an enraged lover, but a fundamental instinct of self-preservation she ought to have listened to far earlier, though she had refused to make peace with it until now. Court was not a place for common little people, it was hardly a place for anyone, though some could not escape it. For years Colette had been fighting against this truth, desperate to be a part of that shimmering world despite the ugliness that lay underneath the surface, glorifying the people who inhabited it despite their high-minded views.

The boiling in her stomach had cooled to an unpleasant, lukewarm nausea. *That's what I am: a common little person. People like me can't be running about having affairs with people like her. How come I never fully understood that until this moment?*

A few days later, the company travelled back to Paris. Rigaud gritted his teeth in dangerous silence, pondering who the rascal who had caused such ruination might be, while Colette sat across from the two blank-faced students in another carriage, desperately longing to return to the peaceful life of taking care of the house at the *Rue Saint Antoine*. Monsieur Lemaigre was paler than ever, almost transparent, and had taken to his bed again shortly before she left. At this point it was as though he did not exist—they only saw one another when he signed one of the paintings and spoke only a word or two, for he took his sparse meals in his rooms.

As the carriage shook, bouncing over uneven rocks on the road, Colette began to truly accept that that life would be her only life from this point onward.

'Rest assured, my doll, we shall find whoever did such a disloyal thing,' the King exclaimed.

'Vandals! Some people can be as insensible as cows,' was Madame's only comment. She had become even more blatantly critical since the death of Monsieur; now that she was a dowager, however, she had turned to only speaking well of her late husband. This meant that everyone else was a more likely target than before, since the sharp remarks had to land *somewhere*.

Adélaïde shook her head. 'It's alright, Sire. I never liked the portrait anyways—I should not have commissioned it in the first place.'

'Are you certain? You have spoken very fondly of Monsieur Rigaud. Did he do anything to offend you? I always liked the man, but he might have turned wicked and begun carving in his own artwork.'

'I truly am certain,' Adélaïde reassured her King. 'But I'm glad you sent him and his little entourage back to Paris. I hope there has to be no further complications, Sire—I wouldn't want you to punish an innocent man.'

'Ah! Always the sweet-natured diplomat. If that's what you want, then that's how it will be, though a desire to cause harm to the royal family is an offense to the crown, not to speak of violating property.'

'Perhaps they did it in a fit of rage. It matters not. It was only a painting, I pray you remember that.'

Madame sucked the grease and flakes from a pastry she had recently devoured off her fingers, the courtiers glaring at this display of bad manners. 'Well, it's beyond my comprehension why anyone would be in a fit of rage over you, *Madame la Duchesse*. I repeat: vandals.'

Adélaïde said nothing but twisted her hands in her lap under the grand dinner table. *How could everything go so horribly wrong? And who is to blame? Mayhap I should not have made such a fuss—but she was cruel...Am I truly such selfish person?*

CHAPTER XXXX

8th January, 1707

Another Louis; another son. Adélaïde felt his little heart thudding through the linen swaddling as she pressed him gently to her chest. She could not yet stand to look at his eyes, for fear they might be identical to his brother's large, dark ones, though she knew she would have to eventually. She was not quite certain whether it was euphoria or pain that soared and spired in her—both, perhaps—over this miracle. In one moment, she felt the same delirious joy and triumph she had felt after giving birth to the first Louis, and in the next she was overcome by guilt because she did not know if it was fair to her dead child that she should love this new life so ardently instead.

The courtiers cast long glances at each other, nodding discreetly. The *Petite Dauphine* had not been a bad bargain after all; she had produced not one but two sons in the span of three years, and though there were women who had been far more successful, she had been lucky twice and would probably be lucky again. They craned their necks to get a glimpse of the baby. He was slightly larger than the last one—a good sign—with folds of soft fat on his arms and plump cheeks. He would be anointed *Duc de Bretagne*, as the title was unoccupied since the death of his brother, and become another link in the chain of heirs to the throne.

The curtains had been hastily removed so that a window might be opened to let in a gust of cold air. The frost lay crystallized on the glass in exquisite patterns, like something from a fairy-tale, bathing the room in a blue hue as the sun shone through it.

There were two worlds: that of the stagnant bedchamber crammed with people and hung with heavy tapestries, and that of the crisp outside, where the ground was frozen and the skies the colour of silver without a single cloud. Adélaïde yearned to break out from the first world and into the second, to escape her bedchamber, to wrap herself and the baby in an ermine cloak and walk in the open for as long as her legs would carry them. She had been forced to absent herself from both the Christmas and New Year celebrations because of her confinement;

now there would be another period of waiting before the church and the physicians considered her clean enough to appear at formal gatherings. *Why would anyone willingly go through such a tedious process? For the sake of the child, of course, but still. I wonder if I shall ever do it again.*

These were naught but the thoughts of a dizzy mind though, for Adélaïde knew in truth that even if there was a choice, she would gladly repeat what she had just done if the reward was as worthwhile as the warm bundle in her arms.

Both Adélaïde and Louis breathed a sigh of relief when the new baby showed no signs of illness or convulsions, though the court still tripped like on a bed of needles, knowing that the child's health could decline at any age and at any time. He was a temperamental little thing—more so than the last baby—and would often scream and wail until his face was as red as the sugared cherries that were sometimes served for dessert, his tiny fists clenched and swinging in the air. Some said he was as violent as his father had been when he was a young boy, while others preferred to interpret it as a good sign that he was so forceful.

However, Adélaïde knew this was only one side of her son, because once the attendants were dismissed from the nursery so that she might rock him in her arms privately, the screaming turned into funny little noises and his body relaxed. He would not fall asleep against her shoulder like his brother had sometimes done, but Adélaïde was only glad to see a difference between them. *You have my eyes—the Savoyard black, not the Bourbon coco- brown. And you're so lusty, like life itself.* She smiled down on the new *Duc de Bretagne*, savouring the few minutes they had left together before she would have to summon the wet-nurse and the rocker so that they might care for the child's needs and take her place once more. *They're such a nuisance...though I suppose they serve their purpose. I couldn't bear to stay up all night, no matter how darling you are, not to speak of the cleaning...*

Adélaïde wrote to her sister, Maria Luisa, indulging her in every detail concerning the new prince. The young Queen of Spain was with child herself and devoured every piece of information she could get her hands on like a hungry dog: Was labour as difficult as she thought it would be? How could one best prevent illnesses? How often would the baby have to be fed, and for how long would he suckle his wet-nurse?

Adélaïde did her very best to answer the flood of anxious questions, all while fishing for some detail regarding her sister's relationship with her husband, Philippe. Every time Maria Luisa mentioned him, it seemed to be with a certain caution; she spoke of his affection as though it was not within the bounds of a healthy union. Still, she never wrote a straight-out bad word about him, and Adélaïde gritted her teeth out of curiosity as well as concern, just as she had done from the very day the couple had exchanged their vows.

Rigaud had not yet returned to paint a portrait of any intimate member of the royal family—although he worked for other nobles as well—nor had any of his students been seen at Versailles since the spring of 1705. Adélaïde had several times considered sending him a note asking for one of the youths in particular, but each time she discarded the idea both out of fear that it might make people scratch their heads and wonder what reasons she might have, and out of dread for what Colette would say if they met again. Her lashing out on the portrait had been a clear enough message, and Adélaïde had no desire to provoke that anger another time.

Perhaps it was never meant to be, anyhow. Perhaps it's for the best...if it was meant to be it would have happened. But it didn't, and it never can. It felt odd, terribly odd, to let go of the perfect picture she had built in her head—a shiny picture where anything was possible as long as it gave one happiness—and step into the harsh reality where the few realistic life paths one could take rarely had anything to do with happiness. She longed for the days when she had been ignorant; she longed for Colette in spite of everything that had happened, in spite of her recent realisations.

After having escaped her confinement, Adélaïde successfully numbed this longing though, by engaging in a series of flirtatious escapades—none of which progressed any further than the flattery and jokes the courtly game of love allowed. It was expected that a young woman of her status would grant the gentlemen that tugged at her heels some attention, play along in their gallantry, although naturally she must never take it a step too far and risk scandal.

Louis hardly noticed, and if he did, he knew better than to make a scene of something so commonplace. They were all just a way to pass the time. Adélaïde knew this as well as anyone, and discovered to her surprise that it was difficult to develop any true emotions for the string of beaus despite the merry company they provided.

Less than year after the birth of her son, she found herself with child again. This time—the fourth time—it provoked annoyance as well as joy. The joy was inevitable, while the annoyance sneaked up on her like a strange rash, as she realised she would have to go through the emotionally draining process once more: another pregnancy to change her body before she had had the chance to grow accustomed to it after the last one, putting her at risk of mortal danger just as it would do to any woman, regardless of social standing. Another pregnancy to make people treat her like a glass flower about to break, keeping her from participating in various activities that were considered too dangerous.

One of the court doctors, Fagon, emphasized this in particular. The King, however, was not of the same opinion, for he was bored with Versailles and yearned to move the court to Marly once more in April, sweeping all his favourites off their feet to take them with him, like a stubborn child with his collection of rag dolls.

'Your Royal Highness ought not to travel in your delicate condition,' Fagon said.

'The *Duchesse de Bourgogne* already has a healthy son—she can be in no hurry to beget another one. Isn't that right, dearest?' the King overruled.

Adélaïde glanced from one man to the other, uncertain as to what she could possibly say to any of them. *I want to travel, I do. But not at such an expense...I want a daughter this time though. A perfect daughter. That will answer his question well enough.* 'No, Sire, I'm not in a hurry to have another son.'

'There.'

Madame Maintenon, who had been standing in resigned silence, stepped forth and placed a gentle hand on her husband's thick arm. 'Sire, I urge you to head Monsieur Fagon's advice. He's a doctor—he knows better than we do.'

'You're mistaken if you think I question the good man's authority, Madame. Nonetheless, I stand by what I said. I shan't go without my darling girl.'

Thus, it was decided, and there was nothing anyone could, nor dared, say to alter the Sun King's mind. Towards the end of April though, when the caravan of courtiers had only just begun to unpack their belongings and settle down for the stay at Marly, the consequences of the bumpy, rough ride in the carriage caught up with them.

As Adélaïde was told by Madame Maintenon the day following the miscarriage, the *Duchesse de Lude* had been seen hastening to the King, who was enjoying a walk in the gardens, to deliver the news personally. The King's companions had expressed adequate sympathy, while the King himself had burst into a fit of anger, exclaiming, 'And if it should be so, what difference would that make to me? What does it signify to me who succeeds? Has she not already a son? And if he were to die then the *Duc de Berry* is old enough to marry and have one of his own. Thank heavens that it has happened, since it was to be! And I shall not have my journeys and plans disarranged again by doctors and matrons!'

Adélaïde stared at Madame Maintenon in pure horror once the older woman drew a deep breath after recounting the events. The room was empty of attendants, since the King's wife had dismissed them all for the purpose of a private conversation.

'Did His Majesty speak those words, Madame?'

'I'm afraid he did.'

'I know he loves me as dearly as ever—and I him—but sometimes I think...sometimes I think he has begun to love me the same way he loves his jewels, or his swords. Like a possession. Sometimes I think he has become selfish over the years.' She hesitated to say anything more, because she had already spoken far too boldly.

'He's the King, my dear.' Madame Maintenon's smile was dry, on the verge of bitter even. 'He regards us all as his possessions, whether he knows it or not, at one point or another. If your own health had been damaged by, well, by what has happened, then I'm sure he would be mad with worry. But he cares little for a baby that was an obstacle in his eyes.'

'How can another heir be an obstacle? Ever since I married...'

'I know—and most would share your view. But the King...the King thinks the Bourbon dynasty is safe enough now, and that you're young enough to make it even safer in the future.'

Adélaïde plucked at the ruffled lace on the sleeves of her chemise and sighed. 'I wish I was as young as he seems to think I am. I wish I was still the child I sometimes feel like.'

'You must think *me* an old woman indeed, if you think your own twenty-two is not young!' Madame Maintenon exclaimed, her face gravely scolding but her voice bearing an undertone of laugher.

'Never, Madame, never!'

Once the King's wife left her bedchamber again, Adélaïde was in brighter spirits than she had dared to hope. The loss of the child—though it pained her—did not put as deep a wound in her heart as the two previous losses, partly because she still had little Louis to find comfort in and dote upon, partly because the circumstances had not been nearly as traumatic.

As soon as it was allowed, she was once more riding at the head of the hunting entourage with the King and her husband, chatting idly about everything from the choice of tapestries at Marly to political matters, offering the blinding smiles that had gone from being effortless to becoming more of a well-rehearsed show. Many of them were still genuine, but some derived from the pressure to maintain the giddy atmosphere she had brought to the court all those years ago.

CHAPTER XXXXI

I n the beginning of January, the temperatures suddenly plummeted lower than they had done for as long as Colette could remember, lower than anyone she spoke to could recall. The river Seine froze; it did not freeze the way it usually did—thin patches of ice swimming on the surface—but so thoroughly that one could walk from one bank to the other without setting foot on a bridge. The merchants, whose trade depended on transporting goods down the river, were in an uproar, but of course nature did not care about their desperate complaints.

The frost had destroyed the crops as well, which proved to be far worse. Every day, Colette listened to stories of how the peasants were starving; every day, she witnessed for herself how the Parisians fought over the little food there was on the market and heard her own stomach growl loud enough to turn the heads of passers-by. The death toll kept rising with every day, due to the inevitable famine and the cold itself, both of which struck the lower classes hardest but pushed into the wealthier bourgeoisie households as well. As the weeks crept by, it was not a matter of hundreds or even thousands of lives, but tens of thousands—and those were just the deaths in Paris alone.

A few months had passed since Colette had at last abandoned her disguise as a boy, dismissed Madame Sylvester, and put an end to her regular visits to Rigaud's studio—all in order to live an honest, uncomplicated life. Monsieur Lemaigre had finally slipped into an eternal sleep during last year's spring and left her the house on the *Rue Saint Antoine* to do with as she pleased—a strange act of kindness on his part. The commissions still arrived in a steady stream though; the money Colette earned was sufficient to pay the necessary repairs on the house when the winter took its toll, and she held her head above the drifting line of poverty, living in relative comfort although there was a difference between this comfort and luxury. Of course, the paint also stood for a large chunk of her expenses, but it was something she refused to do without, and it was a necessity when making her livelihood. These days, she signed the paintings with her own name, and to her astonishment, the demand only dropped the slightest bit.

By the time January reached its midst, Colette eventually accepted that the clothes she wore were far from adequate to the weather and sought out a modest little shop run by a tailor and three seamstresses.

'Allow me to guess, Mademoiselle: you're in need of a thicker woollen gown,' the seamstress said when Colette closet the door of the shop behind her.

'Yes, yes, thank you, Madame. The warmest garments you can offer me.'

The seamstress shook her head, compressing her lips to a thin line. 'You should have come sooner, Mademoiselle—I'm afraid the best fabric has already been used and sold. I can make you...' She turned around and started to flick through the thin stacks of linen and wool in one of the cabinets. 'I can make you an extra underskirt, or perhaps a shawl? I don't have enough for a coat or a gown, see.'

Colette swallowed her disappointment and stuck her hand in the pocket of her skirt to extract the money she had taken from the wooden casket of savings she kept on the table in her bedchamber. 'A shawl, then, Madame. Thank you.'

The seamstress nodded, accepted the due sum, and noted the purchase in a book that was filled with similar orders, all scribbled down to keep track of the business.

There was no use for specific measurements, since something as simple as a shawl could be crafted from a general pattern, and Colette departed from the shop with instructions to return the following day. She steered her steps towards the market place, though she had forgotten her basket at home, and silently rehearsed the list of groceries she would need to cook anything other than soup for dinner. It still felt rather strange to visit the cluster of booths with solely honourable intentions—especially since she knew how easy it was to slip an apple down one of the pockets hidden in the folds of her skirt—but each time she thought about her clear conscience, the pleasure grew.

I ought to find a kitchen maid, if not a new cook. Madame Sylvester was too expensive to be worth it, but perhaps I could find someone else. The company would not be so bad, either.

The market place was buzzing with hollow-eyed people with empty bellies and hands thrust deep in their empty pockets, mingling with yet another group, who had enough money but were unable to find anything to buy with it. Both crops and livestock were in a poor state, and the farmers who usually travelled to the city to sell their eggs, milk, and fresh meat at a reasonable price had little to offer their baffled clientele.

The prices would have been high during a regular shortage, naturally, but now they did not have anything to sell in the first place.

Colette slowly went through her list and managed to find, to her rough estimation, half of the supplies she had intended to purchase. With the packages feeling light in her arms, given her an unpleasant feeling as she knew they contained too little, she returned to the red brick house on the *Rue Saint Antoine* and the quiet life she led there. The winter would simply have to hit her as hard as it pleased; she had survived ordeals before, and though the discomfort was definite, she did not doubt she would survive this, too.

CHAPTER XXXXII

In February 1710, Adélaïde gave birth to a third son: Louis *Duc d'Anjou*, a title previously held by Philippe, who was now King of Spain. Adélaïde cringed in secret when she first realised this would be the name her son would be recognised by—there would be no use in referring to him as simply Louis, considering the numerous people at court who shared that name. However, the newborn *Duc* was nothing like his tedious uncle, but a sweet-faced baby with a curious glint in his eyes. Adélaïde felt that familiar warmness each time she laid eyes on him—though she hoped he might be the last addition to the family for some time to come. *This must be the last time...I'm too worn out to carry another child. Too worn out—perhaps age really is coming on fast! But I've done my duty. An heir and one to spare.*

Early that same year, the matter that had been on the courtiers' lips was raising even further interest: the *Duc de Berry*, soon to be twenty-four years of age, was still unmarried and in search of a suitable wife. Had he been of more modest rank, his age would not have been worth mentioning, but being a *Fils de France* and thereby an advantageous match for as good as any member of the nobility—both in France and in foreign circles—it was crucial that he both produced an heir and helped create another political alliance as soon as possible.

Adélaïde watched with a knot in her stomach as countless young women and girls exchanged their trivial pining for a deadly serious hunt, each convinced that the title *Duchesse de Berry*, granddaughter in law to Louis XIV, was hers and hers alone to claim. Their mothers and fathers rallied to their assistance, of course, for it was often they who had thought of the opportunity to begin with. Charles's impeccably fine clothes and reputation of being a promising military man only spurred them on, although everyone was perfectly aware of the silent agreement stating that marriage was rather unrelated to one's infatuation under circumstances like these.

*They don't know any better. They don't know what kind of a person he is, they haven't seen...*Adélaïde pitied the hopeful, potential brides—all except one. Nantes's second eldest daughter, Louise Élizabeth, had blossomed into a seventeen-year-old beauty, taking the place Nantes had once held as one of the most popular young ladies on the noble marriage market. With her serene face, pleasantly soft features, and skin like fresh cream, there was no denying that any man who was attracted to women in general would be attracted to Louise Élizabeth in particular.

Although Adélaïde held no personal grudge against the girl, Nantes held her daughter like a puppet doll, pulling the strings relentlessly according to her own fierce ambitions, and Adélaïde had no intention of allowing one she had been plagued by for so many years to creep any closer to the throne. Hence, her gaze fell on another young girl: Blois's eldest daughter, Marie Louise. The idea was fuelled by the singular malicious emotion Adélaïde had grown accustomed to feeling over the years: vindictiveness. She had pushed it away sometimes, as she had done with her burning hatred towards Charles, but it was difficult to always do so.

That harpy would be beside herself...her own sister, whose dowry she was always so envious of, succeeding in this. Her own niece, snatching the position she thinks she can reserve for her daughter. Blois was not high in her graces, of course, but Nantes was even less so.

One evening, she summoned a selected group to her private chambers, inviting them to dine with her exclusively—an offer no one at court, or in all of France, felt entitled enough to decline. The company included Blois, Charles, Louis, and a few additional men and women to fill the table; men and women Adélaïde knew remained loyal to the Bourgogne faction. The bride-to-be herself had received no invitation though, because Blois had promptly stated that her daughter should not be given the opportunity to scare the *Duc de Berry* off with her headstrong ways. It was better if she was simply the conversation topic of the evening, a glorified figure, and Charles could interpret what was said about her as best he liked.

Once the servants had placed *les hors d'œuvre* on the table and every guest had been served, Adélaïde took a deep breath and leaned discreetly towards Charles, to whom she had assigned the chair on her left. 'You're searching for a suitable bride,' she stated in a voice low enough to keep her from being overheard.

'Obviously. I've been told it's high time.' The sarcasm was unmistakable as he began carving the food with the silver knife, his eyes fixed on his plate.

'They're right, Charles. And…and I know we have not been as close these past few years as we once were, but I hoped you might take my advice when you make your pick.'

'Your children have taken their toll on you,' he remarked bluntly. 'I should think there is a certain distance between us.'

Ah, yes, five pregnancies of mine, and eight years of scattered amorous affairs of his. No wonder the distance has grown. In that moment, Adélaïde was eternally grateful for having remained true to the silent vow she had made to herself at the birth of her first son: to cleanse her mind of grudge and focus her thoughts on other things. With the passing of the years, neither of them had spoken a hostile word to one another, and though she knew every fragment of the blame was his, she also knew better than to express anything of the sort. At first it had felt like carrying a large, sharp rock in her chest, but as time went by, the rock had been polished, and though it was still as heavy, the edges no longer cut her. Nantes was a different matter; mayhap it was because that rivalry had never hurt as much that she could allow herself to nurture it.

'Perhaps. But I would like you to heed my advice nonetheless. I know a little about girls, mind you, I used to be one.'

'Who would you have me choose, then?' Charles tucked an impressive amount of food in his mouth and chewed thoroughly, then took a deep sip from his wineglass.

'Marie Louise d'Orléans, the eldest daughter of the *Duc* and *Duchesse d'Orléans*. Your cousin. Do you fancy her, Charles? I think she would...well, she wouldn't bore you, at least.'

'Didn't she suffer of smallpox as a child? Is she marked?'

'I would never have guessed she had been affected, had you not mentioned it,' Adélaïde lied. 'We can get a papal disposition—it won't be an issue. She's young, too, and would bring a considerable dowry.'

'Such a dowry is a good thing, I suppose, but there are many girls who can bring me that. I want someone...someone stimulating.' He wiped the corner of his mouth with the napkin and smirked.

Stimulating—I should have guessed. 'Well, as I said, she won't bore you. She's not as bleak as some of the other contestants. Don't you trust me to find you a wife, Charlie?' The old nickname was sour on her tongue but appeared to wake some old sentiment in Charles.

'All right, then, I shall think of it. But you will have to speak to His Majesty, too, though I don't doubt he'll yield to you.'

'Don't worry about it.' Adélaïde's smile was genuine; the evening had gone as

404

smoothly as she had hoped, and she knew she had not only succeeded in quashing Nantes, but in gaining Blois's unconditional gratitude in the process. Though she might never have to use it, it granted a certain feeling of security.

Once the dinner had come to an end and the guests were departing one by one from her private chambers, the *Duchesse d'Orléans* lingered at the door, her lips curved, for she knew precisely what the purpose of the evening had been. 'Thank you, Your Royal Highness, for being so kind as to invite me.'

'It was my pleasure, *Madame la Princesse*. I hoped you enjoyed the crab soup—and I pray your daughter is well?'

'Oh, yes, she's in good health.' Blois tilted her head. 'Madame, you have greater influence than you perhaps realise.'

Adélaïde allowed a giggle to escape her lips. 'Ought not the First Lady of France have great influence?'

Blois nodded. 'I bid you a good night, Madame.'

'Good night.'

On the sixth day of July, the marriage was a fact, having passed the approval of the King once Adélaïde had leaned in to whisper the idea in his ear, placing her words carefully.

The bride reminded Adélaïde of her own wedding all those years ago, as she watched Marie Louise stride down the aisle decked in pearls and lace, her auburn hair fastened with a mother-of-pearl comb. The girl was not yet fifteen years old; one might easily have taken her for a fainthearted little thing, comparable to a glass vase or an obedient child, but Adélaïde knew this was naught but an illusion. Marie Louise would keep her husband in his place despite his brazen habits. If one looked closer, one could see the knowing glint in her eyes, and it did not take long to discover how cleverly she bargained with those around her to get what she wanted—whether it was another person's affection or a valuable possession. She was not by any means the most beautiful bride, despite the countless ornaments and the precious gown, but her smile was compelling, and she knew what to show the world and what to disguise.

Marie Louise kept her chin elevated as she approached her spouse. The two of them exchanged a quick look, appearing as though they were calculating the conditions of their future, and Marie Louise's eyes were as unyielding as steel.

I hope she'll be able to handle him. I hope...I hope he's fond of her, but not too fond. Adélaïde shuddered as Charles knelt by his future wife's side in front of the cardinal who would perform the blessing. He was a head taller than she, not to mention nine years her senior, but the differences could have been far greater. *Better she than someone who he can step over as easily as he steps over the gravel paths in the gardens. Better she than a girl who wouldn't be headstrong enough to survive it.* Although she had originally promoted the match to spite Nantes, Adélaïde realised there had perhaps been an underlying reason, an instinct that had made her pick this particular candidate.

The wedding proceeded smoothly, as did the banquet and the celebrations that followed. Once it was time for the ceremonious bedding, Charles was already drunken as a sailor on leave, which would perhaps be an advantage to his poor bride since he had drunken himself past the stage of unreliability and well into half-unconsciousness. This union would be consumed at once; there would be no loitering around for years, as had been the case with Adélaïde's own marriage. She could not help but smile at the memory of the flustered young *Duc de Bourgogne* who had spent fifteen minutes in her bed, blushing and trying to force small-talk. *How young we were! Me, especially. And I was so disappointed I was not passionately in love...I thought there was only one kind of love. And now...now I have had that passionate thing, and I have had my flirtations, and still the cousinly love is the only love that won't be taken from me. It's not so horrible, cousinly love.*

Her thoughts were interrupted by the King as he raised a crystal glass to the young couple's good fortune. 'May your union bear fruit in the shape of healthy sons and beautiful daughters.'

A wave of snickers and murmurs swept through the mass of courtiers present in the room, before they all shuffled out like sheep.

'He appears very affectionate towards her,' one of the ladies mumbled in Adélaïde's ear. 'Though perhaps not entirely sober.'

'No, not entirely. Do you think they make a fine match?' Adélaïde responded.

'Well—she's a bit...different, isn't she? But she's young. And he's handsome. What could be finer?'

Adélaïde sighed. 'I hope she'll be alright.'

'Is there any reason why she shouldn't be?'

'No—no.'

The lady tapped her nose and floated back into the collective mass again.

*Does she know? Of course she doesn't.
But maybe they all know there is* something,
maybe they are not as ignorant as I thought.

Three months of genuine fondness from
Charles's side and business-like responses
from Marie Louise passed before Charles had
a change of heart and fell in love with *a
femme de chambre* instead, which was not
surprising for a man of his nature. Adélaïde
summoned Marie Louise to her chambers,
watching with amusement as the girl's eyes
grew round from beholding the rooms that
had once belonged to the late Queen. She then
cut to the chase, just as Adélaïde had hoped
she would. 'Your Royal Highness, my
husband, the *Duc de Berry*, has shifted his
affections.'

'Oh.' Adélaïde practically lunged
forward, taking Marie Louise's hands in her
own, uncertain whether she ought to be glad
for her or if this was bad news. 'How so?'

'An ugly little thing, with rat-coloured
hair. A *femme de chambre*. But it's all right, I
think.'

'How like Charles! But you mustn't
lose heart.'

'I know—I told him that he might
continue with the frivolity as long as he
pleases, but if he ever...if he ever acts

unkindly towards me, I shall tell the King all about it.'

'You really are a gem!' Adélaïde blurted out, feeling kindlier toward the girl with every second that passed. 'Do be careful though. You don't want to attract his wrath— believe me.'

'Sometimes, Madame, you make it sound as though I should be afraid of him, but I'm not. He's just like any other man: high-minded and capable of cruelty, but like clay in your hands if you have anything to threaten him with, anything to use to your advantage. He'll leave me to do as I please.'

'I wish I had your wits when I was your age.'

'I wish I had your marriage, Madame.'

Adélaïde laughed, squeezing Marie Louise's hands, then released them and took a step back. 'I've been lucky. Now, do you like biscotti?' She gestured towards a porcelain plate that a servant had brought to her antechamber a short while ago.

Marie Louise shook her head. 'I must be journeying back to the Palais Royale—with your permission, Madame. My husband will be expecting me for dinner, although I'm not sure he'll be there himself.'

'Then you must go. Thank you for confiding in me. You have my most heartfelt best wishes.'

Thus, they parted, and Adélaïde spent the following fifteen minutes strolling back and forth in her antechamber with a broad smile on her face, relishing the feeling of contentment. *It's not such a bad thing to be twenty-five. The older, the wiser, they say. At least the happier. Two thriving sons, Charles kept in place, Nantes humbled...the King frightfully old...*She stopped herself before her thoughts began to stray in a treacherous direction, before she had the time to think any further about the King's declining health. Not only was it forbidden, but Adélaïde dreaded the fraction of her subconscious that relished being one step closer to the throne more than it loved the current monarch. *I mustn't think horrid things like that—never.*

CHAPTER XXXXIII

Adélaïde clasped her husband's hands and beamed at him, searching his face for anything that might reveal his sentiments. 'How is the *Dauphin*, your father? Is he improving yet?'

Louis shook his head, slowly, then tore his gaze from something far away and met her eyes. 'The *Dauphin* is dead. My father has passed, God bless him.'

Adélaïde's grip on his hands tightened and she felt her breath twist into a knot in her throat, making it impossible to exhale for several seconds, as she grappled to comprehend what this meant. *I'm the new Dauphine. Louis is first in line to the throne, there is nothing standing in the way. But that poor, dear man...*Though there had never existed an exceptionally strong bond between herself and her father-in-law, the Grand *Dauphin* had been kind towards her—not clever, perhaps, nor very interesting, but kind nonetheless—and the initial triumph was dampened by grief.

'I thought...I thought he was improving, but then...' Louis swallowed, his Adam's apple bobbing.

Tears sprung to Adélaïde's eyes. 'The children will be so awfully sad, Louis. We shall have to tell them soon. Could the doctors do nothing?'

'Once the pox had progressed so far, well, they tried to bleed him, but perhaps they didn't take enough. Perhaps they were afraid to contract the disease themselves. I don't know.'

Overcome by an urge to comfort, Adélaïde flung her arms unceremoniously around his neck, allowing him to hold her while they both struggled with the tangle of emotions.

'You're almost Queen now, dearest,' Louis whispered, his voice hoarse.

'Hush. We must not think of such things—we must think of your father. But it's true, yes, and you're almost King. Imagine that!'

Then, before either of them could say another word, the door swung open, and the usher announced the arrival of the king The man who was supposed to be a father mourning his oldest legitimate son stalked into the room with the rest of his entourage, his brows furrowed but not a trace of a tear in his eye. Of course, it was not the Sun King's habit to weep in public—which meant he did not weep much at all—but despite this, his face was surprisingly pragmatic, his posture upright. Neither he nor any of the attendants had had the chance to change their lavish garments for black replicas, for the Grand *Dauphin*'s body had not yet cooled, and the King would have reminded a common man of a peacock strutting about his apartments just like any other day of the year.

'Sire!' Adélaïde exclaimed and unclasped her hands from around Louis's neck, taking a few steps back. 'I've had word of our loss. Are you terribly upset? Is there anything I can do to comfort you in your grief?'

'Nothing, my doll, nothing. My son was weak, succumbing to the small pox. He was never a very vigorous man.'

'I suppose not, Sire,' Adélaïde replied, her heart sinking like a lump of lead in her chest. *I knew he did not think particularly highly of him, but still...perhaps it is true, then, that he has become selfish with age. Selfish and a little bitter.*

Louis stood in silence with his eyes glued to his glossy shoes with the golden buckles. He was forced to raise his glance though, as his grandfather approached, surveying him from the top of his hat to the heels of the very same shoes.

'You shall be my direct heir from this day. Do you realise your responsibilities? Methinks you will serve your nation better than your father did, and with greater eagerness.'

'Yes, Sire.' Louis swallowed again to keep his voice from cracking. 'I have proved to you many times that I have a keen interest in the well-being of France, and the necessary politics. I pray I shall be worthy, Sire.'

The King grunted and smiled his toothless smile at this, then squeezed Louis's arms and shoulders firmly. 'I know it. Now, we must all prepare for the period of mourning. We must give my late son the same show of respect we granted my brother, the *Duc d'Orléans*, for he was no less in standing.'

But his standing is the only reason, isn't it? And here I am, a part of it all, this secret rejoicing. What's the matter with me? Adélaïde was careful not to express any of these thoughts but simply offered the onlookers her most solemn expression, so that they would only see the side of her she wished them to see.

Although a great deal changed for Adélaïde and Louis officially, the everyday life they led remained similar, with a few additional ceremonies and rules of etiquette that were required. True; according to the documents they were now not second but first in the line of succession, but they had enjoyed the privileges that came with that rank far earlier than they achieved the promotion itself. However, the King made certain to double Adélaïde's entourage and increase her guards, so that she would now possess everything a Queen might expect to have.

Adélaïde already knew the drill of being First Lady of France; Louis was no stranger to being one of his grandfather's primary advisers and confidants in matters concerning the governing of the country. The general mood at court was not as dire as one might have expected following a tragedy, but rather expectant, as its members anticipated the possibility of their next King and Queen being two youths and not a lazy man approaching fifty. However much they venerated and respected the current King, it was undeniable that there were some who hoped that the less stern rule of the *Duc de Bourgogne* would give them greater freedom to move around in their own palaces instead of being tied to Versailles under constant supervision like naughty children. Louis XIV was no fool, and there was—obviously—an unspoken purpose behind the move to Versailles that had occurred several decades ago: to gather all of France's powerful men and women under the same roof, making them dependent on it, so that he might control their every move through etiquette and distract them with silly games. Over the years, nobles had accumulated debt towards their monarch as they struggled to pay for the extravagant clothes he required them to wear, and now they found themselves trapped in a web spun by a spider they had to please if they were to keep any favours or privileges.

Adélaïde spent hours walking in the garden in silence; her ladies gave one another concerned glances, but the truth was she was simply too preoccupied to speak much. She pondered the possibilities that were sure to come once she was crowned Queen—which could not be too far ahead—and how she wished to manage the nobles that would fall to their knees in their fancy silk stockings, pouring flattery on her in hope of her friendship. She quickly concluded that she would do everything in her power to bring them satisfaction and joy, all while improving the living conditions of the common people. Once again, she remained blind to the necessity of redistributing wealth, unable to grasp that it was impossible to raise the little people without first lowering the upper crust. *It shan't be a problem. All those great sums wasted on waging war against England and*

Austria...perhaps we can pull out of the fighting, and everyone will be happy. And France will be prosperous, and...

In that moment, Nantes passed the entourage and dipped into a forced little curtsy before continuing with hurried steps, head turned forward as if her neck had been locked in that position, the profile of her face captivating despite the lines that had begun to gather at the corner of her eyes over the past few years. She resembled a withering flower that still maintained some beauty—she was thirty-eight years of age but carried herself proudly like the twenty-three-year-old she had been when Adélaïde first saw her.

She'll have to go, I'll dismiss her from court. We will all be better off without her poison and her snobbery.

The mourning court travelled to Fontainebleau as January shifted into February the following year, and with the move came the pleasant breeze of refreshment that always followed when they switched scenery. Adélaïde rejoiced to see both the King, Louis, and her own ladies fluster at the prospects each new year seemed to bring—although, of course, nothing had actually changed. However, her greatest pleasure came from watching her two boys tumble in the nursery, and she was swept

418

back to what felt like another lifetime when she had been a child herself, playing in the sun-chinked halls of the Palazzo Madama in Turin with Maria Luisa. Their games had not been as frivolous or rough—such a thing would have been considered terribly unsuitable for two little girls—yet they had possessed the very same playfulness Adélaïde saw in Louis and Louis.

The *Duc de Bretagne* was responsible for most of the running about, for he was five years old and as lively as he had been as a baby, while his brother, the *Duc d'Anjou*, was approaching his second birthday, and so he waddled on unsteady legs rather than ran.

'They show no signs of illness or...or defects of any sort, do they, Madame? Nothing like the late *Duc de Bretagne*?' Adélaïde asked one afternoon during her regular visit to the nursery.

'They're both as healthy as I ever saw a child, Your Royal Highness. I urge you not to worry yourself when there's no need,' one of the nurses replied, scrambling to her feet from the floor, where she had been wiping spit from the *Duc d'Anjou's* lips with a linen napkin. 'If your sons were suffering from convulsions of that sort, Your Royal Highness, they would have shown symptoms already, but they haven't.'

'I suppose you're right. Thank you, nurse.'

While the boys' well-being ceased to worry Adélaïde, as she now felt assured of it, she soon began noticing changes in her own physique—changes unlike anything she had experienced before.

Her limbs were like heavy lumps, making it an effort to walk with the precise posture and small steps she had been told to use ever since she was a little girl; her thoughts were slow, as if muffled by a fever. Despite these symptoms, Adélaïde could not quite believe what she was hearing when Charles pointed out the following evening how disturbingly red her eyes had become.

'Didn't you look in the mirror before making your appearance at the table?' he asked.

'Well, I—' Adélaïde was interrupted by her own lungs as she fell into a fit of dry coughing. Once she had regained her composure and was breathing normally, five or ten pair of eyes had turned to her, the courtiers astonished at this show of bad manners.

'Perhaps you should see a doctor,' Charles continued before returning his attentions to a young lady further down the table, gazing at her décolletage over the edge of his wine glass.

That's ridiculous—I don't need a doctor. I'm never sick, at least not like this. Louis would react too strongly, not to speak of the King!

As it happened, Adélaïde was not entirely mistaken in this premonition. As soon as it became commonly known that the *Duchesse de Bourgogne's* health appeared to be on slippery ice, she was forced to take to her bed, and though the King whined childishly about how he lacked his doll's company, even he appeared to realise the graveness of the situation. Urged to avoid her presence by the doctors, who had already agreed that the disease was most likely contagious, he gritted his teeth and heeded their instructions, for he dreaded what might happen to the nation if he were to be infected as well.

Louis, however, did not suffer from any such self-important thoughts, and insisted upon visiting his wife instantly.

Adélaïde's heart leaped with warm fondness as she spotted his frankly unattractive person in the doorway to her bedchamber, and pushed herself up in a sitting position against the pillows. 'Louis! Won't you come and sit with me? It's so dreadfully dull here—almost like confinement.'

'Are you not too tired, dearest?' Louis voice was tinged with anxiety. He ignored the chair that one of the servants offered him and simply knelt on the cold floor by the bed.

'I don't...I don't feel very well, to tell you the truth. But once I recover, I shall make them bring me something to entertain myself. I will recover.'

'Of course, of course. The boys want to see their Lady Mother but His Majesty forbade it.' Louis patted Adélaïde's hand awkwardly. 'He's terribly enraged.'

'He would like to be the master of nature, too, I'm sure. Have you ever had these kinds of rashes before, Louis? They appeared this morning—I haven't shown the doctors yet. Have you had anything of the sort?' Adélaïde used a finger to sweep her hair behind her back so that her throat was exposed; the skin had erupted in a cluster of flat, red patches stretching from her collar bones to her jaw. It had begun on her face, but had been too subtle to notice—until now.

'I...I haven't, dearest.'

'But you know what they are, don't you?' Fear made her stomach cramp as she waited for the answer that might confirm her own suspicions. *Please don't say it, please...I can't risk it, not now.*

Louis's voice was a mere whisper. 'I'm no physician. The measles?'

Please, no. It cannot be. 'Does the King have to know? I would hate to worry him when there's no reason. I'll be alright—won't I, Louis?'

'The King is already worried, and with good reason.' A mask seemed to have replaced his face: a mask of stone, frozen in fright, only the dark eyes moving. He sank his elbows into the thick mattress and rested his forehead heavily on his fists, his breaths deep and trembling.

Adélaïde wanted to shake him and urge him to tell her everything she wished to hear, tell her what must surely be the truth as well—that she was not necessarily doomed— but Louis had already retreated too deeply into what she assumed was a prayer, and did not stir for several minutes. When he did though, he placed a kiss on her cheek and left the bedchamber without another word.

CHAPTER XXXXIV

T hree days passed, and each day it became more difficult to smile, to talk, to stay awake; each day the fever and the coughing was worse than it had been the day before, the rashes more agonising. Adélaïde spent the hours drifting in and out of a state which was not so much sleep as disturbing dreams and hallucinations. Often, she would see the places she adored and the people she loved in bizarre situations, always in complete silence, always in the same decline she felt creeping upon herself.

The mirrors were all cracked but remained in their frames without shattering or falling to the polished wooden floor in pieces. The cracks spread across the glass like intricate spider's webs though, and Adélaïde felt the urge to lunge forward and press her hands against the glass to keep it in place. She was convinced that if they did indeed fall to the floor, everything else would

*break as well, whether it be furniture or
people.*

*A small army of men, women, and
children strolled leisurely through the hall,
decked in absurd clothes in garish colours.
The jewels around their necks appeared to be
dragging them down; despite the light-
hearted walk their necks were bent with
effort, threatening to snap any minute unless
they were relieved of their burden.*

*There was Louis, with four boys
clinging to his hands and tugging at his
cuffs—their two sons accompanied by the two
others that might have been, had they only
been allowed to live. Their faces were pale,
ghost-like, their lips the colour of prunes, and
the desperation with which they held onto
their father made Adélaïde's chest bubble
with panic.*

*There was her mother, and her
grandmother, Marie Jeanne. Both were
skeleton-thin with the contours of bones
poking through the transparent skin that
stretched over their cheekbones and wrists.*

*There was the Sun King sitting on a
blackened silver throne with his head
hanging limply against his chest as if he
were already dead, dressed in solely cloth of
gold which made him shine as brightly as
when he had played the role of Apollo in a
ballet before age took its toll.*

And there, by the Sun King's feet a young woman sat cross-legged with red hair falling down her back, a sketch book in her lap. When the young woman turned up her face though, Adélaïde did not see what she had been expecting—for her face was twisted in a grimace and completely void of love.

Adélaïde awoke to see three grim-faced doctors leaning over her bed, each frowning more than the other, without doubt fearing the blame they would have to fend off best they could if they failed to cure the *Dauphine*. Perhaps they had attended her before—perhaps they frequented the court—but Adélaïde failed to recognise any of them, her thoughts drifting and wavering like one big blur. However, she distinctly felt the cold metal one of the doctors placed against the area between her wrist and elbow, where the skin was as soft and pale as white satin, the purple veins bulging through.

They're going to bleed me, to purge me of unbalanced humors. Too much yellow, too much black...it's going to hurt. Although she knew what was coming, Adélaïde shivered as she studied the triangular blade and realised it must be the largest fleam in the doctors' collection. Then, one of the men extracted the fleam hammer from a leather casing, rested it against the top of the fleam, and with a swift flick of his wrist, hammered down the blade and punctured her skin. The shallow vein underneath broke—just as it was supposed to—and a steady stream of hot, red liquid began pouring out, filling one cup and then another.

Adélaïde winced at the pain, which was strong enough to make every other impression fade, worse than it had been when she had been bled before, and forced back the disgust that came from feeling her own blood running over her arm. *They know what they're doing. It's for the best.* Yet the little strength she had left was being drained from her veins quite literally; she began to swoon back into unconsciousness, though this time it was not mere sleep but something she suspected she might not wake up from.

'Would that be sufficient?' one of the doctors said to his colleagues.

'A few more drops—then we can repeat the process tomorrow at noon, to ensure it has done its purpose,' answered another.

'Careful with the sheets.'

'I know my business, *Docteur*. Will you hold the cup for me while I manage the bandages?'

Minutes later they had departed, leaving Adélaïde to stare at the canopy through a haze. Her arm throbbed; it was already beginning to swell under the tight bandages and the redness that surrounded the place where the fleam had been inserted was as red as the rashes on the rest of her body. To run, to dance, to move with ease...all these things were naught but absurdities now, too distant to seem real, and Adélaïde marvelled at how she had once been able to do all of them with light steps and even lighter heart. With considerable effort, she brought the arm that had not been bled up to scratch the rashes on her throat and face—they had now spread to her arms and, though she could not see it, her legs—and listened to the heated conversation that was going on in the antechamber.

The King's unmistakable voice was dominant, while the doctors did their very best to defend themselves without risking their own lives in the process.

'We have bled the *Dauphine* now, Your Majesty. We shall try again soon, and pray that it stabilises the humours in her body.'

'Praying is not enough, Monsieur. We all pray to God but that was not why I summoned you! I summoned you to cure the *Dauphine*. You *will* cure her.'

'Your Majesty, there are limits to our abilities.'

'Are you opposing your sovereign? Would you like it better, perhaps, to practice your abilities in the homes of carpenters and

428

common workers, where your skills are adequate?'

'No, Sire. Forgive me.'

'You may attend my grandson, the *Dauphin*, now. With the grace of God, he'll benefit more from your treatments. You are dismissed.'

Adélaïde creased her forehead in a frown. *The Dauphin? Louis? Why on earth...is he ill? Has he caught it from me, because of me?* The possibility was an alarming one; it filled her with a guilt that was beginning to poke at her like a sharp needle. If Louis had taken ill as well, then it meant the measles has begun to spread, and it might only be a matter of time before it was devouring the court like an open fire without discriminating between any two people. The *Duc de Bretagne* and the *Duc d'Anjou* were strong, healthy children—but they were not immune. *If they are infected I shall never forgive myself, even if they recover. They should be taken away for the time being, until we are all up and well again.*

The following day, after another session of bloodletting, the King himself finally came to sit by Adélaïde's bedside, for he had decided that the emptiness she had left was worse than the risk of being taken ill with the measles. Hence, he abandoned his attendants

429

in her antechamber, leaving them to bicker and gossip amongst themselves, and ordered a plush armchair to be brought to the bed.

Despite her condition, Adélaïde was jubilant within: the Sun King's golden rays still shone on her even in this hour, and as she basked in them it felt as though she was the luckiest person alive, just like before. She managed to reward him with a smile and drew a faint breath. 'I hear the doctors speak of my husband—has he been contaminated? Is it my fault?'

'He's not well, my doll—I won't lie to you about that. But to say it is your fault? No, I should think God will do what He deems just.' The King shifted in his seat, his fleshy lips pressed tightly together so that they appeared slim.

'And the boys?' *Dear Lord, let them be safe. Don't take them from me. You have taken enough already.*

'Nothing alarming—yet, at least. Now you ought to concentrate on your own well-being, understood? Methinks you made a young man out of me again, my doll, and if—God forbid—you should leave us, I will age many years in the course of one night.'

'Sire, you look the very same as when I first saw you,' Adélaïde lied. 'Do you remember? It was November, and I was bursting with fright and excitement at the same time. Do you remember that?'

The King smiled tenderly. 'I remember a little girl with the most pleasant airs I had ever seen. I remember she curtsied deeper than she was required to.'

'And you raised me up, Sire. I was very glad when you did. I think I shall sleep now.'

'Yes, yes, of course. You sleep, my dearest girl, and I'll hear with the doctors. Perhaps they have figured out some new method.' On that note, the King stood up with cracking joints and several displeased grunts, and walked slowly towards the door. Once he was gone, Adélaïde allowed her eyelids to finally close, pulling her back into the comforting darkness that had become her habitual state. However, she found herself unable to drift into sleep, as her thoughts kept returning to the one person she truly wished would come to her bedside at this grave hour: Colette. Though she did not say the name aloud, she repeated it in her head until the other girl's face became clear for her inner sight. *Colette. 'Ette. I shouldn't have let you go—never...If I can't have your love, I only wish for your forgiveness. I should have asked for it. I should have asked you to stay. If I could tell you that, if...*

CHAPTER XXXXV

The bells chimed with a deep, melodious voice. The mist lay thick over Paris, creeping through every slit in doors and windows, soaking the streets in an icy haze. The sound of the bells penetrated rather than crept; it was strong enough to make Colette press her palms over her ears and squeeze her eyes shut as she realised what it meant. There could be no certainty yet as to who it was—not until it was publicly announced—but rumours had been circulating in the city. The court was ridden with measles. The *Dauphin* and *Dauphine* had both been contaminated, as well as their little sons. These were the chimes of doom: the disease had taken one, or several, of their lives.

Six days later, the bells tolled again. On the eighth day of March, the sound filled the streets anew. By then, it was common knowledge that the *Dauphine* had been the first to succumb to death's grasping fingers, then her husband had followed, and finally the oldest of the two boys—the *Duc the Bretagne*, who had been *Dauphin* himself for little more than two weeks following the death of his father.

Paris waited in silence, trapped under an atmosphere of tension, wondering whether the last member of the ill-fortuned family would face the same fate. Those who favoured the monarchy wept for the idolized sweetness of the Savoyard princess, of whom they had heard all the kind things that could be said of a person, while those opposed to the entire mechanism that was the royal family gritted their teeth, perhaps wondering why the measles could not take the King himself. Regardless of which, they all gaped at the turning of fortune's wheel and the mortality of those who had been promoted as divine creatures anointed by God.

However, there came no fourth death report, and the bells remained silent. Louis, the sole surviving son, was now the direct heir to the throne of France at the grand age of two—and it was not likely that he would grow much older before he would have to take his great-grandfather's place as King, for time was chasing Louis XIV at the heels and making him weaker for each month that passed. Yet another boy King—the third in a row—would require a regent, which in itself threatened to spark grave quarrel within the walls of Versailles. Who could be chosen? The little boy's cousin, the *Duc d'Orléans*, or perhaps one of the current King's legitimized sons by Madame Montespan?

None of this political crisis interested Colette though. She found herself too preoccupied with the first death to care about those that followed, nor the consequences. She stood by the window at the *Rue Saint Antoine*, clenching the paintbrush tightly in her hand as she drew the first strokes of yellow on a painting—this time the motif was not a face, but a raps field billowing in the imagined breeze—when the brutal reality came as a slap in the face once more. *Dead. Dead. How can it be? Dead. But it is, I know it is. She looked so...so luminous the last time I saw her.* Of course, the last time they had laid eyes on one another had been that fateful night in Adélaïde's bedchamber, when the pillars of sand their relationship had been built upon had crumbled down in the course of minutes. The candlelight had indeed illuminated the figure on the bed, almost like a statue of gold, but that was seven long years ago. During those seven long years, the burning grudge had cooled and faded into bitter nostalgia, and once the bitterness had faded as well, the nostalgia had been a loving one. Colette had caught herself thinking of the dead *Dauphine* often, although she could not remember when she last had wished to return to that whole world. She had concluded— slowly and tortuously—that this love story had no happy ending, because such things only ever existed in fairy tales, at least under circumstances like these. *It was like a painting of love: sometimes the picture is even prettier than reality, but it's still just an illusion, a resemblance.*

Still, she felt an indescribable pain shoot out in every limb, paralyzing her, as she imagined the lively girl she had once known sunk deep in the stale sheets in her bed like a helpless doll, her heart no longer pumping blood in her veins. Her skin was already cool, of course, and soon she would be buried during a procession as grand as the life she had led, though far more solemn and perhaps not what she would have wished, had she been in a position to object. *At least she didn't have to watch her son die, not another time. Maybe that would have killed her if the measles hadn't already.*

Locked in the tight grip of melancholy, Colette abandoned the paintbrush and swung the door open, then stepped out on into the ghostly atmosphere of the street. The city— which was usually bustling with life, a cacophony of horse hooves against cobblestone and rowdy shouting from one window to the other—was as silent as a grave, quite literally. The mist still lingered, making the contours of the buildings appear obscure and pale; a fat rat sped across the gutter on tiny, pink feet, sweeping the street with its tail as it passed. Except for this scurrying animal, the only visible life on the *Rue Saint Antoine* was a couple of hunch-backed old women and a grim-mouthed young gentleman.

Colette inhaled the crisp air, filling her lungs until she thought they might burst in a thousand pieces, and followed the rat with her glance. She recalled a passage from a play written by an Englishman—a William Shakespeare—that Adélaïde had once shown her. It said something about how the fault lay not in our stars, but in ourselves. *It cannot be true...the fault lies very much in our stars.* The *Dauphine* would never be Queen of France, for the world was a cruel place, whether that world was Paris or Versailles.

The rat had disappeared, blessed in its ignorance, possessing a greater fortune than the red-haired young woman who had looked down on it and thought herself a higher being.

ABOUT THE AUTHOR

Saga Hillbom is an author of historical fiction, as well as an avid reader, and her debut novel *A Generation of Poppies* was published in February 2018. Saga currently studies history in Lund, Sweden, where she lives with her family. You can visit her online at http://sagahillbom.blog/ or on Instagram at @writing_history_.

Printed by Libri Plureos GmbH in Hamburg, Germany

9 789151 908878